The Wind Came Running

Marianne Gage

Plain View Press
P.O. 42255
Austin, TX 78704

plainviewpress.net
sb@plainviewpress.net
512-441-2452

ISBN: 978-1-935514-46-6
Library of Congress Number: 2010925799

Cover art by Ed Diffenderfer
Cover design by Susan Bright

Disclaimer

The Wind Came Running is a work of fiction. Any likeness of its characters and events to real people or situations, past or present, is purely coincidental and unintentional, except for references to well-known historic personages and circumstances.

This story contains offensive language, including racial epithets that are an intrinsic part of the storyline. The language and racial attitudes were those of the time and place, and it seemed necessary, in the pursuit of veracity, to leave them in the novel.

To Alan Rinzler, Sofia Shafquat, and
Michael Carr, my editors

And to my husband Ed, who stayed
steadfast through it all

To Martha
from Marianne Gage
with best wishes!

Marianne Gage

Contents

Over the windy mountains
Over the windy mountains
Came the myriad-legged wind
The wind came running hither

—Wind Song
Pima

Part One

1935

1

When I was single, went dressed all so fine
Now I am married, go ragged all the time.
I wish I was a single girl again, Oh, Lord,
Don't I wish I was a single girl again.
—Folk song, "The Single Girl"

Cassie lay in bed, her head next to the open window. The mourning doves were making their low cooing sounds just for her, and the commingled scents of spirea and lilac drifted from outside. The birds were already making a racket—mockers and meadowlarks, and a crow or two, singing in all their languages and cadences from the trees, and insects were cranking up their daily chorus, one cottonwood or elm offering up the thrum and buzz of its cicadas and grasshoppers to another harboring the same tiny, boisterous creatures.

It was getting to be the time for bugs. At night you could catch fireflies in bottles and have your own display of flashing lights, and once in a while, if you were fast and lucky, you could snatch a grasshopper. If you went out in the grass you got chiggers, bugs no bigger than a speck of pepper, which would bore into your skin and you'd never know till tomorrow. She already had a few red welts on her legs. She held them up in the air, one at a time. They were ugly, she thought, with bumps and faint hairs rising from the tanned skin. She wondered if they would ever look like her mother's, which were slim, shapely, and often sheathed in silk.

She got up and stood in the door of her brothers' room. Mitch was turned on his side, as far as he could remove himself from Dan without falling off the bed. A gangly arm and leg hung over the mattress, a faded quilt half-covering him. Cassie walked around the bed to see if he was awake. The older of her two brothers was handsome. She envied him those long black lashes, so at odds with the chiseled jaw line. He was definitely asleep. Dan was uncovered except for his pajamas. He had one arm thrown over his brother, and his legs were brought up tightly under Mitch's backside. Even asleep, he looked intense and unhappy. Cassie saw the hilt of his knife gleaming under the pillow.

She went down the hall, opened the door to her parents' bedroom, and tiptoed in.

The oak rocker sat draped with her father's trousers, white shirt, and underwear from the day before. Cassie eased down into the rocker and rocked back and forth a couple of times, but it squeaked, so she stopped.

Her parents seemed to float comfortably in their own private worlds. Her father's pajamas wound about his body, the stripes garish in the morning light. He snored peacefully, his mouth open under his black mustache. He was on his back, one arm thrown sideways and resting on Liddy's chest. Her arms, too, were thrown upward, and long strands of copper-colored hair pillowed her head. Cassie thought they looked as though they belonged together, looked happy—an impression they never gave when they were awake.

Cassie wandered out of the room, through the kitchen and into the backyard. The wind had died, and the sky was a light gray. Sun streaks of lighter gray in the east could almost be taken for clouds. The air was soft, and the grass dry and springy under her bare feet, even this early. Right now the dust didn't catch in your throat or sting your eyes. She breathed in as she passed the blossoming pear tree by the garage, wishing she could taste such a heavenly scent. The morning glory vine—her mother called it a weed—not yet blooming, wound up the trellis her mother had hammered together. Mama did the fixing around the place; Daddy was all thumbs.

Turning at the sudden ruckus, Cassie saw Jim and Sadie, her father's English setters, bound out of their house with wagging tails and lolling tongues. Sadie's week-old puppies mewled and wiggled in a little heap inside the doghouse. Caught in the sun's slanting rays, they looked like fat white worms with tails. Cassie roughed both dogs behind the ears and headed back to the house, carefully stepping around goatheads and grass burrs, as the dogs set up their rackety morning barking. Her parents would hear from old Mrs. Pinkerton about that.

In her bedroom, she pulled her paper-doll book from under the bed and sat sorting through the pretty ladies and dresses she had cut out yesterday. Now another early morning sound reached her ears—her brothers wrestling and thumping each other on the floor of their room. She left the paper dolls to watch. Dan was getting the worst of it, as usual. Mitch had Dan's head jammed under the bed, and Dan was kicking Mitch wherever he could, as dust swirled with them on the floor and clung to their pajamas.

"*Boys!* Get out here before I throw your breakfast to the dogs," Liddy yelled from the kitchen. "You're gonna wake the dead!"

○

Later in the morning the dust kicked up right on schedule. Liddy, her hair tied up in a rag, flew through the place like a dervish; Marvin always said she cleaned house like she was fighting fire. Liddy took great pride in her home. It was big, two stories, one of the more substantial residences in Cato. The only bathroom and the three bedrooms, one of which the boys shared, were upstairs. Downstairs was the kitchen, a breakfast room where the Field family took all their meals and did most of their congregating, and a dining room and living room, both devoid of furniture.

Liddy was Scotch-Irish. She knew what people said about such folk: that they were a race that kept God's commandments and every other thing they could get their hands on. But she didn't care; she carefully preserved her nice things in her cedar chest—her lace-trimmed sheets and pillowcases, her finely worked dish towels and crocheted doilies, the beautiful tatted tablecloth Aunt Julia had made her. Liddy didn't quite know what she was saving the things for, but Cato in spring was too dirty to bring them out. Besides, there was no one in town she wanted to impress. The cavernous living room took no time to clean. Maybe she'd have furniture someday, but they couldn't afford it now. Marvin kept promising he was going to trade a bird dog for some. And the house needed painting, but what was the use of slapping it on when the westerly gales would just sand it right back off?

She gazed into the boys' room—what a pigsty. Merely changing the bedclothes would be like bailing out a single pail of water from a sinking ship. Dan's motley collection of cigar boxes filled with rocks, arrowheads, bird feathers, and marbles flanked Mitch's stacks of comic books and Western magazines, paper-weighted with various balls, bats, and baseball mitts. A BB gun stood in the corner, in easy reach if Mitch wanted to shoot a crow. Maybe if she cleaned it up *just once more*, they would get the idea. With the dust mop handle she fished out several dirty socks and undershorts from under the bed, along with a considerable pile of house moss and fine sand.

As she worked, the wind tore and whipped around the house, thrashing the bushes and trees. Drafts of dust-laden air snaked through the windows and under the doors—not cold, just blustery. Taking a throw rug into the backyard to beat it, Liddy paused to look up in the sky. Mares' tails scudded high above, but there was no sign of rain.

Just two days ago the children and she had had to dash to old Mrs. Pinkerton's storm cellar.

That black Sunday, Marvin had been at the store. He'd heard on the radio that the storm was coming—how people up in the panhandle were already being lost in a huge, choking sea of dust, so he had called Liddy and told her to take the kids and hightail it next door. Mitch swept up Cassie, and Dan nearly blew away as they staggered across the yard. Liddy would never forget the sight of his skinny little body suddenly lifting off the ground in the thick, swirling dirt. She'd had to grab his belt to hold him till they made it to where the old woman held the cellar door open; then they all stumbled down the steps of what was little more than a roofed-over hole in the ground, and sat huddled against the dank, rough concrete walls, amid the rows of home-canned pickles, tomatoes, okra, and green beans. When they emerged two hours later, the air was ugly, foul stuff, and the light was like no daylight Liddy had ever seen—a yellow opaque haze. Curtains of dust swirled around them menacingly, making them cough and gasp for breath as they crossed toward home. Out on the road, piles of fine silt had drifted into little dunes.

The next day she and the boys took all the bedding from the house and shook it out, with Mitch singing, "California, here I come!" At supper Dan asked, "How come *we* can't go to California?" and Mitch chimed in around a mouthful of french fries, "Yeah, how come? I hear the sun shines there *all* the time!"

Liddy said, "*No, thank you!* Those poor tenant farmer families don't know where their next meal is coming from. They have to pack up everything they own and take off for a place they don't know a thing about!"

Marvin blew out the smoke from his cigarette in a lazy, drifting circle. "You boys think I wanta join up with a bunch of hard-up, stony-broke farmers, people who don't have enough smarts to scratch out the barest kind o' living?"

Amazed to think they might have it all over the farmer kids, Mitch sat up a little straighter, and Dan looked down at his knees, spreading his hands over the patches on his overalls.

Now, holding the rugs, Liddy stood looking at her lifeless backyard. Her spirea drooped, more gray than green, and the lilac bush she'd planted last year looked dead. The sparse yellow grass was interspersed with prickly burrs.... The drought wasn't finished yet. Dust blew in her eyes, and she went back inside.

Suddenly she remembered she'd promised to meet Winifred Weston at the church. And today was the day Marvin was going to raffle off two Sunbeam Mixmasters to stir up business at the drugstore. Liddy had put up strong objections about it. The mixers—the new model with the bakelite handle—cost $5.95 apiece, $9.95 retail, and they couldn't be frittering away that kind of money! She didn't have an electric mixer herself, and besides, it was gambling. What did they need a promotion for, anyway? Business was steady, and steady was what Liddy liked. Let the theater have the lotteries. It was just another in the long list of arguments they were always having.

Why had she married anyway? she wondered as she wrung out the filthy mop water. To have children, she supposed.

Cassie came running in from the backyard. "Mama, I got a splinter!"

"Why do you go outside in this wind, anyway, child? How'd you get a splinter?"

"I climbed up on the fencepost to watch Sadie's puppies, and then I kinda slid down, and the splinter went in—it hurts somethin' fierce!" Cassie held up the knee, whimpering. Liddy scorched a needle with a match and teased out the splinter, then went upstairs to get Merthiolate from the medicine cabinet. She painted the knee, and Cassie whined, "Mama, it's ugly! It's all orange!"

"You go in your room and color," Liddy replied. "I've got work to do."

It was nice to have the kids around, even if she was always losing her temper with them. Her temper was nothing compared to Marvin's, though—he was going to kill the boys someday! But he'd never laid a hand on Cassie.

Liddy dropped down on the old brown couch in the breakfast room. She raised her hands to her face and sat, shoulders slumped. Lately an unease, a feeling that all their hard work was, in the end, not really worth it, had descended on her. She and Marvin ought to get along better; they ought to try to get more fun out of life.

She had gotten in the habit of *never* having any fun. As long as she had the kids, though, and her church, she could keep on scrimping and sewing all their clothes and wearing hand-me-downs that her sister-in-law sent. She could even live without dancing—never mind that she had been the best dancer in Paul's Valley. She would gladly do without and work like a slave—*if he did, too.* But Marvin was taking more and more time off to train the dogs. He was gone for days at a time, even during wheat harvest, when every able body was needed to work. The dogs were the thorn in her side, the curse to test her Christian soul. Not only did they smell bad and cost money to feed, they got under the fence and ran through old Mrs. Pinkerton's yard, then came home and peed on the lilac and snowball bushes in hers. When there had been rain and she'd had a vegetable garden, her okra, cabbage, and asparagus were always being anointed. Marvin was down to only two grown dogs now, but here were eight messy, noisy puppies coming along.

The war had changed Marvin—hardened him. Before he went off to France they had had the same goals, wanted all the same things. *They would build a decent life based on their love for each other.* Now he did what he wanted to, without even bothering to consult her.

And the guns—that was the worst part of the whole business! In the early days he'd been in the habit of cleaning his hunting guns in the drugstore apartment where they lived. *BAM!* He'd shot the rung out of one of their chairs, and once, only a few seconds after Cassie'd been standing in front of it, he shot a hole through the refrigerator door! She had *never* been as angry as she'd been the day that happened, and Marvin had never cleaned his guns inside again.

Amazingly enough, the refrigerator still worked.

She finished the mopping and scouring in the bathroom. There were black hairs everywhere. She straightened up the medicines and hair pomades in the medicine cabinet and wiped off the mirror. Marvin used more beauty aids than she did. Well, he was handsome—always had been—and he knew it. Knew that, when he wanted to, he could wrap her around his little finger. Knew that when he made love to her, as he'd done last night, it almost made everything all right.

After they married she had found out about passionate love, something she'd never dreamed even existed. You could well nigh get *addicted* to it. But she wasn't a woman to be addicted to anything, not even Marvin. She was getting too old for it, anyway. The kids were growing up, and there wasn't much privacy.

Mitch was getting taller, and he was so good-looking with his black hair, ruddy Scotch-Irish coloring, and the beginnings of a muscular build, the girls were already chasing him. But the drugstore was going to take a toll on the boys. Marvin was expecting them to work longer hours, and they still had growing and playing to do. She was afraid Mitch would confront his father about the whippings someday…

Everything would be worthwhile, though, if Marvin still loved her. But if he did, why would he spend so much time with the dogs and that awful Joe Kelly from down at Ardmore—manager of a Kress's five-and-dime! All he liked to do was train dogs and hunt, then bring the damn quail home for *her* to clean! She didn't even know if they were getting ahead financially. They wouldn't have this nice big house if she hadn't told Harold Cutter she could come up with the extra four hundred and fifty dollars they had to have for the down payment. Marvin didn't know she'd been sneaking out a dollar a day from the cash register for years to pay herself for slaving away down there. They'd gotten this house because she outsmarted him, and Harold was the only person in town who knew. Once she had almost told Rowena Richards, her best friend, but at the last moment changed her mind. It was too bad, outsmarting your enemy that way and not able to brag about it to anyone. She supposed someday, when they were old and gray, she would confess to Marvin. He would hate it; he would say she was a manipulator and a conniver, the worst thing a woman could be!

Harold Cutter was an older man—upright, moral, and a widower now for several years, with no children. He and she had developed a friendship last fall when they'd worked together to raise funds for a new parsonage roof at the First Methodist. Harold loved to walk. People would see him out in the country, striding along, swinging his arms. He told Liddy it was the only way he'd found to stop grieving over his wife.

All Marvin cared about was calling long-distance to Georgia to order a new puppy! The whole country was in a depression, she hadn't gone dancing or had a new dress in three years, and he was calling *Georgia* to pay God-knows-what for a new bird dog puppy! She thought of the words to a song she used to hear at the Chautauqua Assemblies:

"When I was single, went dressed all so fine;
Now I am married—go ragged all the time…"

If Marvin and Joe Kelly thought they were running off for five days in July while she ran the store, they had another think coming. She wasn't filling any more prescriptions like last summer! If they got caught, Marvin would lose his license; *then* where would they be?

The phone rang. It was Principal Cantrell saying he was going to have to keep Mitch and Dan after school for fighting on the playground, maybe even give them paddlings.

"Oh, no, Fletcher! *Now* who are they fighting with?" she cried. Mitch was in ninth grade and Dan was in sixth, but the school's small enrollment dictated one playground for all.

"Liddy, are you sure you want to know? It seems Dan was playing baseball with Sean O'Herlihy, and Sean said Dan couldn't hit a bull in the rump with a fiddle. Then Dan said Sean ran like a striped-ass ape. Sorry, Liddy, but I have to tell you the words so you'll see the seriousness of the situation. They got into a real fistfight— I guess Mitch piled in to help Dan. Now, Liddy, I know you and Marvin don't talk like that at home."

Liddy's face had turned scarlet. "Do me a favor, Fletcher. Don't tell Marvin. He always whips the boys once more for good measure. You keep them after school, and I'll talk to them."

"Okay, Liddy. I'll try to straighten 'em up."

Liddy sighed. The dusting was finished, and all the bare floors had been mopped. No sooner had she thrown the last bucketful of dirty water on the spirea than the phone rang again. This time it was Marvin. "Liddy, I want you down here today for this Sunbeam drawin'. No tellin' how many people this thing is gonna pull in!"

"All right. I'll be there about two. But I still think you're wasting your—*our*—money!"

"Never mind what you think. Just be here." He hung up.

○

She and Winifred Weston were alternating the duties of decorating the church altar through April and May. This week it was Liddy's turn, but she didn't want to stop at the church—she was already in a bad enough mood. Not only had she cleaned the entire house, with the dust starting to settle on everything before she'd even finished, but she hadn't been able to find a pair of stockings without a run, she had a pulsing, throbbing headache, and she couldn't do a thing with her wiry waist-length hair. After working with it for five minutes with a curling iron, she gave up, wound it up tight in the usual bun, and stuck a bunch of pins and combs in it. She threw on a white organdy blouse that had seen many a season, and a skirt with Coca-Cola spots she couldn't get out.

Then, going out to the garage, she found the clippers, went to the pear tree, and carefully trimmed off some of the long branches that were heavy with white blooms. Why they weren't blown away she didn't know—she supposed it was because the tree was sheltered on the east side of the garage. She tossed Cassie and the branches into the Model A, then drove to the church.

Scrawny Winifred was the wife of Floyd Weston. They had a little farm northwest of town, 160 acres, mostly in wheat and cattle. Mrs. Weston was not the typical farmer's wife. She spent a lot of time in town delving into community and church affairs with a particularly meddlesome hand, and she seemed pretty interested in people's private business, too. Violet Shafer, the plump widow who ran Shafer's grocery, had told Liddy that she thought Winifred was the worst busybody she ever met. Liddy silently chastised herself for having such uncharitable thoughts as she parked in the church's dirt parking lot.

Carefully lifting the blossom-laden pear branches out of the backseat, she took Cassie's hand and made her way down the aisle between the dark pews. She was disappointed to see that the two tall altar vases were already filled with white lilies.

Winifred Weston, standing back to admire her arrangement, saw Liddy walk down the aisle and nodded in perfunctory greeting. She didn't like this feisty redhead, whom she had tangled with several times on church matters.

As for the Field children, she thought Cassie much too independent for a child her age, allowed to loiter around her parents' place of business at all hours. She should be watched more carefully, because those impudent dark eyes would get her into trouble. And the Field boys were turning out poorly, too; you could tell the younger one was a born troublemaker.

Winifred was sure Liddy Field was a devout Christian, but perhaps she was one of those people who shouldn't have been allowed to *have* children. The Westons had never been blessed with issue, but if they had, their children would be strictly supervised and not allowed to run hog wild. The father Marvin Field never darkened the door of the church, and there was something about the man… At the post office he always smiled at her, and kept smiling until she had to respond. He should take his place at his wife's side in God's temple—then, thought Winifred— *then* she would smile.

In a fluty voice she said, "Oh, hello, Mrs. Field! I didn't expect to see you. I heard about the lottery at the drugstore—I assumed you'd be busy with that. Hel-*lo*," she said to Cassie, looking down her nose.

Liddy thought the way Mrs. Weston said, "lottery at the drugstore," it sounded like "orgy at the brothel." Winifred showed her teeth briefly and twitched her long nose. Not a strand of hair escaped her stiff hairdo, and her black print dress with its ruffled peplum was immaculate.

"Mrs. Weston, remember I said I would bring some branches from my pear tree for the Easter service? But I see you've got these lilies—they're beautiful!"

"Yes, Floyd had to run over to Red Arrow, and I told him to pick up some flowers at the Blossom Bower." She smiled the complacent smile of a woman who could afford to buy flowers at a florist's during a depression, smack-dab in the middle of the Dust Bowl. "Why don't you just take those cuttings back home and decorate your *own* home with them?" she added. "I'm sure they would add something."

"All right, I guess I will." Liddy gripped Cassie's hand harder and, pressing her lips together, led her back up the aisle.

Winifred spoke to Liddy's back. "We'll see you tomorrow morning, and remember, God *so* appreciates your hard work!" She sounded as if she were speaking as His own private ambassadress.

Liddy turned.

Winifred held up a finger. "Oh, Mrs. Field, wait. There *was* something I was considering telling you. I don't want to worry you, but…" Winifred's head wobbled on her long neck, and her thin mouth curved in a vicious, anticipatory smile. "It's just that I heard…"

"Yes? Go on," challenged Liddy.

"Well, Mrs. Curtiss Billings—you know, Hazel…"

Liddy waited. Mrs. Billings, as the widow of the original builder of the Cato grain elevator, was the richest woman in town, and consequently the highest in the town's social order.

"Yes?"

"She saw your husband and that Sally—Sally Scruggs, the mayor's wife—somewhere, and your husband was kissing her—on the *lips*."

Liddy gripped Cassie's hand. "Where did she see them?"

"I believe…" Mrs. Weston paused again and licked her lips. "I believe it was at Veterans Hall."

"Oh, of course." Liddy moved away, pulling on Cassie's hand. "They often meet there. Mrs. Weston, you're wrong in your inference about my husband and Mrs. Scruggs. Please pass that on to Hazel Billings." She and Cassie walked quickly to the car, where she settled Cassie into her seat and threw the branches behind her with a force out of all proportion to their weight.

She revved the motor and drove away.

O

Field's Drugs was one of about a dozen viable business establishments on Main Street, which began just a few yards down the hill from the train tracks and ran north and south. Times were hard, and there were five or six vacant storefronts.

Cato, now grown to a population of 750, had sprung up in the early part of the century because the Atchison, Topeka and Santa Fe Railway traversed this section of prairie. The tall grain elevator was built by Curtiss Billings in 1912, when wheat was growing gloriously and splendidly in this part of the state. The cattle business was thriving, too, and the railroad shipped all over the United States. Near the grain elevator was the other Cato high-rise, the spindly- legged water tower, whose huge faded black letters announced the name of the town to a sparsely inhabited world.

At the southern end of Main stood a tall flagpole holding a weathered Old Glory and a tattered Oklahoma flag. The state flag, an Indian shield emblazoned with eagle feathers, crosses, peace pipe, and olive branch, was a symbol of the state and not the town, for no tribes were represented here. Cato's residents were descended from tough old sodbusters, mostly of German, Scotch, or Irish stock, with an occasional Scandinavian or Russian thrown in.

The town boasted a hotel on the other side of the train tracks, a rambling two-story wood structure that looked ready to collapse in the next high wind. Obviously this seedy establishment had seen better days, but it still served a few traveling salesmen, government men, and roaming oil and gas prospectors. Off the lower end of Main was the big fieldstone Veterans Hall, and to the north, the town's only gas station.

At that end of Main, a short stretch of unpaved road led to the quarter-mile-long bridge spanning Wolf Creek, a tributary of the North Canadian River. The creek was usually low, and now, in the mid-1930s, it was so low it had dried up altogether. But in the past it had roared with torrents of water; in fact, in 1915 a young woman had drowned there, a tragedy Liddy used as a cautionary tale to the boys. But they had scoffed at the idea that anyone could drown in a mud wallow that wouldn't keep a catfish alive.

Scattered about town were six churches. There was no Catholic church and no synagogue, for the town was unrelentingly Protestant. However, there were differences enough among the Protestants to keep religion interesting.

The town was well enough equipped to fight sin, but it hadn't organized much against fire. The fire department consisted of a single Model T fire truck, parked at the gas station, and a volunteer fire department. In the alley behind Field's Drugs was a fire whistle, used to signal when it was twelve noon and also to alert the town to emergencies. The fire whistle blew every day except Sunday, when the church bells took over. Cato was lucky; only three houses had burned down in recent history. Lately, dust storms and drought took all the town's attention. There had been droughts in 1890, 1900, 1910, and 1917. The years of the Great War were good for the wheat farmer, and by 1924, in spite of dry spells, farmers were growing seventeen million more acres of wheat than they had in 1909. But arid shortgrass regions of most of the plains states, where plow should never have broken sod, were being farmed, and the day of reckoning had to come.

Well, that day was *here*. Roosevelt and his administration had begun to look for solutions to the farmers' problems, but most rural Americans still thought they could work out their problems for themselves—if it would just rain.

Field's Drugs was situated between the feed-and-grain and Cato Mortgage and Loan. Next to this granite building with its wide concrete steps stood Reuben Hargraves's Mistletoe Café, advertising HASH FOR CASH. Marvin had picked up some advertising tricks from somewhere, and all through the thirties, while the depression dragged on and the dust storms blew, he used them. Out on the dusty roads, wooden signs with his ornamental lettering—the only billboards for miles— proclaimed, FIELD'S DRUGS—WE HAVE IT! The family's Model A, painted olive-drab with white splotches, bore the same slogan. This motif, army-green paint with white splotches, also decorated an old upright piano that Marvin had donated to Veterans Hall. He'd acquired several hundred gallons of the surplus war paint, and after using what he needed for the store and the car, he had enough left over for the piano.

Cassie loved the spotted piano. She liked to look at it for long stretches of time, like the stained-glass windows at the First Methodist.

O

When Liddy and Cassie arrived at the drugstore, it was thick with bodies, and Mitch was busy serving drinks. People didn't want to buy any merchandise, but the fountain business was good. Among the assemblage was Sally Scruggs, dressed in a Pepto-Bismol pink taffeta dress. Fat round curls the size of dog turds covered her head, spit curls snaked in front of her ears. Liddy went behind the cosmetics counter and began to straighten jars of Pond's Cold Cream, refusing to look at Sally or anyone else.

The drugstore was divided into distinct parts. At the front, to one side, was the fountain area. Across the aisle was the cosmetics counter, and down the middle were marble soda fountain tables with their matching spindly wrought-iron chairs. The back of the store held perhaps a dozen tall shelves filled with medicines, first aid supplies, and such. The prescription area was an enclosed space in back, fronting the family's old apartment.

Marvin kept it scrupulously neat. Large green and brown glass tincture bottles were lined up on the marble counter where he hand-mixed his powders and ointments. Each of his spatulas, mortars and pestles, and glass beakers was in its proper place. At the end of the counter were six green tin canisters with gilt lettering—LACTOSE, CALCIUM CARBONATE, BELLADONNA, CASCARA SAGRADA, QUININE, SULFUR—and nested beside them was a collection of a half-dozen tin funnels he used to pour concoctions from one bottle to another.

Five minutes after Liddy arrived, Marvin started the drawing for the mixer. The raffle tickets were in one of the big syrup vats, cleaned and scoured for the purpose, and he stirred them around with a long wooden spoon. He tossed his head, obviously enjoying his "Lord of the Merchants" role.

"Is everyone ready?" he asked, looking around at the crowd.

"Ready as an old maid at a cakewalk!" yelled Stuffy Byers and everyone laughed.

The first winner was Inga Sundersson, Sven Sundersson's hardworking wife.

"Oh! It's *me*!" shrieked Inga. She made her way through the tables and took the large carton from Marvin, her florid face redder than usual. "Oh t'ank you, Mr. Field! *T'ank you!*" She returned to her seat, holding the box to her chest and beaming at the crowd.

Sally Scruggs won the second one. Sally pranced up to Marvin on her high heels, curls bobbing, and he handed the carton over to her with a flourish. It was too much for Liddy. She dropped down and knelt out of sight behind the cosmetics counter.

Cassie was behind the counter, too, sipping Coke. Her mother was acting mad, she thought. Her mood must be left over from the church, when she got so cranky after that old witch had talked about Daddy.

Cassie whispered, "Mama, did Daddy really kiss Mrs. Scruggs?"

Liddy glared. "Hush! *Be still!*"

The drawing was over, and Marvin intoned, "That's it for today, folks. Hope you've enjoyed yourselves! Come again!" He smiled and nodded at everyone as they filed out.

Stuffy Byers and his wife, skinny, fair-haired Charlene, were the only customers left. A rotund fellow and a regular drop-in customer at the drugstore, Stuffy was the local broomcorn merchant, and Marvin's good friend. He also dabbled in bootlegging, a fact of which Liddy was ignorant. The Byerses had one child, Betsy, who was Dan's age.

Stuffy and Charlene sat down on the revolving stools at the soda fountain and ordered root beers from Mitch. Stuffy's buttocks sagged on either side of the stool like two full sacks of flour, while Charlene's barely took up half the seat.

"Now, that there was a real successful drawin'. Don't you think so, Liddy?" Stuffy boomed.

Stuffy was addressing thin air; Liddy was still crouched on the floor. She could be seen, though, through the glass showcase.

"Don't you think so, Liddy?" Stuffy repeated.

Marvin lit a cigarette. Seconds passed; then Stuffy noisily sucked up the last drops from his copper mug, and he and Charlene left.

Liddy emerged from her hiding place. "I'm going home. You don't need me anymore for the big crowd, do you?"

"What's the matter with you? Why is it you have to ruin everything?" asked Marvin.

Cassie looked at her father's face, then back at her mother's. Here came another of their spats.

"*Ruin* everything? *You're* the one who said this would do business so much good— how we'd be raking in profits today! Maybe you noticed— nobody bought a darn thing!"

"You don't think all these people will be back here to buy things, like…like at Christmas? *You don't think this built up an awful lot of goodwill?*"

"No. I think they'll all drive over to Red Arrow or Antelope, like they do every year, and we'll be out the price of two mixers!"

She stomped out, for the second time in one morning dragging Cassie along. When they got home, she sent Cassie upstairs and told her to take a nap. Then Liddy went into her bedroom, closed the door, and threw herself on the bed. She felt so tired…. She thought about leaving Marvin, and not for the first time. If he was going to worry her with these indiscretions, acting intimate with women all over town, she couldn't stay—*wouldn't* stay! Had he really kissed Sally, or was that just Winifred Weston making trouble again?

She stripped to her slip and took the hairpins out of her hair, then buried her head in a pillow and let the tears flow. At last getting up for a handkerchief, she saw herself reflected in the dresser mirror. *Can that possibly be me?* she wondered. She'd once been pretty; now she was nothing but a dried-up country hag. They said Englishwomen had beautiful skin because they lived near the water, so the opposite must hold true, and her skin was living—or half-dead—proof of it. She grabbed the Pond's off the dresser and smeared a glob over her face, blotted it, and threw herself down on the bed again. Once more she began to cry, for herself and for all the other women in this godforsaken dust pocket of the world.

Finally she went to sleep.

She woke an hour later and went down to the kitchen, barefoot, to fix a cup of tea. Out the kitchen window she saw Cassie swinging in the backyard. The wind had died down, and the child looked contented and happy.

I should thank the stars above for what I do have, thought Liddy. She stood offering up a silent prayer of thanks for her blessings: her irrepressible daughter, her smart handsome sons.

But sometimes she felt she couldn't deal with it all. Children were supposed to get easier as they got older. The human race would die out if the secret were ever told—that offspring became more difficult with each month that passed, and even though she had Marvin to help deal with some of the boys' peculiarities, their unceasing energy, he was much too harsh with them. Still, she would never be able to cope without his help. But was that reason enough to stay?

Deciding to skip the tea, she padded up to the bathroom, ran a tub of water, and sank gratefully into the warmth. She sprinkled in a lavish amount of bath salts. This was one of her few indulgences—another blessing!

If only she could escape some of the drudgery of her life. She had been offered a job; maybe that was a way out. Harold Cutter had come into the store to see her a week or so ago, cooling off with a milkshake after one of his walks. He'd looked around, seen that Marvin wasn't there, and said, "Liddy, I been meaning to talk to you about something, something kinda important. You know, you're one heck of an organizer—I found out about it when we worked on that church drive. Thing is, I been hired by the Works Projects Administration, the WPA. I just signed the contract yesterday."

Harold brushed back his gray hair with one tanned hand and stirred the milkshake with the other, and Liddy thought how young he looked for his advanced years.

"I'm don't know anything about the WPA, Harold," she said. She was rinsing out glasses and turning them upside down to dry on a towel.

"It's part of Roosevelt's New Deal. I'm gonna be in charge of all the programs for the poor folks in the county, and I could use someone like you, someone real interested in helping people. You'd work at distributing food, or startin' up programs for impoverished farm families. But I'll be real honest with you—there won't be much pay!"

As if Marvin paid her!

She turned away so Harold couldn't see the excitement on her face. *Leave the house behind…leave the store behind!* It sounded heaven-sent.

"I can't sell real estate now," he continued, "with people moving away and the town dryin' up. The only thing wrong with this job is I have to drive over to the regional office at the county seat in Red Arrow, couple times a week."

Now, thinking of Harold's offer, Liddy slid all the way under the water except for her head, giving herself up to the luxury of the perfumed salts and the sensation of hot water on her skin. She had been in the tub for three or four minutes when there was a timid knock on the door.

"Mama?"

"I'm in the tub."

"Can I come in?"

"Can you wait a few minutes? I just got in here."

"Okay." Cassie's voice sounded muted, small, and rejected.

Silence.

Liddy sighed. "Just a minute, I'll let you in." She got out of the tub, put on her robe, and opened the door to Cassie. She didn't believe in nudity in front of the children. She didn't believe in nudity, period.

"Can I get in with you?"

"No, but wait'll I let the water run out; then you can have a bath with the bath salts like I did."

"Mama, you been cryin'?"

"I'm a little tired."

Cassie was unbuttoning her shirt and slipping off her shorts. She handed her clothes to her mother and got in the tub. "The bath salts smells nice."

"Good. Do you want me to wash your hair?"

"Unh-uh...Mama, you have pretty hair. I wish mine was red like yours."

"Oh, Cassie, it's wiry as a mule's! You have pretty black hair, like your dad's. I always said the reason I married him was because I wanted black-haired children, and I got three!"

Cassie covered her little mound with the washcloth. "Mama, should I wash down here, or my feet first? Which is dirtier?"

"Cassie, your *feet* last, of course! Of all things to ask!" Liddy's eyes were averted from Cassie's body, and she drew her robe closer around herself. "You just have to soap yourself there, no need to *rub*."

Why was the child so preoccupied with that part of her body? She'd once seen Cassie, as a four-year-old, touching herself, and to put a stop to it she'd threatened her with a spanking.

"You can get out now. Step out."

Cassie reluctantly got out of the tub. The intimacy she had sought with her mother had been spoiled by something, but she didn't know what. As Liddy toweled her, she tried to recapture the moment. "Mama, how come you don't wear lipstick? Mrs. Bannister wears a *lot*, an' she looks jus' like Jean Harlow!"

"My father always said a woman wearing lipstick looks like jaybirds at pokeberry time.... Let's go, Cassie; we're through getting clean. Put your clothes on by yourself—you're five now; you're a big girl."

Sensing that Cassie wanted more, Liddy gave her a hard hug, holding her for a few moments and patting her on her little behind. She felt a rush of maternal love, a different feeling than she had for her boys—something indefinably softer and more protective.

○

That night Liddy stood behind the closet door with her back turned, and Marvin sat on the side of the bed, removing his shoes and socks.

"Winifred Weston told me today that someone saw you kissing Sally Scruggs." She spoke in a low, flat tone, hands stopped in midair, ready to remove her slip and put on her nightgown.

"Who in the world saw—*said* that?" he exclaimed, tossing a shoe across the room.

"It doesn't matter who saw it—*someone saw it*," she answered, her voice muffled by the gown.

"I was just congratulatin' her on havin' her name in the Antelope paper, is all."

"*Congratulating?*"

A few beats of time went by.

"What'd they put *Sally's* name in the paper for?" Liddy asked, her voice dry with skepticism.

"She told me she'd been writin' these poems, an' they put one of 'em in there."

"What're her poems about?" Liddy turned around, her nightgown finally on.

"I think they're about raisin' kids."

"What does Sally know about raising kids? She's only got one, and *he's* nothing to brag about!"

Marvin didn't say any more, and neither did Liddy. She opened her mouth once to ask if he'd rigged the contest so Sally would win the mixer, but decided against it. They went to sleep with their bodies turned away from each other, Liddy clinging to the edge of the bed as if, unanchored, she might sail off into the ether.

2

NEGRO: DON'T LET THE SUN SET ON YOU
IN THIS TOWN
—Sign outside many Western towns

Marvin stood in the doorway of the drugstore, looking out at the empty street.

In white shirt and black suspenders, silk bow tie, and dark pants, he looked more like a shirtsleeve city lawyer than a small-town druggist. He was thinking about how Liddy had jumped all over him about kissing Sally—something so innocent, *for God's sake*, he'd forgotten all about it as soon as it happened! He didn't know how long he could keep dealing with his wife's jealousy and bad temper. It was impossible to live with her.

Almost immediately, his thoughts segued from problems with Liddy to his worries about making a living.

He lifted one foot and pounded the heel of his shoe on the doorsill. Dust an inch thick, even on the sidewalks! What a godforsaken place Main Street was, tumbleweeds blowing down it much of the time. If things didn't get better, he and all the other businessmen in Cato would go broke. They'd have to try to sell out and move back to Liddy's hometown, or his. Both were way south of here, and their prosperity didn't depend as much on wheat. But he didn't want to go back to working for a boss.

Was the government ever going to do anything to help? He couldn't tolerate the Democratic Party, and especially that snobbish-sounding Roosevelt. He was proud to be in business for himself, and had nothing but contempt for the New Deal. He and Liddy had come up the hard way, and they had done it through hard work and true grit, with little help from anyone. Well, there *had* been that one small loan from Liddy's mother. When they were just getting started, they had worked late into the nights of the wheat harvests, serving thirsty farm laborers. They were so busy then that they would leave trails of dollar bills scattered on the floor as they carried trays of drinks back and forth, so exhausted they took turns napping all night through in their apartment in back. Those bounteous wheat harvests of the twenties put the drugstore on its feet.

Now they had more than they'd ever had, for they had had nothing. Everyone else might be willing to take handouts from the government, but not Marvin Field!

But if the wind didn't stop blowing and the rains didn't come, the wheat farms would fail, and when that happened the drugstore would fail, too. Marvin didn't see how Roosevelt, who had the brass to call himself a farmer, was ever going to solve the problems of too much wind and too little rain.

O

Cassie sat in the darkened movie theater across the street from the drugstore, clutching a box of lemon drops and her rag doll, the one Grandmother Field had sent her. Liddy hadn't wanted to give it to her, because of germs or something, but after washing it twice, she said she supposed it was all right.

Liddy had spoken once of Grandmother Field's illness—something called "TD" or "TB." Cassie held up her wrist to look at her new Mickey Mouse watch, the one she'd gotten for kissing Mrs. Weston's nephew, Alvin Jonas, in the Palm Sunday pageant rehearsals. Alvin was supposed to be Jesus entering Jerusalem, and Cassie was one of the children who were to throng about him on the raised platform at the church. Alvin Jonas was a sissy classmate of Mitch's who had pimples and pale, sparse hairs on his cheek. Mitch thought Alvin was lower than a snake's belly, and Cassie agreed; she thought he had a face like a can full of worms.

Why couldn't Mitch have been Jesus? But neither he nor Dan went to Sunday School anymore. Liddy had had to bribe Cassie with a Mickey Mouse watch to get her to kiss Alvin. That was last week. She guessed it had been worth it. She'd just brushed his scaly cheek with her lips and got down off the platform, fast.

When she'd asked to go see this movie, *Imitation of Life*, her folks had acted glad to get rid of her, and she didn't have to steal the dime like usual. Mrs. Richards had come into the store and told Liddy that *Imitation of Life* was a real tear-jerker, but it was only when she said there were colored people in it that Cassie got interested. The movie was about a pretty white lady with bangs and a colored maid who made pancakes. The maid had a little girl, and so did the white Liddy. Uncle Fred down in Waxahachie had colored people working for him at the newspaper, and his wife Aunt Bertha had Feemy. Sometimes Liddy called them "niggers"; sometimes she called them "negras"; sometimes "colored folks." There seemed to be endless names to call them, but you could call them anything you wanted to because there weren't any in Cato anyway.

Cassie liked Feemy, who was Aunt Bertha's cook. The last time they'd visited Waxahachie, she had taken Cassie up above the garage, where she and her husband, Jesse, lived with their little boy, Carlton. Feemy gave her ginger snaps, and Cassie and Carlton played Chinese checkers.

The only other colored person Cassie knew about was Little Black Sambo. She adored Little Black Sambo, the main character in a cartoon strip in Dan's *Weekly Reader*. While Dan read the words to her, she would gaze at Little Black Sambo's red coat, blue trousers, green umbrella, and purple shoes. The bright colors against Sambo's black skin made him seem powerful and magical, and the tigers didn't seem to scare him at all.

The movie ran on and on and wasn't as interesting after the first hour.

Now Eula the ticket girl was shaking her to tell her the movie was over, and picking up her rag doll off the floor and handing it to her.

Cassie squinted her eyes against the bright light outdoors and said good-bye to Mr. Gruber, who was already on the sidewalk smoking. Mr. Gruber owned the theater and ran all the movies from a dark room upstairs. He was always bragging on Cassie, saying she was one of his best customers.

Cassie crossed the street to the drugstore and found her mother behind the cigar counter, stacking boxes of cigars. Her dad was at the cash register.

"Can we get a colored maid, Mama? Like Aunt Bertha has?"

Liddy's face showed astonishment as she raised her head from stacking Roi Tans.

"What?"

"The white lady in the movie had a little girl, and she had a Negra maid who had a little girl, too. The girls were friends until they grew up and—somethin' about passin'—I dunno, but if I had a friend like that who lived with us, then I wouldn't be botherin' you so much!"

"*Botherin'* me! What makes you think that? I've got a surprise for you. We *are* going to get someone to live at home and cook for us. Her name is Mabel!"

"Is she a Negra?"

"No!" said Marvin. "She's big and white and ugly as a mud fence in a thunderstorm!"

"Marvin, hush! Cassie, how did you like the movie? Did you cry, like Mrs. Richards did?"

"Nunh—uh. I just liked the first part. Why don't we have any niggers livin' here in Cato? An' Dan an' I was wond'rin' why there isn't any redskins, either."

Marvin and Liddy looked at each other, but neither spoke. A customer came in, and Liddy rushed off.

Marvin guided Cassie to the back table and sat her down; then sat down with her. He put an arm along the back of the wrought-iron chair and leaned back. "Cassie, Cato is just too far away from everything to have any of those kinds o' folks come live here. We don't have any special schools to handle 'em. There aren't any jobs for them here, anyway. The Negras have whole towns to theirselves over around Tulsa—Boley and Taft. They've even got their own college at Langston. And Indians settled in lots o' parts of Oklahoma, but none of 'em want t'come out here."

"Dan says there's *lots* o' Indian stuff around here. He found some arrowheads he says are *real* old! He's been talkin' to Charlie Detwiler about it."

Cassie's tone of voice became assertive. That Dan had been confiding in her was a source of pride.

"Just because Charlie Detwiler's got a big ranch don't mean he knows beans about Indians," said Marvin. "He's always puttin' too much paint on the brush. I wish Dan'd just stick to lookin' for arrowheads and readin' books. There's no Indians for miles around here, and no signs they ever *was* here! Now, you better hightail it on home with your mama."

Her questions seemed to put him out of sorts. Cassie hiked her doll up on her hip and went once more in search of Liddy. She wanted to find out more about the new hired lady, Mabel.

○

Liddy had tried out three other girls before she found Mabel. The first one quit after three days because she didn't like to referee the children's fights.

The second was so slow you had to set a stake to see her move.

And the third one, imported from Red Arrow, had come to work with no camisole on, her nipples showing impudently through the thin cotton of her dress, and Liddy didn't like the way Mitch hung around gazing at her with his mouth hanging open, nor did she like the way Marvin did the same only with his mouth closed. She was ready to give up on having any help at all when Violet Shafer said she'd heard Mabel Farrow was looking for work, maybe would even live in if they wanted her to, because she wanted to get away from her father. Old Mr. Farrow had gotten even more demanding of Mabel since his wife died, and Mabel had told Violet in the post office one day she couldn't take much more of his bad temper.

Mabel came to live with the Fields, all six feet of her. She had a tanned, country-woman's face, big hands, and hair pulled up in a braided knot. One of her eyes had a slight cast, and her mouth, though large, had difficulty containing all her outsized teeth. Her bosoms were abundant, more than filling out her bodice, but discreetly covered in plain, coarse calico.

Liddy fixed up the little spare room off the kitchen, the one she'd been thinking about making into a sewing room. Rowena had an old iron bed she said she'd be glad to lend, and Liddy made it up with bedding and covered it with one of her quilts. She found a bureau in the attic filled with fabric she'd been collecting for decades, and she stored the cloth in boxes and put the bureau in Mabel's room. She found an old rag rug in the garage, and brought home a floor lamp from the store apartment.

She stood in the door when Mabel put her suitcase on the floor and sat down on the bed.

Tears flooded the countrywoman's eyes. "Whenever I said I'd work here, Miz Field, I never 'spected *nothin'* as nice as this!"

"Oh, it's just odds and ends," said Liddy. "I had a good time puttin' it together."

Dan and Cassie were shy with Mabel at first. They looked at her face, high above them.

"You live out n-north o' t-town?" asked Dan.

"More like northwest," said Mabel. "Over the Wolf Creek Bridge is whar my daddy lives—'bout five miles out."

"N-near W-Walt Zimmer?" asked Dan. He hated his stammer, which, of course, made it worse.

"Uh-huh," said Mabel tying on an apron and banging pots and pans while she located things in the kitchen. *"People scared o' Walt just 'cause he's blind."*

Cassie looked at Dan. She could tell he was interested in old Walt.

Mabel seemed to know instinctively how to take care of them all.

The next day Cassie came in sobbing her eyes out. She told Mabel that her best friend Fiona, who lived next door, had kicked her when they argued over the rules of hopscotch.

"She steps on lines all the time," Cassie said, "an' she drops her rocks and picks 'em up like it didn't even happen, an' goes right on jumpin'!"

Mabel patted Cassie and pulled her up onto her lap. She patted her back and talked to her about how, when she was a little girl, she made dolls out of clothespins and painted their faces with berry juice.

Liddy and Marvin thought Mabel was a marvel, a phenomenon, a wonder—a being who seemed to know why she was put on earth: to cook and serve up food, keep a home spotless, and do it all cheerfully for very little pay. Marvin repeated to Liddy Stuffy Byers's remark that Mabel was "big enough to go bear huntin' with a stick," but now he always had ironed shirts. She baked three times a week—delicious sweet cinnamon rolls and light, crusty bread, rich dark-chocolate cakes. Pies of all sorts, with pastry so short it vanished on your tongue. She fixed wonderful stews, mouth-watering chili, and roast pork with fresh-baked rolls and redeye gravy.

After a month, Marvin noticed he was thickening around the middle. The boys' faces were filling out, Cassie was learning to bake cookies, and Liddy almost felt forgiven for firing that third girl.

○

There was a slight complication, however. Mabel had a boyfriend, and he visited her at the Fields' house.

Buck Corkle was a big, raw-boned country boy, son of Ezra and Jerusha. Ezra was a fiddler and wood-carver from the hills of Arkansas who had moved to Cato with his wife, his son Buck, and a retarded younger boy, Harley. No one knew why they'd moved here, but everyone knew the Corkle men didn't work very hard. Only Jerusha really liked to work.

Buck was a hired hand, and occasionally he drove cattle and worked in the wheat harvest, and Ezra spent all his time carving and fiddling and telling Ozark stories. Both of them mostly loitered about town.

Buck was even bigger and homelier than Mabel. Dan and Cassie were scared of him—of those slanted dark eyes under threatening black brows that seemed to communicate, "Keep out of my way," so when he came they stayed out of sight. Mitch was never there for Buck's visits; he was always working or at ball practice.

One July day Cassie sat at the kitchen table drawing a picture of a watermelon. Mabel said she was going to make room for the watermelon in the refrigerator as soon as she finished what she was doing, which was making sweet-and-sour red cabbage and singing in a cracked voice:

"Bile 'em cabbage down,

Bake 'em hoecake brown,

The only song that I can sing is

Bile 'em cabbage down!"

She sliced the cabbage really thin with a sharp knife, then put it in a big, heavy skillet with bacon fat, grated onion, vinegar, and brown sugar. Mabel's face was as red and steamy as the cabbage, and her hair was loosening from its braids. Cassie was about to ask her to sing the song again—she'd never heard it before, or any singing *anywhere* like Mabel's—but just then there was a loud knock.

"Mabel, you thar, honey? I got lonesome fer ya. So here I be!"

Buck came through the screen door and onto the back porch.

Mabel hurriedly pinned up her hair and smoothed out her apron. She shook her head in an aggravated way.

"Buck, I *tole* you not to come here whenever I'm workin'!" Her voice sounded funny to Cassie, shaky and uncertain, as though she didn't really mean what she said. She always sounded like that when Buck came.

Buck loomed into the kitchen, his broad shoulders taking up all leftover space.

"Wal, hello thar, little girlie." He reached down, chucking Cassie under the chin, and peered at her drawing, leaning down really close and grinning. Cassie noticed an odor of sweat, and another funny smell. Sometimes her father smelled like that and seemed happier than usual, like Buck did now.

"Oh, I see yer colorin' a watermelon, huh? Throw it up green, comes down red! Oh—an' Lovie's a-cookin' cabbage! What's a patch on patch an' has no seams? A *cabbage*, li'l gal, a *cabbage*!" He gave one of Cassie's pigtails a heavy tug.

"Her name's Cassie. Now whyn't you git on outta here?"

Buck's only reply was to step over to Mabel and encircle her waist with a hairy arm.

To Cassie they looked like two giants out of one of her fairy-tale books. Inching her way up from the table, she sidled out of the kitchen into the hall and started to tiptoe upstairs to her room, but then stopped for a moment. Sounds of scuffling feet, then a period of quiet, followed by heavy breathing and slobbering sounds, the kind the dogs made when they were drinking water. Slowly Cassie peered around the side of the door, her hand clamped on the doorjamb to brace herself for a fast escape. She would have given anything if Dan were here.

Buck had one of Mabel's big breasts in his hand and was kneading it the way Mabel kneaded her bread dough, bending her over backward over the kitchen sink. slavering and sucking on her neck. Mabel was trying to push him away, but only halfheartedly. She finally shoved him hard enough to escape his grasp. She rushed to the stove, where she grabbed the lid off the pan and stirred down the boiling liquid. The cabbage smell now completely overtook the smell of Buck. It permeated the hallway where Cassie hid, and began to waft its way through the rooms. Buck let Mabel tend the pot while he leaned against the sink, looking pleased with himself, his black eyebrows moving up and down. "Know what I'm gonna do tonight when you git off?" he asked.

"Yer a-gonna git me *fired*; that's what yer gonna do!"

"Honey, that there cabbage reminds me of another riddle! See if you git it! When it goes in, it's stiff an' stout; when it comes out, it's floppin' about."

"Buck! Now I *know* yer tryin' to git me fired! You git on outta here, I said!"

"I wuz jes' talkin' 'bout yer cabbage there!" He continued to recite in a loud singsong voice:

"The ol' man shook it an' shook it,

The ol' woman pulled up her dress an' took it;

The ol' lady pitted it an' patted it,

The ol' man down with his britches an' at it."

Mabel grabbed Buck's cotton sleeve and hauled him to the back door. "Now you git outta here or I ain't never goin' to have nuthin' to do with you ever again, Buck Corkle! Now, git!" Cassie had never seen Mabel's face so twisted-looking, and the eye with the cast looked like clouded glass.

Buck was still guffawing as Mabel propelled his huge frame to the door. "You sure are one riled-up woman! I was jes' talkin' 'bout a man shakin' apples out of a tree and his wife catchin' 'em in her dress! An' the same ol' wife makin' the bed and th' same ol' husband gittin' in! Wha'dja think I meant? You better not let folks know what a downright dirty mind you got!"

Mabel shoved him as hard as she could across the back porch and down the steps. Buck straightened himself up, laughing louder than ever. He climbed into his pickup, backed out of the driveway, and was gone in a cloud of dust.

Cassie had disappeared up the stairs.

For supper that evening Mabel served sausages and the red cabbage, and when she put Cassie's plate in front of her she squinted at her real hard with her good eye. Cassie smiled a saintly smile right back. She knew better than to tell about Buck's visit. Mabel might change her mind and tell about the black eye she got last week when Cassie and Dan were playing catch with a potato and hit her in the eye. She'd told Liddy she got the black eye from a closet door.

○

One day Mabel abruptly hung up the phone after talking to her father. She grabbed Cassie and braided her hair tight before bundling her into her pickup and taking her with her out to the country. Mr. Farrow was complaining again that neighbors had stolen water from his trough, and since her cousin, Duke Farrow, wouldn't get involved, she'd promised she would go out and have a talk with Verley Hoffman. Mabel talked to herself on the way. "How come Duke cain't take no responsibility fer his uncle! He's a whole sight meaner than I am! He could put a scare into Verley, that's fer sure."

They traveled over some good bumps on the way, Cassie's stomach doing pleasurable flip-flops over the hills of the dirt road.

"That was a good one!" Cassie squealed, after they had flown over one exquisitely stomach-floating rise. "Let's go back an' do it again!"

Mabel ignored her and drove without talking. Finally they turned into an opening in the barbed-wire fence. They had to drive a long way into the property, then Mabel turned off the engine. They sat for a minute as their dust settled slowly into the dust of the farmyard.

They were at the Hoffman farm. A few scrawny chickens eyed them warily, but no humans were in sight. Tumbleweeds, looking as if they had taken root, crowded just outside the fence enclosing the yard, and tall piles of sandy dirt were banked against every outbuilding. Mabel got out of the pickup and waded through the dust to the front door, her cotton dress sticking to her broad backside. Cassie saw a skinny woman come to the screen door with a baby in her arms; soon a man in dirty overalls joined them. The wind was kicking up again, and Cassie could hear their voices but not their words.

A little girl slipped out of the cabin, and Cassie climbed down from the pickup cab. She had seen Lally Hoffman before, in town. Lally was about her age, maybe a year older, and she had straight brown flyaway hair. She was real skinny and dressed in a faded calico print dress that reached almost to her ankles.

"What you wanna do?" asked Lally.

"I don' know."

"We got baby pigs." This was offered tentatively, as if it might not be up to Cassie's standards of entertainment.

But Cassie had never seen baby pigs. "Where are they?"

"Come on." Lally was barefoot, but for once Cassie wasn't, and her shoes scuffed up the dirt as they walked around to the back of the cabin and down a gentle slope to the pigpen. This stood —or leaned—next to a tall windmill and water trough. They stood silently contemplating the sow and a dozen baby pigs nuzzling her in the dried mud.

"We keep it wet from our own trough."

It sounded like Lally was making this statement to the world.

Cassie hadn't thought about where the water came from; she only knew she had never seen anything cuter than the way the baby pigs pushed and squealed next to their mother. The little girls stood close together, leaning on the railing and gazing at the squirming little black-and-white-spotted porkers. They were grunting as they suckled, emitting high-pitched squeals unlike anything Cassie had ever heard. Especially the ones that had lost their place.

"They're nice," was all Cassie could think to say. "Where's the daddy?" she asked finally, thinking of Jim, her current favorite of Daddy's bird dogs and sire of the puppies at home.

"We et 'im.... Your daddy's got the drugstore, han't he?"

"Uh-huh. I get ice cream all the time. When you come to town I'll give you some."

"We only come Sattidays. Whenever I go to school I come right home on the bus. I don't git to town much."

"Do you like livin' in the country?"

"I never knowed nothin' else. I reckon I do. Pa says we may not be able to stay."

"How's come?"

"The land ain't payin'. There han't been no rain, and the wheat didn't come up last year, an' my pa couldn't buy no seed. My cousin an' aunt an' uncle in Cimarron County done left for Californ-y."

"Where's that?" asked Cassie.

"You know, where they make the movies. There's lot o' crops there to pick. My cousin and her folks and little sister done left last month. Lots o' people're goin'."

Cassie thought Lally was pretty. She had big shy blue eyes and wispy hair that blew all around and in her face. Her gesture of reaching up to brush it back was graceful and slow, and her face and arms wore a light covering of dirt.

"I got puppies at my house," Cassie said. "You wanna come see 'em?"

"I don' know. Pa don't have gas to come in, 'cept Sattidays, like I said. But I'll ask. Pa ain't in much of a good temper lately, though—he'll prob'ly say no."

Just then a black dog with a stick in his mouth ran up to the girls, dropped the stick, barked, picked up the stick again, and ran away, looking back, daring them to chase him. They ran after him down to the sandy pasture, then chased him back together, running arm in arm.

On the way home Cassie sat up close to Mabel, confiding, "Lally's nice—nicer'n Fiona is sometimes. She might come see my puppies, 'cause I saw her pigs."

"Don't think they'll be havin' those pigs much longer. Don't think they'll e'en *be* thar much longer."

"How's come?"

"Those folks is *pore*—they're tenant farmers, y'know. The land don't pay no more, an' the bank's takin' it over. That's just 'tween you and me."

"Lally says they might go to Californ-y—*California.*"

"Might's well. Seem like lots o' folks goin'. Buck's e'en talked 'bout it." Mabel's neck got red; then the bright scarlet traveled up into her face. She swung the pickup violently around a curve.

"If *he* went, would you go, too?"

"Heck, no, chile! Don't you know I hafta stay here an' take care o' all you Fields? Not to mention my pa, who allus seems ta have somethin' fer me to fret over. Like the poor ol' Hoffmans usin' his water. I don't see how he's goin' ta prove they's usin' it. He'd hafta git th' sher'ff out there night and day to watch 'em! And it ain't like they don't have more'n one mouth to feed."

They arrived back home, and Cassie jumped out of the truck to go visit Sadie's and Jim's puppies. They were getting big now, jumping on the fence and trying to get out to play with her. Their legs were getting longer, and so were their ears and tails.

She hated to admit it, but Lally's pigs were cuter.

3

Courage is doing what you're afraid to do.
There can be no courage unless you're scared.
—Eddie Rickenbacker

The fact that Dan slept with a knife under his pillow was an indication that he was afraid of something, but nobody knew what. Liddy and Marvin had tried to talk him out of sleeping with it, and Mitch had kidded him endlessly about it, but he screamed when they tried to take it away. He didn't carry his knife around during the day, but it was always there, under his pillow.

Dan was afraid of a lot of things, and he was more than a little afraid of his father. And although he worshipped Mitch, he was also cowed by him, because Mitch could always get the best of him in a fight. At fifteen, Mitch was four years older, sturdy and strong, while Dan had a skinny, string-bean frame—there was little doubt about the outcome of any scuffle.

On top of all this, or maybe because of it, Dan stuttered. Grandmother McIvor, Liddy's mother, who came to stay for a few months every year and who was Dan's champion, said the reason he stuttered was that he couldn't get his thoughts out as fast as he was thinking them.

Everyone knew that Dan was the smartest one in the family.

O

At breakfast, Mitch was reading the sport sheet from the *Daily Oklahoman*. "Dad, did ya know one of the high school players from up at Boise City is goin' to a minor league team down in Alabama?"

"That so?"

"Yeah, Coach Lansford said they offered to sign 'im up." Mitch waited for a response from his father, received none, and dropped his eyes back to his paper.

Marvin's head jerked up. "Mitch, you better get your mind off baseball or you're goin' to end up pumpin' gas somewhere till you're old and gray. Now, school's out this year, and you did barely passable—with help from some o' your girlfriends"—Dan snickered audibly at this—"and next week you're goin' to be in the store full-time, but you got two more years o' high school, and next year I expect some *real* grades." Marvin lowered his voice so the women wouldn't hear. "You better prove to me you haven't got shit for brains!" He stood up. "And today I want you to clean out the dog pens, and rake up the yard—the front and sides. Dan can do the back. There's two rakes." He picked up the keys to the Plymouth and yelled to Liddy that he was ready to go. Liddy left hurriedly after giving Mabel a few instructions.

As Marvin left the room he heard Dan say, "Guess you better start doin' some of your *own* homework, huh, Romeo?" Once more Cassie noticed how Dan's stutter disappeared when he was being mean. Neither boy noticed Marvin still standing in the doorway, although Mabel tried to signal them from the kitchen. Mitch flipped his spoon end over end at Dan, breaking the cereal bowl and causing Dan to knock over the milk pitcher, sending it crashing to the floor as he tried to dodge the cascading milk and corn flakes.

Marvin came back into the room, grabbed Mitch by the shoulder and shook him like a rag doll. "You clean this up—I won't have Mabel doin' it! Then get in there and make your bed, and then go clean out that dog pen!"

Mitch left.

Marvin turned to Dan. "Guess you haven't learned about folks with big yaps! Guess I hafta teach you again!" He took Dan by the collar and dragged him upstairs to the bathroom, and Cassie followed to watch. She had endured the same punishment from Liddy for saying she had seen Amos Hicks take a shit outdoors. Amos was Ol' Mrs. Pinkerton's grandson, and Tootie and Perry Hicks' son. Cassie had gotten no credit for telling the truth or for giving an accurate report of neighborhood events. Just humiliation—and the soap taste that wouldn't go away all day.

Marvin grabbed the soap and rubbed inside Dan's mouth while the boy choked, coughed and spat. Then, with his hand on Dan's shoulder, he gave him a hard, teeth-rattling shake and left.

Dan's face ran with tears, and Cassie went in and patted him on the arm. But he yelled, "Get outta here!" and shoved her out of the room, slamming the door.

That afternoon Liddy took time off from the drugstore to climb up to the attic and store some of their winter clothes. She sat on the floor folding woolen knickers, thinking about the way Marvin treated the boys. Should she speak to him about it again or just let him go on punishing them for every little thing? Or maybe he was right—maybe the only way to get their attention was to beat on them. Maybe they'd be better citizens when they grew up if they had his heavy-handed discipline. Marvin had hated his own violent father, who had started to drink after he lost his money in a land development scam down near Ada, near the Red River. Enraged at the world, he had taken it out on everyone around him, including his saintly wife Letitia. Marvin had been beaten and thrashed many times before he ran away from home at sixteen, never to return.

O

Cassie thought when school let out that her brothers would play with her; her mother had encouraged her to think so. They would all three play hopscotch, or jacks or tents. The boys sometimes included her in a game of hide-and-seek, but as for the things which were the most fun—tree climbing, bicycling, kite flying, snake catching—she was always left out. Now, as the long hot days of summer came on, it dawned on her that they were leaving her out of something secret, mysterious, and no doubt thrillingly criminal.

Mitch and Dan had been coming home dirtier than usual these past few days. Mabel said she didn't want them looking like they had the swamp measles, so they had to hose themselves off before entering the house. Cassie watched them wash themselves one day just before supper. The water gathered in the dust and dirt on the ground and made a sludgy pool.

"Where you two been, anyways?" she asked.

Mitch just looked at her, stony-faced, and Dan got that smug smirk she hated.

"Dan, where you been? *Where you been, Mitch?*"

Mitch went up the porch steps and into the house. Dan was still trying to dry off the front of his overalls where he'd slopped water from the hose. His face was smeared with dirt, and his hair was adorned with a sprig of buffalo grass.

"You and Mitch been down to the river?"

Instead of answering, he rubbed his hand on his overalls and waved it in the air, snapping his fingers. "What's this?" he asked.

"I dunno! Where you *been* today—you and Mitch been gone for hours!"

He waved his hand and snapped his fingers again. *"A butterfly with hiccups!"* And he ran into the house.

Standing in the backyard, with the evening's first fireflies blinking yellow-green around her, Cassie was aware of something hardening inside her, something like a steel spring. She didn't yet know what to call it.

The next morning Marvin told the boys they had to rub down the dogs with a solution for fleas, so they were home all morning, and the carbolic acid solution stunk up the air all around the house. But that afternoon Cassie heard noises outside the bathroom window. She climbed up on the clothes hamper in time to catch a glimpse of Mitch and Mike O'Herlihy heading down the road, with Dan trailing.

Her mother was ironing, and Mabel was off that day. Cassie stayed in her room a few seconds; then, when her mother turned her back to shake out a shirt, she sneaked out the back door. She didn't ask permission, knowing none would be given. She darted behind the house and out onto the street. The wind was blowing, sending the dust rising up in thick whorls, and the sky was the usual dirt color. She walked and walked and finally arrived at the fenced pasture. The giant cottonwoods swaying in the wind stood guard over the meadow like great, stern sentinels shaking their heads.

Cassie was able to see where bodies had dragged in the dirt under the barbed wire, so she scooted under at the same place and walked until she arrived in the middle of the pasture. By now her pigtails were studded with little burrs, and her dress was torn where it had caught on the fence. Some distance away, two brown-and-white cows stood chewing; one had a calf nuzzling under her. The wind rustling through the trees suddenly died down, and she heard muffled sounds of boyish giggling. With an ear cocked toward the voices, she headed in that direction, trying to avoid the cow plops on the way. Walking as silently as a deer, Cassie came upon a rectangle of boards nailed together and covered by a small tree limb. Now she could *really* hear them! She struggled, pulling up the heavy boards, and knelt down to peek in.

Five faces peered up at her.

"Cassie! What're you doin' here? You git on back home!" yelled Mitch.

"I ain't *goin'* home. You let me in, and then I won't tell."

There was a long pause while the boys looked at each other.

"Ben, move the trapdoor."

She shinnied and slid down on dirt steps that were almost like real ones. The cave was big; it must have taken a lot of digging.

Hunkering down next to Dan, she pointed to a corner of the dugout. "There's Mama's shovel she's been lookin' for!"

The cave was full of bluish cigarette smoke and the smell of burning wood. Mitch's friends Dooky Schlanaker, Ben Hargraves, and Mike O'Herlihy were here. None of Dan's friends were. He only had one, towheaded Pauly Stone, whose folks ran the Cato Hotel.

"You better not blab about any o' this," said Mitch. "I swear, Cassie, you ain't got the brains God gave a squirrel, followin' us down here."

"I won't. Those cigarettes smell good. Can I have one?"

"You sure *can't*—it'll make you sick!" Dan said. He did look a bit queasy; so did Ben.

"Boy! Daddy and Mama would sure be mad if they knew you dug a hole in this pasture. Who's it b'long to, anyway?"

The boys exchanged another look. Their biggest fear was that someday Mr. Brandenberg would stumble across them.

"Okay. Here. You can smoke some of the dogwood—you're too young for real cigarettes. See if you can get it lit." Mitch handed her a short, slim stick of grayish wood.

Dooky held a match, and she sucked in with all her might, but nothing happened. For now, however, her moral victory over her brothers would suffice. She crawled over to the side of the cave near Mitch and curled up, letting the stick hang out of one side of her mouth the way she'd seen movie stars do. The dirt walls felt cool and hard.

"Okay, I heard a new one." This was freckled, red-haired Mike. He was Irish, and lived down near the water tower with his dad and four little brothers. He didn't have a mother, ever since she ran off with the Singer salesman. Mike was the raggediest of all Mitch's friends, but he had an endless stock of riddles and funny sayings.

"What vegetable is it you throw away the outside, cook the inside, eat the outside, then throw away the inside?"

No one had an answer.

"Corn, you dumb-butts! What's in the water, under the water, over the water, and never gets wet or cold?"

No one knew.

"A duck egg!"

"You told that'n last week," objected Dan.

"Then why din'tcha remember it?" asked Mike.

Mitch had one. "Why is a thief in an attic like an honest man?"

Silence.

"Because he's above doing a mean thing."

The boys liked that one, but Cassie didn't understand it.

"If a man was born in England, raised in Kansas, and died in Pee-king, what is he?" Mike sucked hard on his cigarette, blew out the smoke, and waited. The smoke circled around their heads and hung in the narrow shafts of light piercing between the boards.

"Dead!" he chortled.

The boys groaned, and Cassie felt herself growing sleepy. The smell of the cigarettes, hot bodies, and sweaty, smelly hair of the boys was intoxicating but soporific.

"My dad said if'n it don't rain soon we're goin' bust." This was tall, skinny Dooky Schlanaker, who lived a mile out of town but managed to come in almost every day to see his friends.

Dan spoke up for the first time. "If you k-kill a spider, i-it'll rain."

"We tried that," responded Dooky. "I killed *lotsa* spiders, an' my pap's kilt nigh on to twenty snakes, an' nothin' like rain's showed up. None o' you know beans from buckshot 'bout how to make it rain." Dooky tried to straighten his long legs, but gave up and folded them back under.

There was a long minute of hanging quiet. After this, the talk changed to a discussion of all the teachers they all hated and some of the awful mean things the boys had done to them before school let out, plus the awful mean things they planned to do next year. The older boys said they hoped they'd made Miss Thornhill so miserable she would throw in the towel and quit.

Stocky, pale Ben, the gentlest and best-natured of the boys, didn't say much. He was too kind to make fun of Dan for stuttering, and much too nice to try to make teachers quit teaching. He enjoyed the other boys' jokes and riddles, but he himself didn't know a single one, nor was he good at remembering the ones he'd been told.

The last thing Cassie remembered was Mike's joke with the funny word "Pee-king"; then she was being shaken by Mitch. "Come on," he urged, "we got to go."

They climbed out of the dugout and into the blinding daylight. Mitch and Mike replaced the board and tree limb over the opening. The other boys scattered, and Dan, Mitch, and Cassie headed for home.

While all three washed off with the hose by the back porch, Liddy waited nearby with her arms folded, hopping mad at all three. And when the boys protested that it hadn't been *their* idea for Cassie to follow them, she flew off the handle.

Didn't they know they were Cassie's big brothers and *responsible* for her?

Marvin, home for supper, finally extracted from Mitch where they'd been and what they'd been doing.

"August Brandenberg's pasture!" he yelled. "That's trespassing, and you know it, Mitch! I won't have you boys shamin' me this way—you'll both remember *this* whippin', goddamn it! And you both been smokin', too—I can smell it!"

Dan ran outside, and they could hear him throwing up.

Liddy dreaded what was coming. She said, "But Marvin, *you* smoke!"

He ignored her, and her stomach gave a sickening lurch when she saw him drag Mitch by one arm, twisting it painfully as he pulled the boy down the back steps and into the garage. Listening to the loud whacks of Marvin's belt, Liddy shuddered. Being pulled along by his father, Mitch looked so sullen and rebellious, and Mitch was not a rebellious boy. Marvin was going to ruin him! Thrashing Mitch was just plain wrong— he wasn't a boy anymore, although she had to admit that this prank made him look like one.

Liddy was doubly angry with Marvin for beating Dan while he was so sick to his stomach.

Cassie was put to bed without any supper. The unhappiness of the household fell on her ears for some time, and she mourned and sobbed because she was the one who had got her brothers in trouble. Finally, by hugging her rag doll tight and pulling the covers over her head, she managed to go to sleep.

Liddy took trays of food to their bedroom, but the boys wouldn't eat. Dan lay on his bed, hiccuping sobs; Mitch was turned toward the wall, his shoulders twitching in pain.

When she and Marvin finally sat down to eat, she could barely chew. They ate in silence, Marvin's face impassive as he spread jelly on a square of cornbread. Finally Liddy pushed her plate away, smoothed her hair, and placed her hands on either side of the table.

"Marvin, can't you think of some way to punish the boys without the strap? I swear, sometimes I think your heart is stuffed with sawdust! Mitch is gettin' too big, and Dan's scared to death of you! I don't want them growing up hating you!"

Marvin's voice was harsh. "They have to learn to behave and stay out of trouble. If you don't like it, I'll just leave, and you can raise them alone."

Mabel was spending the night with her father. In the middle of the night, Liddy allowed herself to cry for a long time in the bathroom, where no one could hear her.

That night Dan had bad dreams and woke Mitch with his screaming. Sobbing and hysterical, he went in to Liddy, saying he'd seen some terrible animals in his sleep—awful-looking beasts, with bodies like bears and heads like tigers. Marvin merely turned over in bed.

The next day Mitch's arm was swollen; it looked sprained. While Marvin was shaving, Liddy went into the bathroom and closed the door, tears brimming in her eyes, and said she thought Mitch's arm should be looked at by the doctor. Marvin dropped his shaving brush into the mug with a loud plunk.

"There's nothin' wrong with that boy's arm, Liddy. You're makin' a mountain out of a molehill."

But she caught the look of worry that flitted over his face, and she was certain of one thing: he didn't want Doc Ledbetter to see what he'd done to his son.

O

Marvin laid down new rules. From now on and throughout the summer, both boys would come to work at ten a.m. and work until three, each day and every day. No more larking about in other people's cow pastures, no more climbing trees and whittling on dogwood; in other words, no more having fun.

After she and Marvin had the fight over Mitch's arm (the swelling went down in a couple of days) Liddy spent hours thinking over everything that was wrong with her marriage, most of it having to do with the way Marvin treated the boys. But she didn't like the way he treated her, either— forever putting himself and his own wishes first, never hers. She'd always prided herself on her independence of thought and self-reliance, but those qualities had receded into the background for some time now. Realizing this, she made up her mind: she called Harold Cutter and told him she would take the WPA job.

He said, "That's great, Liddy. I know you'll be a real addition to the program. Come over to my office and we'll sign your work contract."

After she'd signed the contract and the salary of ten dollars a week had been decided on, she went home and told Mabel the news, cautioning her not to mention it to Cassie, who couldn't keep a secret. But the boys were old enough to know, so when they got to the drugstore and Marvin was at the post office, she told them about it, saying, "I haven't told your father yet, so don't mention it until I do."

Mitch and Dan were tying on their fountain aprons. They looked at her and at each other, at first speechless. Their mother with a real job!

"What're you gonna *do* for the WPA, dig ditches?" asked Mitch.

"Pauly's dad calls it the Worthless People's Army," spoke up Dan.

She gave them a hard look. "It's a *very* worthwhile organization, and I don't want to hear silly talk like that. I'm lucky to get a job! Hardly anyone gives women employment these days, so Mr. Cutter must think I'll be better than any of the men around here!"

She would never say anything like that in front of Marvin, of course. She dreaded telling him, and knew she was being a coward.

Three days went by.

She told Harold she was almost ready to go to work, but not quite, and the boys seemed to tiptoe around with their secret. Finally she made the announcement in the privacy of their bedroom. She said she was starting work the very next day.

"Oh, no, you don't!" he snorted. "I need you at the store. You won't make any money; you know that!" He went on and on, yelling, certain that he was right. "People don't have to be on relief, and you shouldn't be helping them get any! Besides, they got plenty other folks, men out of work, can do that job."

Liddy stood across the room, glaring back at her husband. "I don't care *what* you say, Marvin, I'm going to start; besides, you're only thinking of yourself."

He strode off to the bathroom, flipping the toilet lid up so loud she heard it all the way down the hall. Liddy's hands shook as she brushed out her hair, shaking almost as bad as they did on the day she got married. But she could already think of three or four ways to spend the extra money.

Next morning, Liddy told Marvin the entire story. He was tying his tie and admiring himself in the mirror when she said, "Marvin, I have to be gone for three days and nights to a government conference in Red Arrow. Harold wants me to go to some meetings over there. I'll be staying with one of the WPA women employees, and I'll be learning—"

"*What?* You're actually goin' to leave the house and the kids and go out of *town?* That's a pile of crap, Liddy, an' you know it! Why can't Harold train you right here? The gov'ment sure is spreadin' it around—usin' tax dollars to coddle people who brought their troubles on theirselves! Traipsin' off to another town with an unmarried man, to boot!"

She couldn't believe how calm her voice sounded. "Harold won't be there, he'll be here, and I'll be taking a course on all the WPA agencies, especially food distribution and sewing programs—those are the ones he wants me to know all about."

"All right, but remember this. When the kids start goin' to hell in a handbasket, it'll be your fault!"

"It will not," said Liddy. "We have Mabel; besides, *I'm* not the one they're afraid of."

They exchanged a glare of mutual challenge, and something not far from hatred.

He walked out, and she finished pinning up her hair. She was so pale she was the color of barley flour, so she rubbed a little Tangee rouge on her cheeks. But it gave her such an unnatural glow she ended rubbing it off.

She drove over the corrugated concrete roads to Red Arrow in Harold's old Studebaker coupe. Marvin had refused to walk the few blocks to work, not even for three days, so she had to use Harold's car. An hour after starting her journey, she turned into a parking space near the Bliss County courthouse. When she got out of the car, her dress stuck to her thighs, and her slip felt as if it was riding all the way up to her shoulders. She pulled her dress down well below her knees, where it was supposed to be, and yanked her slouch hat tighter on her head. Trying to quiet the butterflies in her stomach, she climbed the granite steps.

○

The August weather had warmed up even more. Cassie was playing with paper dolls in her room. It was lonely without her mother, even with Mabel there. Fiona had gone away, too, to visit an aunt. Mabel said to keep the shades drawn and the windows down, so the coolness of the morning air would stay, but it wasn't working. At least she had the electric fan. They only owned two, and she was seldom allowed to use one. Even so, she had to keep wiping the sweat off her hands to keep the scissors from slipping.

Mabel was in the backyard, picking peaches. She'd allowed Mitch to play catch with Dooky Schlanaker, even though he was home with a summer cold.

Sweat dripped off Cassie's nose as she painstakingly cut out Carole Lombard's legs. It was hard to do the toes of the shoes—she'd have to borrow her mother's sewing scissors. Passing the bathroom on the way to the sewing basket in her parents' bedroom, she found the door slightly ajar.

"Mitch?"

"No. It's me. Come in." It was Dooky. "I hurt my thumb catchin' a ball. C'mere an' look at this, Cassie."

She pushed the door open and went in. Dooky stood leaning against the washbasin. His face was flushed, and he had a dreamy smile on his face, as if he were pleased with himself about something. Cassie lingered just inside the door.

"Close it."

The hinges creaked in the silence.

"Look at this." A thick cylinder of pinkish-purple flesh stuck out of his undone trousers. He hadn't dropped his pants, only pulled the thing out of an opening down there.

"That's not your thumb," she said.

Dooky took several steps toward her. "Feel it! Here!" He took her hand and placed it directly on the smooth flesh.

Quickly she withdrew her hand. Dooky's hair was sticking to his forehead, his eyes wide and kind of spooky.

She said, "I'm goin'. You better not let Mitch or Dan see you doin' that."

"I just thought you might *like* to see it. It does this ever' now and then. Just wait; sometime you'll be wonderin' if I can do it again, an' you'll never git to know." He zipped up his pants and patted the bulge with a smug grin, his mouth still open and wet-looking. "But don't tell anyone, okay? If you do, I'll tell 'em you *asked* to see it."

Cassie shut her eyes tight, backed out and closed the door. She got the scissors from her mother's bedroom and went back to her room. She sat on the floor in front of the fan for a long time without moving, then began to cut around Carole's shoes. She wasn't real *real* mad at Dooky. But she wished she could have been a better audience for looking at his sticking-out thing. She knew it would have meant a lot to him.

O

It was Sunday.

Liddy was still in Red Arrow, Marvin had closed the store for once and was out in the country running his dogs, and Mitch and his friends were teasing Dan again. They got a lot of enjoyment out of it, always inventing new ways to bedevil him. He would put on such a show of temper that it made all their efforts worthwhile. They would hide from him, shoot arrows at him, tie him to trees—whatever it took for him to come completely unhinged, stuttering and spluttering away.

Cassie was pulling a doll buggy filled with bird dog puppies up and down the sidewalk while listening to the boys tease Dan in their singsong voices.

"Fernie May loves *Da-a-ann-e-e!* Fernie May loves *Da-a-ann-e-e!* Fernie May is gettin' into Danny's *pa-a-ants!*"

Fernie May Applebaum was Dan's age and lived down the street. Her dad, Smiley the trash man, was a bantam rooster of a man: a runty, begrimed creature who spent all his free time loafing downtown. Although you couldn't by any stretch of the imagination call Smiley hardworking—he collected only once a week and was a charter member of the Main Street Strollers and Spitters—he was an indispensable member of the Cato working community. Fernie May's mother was a silent backwoods woman. Folks said she never left the house because she didn't want to associate with Smiley. Their family gave new meaning to the word "unwashed," and Fernie May was cross-eyed, besides. Teasing Dan about her was nothing new.

Dan ran after the boys, his face streaming tears, yelling curses while he brandished his knife and threw one rock after another. Finally Mitch and his friends left to go farther up the street.

Dan stood, shoulders slumped, a few feet from Cassie and the doll buggy.

"They are *bad*," said Cassie.

"I'll get even w-with them. Swear to G-God I will. They'll be s-sorry."

One day a few months before, old Mrs. Pinkerton had stood near the snowball bushes that divided their yards and talked in a confiding tone to Cassie about Dan's stutter. She said that if Marvin or Liddy would just throw something called 'milt' on Dan at hog-killing time, he'd never stutter again. Cassie looked up at the tall old woman with her bun of gray hair and her craggy, wrinkled face, not sure how to reply. She didn't want to admit that she didn't have any idea what 'milt' was, but she did wonder why her parents hadn't tried it.

Now she asked Dan, "What're you gonna do?"

"None of your b-beeswax." He went inside, and in a few minutes came out carrying his knife, a Mason jar of lemonade, and his Boy Scout knapsack packed to the gills.

"Where you goin'?" she asked.

"Shut your trap and go take a flying leap to Rio. It d-doesn't m-matter to n-n-nobody anyway." He talked tough, but he looked pitiful, his scrawniness emphasized by the overalls that seemed to envelop him.

Cassie went over and hugged him around the waist. He let her hug him for a moment before yanking himself away. Then, stuffing his knife and the Mason jar into the knapsack, he walked off in the opposite direction from the way Mitch had gone.

"You better be back in time for supper!" Cassie yelled.

Dan wasn't home by suppertime, and he wasn't home by dark. Mabel looked worried, and Marvin began to quiz Mitch and Cassie. "Was he playing with you and the other boys today? When did you see him last?"

"No, sir," Mitch mumbled. "I was with Mike and Ben and Dooky. We went a little ways up the street."

"I'll bet. Did you see him at all?"

"Uh, yeah, I saw him this afternoon. He got mad about somethin'—he always does."

Marvin and Mabel nodded, knowing this to be true. "Cassie, think. When did you see Dan last?"

"When he left."

"Don't be smart, young lady. When *was* it?"

"When he took his knife an' lemonade an' stuff."

"*What?* Where did he take them?"

"I dunno."

"Well, do you know *why* he took them?"

"No."

"Think real hard, Cassie. How did he act? Did he act like he was coming right back, or what?"

"I dunno. He was cryin', 'cause they said Fernie May wanted to get in his pants, an' he took his knife an' went away."

Marvin's mustache quivered, and he shouted, "Mitch, you get your flashlight and get out of here. I don't care if you have to go get your friends—you get out of here and find Dan!"

He shoved Mitch on his way.

"I'm surprised at you, Mitch, " said Mabel, "lettin' your friends talk dirty like that in front of your little sister!"

Cassie went out on the screened-in back porch and lay on the cot they kept there in warm weather. She heard her dad say to Mabel, "I'm going to see if Dan's over at the hotel with Pauly Spokes, and if he isn't, I might drive out to Walt Zimmer's place. The other day the sheriff and a bunch o' fellows were in the store and they were talking about how Walt had maybe killed his wife—how she disappeared a couple years ago. You heard about that, Mabel?"

"Shore have, Mr. Field."

"It's all just small-town rumor—how nobody's never found her body."

"Why do folks think he *murdered* her, Mister Field? I just cain't *imagine* it!"

"Because—and this is all rumor— the rumor is he thought she was fooling around with Tom Thatcher on the next farm. Folks think Walt buried her under the cow shed. Barney Scruggs told Sheriff Bartlett that Walt ordered a whole lot of expensive wire fencing to put around the shed, not long after Charlie Detwiler said he'd stopped seeing Miz Zimmer out there. He always used to see her out ridin' her horse, coupla times a week."

Barney Scruggs, Sally's husband, was not only Cato's mayor; he ran the lumberyard too.

"Anyway, Dan was dryin' glasses that day, and you should have seen his eyes! They got big as saucers, and he wanted to know what direction from town the Zimmer place was. You don't think he'd go out there and start snooping around, do you, afraid of his own shadow like he is?"

"Mr. Field, I wouldn't leave no stone unturned—maybe you better look out there! I jes' feel so bad. I shoulda been watchin' 'im better. It was my 'sponsibil'ty and I didn't take care—I didn't do my part!" It sounded to Cassie like Mabel was about to cry.

"Mabel, it's not your fault. Kids get crazy ideas!"

"He gets so mad at ever'body! He shore has a temper—poor little guy!"

It was quiet then, and Cassie fell asleep.

O

Dan crossed Wolf Creek a few miles east of Walt Zimmer's farm, picking his way across on a collection of flat rocks and only getting his shoes and socks a little damp. Then he began to hike across the open prairie. A covey of speckled quail dashed out of clumps of buffalo grass, and headed away from him in that funny running walk. Overhead, a pair of red-tailed hawks soared above his head on the early morning breeze. He stopped to watch them—they looked so free and easy gliding up there.

He rearranged the knapsack on his shoulders so the weight was more evenly distributed. The knapsack was the only good thing he'd gotten out of his three months in the Boy Scouts, which he'd quit after a few meetings because they had to do all these dumb-shit indoor crafts. The straps dug into his shoulders because he'd taken so much food—enough so he could stay away from home a long time. He'd also brought his short-handled spade.

They would find out—he didn't need *any* of them!

He walked faster and faster as his mind simmered over his troubles and the monumental injustices of life. Reaching a fallen cottonwood, he sat down on the trunk, panting. He'd been walking for an hour and a half, and he would keep right on walking until his legs gave out. If he walked far enough, maybe he'd get blisters, and if he got blisters, they would be sorry.

He gazed about; he'd never seen this part of the country before, and it was interesting. He had crossed over Wolf Creek heading northeast, the way he usually went, following the stream as it headed through the sandhills and low banks. The tall trees and shinnery oaks seemed to stretch for miles, with tangles of catclaw and mesquite clumped in between. The knapsack was heavy, so he decided to eat some of his provisions. He took out a too-ripe banana, a chunk of yellow cheese, and a baloney sandwich. It all tasted delicious, but it made him thirsty, so he got out the lemonade and guzzled most of it down.

A few yards away he spotted an old cow skull. That would be great to put up in his and Mitch's room, but his mom probably wouldn't let him—the deer skull he'd found months ago had disappeared. He threw away the banana peel and stuffed the waxed paper from the sandwich back in his pack. Walking over to the cow skull, he picked it up and gave it a closer look. It was a big one with perfect horns, bleached alabaster white by the sun and remarkably free of ants, beetles, and other crawlers. If only he could find a *buffalo* skull! Charlie Detwiler said he could make some money on one of those.

But the buffalo had been almost gone since the 1880s. Charlie had told him the buffalo hunters had shipped out 250 cars at a time, each car loaded with many tons of bones for fertilizer, until they'd stripped the prairies.

He decided to leave the cow skull and try to memorize where it was in case he wanted to come back. Maybe he could remember his exact route here: the tree stump where he'd eaten, the look of the rocks where he'd crossed the river. He walked on. Clumps of red sorrel, beautiful dark brown curly dock, and acres of pokeweed spread out ahead of him. The pokeweed had poisonous berries and leaves—he'd learned that the hard way.

It would be nice to have a dog to walk with, but Dad would never allow him to take one of his bird dogs along on a plain old hike. They were considered prize specimens, and a hike might do something to their finely tuned hunting skills. He and Mitch had been out hunting a couple of times with their dad, but it hadn't been any fun. Even though Mitch was good at shooting crows with a BB gun, their dad said neither of them knew enough about shotguns, and he'd been critical of the way they handled his dogs, too. It seemed like they couldn't do anything right.

Hearing something scurrying nearby, he figured he'd disturbed a covey of quail, maybe a pheasant or a prairie chicken. Or possibly a rabbit or a skunk, making its home in that pile of brush. He recalled that he had found a tiny baby rabbit once, all alone and limping along, and taken it home for a pet. But it had gotten loose, and the dogs ate it.

He came to some low, sandy cliffs he thought he recognized. Maybe he had hiked here before, after all. Somehow they looked different, though, as if their outline and shape had been recast and remodeled. Must have been some earth movement here—this change couldn't be from only wind and rain. Carefully he climbed up the side of the sand and limestone slope. On top was a scrubby growth of jimsonweed and a cluster of large boulders, and between two of the biggest boulders was a deep crack in the earth, with several smaller cracks branching off it.

As he peered into the largest of the crevices, something caught his eye. It looked like part of an animal skin, slightly paler than the dirt around it. He got down on his hands and knees. On the skin he could discern a series of reddish-brown stripes. He threw his pack on the ground, took out the spade, and knelt down and began to dig, unconsciously holding his breath. Carefully he scraped down, removing the encrusted soil from around the skin, using his hands and a small twig when the spade seemed too clumsy. At one point he had to stand up and heave a few big rocks out of the way. Two were so big he couldn't budge them. Suddenly he wished Mitch were here—*he* would be able to move them.

The animal skin was about ten inches below the surface of the earth. He knew enough to take great care; he'd learned that, digging for arrow points. The skin seemed to be from a really big animal, at least five or six feet long. By the time he had excavated around the length of it with his spade, he was drenched with sweat, and the sun was high overhead.

He was so excited he could hardly contain himself. Now the top of the hide was completely exposed. It was decorated with a kind of russet or sepia color, almost worn off, but still visible. It had been painted in a striped pattern toward the middle, and at each end were faded drawings of buffalo, deer, the sun, and the moon.

Dare he reach down inside the trough and pull it out?

Still forgetting to breathe, he took out his knife and cut the leather thongs wrapped around the hide, then lifted an end. Bones…*human* bones! There wasn't any doubt about it—this was the skeleton of an Indian! He had uncovered the man's fringed leather shirt and leggings, leather moccasins, and some silver disks that were tied to what was left of his hair. Buried with him was his shield, also decorated with an animal designed with beads, clearly a bear. Between his leg bones, in the leather leggings with their crumbling fringe, was an empty yellow-brown fur case—a quiver. The bow was nowhere to be seen. Had the hunting or fighting companion who'd buried him taken his bow and arrows? Then why not his quiver, too?

Dan sat back on his haunches, looking at the find: the ancient bones, with the yellowed skull the most macabre sight of all; the fringed leather shirt and leggings, the leather moccasins, the silver disks, the buffalo hide shield, the quiver, and what looked like a slender whistle carved from bone, with a beaded pendant attached. He picked up the whistle and put it in his knapsack. He shouldn't leave the skin exposed, not with the possibility of rain—or sleet and snow in the winter. There could be a sudden torrent like they'd had last week, and it could last for twenty minutes or three hours. He could feel the wind coming up now.

Thoughts raced furiously in his head, one idea rapidly replacing another.

He finally decided he would keep this a secret. It would be *his* Indian, and his alone. Mitch had made fun of him for even *thinking* there were Indians around here. Boy, would he love to show him this! But if he told, they'd just dig the guy up and take him away.

Out loud he said, "I don't know how you got here, Mister Indian, but I'll protect you; I promise I will! I'll leave you here, and it'll be just you and me knowin'."

Slowly and painstakingly, Dan replaced all the dirt and tiny stones around the skin; then he put his knapsack back on and climbed and slid down the hill to level ground.

Walking to a small cottonwood nearby, he cut off a dozen or so of the straightest branches. He spent a few minutes whittling the ends with his knife so they'd go into the ground easily, then stuck them several yards apart, leading back the way he had come. The stakes would lead him back here —something he'd learned in the Boy Scouts. Then, shouldering his knapsack, he started for the Zimmer farm.

He got there early in the evening, hungry again but determined to stay away from home half the night, long enough to make them all sorry.

He didn't go near Walt Zimmer's well until dark. The well was about twenty yards from the house. He crept over to it and stood crouching for a long time, waiting to see if Walt had heard him. He knew that blind people's other senses grew keener to make up for their lack of sight. He waited and waited, and waited some more. Finally, when no sounds of movement came from the house for a half hour, he let down the well bucket as quietly as he could, brought it up and filled the lemonade jar. Then he headed back toward town. No more hiking cross-country now; it was too dark. He groped his way up the dusty moonlit driveway and finally arrived back on the main road.

○

The birds woke Cassie, and she sat up. Someone had thrown a sheet over her in the night. She walked through the house barefoot, feeling the quiet, then remembered about Dan running away. She padded quickly to the boys' room, holding her breath. There they were, both of them. She hurried back to her room, got a pillow and a blanket, and came back, settling herself on the floor on Dan's side of the bed. She would watch his face until he woke up.

Instead, she woke to find him looking at her.

"What are you doin' down there?" he whispered.

"Where *were* you? Did Daddy find you?"

"Shh! Mitch is still asleep!" Dan checked over his shoulder to be sure.

"Can I get up there?"

"Okay."

She climbed up, feeling the hardness of Dan's body and breathing in his smelly warmth.

They huddled together, facing each other.

"Where'd you go?"

"F-first I just started walkin' an' didn't know where t-to go. I walked past the bridge and then I went f-further out— and I found somethin' out there. Then I ended up at ol' Walt Zimmer's."

His large gray-green eyes studied hers to see if she was impressed.

"How's come you went out there?"

"I just did. He's a murderer; you know that, don'tcha? *He murdered his wife!* I b-bet Mitch an' those guys would never've h-had the nerve to do what I did! I got some of his well water! Look! I'm gonna put *curses* on all those guys!" Crawling over Cassie, he reached behind the chair and pulled out his knapsack. He removed from it a large jar of dirty-looking water.

"That's what you had the lemonade in!" said Cassie.

"Yeah. All's I have to do now is get thirteen n-nails, all d-different sizes, and put 'em in a bottle filled with well water. Then I write the names of my enemies thirteen times on s-separate pieces of paper and put 'em in the bottle, and then I bury the bottle upside down in front of my enemies' gates, or under their steps. And that puts a curse on 'em for *life!*"

Cassie didn't have to ask who Dan's enemies were.

"Where you gonna get all the bottles?"

"Mama has lotsa jars. She'll never miss a few."

"Are you gonna put a curse on Mitch, too?"

"I dunno yet. Depends."

"Where'd you learn how to do it?"

"I been readin' about ol' folk cures and curses at school. There's a book."

"What'll happen to your en'mies?"

"They'll get a terrible disease and die, or they could maybe g-get run over by a train or thrown off a horse and be paralyzed fer life."

Cassie thought about Dooky making her touch his thing.

"Can I help you do it? I could help find the nails."

"Maybe. And besides the well water, *guess what!*"

He stopped talking and squinched his eyes together really hard, shaking his head at the same time. Then, "Let's go back to sleep," was all he said.

Cassie closed her eyes and was asleep in three breaths. An hour later Mitch wondered why he was being shoved out of bed, until he discovered that not only Dan but Cassie was sleeping with him.

That morning at breakfast Dan got two cinnamon rolls. Mitch only got one, and when Mitch caught hold of Mabel's apron strings as he always did, she slapped his hand. Mabel put a pat of butter on Dan's plate and said, "You *crazy*, Dan, goin' out to that ol' man's?" But as she said it she rolled her eyes and grinned.

Marvin looked straight at his son. "Dan, if you ever do anything like that again to scare us, I'm taking all your arrowheads away, *and* your knife *and* your BB gun! And you'll stay in your room a week for punishment," he added.

Thank God Liddy hadn't been here when this happened. He'd probably get blamed anyway, when she found out.

Everybody made up to Dan, until Marvin said that if they spoiled him like that for running away, he'd be doing it every week. Mabel stood at the stove, one hand on her hip, stirring bacon. The only sound in the room was the hiss of fat in the pan, and Cassie had a feeling they were all breathing together for a few seconds, as if all five of them were just one person.

O

On a hot afternoon three days after she'd left, Liddy parked the Studebaker in front of Harold's office. The HAROLD CUTTER REAL ESTATE sign outside had been replaced with WORKS PROJECTS ADMINISTRATION. She went in and handed his car keys over the desk.

"Liddy, you're back!" He put a tanned hand up and rubbed his eyes. He looked tired.

Once again Liddy thought what a shame it was that Eugenia had died. She spent a few minutes reporting to him on all the meetings, and said she would write it all up in a report later on. "Right now I need to get home."

"Sure, Liddy, but I'd like the report in just a couple of days. Incidentally, yesterday I got a pretty big check from Washington. We have to do some plannin' and see how it can best be used." He smiled at her. "You go on home—I'm sure your family needs you."

She nodded, left and walked past Schonberger's Dry Goods, carrying her battered old suitcase. She looked in and waved at Flo, who was busy cutting out yard goods, then crossed the street and went into the drugstore. Sara Jane Collins, the pretty high school girl Marvin had hired to replace her, was standing behind the fountain. Liddy said hello, then walked back to the prescription counter.

Marvin was shaking some sort of mixture in a tall beaker. He looked up and saw Liddy, and his face changed from sober concentration to happy surprise. She walked around and put her arms around him, held on, and squeezed.

"Honey, I'm sorry we're always fighting. We have to try harder."

"I know." He put the beaker in a holder and grabbed her in his arms. This time when he kissed her, she didn't mind his scratchy mustache.

"I returned Harold's car. Guess I'll walk home and take a bath, I'm tired and dusty from the drive. Could you bring my suitcase when you come for supper?"

"Why don't I take you home? Sara Jane can handle things. Let me get the keys."

"That'd be nice."

When they pulled up in the driveway, Mabel and Cassie were in the backyard. Cassie hugged her mother around the legs and asked, "Where were you? Mabel said you were talkin' to somebody about poor people!"

"That's exactly what I was doing, sweetie. Later on I'll show you something I brought you!"

She had a few paper napkins, toothpicks, and straws she'd brought from the diner in Red Arrow—maybe the child would be happy with those.

Mabel must have sensed something about the way Marvin was standing there.

She said, "Why don't I take Cassie out for a visit to my pa? He's been wantin' me to bring her out fer the longest time, and I need to take 'im some o' his mended long-johns. He'd as soon be shot as buy new 'uns."

Cassie objected to being removed from the scene when her mother had just returned. She said, "Mama…*mama*! Fiona got a Beano game! When am *I* gonna get one?" But Mabel was already herding her away.

As they went inside, Liddy asked Marvin, "Where are the boys?"

"Mitch is at baseball practice; he'll be at the store by four. Dan's out explorin' somewhere. But I told him to be home right on time for supper!" His tone was so emphatic, Liddy wondered if he'd taken a new interest in Dan. She turned and looked at him. Slowly she walked up the stairs, and Marvin followed.

O

While Liddy sponged herself, Marvin stretched out on the bed.

Liddy never initiated things, but it seemed like she was doing it now. He pulled a cigarette pack out of his pocket, then put it away. She didn't like him to smoke in the bedroom, though he usually did anyway.

He took off his shoes and let down his suspenders, leaving on his shirt, bow tie, and pants, then piled the bed pillows behind his head, lay back, and waited. He thought of Liddy's smallness and her red, crinkly hair. Her little mouth was so prim and tight most of the time, but it softened for him when he wanted it to. He was crazy about the flustered, abashed expression on her face when she wanted his lovemaking but didn't want to show it. Her body wasn't as willowy as when he'd first married her, but she still had small hips, and the breasts that only he knew about, with their rosy tips. Breasts that were small, creamy, slightly drooping—breasts that changed so dramatically when he caressed them.

God, it had been a long time! Why didn't they figure out a way to do this more often?

She slid into the room a few minutes later and sat down on the side of the bed, wearing a rose-pink negligee he'd given her two Christmases ago. He'd never even seen her in it before.

Slowly he undid his tie. Leaning over and burying his face in her hair, he whispered, "Liddy, how come we don't—" But he never got to finish the question.

Maybe it was because it had been such a long time, but it seemed to Marvin as if he was more potent than he'd ever been. Liddy seemed to think so, too. He lasted for a long time, and when he finished she murmured and moaned, wanting him to stay inside her.

Later they lay in quiet, familiar intimacy, returning gradually to the reality of their surroundings. The late-day sun filtering through the drawn blinds gave the room a yellowish glow. Their bodies and the bed were damp and sticky, but they stayed clinging together.

For three whole days Marvin had been worried about his primacy in Liddy's life. Trying to keep the sounds of doubt from his voice, he asked, "I guess you stayed with that woman's family, like you said you were goin' to?"

"Uh-huh. They don't have any kids, and it was so quiet! Anything much happen while I was gone?"

"Not much. Dan took a long hike. I'll tell you about it some other time."

She didn't feel like asking more about the subject. Pulling the sheet up to cover their nakedness, she cradled her head on Marvin's damp, hairy chest, and they went to sleep.

O

After supper Marvin and Liddy lounged together on the sofa downstairs, holding hands and talking. Dan was in his room, sorting arrowheads. Cassie wanted to be with her mother, but Mabel wouldn't let her. She made her help dry dishes, then hustled her upstairs to play Slap with an old worn-out deck of cards.

At the drugstore, Mitch couldn't believe his good fortune. His father called and said he'd give him the grand sum of two dollars to stay and close up that night—an offer he accepted eagerly. The timing couldn't have been better; he'd been wanting to buy that new Lou Gehrig baseball mitt he'd seen in a catalog.

4

It's a mighty hard road that my poor hands has hoed
My poor feet has traveled a hot dusty road
Out of your Dust Bowl and westward we rolled
And your deserts was hot and your mountains was cold
                    —Woody Guthrie
                    Pastures of Plenty

Pioneer Day in Cato was always celebrated on the Fourth of July. The fire whistle, instead of shrieking out the noon hour, went off at nine in the morning, and everyone came into town in their flatbeds, pickups, flivvers, and mule-drawn wagons.

Main Street was where the parade went by, and where they held the greased-pole climb and the greased-pig chase. Luckily, although the town and farms were desperate for rain, there was no shortage of grease—a lot of it was needed on the Fourth.

In the drugstore, the entire Field family was supposed to work all day—Marvin had made that clear several days before, and of course Liddy agreed. The boys and she would take turns behind the fountain, and she would sell cosmetics and general stock while Marvin would handle all sales of medicines and all prescriptions.

O

Cassie knew even before she opened her eyes, before she heard the doves cooing, that something wonderful was going to happen today. She blinked her eyes and remembered what it was: parades, music, flags, *fireworks*! Lying in bed, she stretched out her legs and put her arms behind her head, looking up at the ceiling.

Puckering her lips in various ways, she experimented with her whistle. Her brothers had been teaching her how. They were accomplished whistlers, as were all their friends. Mike O'Herlihy was the best; he could even imitate a few birds. Dan and Mitch had told her all it took was practice. She liked to work on "The Music Goes Round and Round" and

"Pop Goes the Weasel," but she could get a good, shrill whistling sound only once in a while. Mitch and Dan were right—it took practice.

Downtown later that morning, wearing her blue-checked cotton dress, Cassie held on to Mabel's hand. She had never seen so many people! Most of the time you could look all around and not see a soul, but now there were bodies everywhere. Everyone kept saying the same thing to everyone else—wasn't it nice there was no wind!

Buck Corkle was there, lounging on the bank steps with all the other loafers, and seeing him, Mabel ducked her head as she led Cassie into the drugstore, past the displays in the windows flanking the front door: a huge pink hot-water bottle on one side and a giant thermometer on the other. Right away Cassie asked Liddy if she could have an ice-cream cone, and she said yes.

A few minutes later, licking the mound of peach ice cream scooped grudgingly onto the cone by Dan, she went outside to watch the parade. People were crowded around watching a lineup of old soldiers in brown uniforms go by. The soldiers were dressed with leather socks on their legs and brown caps on their heads, and two of them carried flags. Next came the marching band, with three twirlers and the drum major, whom Cassie recognized as Alvin Jonas. She still had her watch, thanks to him.

The band was playing a loud marching song, which Barney Scruggs announced over the microphone as "Stars and Stripes Forever." Alvin stepped high, his baton flashing in the sun, his pimples almost as red as his plumed red hat and uniform. The girl twirlers wore shiny little skirts, so short you could see their round white thighs. Their spangled jackets over satin shirts flashed in the sun, and the men and boys in the crowd let out loud whistles and cheers.

Pulled by a team of horses, the Pioneer Wagon rolled by, with three ladies standing on it in white bonnets and long calico dresses. Cassie knew them all: Mrs. Schonberger, Mrs. Scruggs, and Mrs. Byers. One was pretending to churn butter, another mimed milking a cardboard cow, and the third was working an authentic old water pump up and down. Three men pioneers stood on the wagon also, leaning on long rifles or pitchforks and not doing much of anything. Cassie recognized her mother's friend Harold Cutter, Reuben Hargraves, and Heck Purvis the barber.

Six beautiful horses pranced by making a loud show, with silver decorations on their saddles and carrying riders in real Western outfits.

One of the riders was blond-haired rancher Grace Sampson; she wore a black pearl-buttoned shirt, tight-fitting black pants with lots of metal trim, and a white Stetson.

Most of the horses had forgotten to go to the bathroom before they came. Cassie remembered that happened last year too.

Dogs pulled kids on decorated tricycles, kids pulled dogs in spangled wagons, and teenaged girls pedaled by on bikes with red, white, and blue crepe paper woven through the spokes. One dog pulled a shiny new Radio Flyer wagon with a baby strapped inside. The baby was wearing red-and-white-striped diapers, had a big blue star taped to his bare chest, and was screaming bloody murder.

Cassie had known that Fiona was going to be in the parade, but she was astonished to see her tap dancing on a wooden platform attached to a cart. The cart was dripping with red-and-white bunting, and since Fiona didn't have a big enough dog, it was pulled by her mother. When Cassie waved, Fiona was too busy bobbing her curls and doing her tap dance to wave back. She wore rouge and lipstick, and Cassie thought she looked almost as good as Shirley Temple.

You could tell that the parade was petering out when Amos Hicks and Fernie May Applebaum came by, Amos walking a scruffy mongrel on a leash, and cross-eyed Fernie May carrying her pet mouse in a rusty cage. This time when Cassie waved, both Amos and Fernie May waved back.

Daddy was always saying Amos was one of life's losers, but she'd never heard him comment on Fernie May.

The sack race was starting, and she saw some of her brothers' friends hopping down Main, trying to keep their balance while the crowd cheered them on. Dooky Schlanaker fell over right away, tripped up by his burlap sack, and Ben Hargraves, like a fool, stopped and helped him up, forfeiting any chance of winning. The winner was red-haired Mike O'Herlihy, who let out a big war whoop when he hopped across the finish line. Cassie let out a yell with him.

She came to the end of Main.

Turning the corner, she looked down a side street and saw Lally Hoffman sitting in the back of an old battered pickup. Cassie climbed onto the running board to talk. Lally had her knees drawn up to her chin. Her long dress covered her legs, and she wore a torn, too-large straw hat. Cassie would have given anything to have one like it.

"Hi," said Cassie.

"Hi," said Lally.

"Why're you sittin' here? Where's your folks?"

"They went to look at another pickup. My pa don't think this'un'll make it to Californ-y."

"You all goin', then? To California?"

"I reckon." Lally's face clouded up, and her eyes dropped to her knees.

"Come on. Let's go see the next contest. You already missed the sack race. A friend of mine won it. *Come on!*"

"They tol' me to stay here. If they come back I'll ask kin I go."

Cassie climbed into the back of the pickup, trying not to think how everybody would get mad at her for getting her dress dirty. "How's your pigs?" she asked.

"They're gettin' big. Their mom is sick of 'em."

"Our bitch Sadie..." Cassie stopped. She had never used that word out loud before, though she had heard her father use it several times. Still, she liked the sound of it, so she started the sentence over. "Our bitch Sadie is tired of her pups, too. They're all weaned. My dad may take Sadie to a field trial."

"What's a fiel' trile?"

"It's where all the bird dogs try to outdo each other findin' a quail and pointin' it, and then findin' it again after somebody's shot it, and then retrievin' it so it's not damaged."

"What's 'damaged'?"

"Feathers torn off or body scrunched. They want it dead, but not damaged."

Lally listened, her face shadowy under the big hat.

"Can you whistle?" Cassie asked. "My brothers are teachin' me."

Just then Lally's parents came back, Mrs. Hoffman carrying the baby. In contrast to the Hoffmans' leather-brown faces, the baby was pale and sickly-looking.

"Pa, kin I go with Cassie to see some o' the contests?" Lally's tone was timid. Cassie wondered how she could ever get to do anything, asking like that.

Mr. Hoffman squinted at the girls. "Naw, we ain't stayin' here fer none o' the foolishness. I think we're goin' to turn tail and git on back home." He took a plug of tobacco out of his overalls and bit off a chew.

"Verley, you said we *might* could stay in town a-*while* today." Mrs. Hoffman spoke to her husband in that same whining, servile tone, but it looked as though she might get the desired result. The children didn't breathe. Long moments passed, during which Mr. Hoffman stood looking up at the sky, then turning his head to spit.

"Wal, all right, woman, if'n you think you gotta see the fool goin's-on here. But we *ain't* stayin' fer the farworks! Lally, you keep an eye on this here truck. I might take a notion to go on back home anytime, y'hear?"

The girls jumped out of the pickup and ran away before he could change his mind. Holding hands, they scrambled through the crowds of people, Lally clutching her hat and the ribbons on Cassie's pigtails flying. Cassie's dad was standing in a crowd outside the drugstore with Stuffy Byers. Cassie saw Stuffy hand Daddy something in a paper bag. "You girls been lookin' over the town?" said Marvin amiably. "How 'bout that sack race, huh? You gonna try to tackle the greased pig?" He laughed, louder than usual.

"Aw, Daddy, we're too little! An' Lally has her own pigs at home!"

"Wal, them pigs always got eight acres o' hell in 'em—an' that's no lie!" said Stuffy, one hand caught in the suspenders that were almost losing the struggle to hold up his pants.

"When is the pig goin' to get chased?" asked Cassie.

"'Bout ten minutes. You better be out here if you wanta see it."

Just then Grace Sampson walked up to the men, the white Stetson sitting atop her head at a jaunty angle. She said, "You two gettin' in trouble out here? Marvin, you better get back to the store before Liddy catches you havin' fun!" Grace and her husband Hal owned a two-hundred-acre ranch outside of town. Marvin grabbed her silver belt, pulling her toward him. "Gracie, you don't have no idea what trouble *is*!" Grace lifted her face up close to Marvin's and smiled. Then she pulled back, straightened his bow tie with delicate fingers tipped with painted red nails, and walked away, tight black pants swaying rhythmically.

"Gotta meet Hal. See you!" Marvin stared after her.

Just then Liddy, standing outside the door of the drugstore, spoke up. "Cassie, where you been? How many times I have to tell you to tell me before you run off? Even Mabel didn't know where you were!" Cassie noticed that her mother's hair was falling out of the bun in back and that she looked cross. Her hands were making jerky, nervous movements, as if they wanted to hit out at someone. She said to Marvin in a stinging voice, "We're awful busy—do you think you could possibly come back in and help out?"

Her dad handed the bag back to Stuffy and followed Liddy into the store.

○

Liddy felt annoyed at Marvin for a million and one things. Drinking, of course, and flirting with Grace. Those were two big reasons to be annoyed.

Cassie pulled on her mother's dress. "Mama, this is Lally. Can we have some ice cream?"

"All right. Go on to the back; I'll send Dan—the fountain's full. Hello, Lally." She watched as the two little girls went to sit at a marble table. Why in the world had Cassie chosen this down-and-out Hoffman girl to befriend? But the child had a sweet smile. At the back table was hog farmer Chester Klein's pretty wife Rachel, nursing her baby boy. Her son Fergus, who was Cassie's age, sat with her.

Cassie yelled loudly to Dan, "Two double-dips—make 'em with strawberry and chocolate."

"You come up here and get 'em; I ain't bringin' 'em back there!" Cassie jumped down and hurried to the fountain, and Mitch said, "Why don'tcha bring in some *rich* friends, Cassie? That Hoffman girl's poor as Job's turkey!"

A few minutes later Marvin, weaving slightly, came to stand near Mrs. Klein. He looked down at the baby, ogling the creamy expanse of bare white bosom. "Fine-looking baby you got there, Rachel."

Rachel gazed up at him and blushed. "Why, thank you, Mr. Field."

"We're runnin' out of root beer syrup up here," called Liddy, and Marvin hurried away again.

The girls got their ice cream cones and ran outside. They arrived at the flagpole in time to see the pig, inside a wooden barricade, being greased with one of its own relatives' drawn fat. Cassie wondered how, if it took five men just to grease a pig in a pen, one man could possibly *catch* him while he was running loose! She saw money changing hands all around, with Stuffy Byers doing the bill handling. A boy standing nearby told Cassie the men were making bets.

The men and boys who were going to try to catch the pig came out from behind the barricade. Someone blew a whistle, and the greasy half-grown creature was let go. The crowd began to yell wildly as the pig pounded off in every direction, into the crowd, back again, under the divider and back again! People laughed and whooped as they jumped out of the way, and Cassie and Lally jumped up and down and screamed at the top of their lungs like everyone else.

This was more exciting than the sack race! The pig raced around, squealing, desperate to escape. At long last, one of the men succeeded in grabbing the pig by his two back feet and tying them with a rope. The man's name was announced over the loudspeaker. It was Chester Klein, father of the nursing baby in the drugstore. His prize was the pig and a free meal for four at the Mistletoe Café.

"I need to pee," said Lally.

"We got a toilet at the store." They took turns watching each other, and Cassie saw that Lally didn't wear panties. They started to go back outside.

Mitch was behind the fountain, working hard and hot and sweaty-looking. He intercepted Cassie and said, "I got a job for you. Go down to the grocery and get me some bananas—not too ripe and not too green. Think you can do that? And bring back the receipt and change." He reached over the fountain and handed her a quarter.

How was Cassie to know that the course of her life was about to change, all because Mitch told her to go buy bananas?

Suddenly Lally said, "Oh! *I forgot!* I was s'posed to keep reportin' in!"

"Wait, wait, I'll go, too!" yelled Cassie, but Lally was off and running.

Cassie went to Shafer's Grocery alone, where Mrs. Shafer greeted her, saying, "Cassie, isn't this a glorious Fourth? Considerin' the dust and all. But it's let up for today, at least. Were you in the parade?" She was stacking boxes of Oxydol. Cassie liked to stand and stare at the blue and orange spirals until she got dizzy.

"No, ma'am. But Fiona was. And Amos and Fernie May. Next year I'm *goin'* to be in it, though, with one of my puppies—I don't know which one yet. I need some bananas, please, Miz Shafer; Mitch said not too ripe and not too green."

"Why, sure, honey, I'll go to the back and pick out some good ones for you. Wait right here."

Cassie stood near the cash register, and while she waited she practiced her whistling; there hadn't been time for it all day. Vaguely she heard the screen door open and close, but she didn't turn around. She had only gotten out a few bars of "Pop Goes the Weasel" when suddenly a woman's face appeared startlingly close to her own and said in a loud, nasal singsong voice,

"Whistling girls and crowing hens
Always come to some bad end!"

Cassie was so startled that tears came to her eyes. It was Mrs. Weston from the church, the woman who had made her kiss worm-faced Alvin and who had told her mother about Daddy kissing Mrs. Scruggs.

"My brothers are teachin' me," Cassie said in as dignified a tone as she could muster.

"Is that right!"

Cassie kept looking up at Mrs. Weston, shifting her weight from one foot to the other. There was something about this woman she definitely didn't like. It wasn't just that the old witch thought she, Cassie, would come to a bad end. Cassie didn't like her *looks*. She had a long nose, small, close-together eyes, and hair in a rigid up-do of waves that could have been carved out of road tar. In the heart and heat of summer, she was wearing a long-sleeved dress in a tiny print, a cameo brooch pinned at the collar.

Mrs. Shafer came back with the bananas. Smiling, she put the fruit in a paper bag and handed it to Cassie along with the change. Cassie forgot to ask for the receipt. At the door, she turned and gazed for another moment at Mrs. Weston.

The woman didn't know it, but she had made an enemy for life.

O

People kept coming into the drugstore all day, mostly for soda fountain drinks but also for over-the-counter drugs or prescriptions, cigarettes, cosmetics, or condoms. It was an unwritten law that Liddy was never to be asked for a condom, so when some fellow sidled back to Prescriptions without a piece of paper in his hand, Marvin usually knew what he wanted. Thanks to Margaret Sanger's efforts to legalize birth control, condoms and diaphragms could now be sold in drugstores. There seemed to be an unusually brisk business in both today, Marvin reflected. Must be the holiday and the heat.

Farmers drifted in to talk with Marvin about sick cows or sows. The nearest veterinarian was in Red Arrow, so since Marvin was a licensed pharmacist, he was often asked his opinion about animal illnesses. Liddy was amazed at the store of knowledge he had acquired about hogs and cattle. She doubted that this knowledge was always correct, but since he had doctored his bird dogs with some success, she decided not to worry.

She was busy, too, selling makeup and perfume, though not to farmers' wives—any of their extra money would go toward the children, if there ever was any extra.

Marvin sat on the stool behind the prescription counter, surrounded by his apothecary jars and green glass bottles. Nobody had bothered him for a while, and he could smoke in peace. Stuffy's bootleg whiskey, which Marvin had been sampling that morning, was enough to take the ache out of his back, legs, and feet, the occupational hazard of working twelve hours a day on a concrete floor. Later he had some more, not liking the taste so much as the burning feeling it gave his throat and chest, and the way it raised his spirits. Except when he was out of town with Joe Kelly, Marvin seldom drank, but today he needed it. If you had to work, cooped up inside while everyone else was out celebrating, you deserved a little compensation. And he sure couldn't drink at home, not with his Carrie Nation wife! This was some of Stuffy's Kansas whiskey, the "Just Right" brand. Stuffy said it was called that because it wasn't so bad you couldn't drink it, and it wasn't so expensive you couldn't afford it—it was Just Right.

He'd gotten madder and madder at the way Liddy had embarrassed him—*twice!*—about his perfectly normal behavior, and he was just now beginning to simmer down. Could he help it if good-looking women got him excited? He thought maybe he got them kind of worked up, too—and he sure couldn't help that! He glanced up front, where Liddy stood waiting for Mrs. Billings to decide between two shades of rouge. The woman had enough on already to stop a bull in a pasture, and she was still ugly. Liddy looked annoyed, as if maybe *she* could use a snort of whiskey. She seemed to be getting meaner and meaner as the day wore on. He looked up then to see her coming toward him. She had evidently made the sale.

"*Um-hmm?*" He took a long drag on his cigarette.

"Marvin, I've been putting off asking you about Mitch. Coach Lansford wants him to pitch at four o'clock, against the town regulars. He's got his uniform all set to go. Think we can spare him?"

"Why didn't Mitch come to me with this proposition earlier in the day, or even three days ago? He musta known about it! You know how I feel about the boys' respons'bilities whenever there's a holiday like this!" His words weren't coming out quite right, but he felt sure he was getting his point across.

"Doesn't seem to have kept *you* from doing some celebrating. I saw you out there with Stuffy—I know what you've been up to! Why not let Mitch do this! He's worked all day, and I'll work twice as hard if you'll just let him go pitch!"

Marvin got off the stool and walked back to the little apartment, and Liddy followed him.

He turned on her. "You're always favoring that boy! Why should he get to take off when everyone else is doing their part! When I was his age, *I* worked, God damn it!" A few drops of spittle flew in her face.

Suddenly Mitch appeared beside them in the room. Somehow lately he'd grown to two inches taller than Marvin. "Mom, never mind—it's not worth it. I won't go." Hatred laced his voice.

But Liddy was determined, and she put her hand on Marvin's arm. Marvin pushed her hand away, shoving her hard against the refrigerator. Suddenly, there was Mitch, forcing his father back, his fist cocked. Liddy darted between them. "Mitch, *no!*" She motioned him out of the room. He backed out slowly, eyes narrowed, shaking his head slowly back and forth in frustration.

She and Marvin stood glaring at each other, and finally Liddy said in a low, trembling voice, "I think you're *disgusting,* and no example to anyone." She turned and walked back to the store. There were one or two customers waiting at the fountain, but she didn't think anyone had heard. Her hands were shaking and Mitch's face was flushed and contorted; people might guess there had been trouble.

Marvin stayed in the apartment for an hour, and Liddy supposed he was taking a nap. Customers came in less often now, and she and Mitch were able to handle things alone. Dan had disappeared. Heck Purvis told Liddy he'd seen him trudging out of town with a gunnysack thrown over his back. Someone else said he'd tried to climb the greased pole and succeeded only in messing up his clothes. At the other end of Main, Mabel had found Cassie wandering about, crying because she couldn't find Lally. Mabel brought her in and put her on the cot in back for a nap. Then she said to Liddy, "Miz Field, I was wonderin' if I could get tonight off. 'Course, if you need me, I'll be glad to stay. See, I—uh, I been keepin' company—I been havin' me a boyfriend. You may not o' knowed about it."

Liddy said, "I sure *didn't!* Who is it?"

"Don't know's you know 'im…Buck Corkle."

Liddy stood holding a damp wad of fountain towels, trying to take it in.

Buck Corkle! That overgrown, rough no-good! But Mabel needed to feel love like anyone else, so why *not* Buck? There was somebody out there for everyone, they say.

"Sure, You go on and go."

Since Marvin was either drunk or asleep, or both, she told Mitch to take off the rest of the day, too. "There's still some of the holiday left, honey, you go on," she told him.

Mitch went home to change clothes, taking his baseball uniform with him. He didn't know which made him angrier: his dad's refusal to let him go pitch the game, or the way he'd shoved his mom. Mike had come in and told him that Lloyd Carrothers made a good showing, with six strikeouts, even though the high school team had lost to the more experienced town team.

His dad had ruined his whole high school sports career! But at least tonight he'd see Sara Jane at the dance. His mom was working, so they could both be off.

The Fourth of July committee had decided that spending a lot money on Roman candles, Catherine wheels, and whistlers in the midst of a depression would be sinful, but the five-minute display of flashing lights and rockets, and the popping, cracking, and booming sounds coming from the Cato Shores, the town's swimming and recreation facility a few miles outside of town, were exciting to watch.

Mabel was right there at the Shores with Buck, watching the fireworks, their big bodies packed into the front of his pickup. He said he was leaving soon for California, and he whispered in her ear, soft-talking her, caressing her body, wanting her to show him how much she was going to miss him. But Mabel said it was too crowded.

Mitch and Sara Jane watched the fireworks from the bandstand, holding hands.

Cassie, lying on the sagging mattress in the drugstore apartment, slept through the whole thing.

And nobody knew where Dan was.

Twenty or so townspeople watched the spectacle from Main Street, including Liddy and Marvin who stood without touching, several yards apart.

O

"Mom, didja know Mike O'Herlihy's mom is back?" asked Mitch.

Marvin had left for the drugstore, and Dan and Cassie, half asleep in their chairs, were waiting for hot pancakes and syrup from Mabel.

Liddy was going over WPA directives, and answered, "No! My goodness, how does she have the nerve, after taking off with that Singer salesman— leaving her whole family! Doesn't Mike have four little brothers?" On the words "Singer salesman," Liddy dropped her voice so low that Cassie's and Dan's heads jerked up.

"Mom, they know all about Mike's family and what his mom did— don'tcha, kids?"

Cassie said, "Yeah, and I hear Miz O'Hurley ain't even pretty; she's just round-heeled."

"You mean O'Her-*li*-hy—not O'Hurley!" gibed Dan, snickering.

"Who's been talking in front of this child! Mitch, you *see*?"

"And"—Mitch's voice got louder—"and I hear she's goin' to have a baby!"

Mabel had been silent as she walked back and forth replenishing hotcakes, but now she spoke. "Those five O'Herlihy boys been gettin' along fine. Mr. O'Herlihy done the best he could with all them kids, and some of us from church been takin' food over, and mendin' clothes. They been okay. Mought be worse now their ma's back."

It was a couple of mornings later that Marvin was reading the *Cato Enquirer* and burst out, "Says here Reuben Hargraves's wife is goin' into the hospital for major surgery! Our store's practically next door to the Mistletoe Café, and I didn't know about it."

None of the tables and chairs matched at the Mistletoe Café, and Marvin said the place looked as much like a used-furniture store and sign company as it did a place to eat. The diner was homely and plain, but you couldn't say it was unadorned. Placards were stuck everywhere, pinned to the greasy walls behind the grill, on the walls inside the booths, all around the tables, even in the bathroom. The edges of the placards were curled, spattered and flyspecked, but they spouted amusing adages and jokes about the everyday problems of people. It apparently had never occurred to Reuben to throw any of them away; he just kept adding new ones.

Many reflected the hard times:

> THE ONLY KIND OF CREDIT WE GIVE AROUND
> HERE IS WHEN THE DOG ROLLS OVER.
> THEN WE CLAP.

And

> DON'T TRY TO LIVE BY YOUR WITS;
> HUNGER IS AN AWFUL THING.

Mabel said, "I heard Miz Hargraves has somethin' serious, maybe cancer."

Dan had turned pale. "M-may I be 'scused? I'm f-finished," he asked.

Dan was a picky eater. Marvin peered over his newspaper. "Did you have toast?"

"I cain't eat t-toast; it's t-too hot!"

"All right, then."

A few seconds later, Cassie got down from her chair.

"Where *you* goin'?" asked Marvin.

"I'm finished, too."

Dan was in his room with the door closed. Cassie knocked. "It's me," she said.

Dan was sitting on the floor next to the unmade bed with a box on his lap. She sat down across from him, as slowly Dan removed the lid to reveal a dozen nails of various lengths and several scraps of paper.

"Are you gonna do the curse?"

"I already did it. That's why I'm worried."

"When didja do it? I was gonna help, remember?"

"On the Fourth o' July. I already had the w-well water, and I had to get some more nails and write the guys' names a lot o' times and put the nails and the names in the bottles, then bury 'em at their houses. These here are the leftovers."

"Didja do Mitch?"

He shook his head.

"Where'd you get all the nails?"

"Mr. Brandenberg's buildin' a new barn, and there was some there. I had to buy some at the lumber y-yard."

Cassie sat in silent admiration. "When'd you do the buryin'?"

"I told you, the Fourth o' July! I got tired o' bein' ragged about that dumb greased pole contest. *They* didn't do any better'n I did, but they th-think they're so smart, just 'cause they're bigger."

Dan's face had that worried look he got sometimes.

"Grandmother McIvor's coming for Thanksgiving, didja know that?" Cassie asked. She would comfort him, make him feel better about himself.

"Cassie, st-stop talkin' 'bout the f-future! I'm worried 'bout right now!"

"How's come?"

"Don't you get it? All this bad luck comin' to Mike and Ben— it's *my f-fault!*"

"But Mike's mom came back."

"But Mabel said it'd be better if she hadn't! And she's gonna have a b-baby!"

"I like babies. Maybe Mike'll like it too."

"You're stupid! The baby is prob'ly the Singer man's!"

"Oh."

Cassie still didn't think it was such a dire situation; a baby was a baby, and they were almost all cute.

"Is the Singer man goin' to live with 'em, too?"

He looked at her disgustedly and shook his head. "Cassie, there's no way you're ever goin' to understand about these things. Forget it. I got Ben Hargraves's mom to worry about now."

"Is *she* goin' to have a baby?"

"No—it's a lot worse! She's got c-cancer! And *I* gave it to her! I didn't know this conjurin' and evil-eye stuff'd really work! I'm some k-kinda *s-s-sorcerer* or somethin'!"

"What's cancer?"

"I dunno, but it's bad... I think your brain rots away."

The children sat cross-legged, facing each other, contemplating Dan's unspeakable acts.

Cassie said, "Maybe Mama and Daddy could stop the curses."

"Are you nuts? These things get g-goin' and there's no stoppin' 'em! I keep thinkin' 'bout Dooky—what's goin' to happen to him? Each thing is worse'n the last. Cancer's lots worse than a baby!"

"Maybe you could go to church and talk to Rev'rend Dickens."

"You're the one likes church—you and Mama. Us g-guys don't get anything from it. This thing's bigger than religion, anyways. It's *m-mystical.* I put a jinx on ever'body, and I'll just have to live with it."

Dan put his hand to his mouth and chewed on three fingernails at once, wondering if finding the Indian skeleton had made the nail curse more potent. Maybe he could swear on the Indian's grave that he didn't *mean* the curse, that he didn't really *want* these bad things to happen to Mitch's friends! Maybe he should tell someone about finding the grave—not telling might be more dangerous in the long run.

He could tell Mitch. But yesterday Mitch had twisted his arm really bad for borrowing his best aggie. Shoot, no, he wouldn't tell Mitch. He looked into Cassie's eyes without blinking, and Cassie gazed back, wondering why Dan was sitting there looking scared and proud at the same time. They sat in silence, the cigar box of leftover nails between them on the floor, like talismans of Dan's evil intentions collected all together in one space.

○

Although Liddy only worked for the WPA part-time, going out on her rounds a total of ten hours or so a week and working with Harold at his office another three or four, the drugstore was no longer a priority in her life. Cassie was well cared for by Mabel, and Liddy was never gone when the boys were home.

But Marvin said it didn't look right. He said he had a feeling that the men in town were laughing at him or, worse, thinking he couldn't support his family. Liddy countered that she couldn't help it; she liked her new job and she was going to keep it. He had Sara Jane, and he had Mitch, and although he'd been sure he couldn't, he had managed the store without Liddy.

For the first time in years, Liddy felt revitalized. Harold had found a used car for her that the WPA could afford, and they paid for all her gas. Even if it was in the blowing dirt and dust, driving around the countryside and having a sense that she was doing some good was a tonic.

"At least now I'm not home in the dirt now; I'm out *in* it!" she told everyone. Witnessing the misery and poverty all around her made her feel guilty for ever complaining about her own life. Seeing all these people worse off than she was seemed to put things in perspective.

Harold's job as WPA superintendent consisted of signing up farm families for immunization shots and chest X-rays, and getting food programs and sewing projects started. A whole litany of diseases— tuberculosis, pneumonia, influenza, typhoid, dysentery, whooping cough, scarlet fever, and diphtheria— were killing off children and adults all over the state, and Bliss County was no exception. Two public-health nurses working out of Red Arrow did the door-to-door immunizations and health education; they continually urged folks to get themselves and their kids to the Red Arrow or Antelope hospitals for X-rays.

Harold had asked Liddy to organize the sewing part of the program. Eleanor Roosevelt had started the WPA sewing program; she was always posing with women at their machines and getting her picture in the papers. Once Liddy obtained the patterns, sewing machines, and materials from the headquarters in Oklahoma City and got the women going, the program began to work beautifully. Some women worked at home on their own machines; others came into town and worked on one of the three that Liddy had installed in Veterans Hall. Since poverty and lack of transportation go together, occasionally she had to go out to the country and pick the women up, then take them back home again.

The women sewed men's work shirts and uniforms, children's clothing, aprons, quilted hot pads, coverlets, and mattress pads. These were all sent to the WPA office in Oklahoma City and sold from there. At times the job was difficult, because for one reason or another it was hard to keep some of the women working, but Liddy hung on. Harold gave her pep talks and told her how much good she was doing, and he encouraged her by emphasizing that the pittance the women made was the difference between starvation and survival for their families.

The fact that handsome, silver-haired Harold supervised Liddy bothered Marvin more than a little. Of course Harold was old—fifty-five or so—and Liddy was no spring chicken, even if she was ten years younger. But Harold was refined, the kind of man Liddy most likely preferred —preferred to *him*. Marvin sat up and took notice.

Not that he was jealous, exactly. Liddy would never be unfaithful, and he knew that an upstanding man like Harold would do nothing dishonorable—after all, he and Harold were friends—but just the same, he didn't like it. He had been far happier when Liddy stayed home.

Marvin didn't know what salary Harold made, but his job had been approved by their senator, so it must have been substantial. Liddy hardly made anything, but when Marvin pointed this out, she said she didn't care. She enjoyed the work, and with the tiny bit she made, she could save for something she wanted. She said she wouldn't be spending her money on important things like bird dogs, but maybe she could find something almost as exciting if she looked around.

That shut him up for a few days.

One day as Marvin walked past the bank, Smiley Applebaum spit a long brown stream of tobacco juice into a corner.

"Hey, Mr. Field …" His voice was loud and strident. "I hear yer wife's chasin' out all over the county!"

Marvin walked up two steps and took hold of the man's grimy shirtsleeve. "You're drunker'n a fiddler's bitch, Applebaum," he said tersely. "Close your trap—nothin' you say amounts to a poot in a whirlwind!" The loafers agreed later on that Marvin must be feeling a little touchy about the subject.

O

Cassie, drying cups on a dish towel, learned from Mabel that the Hoffmans were leaving for California.

"Seems like a bad time of year to leave," Mabel said, "it bein' so hot and all, but I guess they got no choice." The farm, which belonged to a man in Antelope, was being taken over by the Cato Mortgage and Loan.

Buck, too, was getting "rared up and ready to go." Mabel repeated his exact words to Cassie, standing back from the sink and raising her eyes to the ceiling. "'I'll miss ya, honey,' was what he said," intoned Mabel. She dabbed at her eyes with Cassie's wet dish towel. She said Buck thought he could make a good wage picking fruit. The Hoffmans were leaving day after tomorrow, piling everything they owned into their old pickup truck (the one Cassie had sat in with Lally) and heading down through the Texas panhandle. Cassie wanted to see exactly where Lally was going, so Mabel found a map and showed her all the towns—Higgins, Miami, Pampa, and Amarillo on Route 60, then, just beyond that, Tucumcari, New Mexico, and Santa Rosa, where 60 joined Route 66. That was where the Hoffmans would join up with all the other Dust Bowl folks, Mabel said.

Cassie thought the towns sounded exciting, especially Tucumcari. She said it over and over, rolling it around on her tongue. It sounded like an Indian drum.

"Can I go say good-bye to Lally?"

"I reckon so. You want me to carry you out there?"

"Mama won't, she hasta work. I wanta take Lally a present for goin' away, like Mama did when the choir director moved."

"How 'bout takin' her a paper-doll book? You love them paper dolls."

"Lally doesn't play with 'em. I don't think she has any scissors."

"Tell you what. Let me finish these here dishes; then we'll get duded up and go down to yer daddy's store and see if he has any idees about a present."

Cassie went outside and swung on the swing for half an hour. She would be so good, so quiet, Mabel couldn't change her mind.

When they got to the drugstore, Cassie asked, "Daddy, what'll I take Lally? I was goin' to give her a puppy, and she was goin' to give me a baby spotted pig."

Marvin said, "I doubt if those folks would want to feed a dog on their trip, honey, they'll be havin' enough trouble just feedin' themselves." As she and Marvin roamed around the store looking over the shelves, Cassie said, "Mitch says a rich Okie is one with *two* mattresses strapped on their car... I don't think the Hoffmans have two mattresses, 'cause I asked Lally."

"Cassie, you better start curbin' your curiosity... Now, what do you think you'd like to take her?"

"How 'bout some bath salts or perfume?"

Mabel and Marvin exchanged a glance. "I don't think she'll be able to use those much on that long trip," said Marvin. "Not many bathtubs on the way. How about a writing tablet and a pencil or Crayolas, or some funny books? Or some licorice sticks or jawbreakers?" They settled on a thick drawing tablet, Crayolas and pencils, and Marvin threw in twelve round pink and white jawbreakers. He wrapped it all up in wrapping paper and Cassie tied a ribbon around it.

Mabel and Cassie didn't talk on the way out to the farm except once, when Mabel cautioned Cassie about asking to see the pigs. "They prob'ly don't have 'em no more, so jes' don't bring it up." When they arrived at the farm, Verley was nowhere to be seen, and they were grateful.

Mrs. Hoffman didn't invite them in. They stood on the sagging porch; Lally, Cassie, Mabel, and Mrs. Hoffman, holding her pale baby, who looked and smelled as though he needed changing. But Mrs. Hoffman seemed peppier than usual; her voice had a chirpy sound Cassie had never heard before.

"Shore do wish you folks all the best on yore trip!" Mabel held onto Cassie's hand while Cassie stood looking down at the splintery porch boards, clutching her gift.

"Is Buck comin' to Californ-y purty soon?... I heerd tell," asked Mrs. Hoffman, peering up at Mabel.

"He's talkin' 'bout it." Even in the shade of the porch, Cassie could see Mabel's face turn brick-colored. "He thinks he'd do better out there than here, f'nancially speakin'."

"Wall, *we* sure hope to. It's got t'git better'n this!"

"Maybe Mister Roos'velt'll come up with somethin' to beat this depression."

"Hope so! But I reckon he just couldn't make it rain. That's the only thing coulda saved us. Guess it was too much t'expect."

Finally Cassie held out the present to Lally, who took it with a shy smile. She looked up at her mother, clinging to her skirt. "Kin I open it now, Ma?"

"O' course. Go 'head. Ain't that nice o' Cassie to do that for you?"

Getting to her knees, Lally untied the ribbon and pulled the package open. Her eyes lit up as she saw what Cassie had brought, but she didn't say anything. Cassie waited. They all waited, but there was only silence.

Lally kept her head down, looking at the gift.

Finally Mrs. Hoffman said, "Lally! What d'you *say?*"

The child looked up at all of them, her mouth struggling to smile, her eyes shiny with water.

"I do thank you, Cassie. I never had no Crayolas b'fore."

No one spoke. The only sound was the rude slobbering of the baby.

"Well, g'bye," said Cassie.

"G'bye," said Lally.

Cassie and Mabel walked to the pickup and climbed in. As they backed up the driveway, dust boiling up after them, Cassie saw Lally dash into the cabin and out again. Mabel slowed down as the little girl ran up the road after them.

"Wait!" Lally held her long dress above her knees, running with long strides.

"Cassie, here! I want to give *you* somethin'!"

It was a little doll made from cornhusks wearing a dress made from the same material as Lally's. Cassie reached for it through the window, their hands touched, and she and Mabel turned out of the driveway and onto the road.

Back at home, Cassie went to her room. She lay on the bed with the cornhusk doll on her chest and thought about Lally's leaving. She wondered if it would be for a long time. There seemed to be no way to understand this parting. There was no way to figure out if it would be for forever, but what was forever, anyway? Cassie tried to imagine it, but it was too big. She got off the bed, tucking the doll under a small quilt, and went to find Mabel.

"Is Lally goin' to be gone from now on?"

Mabel stopped snapping green beans and sat down in one of the kitchen chairs, pulling Cassie up on her lap. "I 'spect she'll be comin' back someday, honey. You dast not worry 'bout it. Lally's goin' to have a better life now, and that's all 'at matters, ain't it?"

She rocked Cassie in her arms for several minutes until the child was drowsy, then carried her to the couch.

5

I'll buy my own whiskey
I'll make my own stew
If I get drunk, madam
It's nothing to you
  —"Rye Whiskey," folk song

As Liddy handed over a few paltry dollars for their months work of sewing, and saw the expression on the women's faces, all Marvin's complaining flew out the window. Pretty Rachel Klein was especially grateful, and soon after she was paid, her husband Chester delivered to the Fields' house a quarter of a freshly slaughtered and dressed hog.

"Now, you see? There are *some* advantages!" gloated Liddy to Marvin, even though she didn't know what to do with all that meat. Finally they decided to freeze some of it in one of the ice cream freezers at the store.

They continued to quarrel about her job, and the worst fight they had was about the oranges.

Four huge crates of oranges, to be distributed all over the county, arrived at Harold's office, but since he had to be in Red Arrow the day after they arrived, he put Liddy in charge of delivering them to the distribution centers—mostly rural schools and churches. She brought the crates home and got Mitch and Dan to help her store them in the garage.

When Marvin arrived home that night, he drove straight into one of the wooden crates, scattering bruised and squashed fruit all over and causing a huge mess. His loud string of curses brought Liddy outside in her nightgown.

"Liddy, why in Hell did you put all these oranges in my garage? Look what you made me do!"

"*I* didn't make you go stone blind so you couldn't see those great big crates! Where were you *looking*? I left the garage light on, just so you'd see 'em!"

"Why do we have to have any goddamned oranges here, anyway?"

"Mr. Roosevelt wants the farm families to get more vitamins, so there won't be so much sickness among the children." Why was she having to apologize for such a worthwhile endeavor? she wondered. Seemed like she was always having to apologize.

"*Damn* Franklin Roosevelt, and damn Eleanor, too, while you're at it!"

So she threw an orange at him, hard, catching him solidly on the cheek.

That night he slept on the cot at the store, and he drank half a quart of Stuffy's Just Right whiskey, which somewhat eased the pain of Liddy's cruel and stubborn independence.

O

Out of the blue, Marvin announced that he was planning to attend the bird dog field trials in Enid in mid-August with Joe Kelly. He also announced, in a commanding tone, that Liddy would have to take over the running of the drugstore. He said that Sadie and Jim were at the peak of their hunting careers, and he had high hopes for them.

Sadie was ready to be in the pointing and retrieving business again. She was penned off from her litter now, and seemed young and frisky and, as Marvin put it, ready for the single life.

Liddy considered telling her husband she would simply close down and they could all starve to death. Why should he get a vacation to show off those despised dogs, while she sat here sweltering and slaving away? He and Joe intended to run the dogs for a few days in their secluded dog camp outside Antelope, then attend the field trial. From there he planned to go to a pharmaceutical convention in Oklahoma City. Liddy knew that he and Joe would eat from tin cans, drink themselves senseless, and Lord knew what else, while she was stuck with all the responsibility. She told him she would not fill a single prescription this time, unless some child was at death's door. If it was for some animal or adult human, she would definitely not risk Marvin's license or being put in prison. They could end up in the poorhouse!

But the pharmaceutical convention was different. Liddy wholeheartedly believed that Marvin should go; it was where new drugs would be displayed, over-the-counter as well as prescription drugs peddled by the manufacturers. There would be pharmacists, doctors, and representatives from all the drug companies. Marvin hadn't gone for two years. A druggist acquaintance of Marvin's from Waynoka was going, too, and the plan was for Joe Kelly to take the dogs home with him from the field trial, Marvin would drive to Oklahoma City, and the other druggist and Marvin would come back together from the convention. Marvin would pick the dogs up later from Joe.

Cassie had never heard such long discussions about future plans. Their family had never needed plans before. Also, she could sense that these discussions excited her dad but not her mother.

Liddy said the only good thing about it was Marvin's decision to buy a used Plymouth sedan. Now she wouldn't be so stranded when he took the Model A, and even though she knew it was a sop, she was glad to get it.

Marvin spent hours oiling his shotguns and packing the Model A, and he had Sven Sundersson build a sturdy dog carrier onto the back to carry the dogs. Liddy groused at the expense of it, six dollars they could have used for shoes for the children, but it got done.

Marvin told Liddy she'd have to work the day before he was to leave because he had to have a day to pack up the Ford. She decided to work in the back apartment, and got busy scrubbing the old range where they made all the syrups.

Marvin packed the car in the parking area in back of the store. He was wearing his hunting boots and plaid shirt, and he looked rugged and handsome. Cassie watched her father pour oil from an oil can into the car's innards, and when he walked back inside, Liddy stopped him. In a carping voice, she said, "How am I going to manage here all that time? If you don't want this whole store goin' up in smoke, you better get back here soon."

"Now, Lydia," Marvin began in a voice smooth as butter, "you've got Mitch and Dan to help, and you know I earn good money with these dogs. This isn't just a *hobby!* Didn't I tell you 'bout that bird dog customer o' mine up in Topeka? He's goin' to trade me a whole livin' room full of furniture just for *one* o' my pups, soon as I get 'im trained! You want that new furniture, don't you? Joe and I have to work these dogs. else they won't do spit at the field trial." His face beamed out with a winning smile. "About the prescriptions, honey, you do what you think best. You know an awful lot about that prescription counter, and I have faith in you. But"—he patted her shoulder, standing at a little distance—"you have to let your conscience be your guide."

It was a lame finish to a rehearsed speech, and he knew it.

"I wish you'd let your conscience be *your* guide. Then you wouldn't waste our time and money on those stupid animals!" Liddy snapped. She slapped the rag on top of the range and walked to the front.

Marvin dropped into the old upholstered chair they kept in the apartment, and Cassie crawled onto his lap, circling his neck with one arm and patting his plaid pocket.

"Daddy, I'll help Mama in the store, and I'll watch the puppies. I'll feed 'em, and I won't let 'em fight."

Her father didn't say anything for a long time. Then he patted her and said, "Cassie, you're my special girl."

He stood, setting her gently in the chair, then went back outside.

O

The days after Marvin's departure were the same as the days before: sticky-hot and uncomfortable. Liddy took a temporary leave from the WPA job, and Mitch and Dan worked longer hours. Liddy said the weather was hot enough to make you melt and run down.

There was a definite loosening of the rules. The store didn't get swept out every morning, and there was other evidence of a friendlier regime. It was almost like a vacation.

Mabel and Cassie brought meals covered by dishcloths downtown to Liddy and the boys, a change of routine welcomed by everyone.

Liddy didn't hear from Marvin. There was no phone at the dog camp, and he'd told her he would have to drive eight miles to call her, so she said what he wanted to hear, "Don't bother."

She supposed that if one of the men shot the other by mistake, she would hear about it eventually.

As if Marvin's absence weren't enough to worry her, Mitch mooned over Sara Jane, and Mabel talked about going to California and marrying Buck.

Then, late in the afternoon of August 15, the town underwent a terrible shock. Will Rogers was reported killed in an airplane crash near

Point Barrow, Alaska. The pilot was another Oklahoman, Wiley Post, famous for the black patch he wore over his blind eye and for his eight-day, fifteen-thousand-mile flight in 1931. Eskimos saw them go down, and one ran sixteen miles to report, "One mans big, have tall boots; other mans short, have sore eye, rag over eye."

At the drugstore, everyone who came in spoke in hushed tones.

"How can Will be dead?" asked Rowena, who came to sit with Liddy. "Nowadays, we all kinda *needed* that man."

Harold Cutter came in to listen to the radio with everyone else, Sheriff Bartlett, Stuffy Byers. And lots of other folks. Mabel had brought a meal, so she and Cassie were there, too.

Liddy said, "He's been all over, everybody needing and wanting him—remember how he came to Oklahoma and Texas and Arkansas couple of years ago, flying all around, raising money to feed people?"

The next day they heard how, when they brought him down from Alaska, fifteen thousand people stood in line all night to see Will's casket at Forest Lawn.

Between carrying all the extra responsibility of the drugstore, worrying about what Marvin was up to, and Will Rogers's death, Liddy's days were long and uneasy.

The only bright spot in her week was when young Tom Thatcher dropped in to buy salve for his milk cows. Liddy had always admired the stocky, muscular young farmer, with his slate-gray eyes and lopsided smile. She didn't believe the rumors about him and Walt Zimmer's wife. All the same, while she was wrapping the salve, Liddy thought that if it *was* true, she wouldn't blame the woman.

She caught herself. What was she thinking!

But that night she dreamed about Tom. She was looking into his eyes and urging him on as he slowly rubbed cow salve all over her body. When she woke up, it didn't seem all that ridiculous at first, and in her semiconscious state she started embellishing the dream. Tom continued touching and kissing her; then he stopped and proudly held up the can to show her the label—DETWEILLER'S COW SALVE. She woke with a start and laughed aloud.

She didn't hear from Marvin for eight days. Things ran along smoothly enough, except for Smiley Applebaum's thievery. She'd asked Smiley to come pick up the boxes and packing left from the shipment of first-aid supplies they'd received, and he had done it, jawing and gossiping the whole time, in and out of the back of the store. Now she was missing a dozen bottles of codeine tablets.

Marvin would not be pleased, but what recourse did she have? She thought of reporting it to Sheriff Bartlett, but decided against it. Smiley would just make more trouble for them in the long run. She knew the sheriff probably wouldn't jail him for it, and she wasn't sure how to prove he'd done the deed, anyway, so she decided to put it out of her mind.

The phone at the drugstore rang one morning around ten. It was the druggist from Waynoka, wondering why Marvin hadn't shown up at the drug convention. He was home now, and he hadn't seen Marvin there.

So frantic she couldn't move, Liddy lay on the old cot in the back while Mitch ran things.

Around four in the afternoon the phone rang. Mitch answered it and said, "It's Dad."

Liddy moved slowly toward the phone, as if crippled by some unseen force, while Mitch and Dan stood like posts.

Immense relief showed on her face; then she said, "Where are you?" That was the last the boys heard for several minutes. "All right. I'll come. I'll start right away."

Another long pause.

"Yes. I will… All right. Are you sure you're not hurt?" Then, "Oh."

The boys exchanged looks.

She hung up the phone and turned to them. "It's all right. He's fine. Just had a little car accident, that's all. I'm going to pick him up in Oklahoma City. Think you two can run things till I get back?"

"Sure," said Mitch.

Liddy motioned for them to follow her into the apartment. Not a single person was in the store, so they knew this must be extra-hush-hush information. She spoke very softly. "Dad's had an accident, but he isn't hurt bad. He and Joe Kelly were on their way into Oklahoma City when Joe's car went out of control."

Mitch asked, "Who was driving?"

"Dad, I think."

"Even though it was Mr. Kelly's car?"

"I think so. We'll find out more later."

"Is Daddy hurt bad?" asked Dan.

"He has a broken nose and a broken leg… He's lucky he wasn't killed." Liddy sank down suddenly into the big stuffed chair.

Dan was having difficulty digesting the fact that the person who had hurt him so many times was himself now injured. He moved close to Liddy and put his hand on her arm. She turned to him. "Dan, you be a good boy till I get back, y'hear? Mitch, you know how I rely on you." Mitch nodded, and Dan wondered why he was always the one being singled out for extra admonishing.

She got to Oklahoma City late that night. The Plymouth ran fine, but the heavily trafficked roads leading into the city made her nervous, and she had to ask three different strangers how to find the police station. After she got there she found out she had to put up bail for Marvin.

When she finally got to see him, he said he'd run into an oil truck outside the city. Joe's wife had already taken him home. Marvin admitted they'd been drinking, and Joe's car had to be scrapped, although Joe hadn't been hurt at all. *Just like him to walk away from a bad accident unscathed,* while her husband had a bandage over his nose, two black eyes, and a cast on his leg.

They sat on a long bench along one side of the room, near the police desk. There were a few rough-looking men—criminals, Liddy supposed—on the other side of the room, but none of them were near her and Marvin, thank goodness. Clutching her handbag to her chest, she could barely look at her husband. His forehead was covered with dried blood, and there were ugly bloodstains on his shirt. The cast on his leg stuck way out into the room.

"Honey, I'm really sorry…" He dropped his head and put his hand on her knee, but she jerked her knee away.

"Marvin, how could you drink and get behind the wheel? You're too old for this! Why would you do this to the children and me?" She knew how that sounded, but she didn't care. How *could* he do this to them, while she was working herself to the bone trying to keep everything together!

"I'm sorry. Can we just get out of here, Liddy? We can thrash it out somewhere else."

"How did you get that cast put on here?" she asked.

"Didn't—went to the hospital first."

She helped him with his crutches, then went to the counter, where she wrote a check for the bail: seventy-five dollars—money they needed so badly for so many other things! Tight-lipped, she picked up the suitcase she'd collected from the officer and started to lead her husband to the car. The young sergeant turned, searching for something under the counter, and called after Marvin, "Sir, how about your daughter's coat? Did you want to take that with you?"

He held up a purple satin jacket with a border of fluffy white fur around the collar.

"No, you can keep it." Marvin's words could barely be heard, and his face told the part of the story that was missing.

As they walked to the car, she said, "I guess that's why Joe wasn't hurt. He wasn't even *in* the front seat... somebody else was." Marvin got in the back seat. Good thing they had this sedan.

Her bitter words were the last spoken until three and a half hours later, when they were past the little town of Seiling. The only reason Liddy spoke then was because they needed to come to some agreement about how to explain this to people at home.

"What are we going to tell everyone?" she asked, abruptly breaking the silence.

"I don't know. My driver's license isn't goin' to be any good for a while."

"How long?" This was a complication she hadn't foreseen.

"Three months."

"The broken leg will come in handy—you can blame not driving on that."

Liddy, exhausted by now with the hours of driving and the emotion of the day, took the news with a certain calm detachment. As she drove through the pitch-black, moonless night, she smiled wryly to herself—she had been so worried about losing the *pharmacy* license!

When they got home at three a.m., Marvin said that, with his cast, it would be easier to sleep downstairs. *Fine,* she thought—*saves me saying it.* She made up the breakfast room couch but refused to help him upstairs to the bathroom to pee. At first she was going to let him figure it out on his own, but then she weakened and got the old chamber pot from the garage and put it next to the couch.

She left a note on the kitchen counter telling Mabel they had gotten in late and to keep the kids quiet. Mabel succeeded, because they were able to sleep in until eleven.

The next morning, after the few details Marvin wanted to share about the crash were told, Cassie and Dan wanted to hear all about the field trial. It turned out Jim had earned more points than any other dog over the three-day trial, and had won an Award of Merit. Sadie had done well, too, although Marvin said that the first day she was too feisty and broke on point. But then she'd settled down, coming in tenth overall among forty-seven dogs! She'd been steady as the Rock of Gibraltar, he said, and every time she brought in a bird, she added a little prance to her finish.

"Mr. Field, you must be mighty proud o' them dogs!" Mabel said from the kitchen.

Marvin had his foot propped on a footstool, and his eyes glistened with pride as he described, with gestures, how Sadie had held point, tail straight out and one paw raised.

Liddy was downing a couple of aspirin with her hot tea. She was positive that if Marvin hadn't had the cast on his leg, he would have stood up and pointed like a dog himself. His face looked even worse than it had yesterday, with black and plum-colored blotches around both eyes and across the bridge of his nose.

"Y'know, I had all kinds of offers to buy Jim. A rich man from Tennessee offered me a hundred dollars for 'im. It was hard to turn him down!"

"So why *did* you?" asked Liddy.

The children gave her scornful looks.

"Where are they, I mean Jim and Sadie?" Cassie wanted to know.

"They're still at the camp with a dog tender; I'll get 'em later."

Dan said, "Dad! We ought to h-have a c-celebration!"

Liddy stood at the back door. "I think your father already did his celebrating," she said.

Her mother's voice sounded like dill pickles, so Cassie knew there was something wrong, but she didn't know exactly what. Didn't she feel sorry for Daddy, with his broken leg and black eyes? And why had she stomped around upstairs, made all that noise getting dressed for work?

Marvin spent most of his recuperation time composing ads for *American Field*. It was true, the hour had come to make a profit on Jim, but he wasn't going to settle for any piddling hundred dollars. Later, after the ad was printed, he read it to Cassie:

MAGNIFICENT MALE
ENGLISH SETTER SHOOTING DOG

JIM ENJOY HOODAH. This one is just one in a thousand. A recent winner Enid Oklahoma Field Trial Award of Merit. Has everything. Sire Nat'l Ch.—Lester Enjoy Hoodah. Dam Astral Aviatrix by Nat'l Champion. 3 yrs. old—White body, black & tan ticking. What does he do—man, everything! This dog finds birds, and how! Steady as a rock of Gibralter on point; backs at sight. Tender, fast, force-broken retriever. Out-birds any and all dogs. Shot over 2 seasons. Minds on command. Mister— I implore, I insist, wire now if you really want that dog which you have always dreamed about!

C.O.D. $175   MARVIN FIELD   CATO OKLAHOMA

Her dad pointed out Jim's name and his own, printed there for all the world to see. The ad made Jim sound so smart, Cassie was sure her dad would sell him, but she hoped he wouldn't.

O

The day after Marvin got back, Mabel left forever. She climbed on the train with every stitch she had and every bit of her hope chest: a set of dishes, a set of sheets, Liddy's gift of two green towels, and two pillow slips.

Liddy finally resigned herself to it, even though when Mabel had said she was leaving, she was sure that Providence was out to show her she hadn't been grateful enough for her Heaven-sent blessings. She gave Mabel her best wishes.

Mabel told Liddy she didn't know how to say good-bye to the kids. It would make her too sorrowful, and she hated for them to see her cry. Liddy said maybe the best thing would be for them all to come to the station and wave good-bye. Then maybe Cassie would be too excited to be upset by her leaving.

Mitch, Dan, Liddy, and Cassie saw her off on the 10:05 going west. Liddy was wrong — Cassie cried, then Liddy cried, then Mabel started to bawl. Even Mitch got tears in his eyes when Mabel hugged him hard and said, "You jes' keep on a-helpin' yer folks, now."

Before she climbed on the train, she tried to hug Dan, too, but he ducked and squirmed out of the way. They saw her through the window, settling into her seat and stacking her meager belongings. Then she stood up and peered through the window, her eyes looking magically in two directions at once, encompassing them all in a final benign expression of love.

O

Liddy moved Marvin into Mabel's room, where he'd be out of the way. For three nights she barely slept, thinking of his selfishness and—she was sure of it—his infidelity. She told herself that she had to come to grips with the fact that his family came last. Obviously Joe Kelly, the dogs, floozies, and whiskey were at the top of his order of priorities. He had told her they only picked up a couple of girls to share a drink in celebration, that there had been no 'bedding down,' but he must think her a downright fool.

Late on the night after his third day home, he thumped his way on crutches up to the bedroom to plead with her. He wanted to be forgiven, to start over; couldn't she see that he loved her?

But she couldn't get rid of that image of the purple satin jacket with the fur trim.

She was mortified that he might have to go back to Oklahoma City. His lawyer had told him the case probably wouldn't even go to trial, but the blot on the family...on her children, and on her! The cast on his leg, and especially the blue and plum mask across his eyes and nose, were dark tokens of what he had done to them. There it was for all to see, the blatant mark of shame and disgrace! It was Marvin's, but she and the children were made to bear it with him!

On his third night home she tossed and turned alone in bed, getting up twice to gaze out the window at the backyard and the dog pens. Sadie and Jim weren't back yet, and the puppies yapped all day and some at night, too. Patches of grass were grey in the moonlight, and branches scraped against the sides of the house like insistent, imploring hands, urging her to act. But if she left Marvin now when he couldn't even drive, wouldn't that be the height of callousness?

Well, he would just have to figure it out—without her.

She returned to bed, but just before dawn she got up again. She sat at the kitchen table and wrote a short note to Harold. *"Family emergency, taking the children to my brother's in Waxahachie. Sorry, I will write later."* Then she went into the boys' room and shook Mitch awake. "Mitch, we're going to Uncle Fred's. Pack a suitcase and help Dan do the same. Take enough clothes for a week or two. And be real quiet. Dad doesn't know we're going."

Mitch sat up in bed, his hair sticking straight up. "Mom, school's about to start! I'll get behind right away!"

"Never mind. I just can't take this bird dog situation any more. Your dad's lost his mind, I think. Now, *get up!*"

In Cassie's room she quickly packed a small cardboard suitcase, then woke and dressed Cassie and took her down to the car. She hurried the boys, shushing them all the while, and packed a lunch of leftover chicken and biscuits, adding some apples and a package of sliced ham. She put the food in two paper bags. They'd been very quiet, but as she slid behind the driver's seat, she heard a noise inside, and she knew Marvin was up. She drove as fast as she could, taking a detour by Harold's house to put the note in his mailbox. Then she drove to the depot and parked.

The six a.m. passenger train to Enid hadn't come in. Homer Botsin, who ran the train depot and the Western Union single-handed, greeted her with a surprised look, processed the tickets, and handed them over the counter. She barely had time to scribble a note and prop it against the windshield inside the car. She couldn't make it too personal—Homer or someone else out early might decide to open the car and read it. Everybody in this godforsaken town was so *nosy*. Sure, they were interested in you and watched out for you, but they wanted to know about it if you got in trouble, and they were always pleased if you did.

She wrote, "Going to Fred's for a while. Emergency. Liddy." She didn't write "Love."

She didn't feel it, and she wasn't going to write it.

The big locomotive approached the station, filling the air with noise and steam. Cassie's and Dan's eyes were open wide in excitement, but Mitch tried to act cool and worldly. The Negro conductor helped them aboard, and they settled into two facing bench seats.

Looking out the window as the train pulled away from the station, Liddy said a silent good-bye to the large CATO painted in block letters on the end of the building. Soon, with the rhythmic click of the wheels on the tracks, Cassie was asleep, her head on Mitch's lap. Dan slumped drowsily in his seat.

Liddy gazed out at the dry short-grass prairie rolling past, with a few poor-looking Herefords standing in the early light.

What will become of us? She closed her eyes, trying to will reality away. Mitch had his eyes shut and his head back. He didn't look happy. None of her children looked happy.

It took six hours to reach Enid, with seven stops along the way, and by then they had eaten all the food. Somehow Liddy managed to get them off the Santa Fe and, after an hour's wait, onto the Chicago, Rock Island and Pacific, which would take them south to Dallas. From there she would call Waxahachie and have Fred come pick them up.

During the layover she herded the children to the station café, where Mitch stood riffling through magazines with half-naked women on the covers. He knew better than to buy those when *she* was around. She bought Dan and Cassie each a box of Crackerjacks, and as she propelled the children back toward the tracks, Cassie held up a little celluloid dog she'd found in the box.

"Look, mama, it looks just like daddy's bitch Sadie!"

"Hush! Don't you be talkin' to me about those dogs! And don't let me *ever* hear you use that word again!" Liddy yanked Cassie's arm hard as they climbed up the steps. The conductor didn't try to help them. He merely stepped aside as the wild-haired woman with the unhappy-looking progeny boarded the train.

They alternately dozed and gazed out the fly-specked windows as they traveled, with no stops this time, past El Reno, Chickasha and down almost to the border where the Red River separated Oklahoma and Texas. They were slowing down to stop just outside Waurika when Liddy saw the little ragamuffin children playing by the railroad tracks, two little boys the ages of Dan and Cassie. Their clothing was torn, their faces were dirty, and their shoes, with no socks or laces, were falling off their feet.

They stopped their play and looked up into the lit-up train with wide smiles, and when Cassie waved they waved back, with large exuberant gestures. As the train moved slowly past the children, Liddy felt something inside of her buckle. Was that the way her children would look, if she couldn't provide for them? She had wrenched them from their father, their home and all their friends. In Fred's house they would be looked upon as orphans, practically, and she would be considered the dependent sister, at least until she could get on her feet. She'd have to find a job, a house, make arrangements for a new life for herself and her offspring. And what about her WPA job? It was just beginning to get going.

Her brother Fred loved her; he was kind; he was prosperous. But he had his own family problems, and Bertha would certainly not welcome them for any length of time. Her sister-in-law was the kind of woman who would make her beg, in the end, for every favor and kindness. She suddenly realized she would salvage more pride, in the long run, by staying put in Cato and working things out. Right now she felt no love for Marvin, but maybe it would come back. Maybe she could *will* it to come back. And who would drive him to work and back home? It really was mean to leave him with that broken leg.

They got off at Waurika and spent the night in the train station, where Liddy bought a paper and read about Huey Long being shot by a man at the Louisiana state Capitol, who had then been shot by Long's bodyguards. Long was still alive, but the account said it wasn't likely he would live for long.

The paper came in handy. She put it over her eyes and went to sleep on the hard bench. The kids found spaces nearby and did the same.

They commenced the trip back home the next morning. It seemed even longer and more exhausting than the ride down had been. When they finally got off the train in Cato around five in the afternoon, dirty, tired, and disreputable looking, they were the only people to disembark. There was, however, one other passenger who arrived. He came in a wooden crate, then sat on the depot trolley where Homer had put him, barking and whining as if he didn't have a friend in the world. Stamped on the side of the crate were the words:

To: Marvin Field
Cato, Oklahoma
From: Tusculum, Georgia
BRIGHT PERKIN'S PERKY
Handle With Care

Part Two

1939

6

You are free to do whatever you like.
You need only face the consequences.

—Anonymous

On a cold day in January, years after Mabel had left for California, Cassie accompanied Marvin on a delivery of insulin to old Mr. Farrow's.

There had been a few nights lately when the thermometer dropped well below freezing. The trees were bare and the ground frozen hard, and as Cassie rode along, shivering in her too-short winter coat, she had to admit that her ugly long cotton stockings at least kept her legs warm. They crossed Wolf Creek Bridge and heard a rush of water. The creek bed was bordered on both sides by sad-looking weeds and brush, but with more water flowing than she'd ever seen down there. As they crossed the bridge and began to drive through the countryside, she gazed at stacks of hay, and horses and cattle grazing. There was a funny scarecrow on the Thatcher farm, with a torn straw hat and a smile made from black yarn. They drove down the long driveway to the house and got out. Standing on the rickety porch with her dad, Cassie remembered Mabel and then Lally.

Lally. She wondered if the Hoffmans had made it to "Californy." Cassie could almost hear her saying the word, could picture her in her long calico dress and straw hat. All these memories flooded her mind in the few seconds before the old man opened the door. He took the package brusquely from Marvin, nodded sourly when Marvin reminded him of his long-standing bill, and started to close the door.

Cassie said, "Wait, Mister Farrow! I was wondrin', have you heard anything from Mabel lately?"

The old man peered down at her. "You wanta read her letter? She was purty stuck on you. Yore brothers, too."

Marvin turned on his heel and went back to the Model A. Lighting up a cigarette, he leaned back, looking out over the half-frozen landscape. Cassie stood shivering on the porch.

"Come in; I'll find it som'ers." She followed him inside, where it wasn't much warmer, but at least there was no wind. He banged the door shut and shuffled down the hall. She looked around. There was an ancient sofa with all the nap worn off, and a faded rag rug. The walls were papered over with calendars dating back to the twenties. She supposed Mr. Farrow kept them because they had pictures—farmhouses, country scenes, pretty girls, and farm animals. One of them depicted a soldier. She looked closer. A torn corner with numbers on it hung off the flyspecked calendar—the year was 1918. *Mabel must have looked at these calendars when she was growing up.* The one Cassie liked best showed the Dionne quintuplets playing with dolls. It wasn't a painting exactly, more like a tinted drawing, dated 1937.

She stepped to the middle of the rag rug and stood waiting. Finally the old man came back into the room and handed her a piece of lined tablet paper:

Calipatria Callifornia

Deer dad,

We are fin. We hope you ar to. Buck is workin evry day so am i he piks chereys an i am kuking for a lot of peeple who work on the farm to. They lik my kukin a lot. we are goin to keep staing here becos the whether is gud all yer round allmost an no sno an jus rite smart of rane. I like Callifornia a lot an Buck an I ar finly goen have a baby. Abowt tim huh! the baby wil com in april. plez say helo to foks ther in Cato if you see enneone. Speshally the Fields. dont sta to yerself to much. let cuzzin Duke tak you in his pickup to town somtims.

Lov, Mabel

p.s. how is yer dibeetis?

Cassie handed the letter back. The old man's hand was covered with veins that looked as if they might burst open and leak blue ink. "That's a real nice letter. Tell Mabel hello for me if you write her."

"You wanta write her? I don't write her much on account o' my hand shakes. You take the letter and tell her the news. And tell 'er I ain't goin' nowhere in that no-good Duke Farrow's truck!"

When she got home, Cassie went straight to Liddy with the news. Her mother was pleased Mabel was going to have a child. "It's been four years since she followed Buck out there. About time they had a family!"

That evening Cassie sat down at the card table in her room and wrote. She told Mabel all the news she knew, and she asked her if she

knew anything about Lally. She wrote, "I would really like to *know*."
But no matter how tightly she scrunched up her eyes, she couldn't
remember Mabel's face. She could almost hear her voice, and she could
remember her long, bony arms and the way one eye looked off to the
side. But Mabel's face just wouldn't appear in her mind's eye. She ended
her letter:

P.S. I am glad you are going to have a baby. So is Mama.
I hope it looks like you.

She decided that might be insulting to Buck. She scratched that out
and wrote:

I hope it looks like you if it is a girl.
Love, Cassie

○

It was the middle of the night, and Liddy, Dan, and Cassie were
traveling to Grandmother Field's funeral. The narrow, rough concrete
highway from Cato down to Ada was dark, and Liddy strained to see
through the bug-splotched windshield. Cassie fought sleep, but after a
few minutes she couldn't any more, and slept for the entire five-hour
journey. Liddy drove all the way; Dan's driving made her too nervous.
Marvin had gone down two days before, when he'd been called by his
mother's doctor, who said that even though the tuberculosis was arrested,
her heart was giving out. Mitch didn't make the trip, Marvin didn't want
him to leave his classes. He had finished high school in 1938 in a blaze
of sports awards and scholastic mediocrity, and was now a freshman at
Northwestern State College in Alva.

In the first hours of daylight, they were shown into the parlor to
view the body. Cassie peered into the casket. For a brief moment she
looked at the ancient face that looked carved out of soapstone, the thin
white hands folded over a dark purple dress. She had never seen this
grandmother in real life. A heavy woman with a contorted expression
bent down to her and said, "*Kiss* her, honey —give her one last kiss!"
Cassie obediently bent over to kiss the waxy cheek. But Liddy stopped
her, putting her arm across Cassie's chest. Cassie started to run out of the
room, and at the doorway Marvin's knees caught her. She stood sobbing

against his legs until Liddy took her away into a bedroom, where she patted her and covered her with a quilt.

The most interesting part of the funeral was meeting Daddy's sister Aunt Hannah, who lived in Seattle, Washington. She had never visited them in Cato, and Cassie was pretty sure it was because she was rich and they were poor. That was what she'd picked up, from her parent's conversations on the subject. Also, she'd detected that her dad was embarrassed because his sister had been married so many times, maybe three or four.

"I don't want Hannah influencin' Cassie. She was *wild,*" Cassie heard him say to Liddy the night before they left Cato for Ada.

She wondered what sort of wild influence she might catch from her aunt, and she wondered it even more after she met her. She thought Aunt Hannah was not just glamorous, but nice. She had long painted fingernails, and she wore more makeup than anyone Cassie'd ever seen. Her clothes were beautiful.

Hannah said, "Liddy! Marvin tells me you're working for the President now. I think that's wonderful. I love FDR, but my husband's not so sure." Hannah's latest husband was a J. C. Penney manager. And she said to Cassie, "Someday I want you to meet my stepdaughter Nell. She's just a couple years older than you. But she doesn't have shiny black pigtails like you have."

A lot of people came to the service. They smiled and nodded, clustering about and expressing affection for Grandmother Field in warm and loving tones. Cassie had never seen anyone shed as many tears as her dad did that day— in the church, then all over again at the cemetery. He kept his handkerchief to his face, trying to keep them mopped up.

Under a slate sky they clustered around the grave. Wind blew through the bare trees, with no green buds in sight. The only pretty things were the chrysanthemums and lilies banked on the casket. The black-suited elderly minister read one of the Psalms he said Grandmother loved.

"The Lord is my light and my salvation
whom shall I fear?
The Lord is the refuge of my life
of whom shall I be afraid?"

Aunt Hannah was crying almost as hard as her dad, and Cassie saw him put his arm around his sister and give her a hard hug. The minister finished the reading, and the casket was lowered into the ground.

○

One Saturday in early spring when Liddy wasn't working, she invited her best friend Rowena Richards over for tuna salad; she wanted to try a new recipe she'd found in the *Ladies Home Journal*. She said Cassie could invite Fiona, too. That was the day Cassie showed Fiona the rag doll Grandmother Field had sent her long ago, consigned to a box under the bed. She was too grown up now for dolls.

"I remember seein' you with this! I've got one almost just like it!" said Fiona excitedly.

Cassie was already jealous of Fiona's blond curly hair, and now she was thunderstruck to see that her best friend was growing bumps under her blouse.

Fiona was only eleven. *How could it be?*

After the tuna salad, which had almonds mixed in, the girls found Liddy and Rowena Richards upstairs. "It's just an idea I have," Liddy was saying. "It's been percolating in my mind ever since I worked with the farm women and the WPA sewing projects. They closed down a lot of women's projects in 'thirty-seven because the government was more interested in construction jobs—they said their hearts didn't palpitate over sewing rooms. What I've been thinking about doing was getting some of the most talented women to run up their specialties, so I could start selling them around the state. I could make a commission, and it would get their handicrafts out to the public, help them make a few extra dollars. I'll bet people everywhere would want to buy their things. The economy's getting better now, and they could make money, and I could too."

Cassie and Fiona stood in the doorway, Cassie waiting to ask if she and Fiona could go downtown.

"Why, Liddy, that would be a real fine thing." Rowena's tone was admiring and respectful.

"I have to investigate all the ramifications, of course." Liddy was busy hauling out her private hoard of quilts, bedspreads, hand-embroidered sheets and pillowcases, dish towels, and antimacassars. There were also a baby quilt Grandmother Field had made for Mitch, a doll quilt she'd made for Cassie, and six or eight embroidered guest towels. All the treasures from the carved cedar chest were spread out on Liddy's bed. Many times in the past, Cassie had seen her mother take them out to show, then put them all away again.

"I have several quilts, too," said Rowena. "Oh, this Lone Star is beautiful!

Liddy said they could go, and the girls ran out into the fresh air. As they started along the gravel road toward Main, they heard the calls of turtledoves and the perky *"bob-white's!"* of a covey of quail. It sounded and smelled like spring. Pungent smells of an outdoor fire came to them as they walked; Heck Purvis was in his backyard, burning a pile of brush. Along the side of the road, bristle grass and jimsonweed were growing taller.

Fiona's and Cassie's arms and legs swung in unison, and the gravel made a crunching sound under their feet. They walked past Cato High's football field, and there was Dan, with Pauly Spokes and Sean O'Herlihy, Mike's younger brother, all looking scruffy and sneaky. They were under one of the trees bordering the field smoking, their shoulders hunched and their heads down. Dan glared at Cassie from yards away, daring her to say one word.

Downtown, they ran into Fergus Klein with his mother. Fergus had sent Cassie a valentine in February through the mail. Fergus had reddish, shaggy hair, blue eyes, and a straightforward gaze. Inside the envelope were a red crepe-paper heart, a drawing of a boy kissing a girl, and the words "Can you go to the picture show with me? I got the money." Cassie had ignored the whole thing and had been careful not to look in Fergus's direction since.

Now as they passed him on the sidewalk. she stared at the ground.

O

Before supper that evening, Cassie went in the bathroom and closed the door. Slowly she took off her sweater, blouse, and undershirt. There didn't seem to be anything happening in the vicinity of her chest, nothing like Fiona. Not a bump, a swelling, or a bulge—not so much as a mosquito bite. She jumped up and down several times… Nothing moved. With a sigh, she put her clothes back on and went downstairs to eat.

"Cassie, what in the world were you doing up there? Sounded like the house was falling down!" said Liddy.

"There was some spiders over the toilet, and I was knockin' 'em down."

○

When business was slow, which was most of the time, Marvin would work on his ads for *American Field*. One day he said to Cassie, "I'm selling two of Tizzy and Perky's puppies."

"Which ones, Daddy? Don't sell Chauncey!" She regretted that her dad had sold Jim after the field trial—she still missed him.

"Nope, I'm sellin' Mick and Baron." He showed her the paper he was writing on, and asked her to correct any misspelled words:

OUTSTANDING BIRD DOGS
OUT OF JIM ENJOY HOODAH EX SADIE
& TIP OF JOYEUSE BITCH

Two beautiful English Setters. Sand Creek Mick and Tusculum Baron Brick; thoroghly broke on quale and prairie chicken. LISSEN! Hard as a rock, stanch and steady, back on command, steady to wing; retrieve, whoa, heel, handle like a glove to whistle or wave of hat. Look them all over! You cannot beat them! $200 each. Contact Marvin Field in Cato Oklahoma!

Cassie was pleased to serve such an important function in the family. She corrected all the misspelled words she could see and gave the paper back to her dad.

○

Marvin had told Mitch, when he started school at Northwestern State at Alva, that he wasn't going up there just to date girls, drink beer, and play sports. He'd better *work* at his studies, or Marvin would yank him out so fast his teeth would rattle. Of course, Mitch hadn't believed it. He'd gone up to the college and promptly fallen in with some card-playing buddies, and when he wasn't playing poker he was taking out some of the freshman girls. He even had a brief fling with a junior—an untamed Chickasha beauty from Anadarko.

Then Sara Jane had turned up, and they'd gotten started again. And then there was the job Marvin got for him in one of Alva's drugstores. It took too much time; every evening after class for four hours! He just couldn't fit it all in.

His dad would have been surprised to find out that sports didn't figure in his downfall at all. He didn't have any extra time to even try out for the football team, and by the time baseball started he was involved in other stuff. The coach knew who he was, though. He'd dropped in at the gym office the second week he was on campus, and the coach said they wanted him to try out for pitcher. The coach had heard of the Cato team and their wins. When spring came, he intended to prove himself with his slider and his curveball, but by then he had Sara Jane and a poker debt, and the only thing sliding was his grades.

He decided not to bother talking to the coach. Why set himself up for disappointment?

When Marvin got the notice from the college that Mitch was failing, he called and told him to get his rear end home *right now*. The bus didn't go into Cato, but dusted its way into Red Arrow, so when Mitch called late the next evening, Liddy went to pick him up. When she saw her son's grim expression, she suggested they go to the drugstore and get all the recriminations out of the way. They pulled up to the store around nine fifteen.

Main Street was deserted, and Marvin was alone, smoking and reading the *Saturday Evening Post*. He took his elbows off the cigar counter and looked up at his tall son.

"Well, that was kind of a botched job, wasn't it, Mitch?"

While Mitch tried to think how to reply, Liddy spoke. "Marvin, Mitch has something to tell you."

"Oh, does he? Let's hear it." Marvin walked out from behind the counter, one hand on a cocked hip, the other holding his cigarette. "Let's hear you explain two F's and two C's in your first college semester, and two F's and two D's in your second! Let's hear you talk me out of tellin' you that your college career has just bit the dust!"

"Dad, I'm not goin' to apologize any more, except for sayin' I'm sorry."

Liddy said, "Marvin, maybe we shouldn't have made him get a job his first semester. Maybe we could have managed."

"God damn it, you know there's been a depression, and Mitch knows it, too. You know I don't make much more'n a livin' wage here. We got three kids, and they're *all* goin' to work if they want an education—*I* sure did."

Nobody spoke for a few seconds, and the silence hung in the air like the gray cigarette smoke. Finally Liddy said, "Why don't we try to be forgiving, Marvin? Other kids have failed at college. You know Mitch is smart; he just got off on the wrong foot." She turned to Mitch. "Honey, would you like to try school somewhere else—maybe down in Texas?"

"*Liddy!*" Marvin sputtered out her name. "That's not gonna *go!* I already told Mitch before he left that if he didn't make the most of this, he was out of luck. Is it my fault he acts like he doesn't have any brains? You're not goin' to stand there and make my word look like nothin' but horse puckey, are you?"

Marvin's face had turned the color of raw meat. He stood with his free hand clenched, as if he was trying not to hit something or someone.

"Wait, wait—Mom, Dad, I don't want you arguin' over me. I know what I'm gonna do. I'm goin' to join the CMTC down at Fort Sill."

"What in the world is that?" Liddy asked.

"Civilian Military Training Corps. Dooky and Mike are goin', too. I'll be there eight weeks; then I'll know what I want to do. I'm thinkin' of joinin' the Army, anyway."

"No, you're not! I won't have you going to war!" The corners of Liddy's mouth turned down suddenly. A sob escaped, but she pushed her fist against her teeth and managed to hold herself together.

"Mom, Hitler's invaded Czechoslovakia! England and France are goin' to fight, and I think we'll be in it soon enough. My political science prof at Alva thinks so for sure."

"Oh, so you went to class at least *once*, huh?" said Marvin.

"Mom, I'm kinda tired. Could we go home now?" Mitch turned to his dad as he left. "I don't think you want to see me around, and I don't want to *be* around. I'll get all my stuff and move out tomorrow."

The darkness outside the brightly lit store swallowed him up.

Marvin stared after him, and Liddy began to cry. "Why do you have to act so hateful toward your son? Don't you know he's heartsick about flunking out? Do you want to lose him—have him go into the Army and get killed in a crazy war—just to get away?"

"Liddy, go on home." Turning his back, Marvin stubbed his cigarette out in an ashtray and said, "He's not goin' to get killed. The service might be the best thing for him. It was the best way for most of us to grow up in 1917."

"*Grow up?* If by growing up you mean getting gassed and getting legs cut off and getting blinded—yes, a lot of fellas did grow up—but some of 'em didn't live to see it!"

She walked out the door after Mitch.

In the car she said, "I baked you an apple pie, honey. You can have a piece when we get there." She was careful not to look at her son.

"Hope you put a good supply of worms in it, mom; that'd be just my dish!"

Dan was reading on the couch in the breakfast room. Mitch threw his knapsack, two suitcases, and a couple of boxes through the back door, then entered the room with a resigned air and a half-grin. He nodded to Dan and ducked into the kitchen. Liddy and Dan looked at each other as they heard the water running for a long time, then the sound of Mitch gulping.

"Well, I booted it!" said Mitch, coming back.

Dan got up and walked over to his brother. They were almost the same height now, Mitch six feet, Dan a little less. "It doesn't matter. The old man's sore, but that's all the difference it makes. Cassie's missed you. She'll be glad you're back."

Mitch sat down suddenly, letting out a long sigh. "I'm not stayin'. Gonna go with Dooky and Mike down to Lawton to the CMTC training camp. But I won't be there long—I'm gonna join up."

Dan's eyes opened wide. "You are? Some other guys I know are joinin', too!"

Liddy had been quiet up to now. "Dan, who do *you* know who's joining the Army?"

"They're older guys from Red Arrow, Mom; you wouldn't know 'em."

Liddy said, "Since you're only fifteen, I wouldn't think you'd know anybody who has anything to do with it. It's not our war anyway. Roosevelt's not goin' to get us into it."

Mitch countered, "England and France are probably goin' to declare hostilities against Germany if the Nazis go into Poland—then they're gonna want us in, too! I might as well get in the action. Now, where's that apple pie?"

The next morning Cassie, still in her pajamas, was startled to see Mitch asleep on the breakfast room couch. She stood for a minute studying him, then picked up a chair and carried it into the kitchen to eat her cereal. When she'd finished and was making toast, Dan joined her.

"Why's Mitch home?" she whispered. "I thought he was at college."

"He didn't like it. He's goin' to try somethin' else."

"What's he gonna try?"

"How should I know? Ask *him!*" Dan poured out a bowlful of cereal.

"What're you two yakking about?" Mitch's sleepy voice sounded from the couch.

Cassie jumped off the chair and went to kneel beside her brother's makeshift bed. "How come you're home?"

"Well, I kinda quit." He sat up slowly and lit a cigarette. "I didn't have time to go to classes and still work twenty-five hours a week at the glorious Alva Drug. Besides, I don't have any brains."

Marvin entered the room from upstairs, and nobody moved.

"Dan, go outside and get the paper. Cassie, you get ready for school. Your mother's gettin' dressed, she'll be here in a minute to fix eggs."

"I had cereal, Daddy. And Dan had Wheaties and a banana."

"We'll all have eggs—give you a good start in the morning. Mitch, put out that cigarette—it smells terrible." No one had the nerve to say that Marvin had been smoking in this room all their lives.

Mitch moved out the next day. He stayed with Mike O'Herlihy for a few weeks before going to Fort Sill, where the two of them and Dooky

Schlanaker spent two months learning how to take fourteen-mile hikes with full packs (seven miles out and seven miles back), stand at attention in the broiling sun in woolen uniforms and ignore the boys that fainted. They learned to make their beds and do their laundry, scrub latrines, and peel potatoes. Mitch sharpened up his poker and crap-shooting skills, learned to drink beer, and got his fill of girlie magazines. He already knew how to smoke.

7

She excelled in needlework, she painted in water colour
—of such is the kingdom of heaven.

—Inscription on tomb of an
18th-century woman

Cassie saw newsreels with a funny-looking man gesturing and shouting to throngs of people, crowds as thick as bees in a hive, and Stuffy Byers and Marvin talked about how curious it was to see newsreels of Charles Lindbergh reviewing German airplanes. Lindbergh was an isolationist, Dan said. That meant he thought the United States shouldn't have anything to do with Europe's war. But Marvin talked about Germany's führer—Cassie was pretty sure that was the funny-looking man in the newsreels—threatening all of Europe. Dan talked at breakfast about how France and England weren't doing anything about it, and some folks thought they should and some folks thought they shouldn't.

Cassie couldn't tell what her dad thought. When she asked him, he just shook his head as though he didn't know. Usually he *knew*.

Dan said maybe Mitch's professor was right about Europe going to war.

O

By the middle of May the wind had died down, and suddenly it was hot. Liddy never knew what made her decide to give a picnic and needlecraft show on Decoration Day. The town never made a big thing out of the holiday—just a small parade after raising the flag, with a few Boy Scouts and uniformed veterans who marched in rows to the Cato cemetery, followed by anyone who wanted to go along. There, the graves of Cato soldiers were adorned with fresh flowers and garlands of leaves. The town didn't boast any Civil War veterans, or any from the Mexican-American war, and many of the town's dead from that war still lay overseas, but eight or ten fighting men from the Great War were buried here at home.

No doubt Liddy's decision to have the picnic had something to do with how fast her children were growing up. All she and Marvin ever did was work—their kids didn't know what it was like to have a party. Cassie had no social graces whatsoever, and Dan was fast becoming a country bumpkin. Mitch was gone to the camp at Fort Sill, so it was already too late for improving him, but then, Liddy thought, Mitch was naturally smooth.

She'd been lying awake nights, trying to think up some way to show off the farm ladies' creations. There were so many county women she knew who sewed, and their work should be *seen*. Then one day she got the inspiration to put on a bazaar, where the women could see what others were doing and possibly make a little money. It would be inspiring to see all their handiwork in one place—it would be like having their own county fair!

Recently the *Cato Enquirer* had run a nice article about Rachel Klein and her church's quilting group at the First Christian. WOMEN SHOW OFF THEIR NEEDLEWORK TALENT, it said. And besides Rachel there was Minna, that handsome Tom Thatcher's wife, with her crocheted afghans. Liddy was constantly surprised at the talent around her. One day Inga Sundersson had shown her a gorgeous Swedish skirt and vest she'd embroidered for her daughter Greta, and once, when Liddy dropped off some washing, she had seen the widow Groves's handmade baby clothes—lovely little bibs, christening gowns, and knitted sweaters and caps—just before Mrs. Groves mailed them off to her grandchildren. How the widow had time for this as well as her laundry business made Liddy feel plain slothful!

Even lazy Ezra Corkle's wife, Jerusha, was an artisan, weaving intricate bedspreads and tablecloths at home on her own loom, although she was shy about letting anyone see her work. Liddy thought maybe she could get her to weave some table runners or buffet scarves. She would like to buy some of those herself, and maybe other women would, too.

But if she put on the bazaar, where would they have it? Not a church—that could only lead to bickering. *She wanted it on neutral ground.* She briefly considered Veterans Hall, but the place seemed so cold and dismal. Now that summer was coming, they should have it someplace airy and open. One of the few places that could hold all the pieces was the Cato Shores dance hall, which never got used for much of anything, and it was certainly airy! The dance hall was a big barn of a place built in the roaring twenties (which in Cato had only mewed a little), with layers of peeling white paint on the outside. It had a splintered wooden floor and a dozen or so rickety wooden tables.

Hank Jenkins, who ran the place, said the town swimming hole would open for the summer two weeks from now, two days before the holiday. It was meant to be! Liddy decided to give a swimming party and invite everyone she liked—the kids' friends, too—and combine it with a needlework bazaar. Her bridge friends, Violet, Flo, and Rowena, could help organize it. They might object at first, but she knew they would pitch in and give her a hand.

She announced the news at breakfast one morning. Marvin pushed back his chair abruptly, making a loud squeak. "Count me out; I have to work." She and Marvin hadn't been sleeping together. Just a few days ago they'd had one of their fights, this time about his not washing his hands after checking the dogs for worms. He had come in from outside, then gone to the kitchen to get a glass of cold water from the jug in the refrigerator. Liddy had been standing right there.

"Marvin, did you wash your hands after doctoring those dogs? Fooling around under their tails and all? I didn't see you wash up."

"Hell, no; I was just gettin' some water, for God's sake!"

"Not in my kitchen, you don't. Go back out there and wash, if you want me to fix supper in this kitchen!"

Cassie was listening from the doorway of the breakfast room. Cleanliness had always been a sore subject between her parents. Her dad was always saying he wished just *one* of his bird dogs had a nose as good as her mom's, and her mom was always saying her dad had disgusting habits. Her dad started sleeping in Mabel's room again, like he'd done after his automobile accident.

"No, you're not working," Liddy said, plopping a plate of eggs in front of him, the words as edged as a shard of flint. "We're closing the store for the picnic. Decoration Day is a Tuesday."

Marvin sat looking at her, his head cocked to one side. She'd been this way ever since she'd worked at that job with the WPA—bossy, always wanting her own way. Months after she'd taken the job he found out from Henry McCallum that she'd opened her own bank account. He'd been angrier at that–a blatant attempt to wear the pants in the family— than at her taking the job in the first place! Henpecked and pussy-whipped, that's what he was.

Henry wouldn't even tell him the amount she had in there!

"You think there's anybody in this town wants to come to some kind o' party out at that old swimmin' hole? We don't even have enough friends to make it worthwhile."

"We do, so! You'll see—besides, it'll be nice for the kids!"

"The kids only care about seein' their own friends, not yours, and not mine. They see people all the time in the store, anyhow!"

But Marvin's newest puppy was arriving any day. He'd seen the ad in *American Field* for these expensive English setter pups in Georgia, and he'd ordered one of the white, black, and tan ticked ones. Apprehensive about Liddy's reaction, he decided for the moment not to argue any more. What was marriage, anyway, but good old-fashioned give-and-take?

They drew up the guest list that evening. At the top of the list were Liddy's bridge club ladies and Flo's and Rowena's husbands, George Schonberger and Herb Richards. She would invite Stuffy and Charlene Byers and Harold Cutter, the only three people in the whole town *both* Marvin and she liked. Marvin said they should invite the Scruggses, since Barney was the mayor, but Liddy refused to have Sally. Harold Cutter would be the only one invited from the First Methodist, because Marvin said he wouldn't come if Reverend Dickens and Drucilla were there. Besides, Liddy was upset with the preacher because he'd helped Mrs. Weston's nephew, Alvin Jonas, get a Bible scholarship to a seminary in the south. Liddy told Cassie that Mrs. Weston had turned inside out, gloating, because the First Methodist was helping Alvin become an instrument of the Lord. Liddy thought it a complete waste of church money.

"Don't you think Alvin'll make a good preacher?" Cassie asked.

"I think he'd make a good doorstop," said Liddy.

Liddy said Dan could invite Pauly, and Cassie could ask Fiona.

"How about Fiona's folks?" asked Cassie.

Liddy said she'd have to think about that, because Mrs. Bannister was "common."

Cassie looked up the word in the dictionary. It said 'mediocre' and 'everyday.' Cassie didn't understand. Anybody who looked like Jean Harlow could never be called 'everyday.' Cassie had noticed that other than the sewing ladies, whom Liddy dealt with all the time, her mother didn't accept many people into her circle of friends. As far as Cassie could gather, by roundabout questioning, the only strikes against Fiona's mother were that she wore makeup, peroxided her hair, smoked, and looked pretty. Maybe that was it—*being pretty*. But maybe not, because when Cassie begged to have her fourth-grade teacher invited, Liddy had agreed, and Miss Gallagher was beautiful.

O

When the day of the picnic dawned warm and mild, Liddy offered up a prayer of thanks. It would be warm enough to eat outdoors, but it was too soon yet for flies and gnats to be a nuisance. Her blooming lilac and spirea exuded wonderful scents, attracting bees and yellowjackets from miles around. The locusts and cottonwoods were in bloom, and yesterday she had gone on a dry run out to the Shores and had seen the redbuds lining the county road. They were filling out with leaves, their coral flowers almost gone. Thank Providence for the Bureau of Reclamation! They'd planted the redbuds two years ago and had even seen to it that they were watered.

Flo, Violet, and Rowena had indeed been helpful. Liddy was in charge of gathering the creations of the sewing ladies. Flo did the pricing and tagging, Violet would handle arranging and displaying the merchandise, and Rowena would see that the booths and tables got set up. After discussing the financial aspects of the bazaar, they decided to give the needlewomen three-quarters of the price of whatever they sold and, if it all worked out, invest the remaining funds in another bazaar. If it didn't pay, the committee would splurge on lunch in Red Arrow.

As she fried chicken early that morning, Liddy wondered if any other families in town were having picnics on Decoration Day. If anyone thought she was being disrespectful of the dead, they could take a running leap off Wolf Creek Bridge!

Dan and Cassie put huge amounts of Liddy's potato salad in a five-gallon cardboard ice-cream container, and they made buckets of tea to be chilled and served with ice. At four o'clock, Dan was to bring all the food and drink out to the Shores.

Marvin said he was going to train his dogs all day, but gave his word he would show up.

Liddy beeped the horn, and Fiona ran out, curls bouncing. Cassie had recently mounted a campaign to get a permanent at Tootie's Beauty Nook, but Liddy wouldn't have it, so she still had to wear her dumb pigtails, whereas Fiona had not only big blue-green eyes and chest bumps, but a golden halo of curly hair. Still, it was nice having a best friend. Their greatest fun these days was in ridiculing people, especially country boys at school who wore overalls and smelled like mouse nests. (Sometimes, though rarely, they made fun of themselves). Harley Corkle was the favorite butt of their jokes. He was three years older and five inches taller than anyone else in the fourth grade, and he liked to carve his initials into his wrists with a pocket knife. Even though they scoffed at him, Cassie and Fiona were a little afraid of Harley.

Fiona had on bright red shorts today. Cassie's shorts had seen better days, but she had a surprise: a new swimsuit purchased at the end-of-the-season sale at Schonberger's. It was yellow with white polka-dots, and had a shirred bodice and gathered skirt. Fiona would get an eyeful in the dressing room when Cassie dropped the old shorts and—*Viola!* a brand new swimsuit!

Liddy couldn't believe how wonderful everything looked. Since she had to fix all the food for the picnic, her friends had said they would handle the rest. George Schonberger and Harold Cutter helped sand the rough old tables and made quilt racks, and since the big room was pretty dim in the corners, they had strung up some lights. Liddy thanked the men profusely.

She circled the room admiring everything. Rachel's silk crazy quilt, in all the colors of the rainbow, was going to be raffled, and they were charging plenty for the raffle tickets—a dollar apiece! Rachel would get three-fourths of that. The First Christian quilting group hadn't consented to sell any of their quilts, but some had given Flo a few small things: quilted Christmas stockings, some delightful quilted dolls, and a collection of tea cozies. At another table, spread out on a red cloth, was Greta's embroidered black Swedish skirt and vest, marked *NOT FOR SALE*. But Inga was willing to part with two delicate drawn-thread sailor collars made of sheer white cotton. Liddy intended to buy one for Cassie when she had time.

The widow Groves and Jerusha Corkle, who were both shy, didn't plan to attend.

Rowena, after declaring for two weeks that she'd never sewn a thing, had stitched up three sock dolls with wild yellow yarn hair and black button eyes, which she put on the table with the widow's baby things. One table after another was filled with beautiful displays of handiwork.

Minna Thatcher contributed some of her intricate crochet work: a diamond-patterned afghan in shades of rose and blue, and a lacy white baby blanket. Minna was no fool; she put a price of ten dollars on the afghan and five on the blanket.

Liddy had driven all around the county, picking up a carful of needlework from farm wives she'd stayed in touch with since the WPA years. A woman outside Caution had contributed knit foot-warmers, several Raggedy Ann dolls, and a clown hand puppet, and another near Antelope had given her six small rag rugs, saying she hoped to make enough money to keep her chickens in feed. Flo was a skilled knitter, and although she wouldn't contribute one of her sweaters, she did hand over six knit caps in bright colors. She said she could turn out one of those in three evenings at home listening to the radio. One table was piled with aprons in every variety imaginable, and some way beyond imagining. There were ruffled aprons, flowered aprons, aprons with pockets and aprons without pockets, children's aprons made from pillow ticking, aprons with appliquéd tulips or cabbages, fancy party aprons, taffeta aprons, aprons made from flour sacks.

Liddy was extremely nervous and excited. Here were all these beautiful things, and people coming through the door in droves! She chided herself for feeling a surge of pride, but it didn't go away; it stayed with her until Marvin's behavior ruined the whole thing.

Cassie wanted for the bazaar to hurry up and be over so they could go have the picnic. Fergus, with his burr head of orange hair and freckles, was there, and he, Cassie, and Fiona ran around the place like the Katzenjammer kids, with little Timmy Klein tagging along behind.

Grace Sampson came without her husband Hal. Liddy usually had harsh words for Grace, who had inherited money from her family in Tulsa. She'd married Hal and they had bought two hundred acres outside Cato and built a ranch house on it, but the acreage wasn't worth much, for cattle *or* farming. Marvin said he didn't know why they didn't buy fifty good acres somewhere else. Mabel's cousin Duke Farrow ran the place, while they spent most of the time at their big house in town. Though Duke was not well liked, Stuffy Byers said Grace kept him on because Duke knew when to sell cows and when to keep them off the market.

Marvin's and Cassie's views of the Sampsons diverged sharply from Liddy's. Marvin thought Hal was a charming no-account, and that Grace was one gorgeous dame. He liked honey blondes, even forty-year-old ones, and he liked her slim figure and languid manner.

Cassie thought that, next to Mitch, Mr. Sampson was the best-looking man in Cato—he reminded her of Gary Cooper. And she admired Grace. If they met on the street, Grace always smiled and asked if she'd seen any good movies lately. Grace was the only woman in town who wore trousers, and Cassie sensed that her mother thought this made Grace suspect in the morals department. Liddy *never* wore pants, not even when digging in her garden or hammering up trellises. According to Liddy, real ladies didn't wear them, and that was all there was to it. But Grace wore jodhpurs and twill pants, or trousers of rayon or silk when she got dressed up. Cassie had once smelled her perfume, and she'd never smelled anything so heavenly. This all seemed to go against Liddy's grain, but she sometimes brought home *Harper's Bazaar* and *Vogue* and spent hours looking at the pictures, so Cassie wondered why she resented Grace being stylish.

Today Grace was wearing beige silk pants and a beige silk shirt with tiny buttons all the way up the front. As soon as she saw Rachel's quilt, she said that she had to have it. Liddy explained to her in an authoritative voice that she couldn't; it was being raffled at the very end of the afternoon, so the suspense would build.

Grace said, "Let me buy forty tickets, then—I need to have that quilt!" Everyone's mouth dropped open while she wrote out a check for forty dollars. Rachel stood there blushing through the whole thing, pleased as could be.

When Winifred Weston came in, she picked up every single thing and looked at it with narrowed eyes, as if looking for flaws. It seemed to Liddy she was there for hours, fingering the merchandise and grilling the women about who did this, and how long did it take them to do that, and why were the rag rugs priced so high, at four dollars? Finally she bought a black net party apron with a red satin bow on the pocket, paid for it with cash, and departed.

Liddy breathed a sigh of relief, and Rowena, who had taken Winifred's money, walked over to Liddy and said, "Wonder if she's goin' to wear that apron for Floyd." For some reason this sent them into paroxysms of laughter.

Ezra Corkle, in overalls, walked into the hall with Harley, carrying a package. Jerusha had given Liddy four table runners in what she called a log cabin weave, and they had all been snapped up right away.

"Howdy, Miz Field," Ezra drawled. "Looks like you got you a fine turnout! Harley, go on over thar and stand agin the wall. The old gal sent some more o' her runners—I got 'em here." He handed over the package.

"Daddy, I wanna play with Fergus an' Cassie!" said Harley in his man's voice, standing there big and awkward, looking like he might cry. Harley's overalls were filthy, but his face was clean and his hair was slicked back and parted.

"All right, go on." Ezra took out a large handkerchief and blew his nose loudly into it before thrusting it in the back pocket of his overalls. "Wife says price 'em like t'others."

"I wish Jerusha was here, Ezra," said Liddy. "People are admiring her things—she ought to *hear* what they're saying!"

"The ol' lady's too back'ards to come here with all o' these uppity Cato folks, Miz Field. Say, you heerd anything about Mabel and Buck lately? That boy o' mine cain't write, but we got some print-work once't from Mabel."

"Yes, Mr. Farrow gave Cassie a letter from Mabel. I'll let her tell you about it." Liddy called, "Cassie, come here! Tell Mr. Corkle about the letter from Mabel."

Cassie ran over. "Mabel said they liked the weather in California. And she said Buck was picking cherries, and she was cookin' for folks. Did you hear about the baby? It was s'posed to come in April."

"Yeah, she writ and tole us I was a grandpappy! It's a girl, name o' Lulu. They're mighty proud about it." Liddy stood nearby, counting bills and at the same time keeping an ear cocked to Ezra's conversation. "That gal al'ays looked like the dogs'd had her under the house, but I reckon even a poor jug don't lack a stopper!"

Liddy said quickly, "Cassie, go get me the receipt book from Violet. Ezra, thanks for coming in." She put a hand on his arm and led him toward the door. He and Harley left soon afterward, which was something of a relief.

O

As it turned out, even with forty dollars' worth of raffle tickets, Grace didn't win the silk crazy quilt. Cassie thought she got gypped, that maybe they should've rigged the drawing so she would win. When Miss Thornhill, the English teacher, won it, she let out a yell like a banshee. Rachel folded the quilt and wrapped it in a big sheet of butcher paper for Miss Thornhill to take home.

"Miz Field," Rachel said, "this was one of the nicest days I ever lived, and it's all because o' you! I don't know how to thank you enough!"

Liddy hugged her. "We couldn't have done it without all your talent and hard work, same as for everybody! Your quilt made the day! Maybe we'll get so good at this, folks'll be comin' from all over the state! I'll bring out your money, Rachel, as soon as we have everything counted out."

"I ain't worried about it," beamed Rachel, and Fergus beamed too.

When everyone had gone, the committee counted up the take. Including checks, it came to $227. 36! They'd never dreamed they would make so much! Liddy made a mental note: if they ever did this again, they would do quilts to get people interested, and hot pads and aprons for quick sales. All at once she remembered the drawn-thread collar for Cassie, but they were both gone. It was four o'clock; time to go to the swimming pond and start the picnic. Dan would be here any minute with the food. Now she would have her reward for all the hard work, family and friends all around her, partaking of food and fellowship. She couldn't wait for Marvin to arrive.

O

The Cato Shores and Swimming Pool had been created from an artesian well, the second largest in the state. The well had miraculously appeared when wildcatters from Tulsa had drilled for oil in 1917. Besides the swimming pond, there was a Snack Shack and a few cement picnic tables with benches. Kids swam in the oblong swimming hole, which had a mud-and-sand bottom. Out in the deepest part, which went down fifteen feet, grew long strands of aquatic plants. The tangled mass of green, floating out of sight beneath the surface, made swimming near it frightening, anyway to Cassie. She never ventured out that far, knowing that the plants wafted there in the depths, waiting to entangle the unwary.

There was a tall wooden diving tower with two diving boards, one four feet from the water and the other up a dizzying twenty-five feet, but only the most audacious boys went there. Daring male showoffs did jackknifes, flips, even double flips. Some could do backward dives into the water.

The only diving board Cassie ever used was the low one by the Snack Shack, and she dived only off the side, where the water came up to her chin. Near this board were lawn chairs where mothers sat to watch their little ones. Dan had arrived and saved three concrete tables for their party by covering them with boxes of food; he and Pauly had already changed into their suits. Cassie thought Pauly's pale skin made him look like some sort of albino cave creature.

Lanky Dooky Schlanaker, who had gotten a short leave from the CMTC to attend his grandpa's funeral, was a surprise guest. The funeral had been yesterday, and since he had another day's leave, Liddy had persuaded him to join them. She hadn't asked Cassie's opinion.

And Miss Gallagher was here!

Cassie's fourth grade teacher was new in town. She wore her dark, curly hair swept up, with little tendrils falling out around her neck and face. On Liddy this hairdo looked messy, but on Miss Gallagher it was exotic. Also, she was the best teacher Cassie'd ever had. She liked Cassie's made-up stories, written when she finished her grammar lessons early, and graded them with red-penciled A- pluses.

As the party got under way, her mother's head was thrown back and she was laughing at something Stuffy Byers had said. Liddy was wearing a bright yellow blouse and a green skirt, and her cheeks were flushed dark pink. She looked pretty. She hadn't given up hose for the picnic, but she wore flat shoes, a concession to informality that she seldom made outside her own home. Cassie didn't think her mother owned a swimsuit, so she probably wouldn't swim.

The ladies were laughing and bragging about how successful the needlecraft bazaar was. Rowena's husband, Herb Richards the postmaster, was nowhere to be seen. When Rowena called that morning and said he wasn't coming, her mother muttered something about Herb being an anchorite, and when Cassie asked what that was, Liddy said it was a stick-in-the-mud.

The girls ran to the dressing room and donned their swimsuits. Fiona had a new suit, too, sparkling white with bright blue daisies. Cassie looked down at her polka-dots, which all of a sudden seemed dumb. And her perky skirt had got all rumpled by her shorts. They ran back to the tables and grabbed some more potato chips, the only thing Liddy would let them eat before swimming.

Suddenly Fiona nudged her. *"Look!"*

Stuffy was approaching the tables, and his belly hung over his bathing trunks, as white as the underside of a snake. They giggled, putting their hands to their mouths.

Now Miss Gallagher and Charlene walked toward them from the dressing rooms, stuffing their hair into rubber caps. Charlene wore a turquoise wool-jersey maillot, and Miss Gallagher, in a clinging black wool suit, looked more voluptuous than a movie star. Both ladies had shaved under their arms, but certain other hair was in full evidence. Charlene's was blond and fine, Miss Gallagher's black and curly, showing a quarter of an inch all around the crotch of her suit. Cassie was stunned. She was used to Joan Crawford's eyebrows and Groucho Marx's mustache, but this was something new. She had never seen hair down there before. Did men have it, too?

There was that time with Dooky, but she'd been forced to zero in on his anatomical wizardry and hadn't noticed anything else.

And that wasn't all: the nipples of both women showed through the thick wool. Cassie turned to catch Dan's expression, but to her amazement he was talking to Pauly, oblivious of the anatomy lesson in front of his eyes. Dooky, on the other hand, was struck dumb, his eyes darting from the blonde to the brunette, his mouth open, a paper cup frozen halfway to his lips.

Just then the noise of a Model A reached their ears. Marvin parked in the lot and walked over to join them. He was wearing his usual white shirt, striped satin suspenders, and bow tie, but today he was sporting a new straw boater. Her dad looked like something out of a magazine, and Cassie ran to him and threw her arms around his legs.

"Hey, this your new swimmin' suit, Cass? It's real pretty. Howdy, ever'body. How's the water?"

Cassie saw her dad notice Miss Gallagher, but he didn't greet her or any of the other women. Instead he walked over to Stuffy and said,

"Looks like you're gonna displace a lot of that cold swimmin' water, friend!"

"Marvin, whenever I go off that divin' board, the whole *county's* gonna hear the splash!" said Stuffy, and everyone laughed.

"Marvin," Liddy said, "come and help me pour this iced tea."

Marvin walked past Charlene and Miss Gallagher, removing his straw hat in an exaggerated, sweeping gesture. He let his eyes drop from the two ladies' faces slowly down to their feet, his manner seeming to convey that it was some sort of beauty contest, and that Miss Gallagher had won. Cassie watched a flush wash over Miss Gallagher's face, spreading down her neck and around her collarbone.

"Marvin," said Charlene, pulling up the strap of her suit, "you gonna join us in the water?"

"No, I leave all the athletics in the family to my two boys. Dan, I wanta see you do some real diving today—you're always braggin' 'bout how good you are."

Everyone laughed again. Dan, reddening, looked down at the ground; then Pauly took him by the arm, and the three boys jumped up from the bench.

"Last one in's a white-livered mule!" shouted Dan.

"Dan! Your *language*!" cried Liddy, but the boys darted away like jackrabbits.

Miss Gallagher and Charlene walked toward the water, and the little girls followed them.

Liddy yelled, "Cassie, you can't swim! Stay in the shallow side! And, Fiona, you stay there, too. I told your mother I'd be sure you didn't drown!"

Cassie turned to give her mother a withering look. Making her look like a kid in front of everyone! What did she mean, saying she couldn't swim! Fortunately, no one was paying attention. They ran up the embankment to the shallow side of the pond.

Maybe she wasn't as pretty as Fiona, but she could outdo her with her athletic prowess. She'd had lessons last summer, and Fiona only knew how to float. The girls locked arms and jumped up to their waists into the cold water. Fiona held on to the wooden framing at the edge of the pond and kicked, while Cassie swam from one side of the shallow end to the other, splashing in the water and moving her arms up and out the way she'd been taught. The only thing she couldn't remember was how to breathe, but that wasn't a problem, because she could stand up anywhere and start all over again. Twice she went out on the low board and dived off the side, remembering to keep her head down.

An hour or so later the chicken and potato salad were uncovered , and everyone was loading up paper plates and chattering like magpies. The grownups talked of the weather, the chance of war, and the fall wheat harvest, which, by all signs, would be a good one. The group agreed that the state was finally pulling itself out of the drought and the depression.

Harold Cutter smiled at Liddy and told her the potato salad was the best he'd ever eaten, and Liddy said if only they had some nice tomatoes, but it was too early for good ones. She talked about tomatoes so much, Rowena finally said, "Liddy, we don't need any tomatoes! Everything's fine, honey!"

Marvin was eating, not saying much.

"I peeled the potatoes," Cassie told Fiona, since her mother had forgotten to mention it.

"How many did you peel?" asked Fiona.

"'Bout forty, I think."

"My mama hates to peel potatoes… We have macaroni."

Dan said, "You did *not* peel forty potatoes, Castor Oil. You peeled twenty! And *I* did the onions—that was the hard part!"

"That's prob'ly the first time you've bawled since Fernie May said she wouldn't marry you, huh?" Dooky jeered.

Dan would never escape being teased about Fernie May Applebaum. Smiley still hadn't corrected her crossed eyes, probably never would.

Charlene sat on the hard cement bench and laughed at the boys and at her husband Stuffy's jokes, shaking her tawny hair in the sun.

Miss Gallagher, sitting with a kimono wrapped around her, was awfully quiet. She was eating tiny little bites, and she didn't seem as sparkling as she'd been earlier. Cassie turned and looked at her mother, who sat at the next table. Liddy was with Mrs. Richards and Mrs. Shafer, with Marvin sitting at one end on a camp seat he'd dug out of the back of the Model A. He'd removed his boater, and his wavy black hair shone in the sun.

Cassie thought her father was behaving oddly. He gave the impression of being self-assured but awkward at the same time. Cassie had never seen her father act awkward before, not in her whole life. There was something funny about her mother, too. This was supposed to be a special, wonderful day, so why wasn't she laughing at Stuffy's jokes, like Charlene? Instead she sat next to Harold Cutter looking bored and distracted, listening to his old stories about trying to sell real estate in the depression. She glanced at Marvin, then at Miss Gallagher, and flashes of a weary sadness came and went on her face.

The food had been decimated, including the cherry cobbler that Liddy had brought out and piled with whipped cream, to the accompaniment of pretend groans. The boys played catch on the dried grass between the tables and the dance hall, while the men looked on, smoking.

Cassie and Fiona played jacks. They knew every game from "pigs in the basket" to "fly around the moon," and all their variations, but Fiona usually won.

Eventually the swimmers went back to the water. Liddy's friends helped her pack up the food; then they walked over to sit in the lawn chairs next to the water. They all agreed that Liddy had crowded a lot into one day. "How's come you didn't plan a square dance for tonight, Liddy?" kidded Rowena. "We could all get together over at the hall and do-si-do!"

Marvin and Miss Gallagher had strolled away, chatting, and Cassie wondered if they were talking about her.

They made a charming picture, her green silk kimono and dark hair next to Marvin's white shirt and dark trousers, his straw hat once again tilted at a rakish angle on his head. They moved slowly on the path on the other side of the big swimming hole, where locust and mesquite trees grew. The water sparkled and shimmered in the sun.

Liddy had the feeling that Marvin was punishing her for something. Was he jealous of the time she'd spent on the bazaar, of her interest and excitement about it? He hadn't liked it when she worked for Harold, either. Suddenly she remembered hitting him with the orange, and she almost laughed aloud. But in the very next second, the sight of him walking with Cassie's pretty teacher filled her with jealousy, a sexual rage that she was finding hard to control. She sat rigid and frozen in her seat, unaware that her friends had noticed her distress.

The thought circled around in her brain, poisoning her soul.

He's doing it again.

Six or seven teenage boys dived off the water wheel in rapid succession, some zooming in a few feet away from swimmers trying to cross the pond. The shouts of rowdy boys and the squeals of teenage girls carried easily across the expanse of water, and no one noticed Cassie walk out to the end of the diving board and dive in.

Liddy felt Rowena's elbow in her side. "Liddy, is that Cassie out there bobbing up and down?"

Cassie's head kept disappearing under the water. She was sputtering and struggling to stay afloat. No one was around her; Dan and his friends were on the water wheel, although Dan's face was turned in Cassie's direction. He stood frozen, like a stick figure hastily sketched and left on a page. Liddy realized that she, too, was sitting motionless, watching her daughter drown. She threw off her shoes and jumped into the pond. She didn't know how to swim, but she waded deeper, pushing against the weight of the shockingly cold water until it was up to her neck. She reached Cassie and grabbed the child's shoulder, yanking her out of the water enough so she could breathe, then clasped her around the waist and carried her back to the edge of the pond.

Rowena and Violet helped them climb out. Liddy sank to the ground; her breath coming in labored, arrhythmic gasps. She squeezed Cassie to her, feeling the limp smallness of her body.

Cassie seemed only half-conscious, but her eyes opened and she coughed up a tablespoon of murky water. Liddy struggled to lift her, but by now Marvin had reached them. He scooped Cassie up and carried her into the dressing room. They put her between them and rubbed her with towels, then propped her on the bench against the wall.

"What were you doing out in that deep water!" Liddy exclaimed. "I told you to stay in the shallow end! *Fiona* wasn't out there; *she* minded me!" Cassie slumped on the wooden bench. Her mother appeared to be half-drowned, herself. Liddy's hair was drooping in long ropes of copper, and her clothes were plastered against her body in soggy wrinkles. She was sobbing, but she seemed more angry than sad. Her father was acting mad too.

Cassie started to cry along with Liddy. Between sobs she wailed, "Dan said I was a sissy if I wouldn't dive off the *end* of the board! H-he said only the *little* kids dive off the side!"

Tears and snot ran down her face, and she reached up with her hand, smearing both together. Liddy grabbed another towel as Marvin headed out the door. She sat beside the sobbing, shivering child, wiping her face, her body shaking. In a few minutes Marvin reappeared with Dan in tow. He held his son's arm in an iron grip.

"Cassie says you dared her to dive off the deep end of the diving board. Is that so?"

Dan looked pitiful. His teeth rattled, his skinny, naked limbs shook, and his hair was stuck against his cheeks. Shivering and fidgeting, he squirmed in his father's clutches. Although he was taller than his father, at this moment he seemed still a little boy.

"*I* didn't make her d-dive off the end of the b-board! Us guys were all having fun diving, and she said she was a good diver, too, and all I said was that was the s-same side she was divin' off last summer—that's all I s-said." He snuffled loudly, and coughed.

"All right. I'll deal with you later. Get out of here!" Dan started to leave, but not before Liddy added her helping of blame. "Imagine! Making your little sister think she has to keep up with you big boys! You ought to be ashamed!"

Dan's eyes filled with tears. "I'm sorry, Cassie. I d-didn't m-mean for you to do it. Honest."

No one said anything. Cassie's sobs were coming more infrequently now, in little muffled jerks.

As if sorry for her words, Liddy touched Dan's shoulder. "Go on, now."

O

Liddy dropped off Fiona, then ushered Cassie into the house. Surprisingly, Marvin had allowed Dan to stay at the Shores. But Dan knew and Liddy knew it wasn't over. Not a beating, she hoped. Ever since Mitch had moved out, Marvin seemed to be trying harder to be patient with Dan. She put Cassie to bed and changed into dry clothes, before putting away the leftover food and washing all the empty containers. She went into the bathroom to towel off her hair, then decided to take a bath. By the time she climbed into bed, it was nine o'clock.

She closed the bedroom door. She wasn't up to talking to Dan when he came home. And after the way Marvin had flirted so openly with

Miss Gallagher, she didn't want to see him either. She wondered why he hadn't come back by now. What would be the point of opening up the store this late in the day? An image flashed—Marvin's expression when he'd seen Miss Gallagher in her swimsuit.

And the way they'd slipped off alone for a walk.

When had she gone back to calling her "Miss Gallagher"?

She got up, went to the phone in the hall, and asked Hetty Saltman, the phone operator, to get her the drugstore. She would reassure Marvin that Cassie was fine, although he should be calling *her* to see how their daughter was doing.

The phone at the store rang and rang.

She went through the house, trying to distract herself by straightening the breakfast room and folding laundry. She wandered into the empty living room—they still didn't have a stick of furniture in there— and walked back and forth, slippers flapping, telling herself that everything was fine and that Marvin would be home any minute.

Finally she went back to bed, but she felt a headache coming on. She got a cool washcloth to put over her eyes and lay down again. She managed at last to drift off into a light sleep, interrupted by nightmarish visions of Cassie drowning. These awful pictures alternated with phantom images of Marvin making love to the beautiful, naked Miss Gallagher. She could see them strenuously engaged in the act of love, their limbs writhing in ecstasy. She could see Miss Gallagher's black bathing suit lying on the floor next to the bed, and Marvin's straw boater sitting on the nightstand, looking very much at home.

O

Cassie couldn't go to sleep right away either. Fiona had never been as nice to her as she had been today, when she almost drowned. She tossed and turned, imagining herself a heroine in a story. Her near death had been the most exciting part of the day!

She began a movie scenario in her head about a drowning episode in which she was the central character. Who could star? *Not Shirley Temple!* This would be a dramatic, near-tragic story. The actress who played her should be a female version of Jackie Cooper, with a trembling lower lip and saucer eyes, or a girl version of Freddie Bartholomew, curly-haired, angel-faced—someone defenseless and vulnerable.

A miniature Jeannette MacDonald would be perfect! Maybe it could be a musical!

Happy with this addition to her lifelong accumulation of silver linings, Cassie threw off the sheet Liddy had pulled over her and fell asleep.

O

The next morning Liddy was up early. She peeked in at Cassie and stood gazing at her sprawled on the bed, completely uncovered. It looked as if she'd gotten too much sun; her bright pink skin contrasted with the white sheets. Her daughter was sometimes an annoyance, but she loved her absolutely—the thought of her almost drowning brought it home once again.

She'd heard Marvin come in early this morning, and had sat up and looked at the clock by the bed. It was five-fifteen. She'd been through this before. Just because she hadn't been able to prove that he had slept with that prostitute in Oklahoma City didn't mean he hadn't.

Marvin came in for breakfast a half hour later wearing work clothes. He kissed her on the cheek, and in her jittery state, she spilled tea on her robe. He poured himself a cup of coffee, then returned to the table. "You won't believe where I went last night, and what I did!"

"I suppose not." She turned away, getting up to blot tea off her robe.

"You know Dooky was home from the CMTC. Well, he needed a ride back down to Fort Sill, and Dan and I took him."

Liddy looked into Marvin's eyes, trying to make him admit he was lying. But how could he lie about *this*, knowing she would ask Dan!

She could still see him walking around the Cato Shores with Miss Gallagher—could still see him *on top of* Miss Gallagher!

"You mean you went to Fort Sill, to *Lawton,* without telling me, and you took *Dan?* Just because Dooky needed a ride?"

"I'm sorry I didn't call. We were takin' Dooky out to his folks' farm, Dan and me, and then Dooky started hintin' he didn't know how he was gonna get back down there, and Dan and I decided on the spur of the moment to take him —I knew you'd want news of Mitch. By the time I thought of calling you, I figured you'd be asleep."

"I thought you were going to punish Dan for almost getting Cassie drowned!"

"He seemed real sorry, and he didn't exactly force Cassie at gunpoint to do it. Cassie sometimes tries things she shouldn't. Besides, Dan's bigger'n me now."

Marvin grinned. The expression on his face was as lovable as a puppy—except she didn't love puppies.

Liddy bowed her head. Tears of relief wanted to come, but she'd be damned if she would show any emotion. She sat up and grabbed the edge of the table with both hands.

"How is Mitch?"

"He looks hale and fit, doesn't seem to mind the regimentation. I remember I enjoyed the barracks life at first, then it got old. It's good Mike and Dooky are down there. He says they work 'em pretty hard. The aide in the office went and got 'im, since it was so late. I had to make it sound like an emergency, so I told him Mitch's sister almost drowned and I wanted him to hear it from me that she was fine."

"He's not going to enlist, is he, Marvin? I worry they're just trainin' those boys so they can force them to go in the Army."

"No, I don't think so. These civilian military camps are just a way of instructin' a bunch of boys in case we have a national emergency. Mitch is gettin' a lot out of it. He looks lean and tough."

"I don't *want* him looking lean and tough. I want him looking like Mitch."

Neither said a word for a few moments. Then Marvin took a deep breath. "Uh…there's something else I been meanin' to tell you. I ordered a puppy…from Georgia. She'll be here soon. I'd like to work on extendin' the dog pen today, like I said I wanted to, if you wouldn't mind handling the store. Dan and I can get started on it right away. And I want to give the dogs a flea dip, too."

Amazingly, she smiled. "I don't mind. After cooking for three days for that picnic, plus all I did on the sewing bazaar, I'll welcome the change."

Now it was Marvin's turn to check for signs of pretense. He looked at her sitting there, her hair floating around her face in coppery springs, her compact body leaning toward him. It had been a long time since she'd been so agreeable. It almost seemed more than he deserved.

O

All day, as he worked with Dan dipping the dogs and rebuilding the pen, he thought about Abby.

Why had he gone by her house yesterday? Sneaking in the back door like a thief! Hell, he knew why! Because he was feeling horny. And she'd certainly encouraged him out there at the Shores. Served Liddy right—always concentrating on everybody but him.

Abby was beautiful! Her body so white, and her hair so black. She'd been so excited—by him! It couldn't be possible that she was a virgin, could it? He didn't think so; nobody that good-looking would have been left untouched this long. And she'd known how to excite him; letting him undress her while she unbuttoned his shirt and started kissing his chest. But she'd been too slow. He'd pulled down his suspenders and pants and thrown them on the floor; then the two of them had dropped on top of the clothes. It was real nice, the way she whispered that she was wearing a diaphragm and he didn't have to think about it.

He'd been so afraid of Liddy wondering where he was, they hadn't had much time, but he'd made the most of it. Good thing he'd thought of a way to keep from going home right afterward, because Liddy would have guessed. *Oh, yes, she would have!* She seemed to have a sixth sense about these things. When he'd gone by the Shores to pick up Dan, Dooky Schlanaker had given him just the alibi he needed.

He'd have to figure out some excuse to see Abby a lot longer next time. But school would be out soon, and she'd be going home to Watonga for the summer.

He hadn't had this feeling for a long time. A man could only hold himself in for so long, and there was hardly any sex with Liddy anymore. She was always finding a reason—mad at him about the dogs, or money, or something. What kind of marriage was that? Probably about average, he suspected. You got together to start a home and a family and you were crazy about each other, and then it wore off and it was all just rote, just habit, with a big measure of hatred thrown in.

By the end of the day he was exhausted. Not only had there been yesterday's strenuous lovemaking, but he'd been up all night driving. Somehow his tired limbs seemed to ease his conscience, he didn't know why. He and Dan sat cross-legged on the grass and shared ice-water while they admired their handiwork. He needed to have a real drink. They'd had a good day working together, and Dan had gotten on his nerves only three or four times, wanting to talk when Marvin didn't, and clumsy with the tools. He'd nailed the wire on all wrong at first, but he finally got the hang of it.

Marvin had been distracted, just wanting to get the job done. Sitting next to his son and gazing up at the overcast sky, he was lost in thoughts of his dark-haired girl.

8

In fool's paradise there is room for many lovers.
—Samuel Hopkins Adams
Tenderloin

It broke Liddy's heart that Mitch wouldn't live at home when he came back from CMTC camp. He moved home at first, but stayed for only three days. The second night he was home, he kept the car out until the middle of the night, and he and Marvin argued about it next morning.

"I've told you and told you about keeping the Plymouth out that late. You better abide by some rules! What do you think I buy gas with—*rocks?* And who pays for the insurance? Not you!"

Mitch shouted back at his father for the first time. "*I* bought the gas last night! And I told you, I had to take Mike out to Charlie Detwiler's ranch—that's why we were so late."

"What'd you buy the gas with, money you made playing pinochle? You sure haven't earned any lately workin'!"

That was enough for Mitch. That same day, he moved into the ramshackle O'Herlihy lodgings, down by the water tower. The last time Liddy could remember Marvin and Mitch being reconciled was when Marvin went to Fort Sill after the picnic. Mitch's flunking out of college was the cause of most of the problem between them. But maybe it was also that Mitch didn't want his father's advice anymore, on any subject. Another reason might have been that he was now so handsome, at six feet one, with straight, coal-black hair and a flashing white smile, that half the women in Cato were beginning to drop in at the drugstore, checking to see if Mitch was "aroun' these days."

Liddy hoped Marvin wouldn't be so childish as to be jealous of his own son. For her part, she wished with a mother's ache that she could see him more.

O

When Mitch, Mike, and Dooky returned from camp, they were all lean, tanned, and to their way of thinking, men. Back in Cato, they took any job that came along, all of them drifting, waiting for the war to start.

When Dooky heard about a combination bartending and barbecuing job with the Sampsons, he passed the bartending opportunity on to Mitch and said he and Mike would take charge of the barbecue. They would make fifteen dollars apiece, which sounded like a fortune.

This was the crowd Liddy had always considered licentious and loose. They drank, seldom went to church, and went through money like water. When Liddy wondered aloud where they got the liquor for all their parties, Marvin said he had no idea.

This fast crowd consisted of banker Henry McCallum and his wife, Barney Scruggs and Sally, Grace and Hal Sampson, and quite a few leftover flappers (Liddy's term) and the male friends they kept turning over like used cars. Stuffy and Charlene Byers went to some of these parties. Stuffy didn't care much for the social whirl, but said it was good for his broomcorn business, and Charlene liked to dress up and show off her figure.

But Charlene wasn't loyal to the crowd; occasionally she gossiped about things to Liddy.

O

The Sampsons' two-story white colonial, the only one in Cato, sat on a large lot surrounded by flowering shrubs and the tallest trees in town. It stood out from the modest brick and clapboard houses around it like a pearl set in mud. A few days before the party, Mitch went there to see what was expected of him, so intimidated by the Sampsons' wealth that he went to the back door. He talked to both Hal and Grace, who told him they wanted the bar set up on a table out on their back patio. Grace was wearing white shorts. Her legs looked tanned and gorgeous, and when she sat down and crossed them, he had to force himself to look somewhere else.

Hal would be going up to Kansas or over to Oklahoma City to get the booze, he said; all Mitch had to bring was the ice. He told them that, since Cato's icehouse made only blocks, he'd drive over to Red Arrow for chipped ice. Hal showed him how to mix a rum Collins and an el Diablo, both of which he said he liked to provide at parties ever since discovering them in a fancy hotel in Mexico City. For the rum Collins you just threw a jigger of rum into Collins mix; and for the el Diablo you mixed a jigger of tequila, crème de cassis, half a lime, and ginger ale.

Mitch felt nervous about making these fancy drinks—he had never even *heard* of crème de cassis, and although he had heard of tequila and rum, he'd never tasted them. The only thing he knew how to drink was beer. If his mother ever learned about him mixing drinks, she'd go into some kind of decline! And Marvin wouldn't be thrilled about him doing it, either, even though he knew his dad occasionally tied one on.

But he had to earn money *somehow*.

He wondered how the Sampsons got away with serving liquor. Mitch knew some of the state's history; Oklahoma had voted dry after Prohibition was repealed in 1933, although you could still get 3.2 beer. But there was a loophole big enough to drive a train through: anyone with a doctor's prescription could get whiskey at a package liquor store. The Sampsons must have a lot of ailments, and know a lot of doctors. Kansas was dry, too, although Mitch knew several people—Stuffy Byers, for one—who went to Kansas all the time to get the hard stuff. Mike O'Herlihy had told him Stuffy was a bootlegger, but he didn't know whether to believe it or not.

It was a sweltering-hot day, and the boys got there at four-thirty, a half hour before the party was set to begin. The barbecue was a huge brick affair built against the back of the house, with enough room to grill a buffalo. Dooky and Mike kindled the mesquite with cottonwood twigs, and soon the delicious scent of burning mesquite filled the patio and backyard.

Dooky had adorned his lanky frame with a cowboy outfit he'd acquired somewhere; he even wore a cowboy hat. Grinning at his friends, he said, "Sure beats Fort Sill, don't it?" He sipped a beer, slipping it under Mitch's bar cloth when either of the Sampsons came by.

Mitch was wearing his usual blue work shirt and new jeans, but since it was a party, he tied a red calico bandanna around his neck. He had his area prepared with a pyramid of glasses set on one end of the long bar table, the bottles on the other end. As he arranged the bottles of rum and whiskey, he thought of Liddy's reaction if she could see him. and a little shiver of wickedness ran through his body. Mayor Scruggs and his wife arrived, and Sally drifted over to Mitch and batted her eyelashes, waving a cigarette, saying he had a great tan, and how did he get it? He mixed her a rum Collins, and she finally waltzed away.

There were a lot of people he didn't know; they must be from Red Arrow or Antelope. Most of the men drank beer or bourbon, except for

Hal Sampson, who right away started testing Mitch on the el Diablos. When he made the first one, Hal drank it standing nearby, talking to some of his guests, then he came over and told Mitch to make him another, lightening up on the crème de cassis. He smacked his lips on that one, told Mitch he was a born bartender, and wandered away. He looked half squiffed already, and the party had barely begun.

Henry McCallum kept in close contact with Mitch's liquor table, while his mousy wife hovered a few feet away. In contrast to Hal's pasty look, the banker's face was florid, but after belting down two or three of Mitch's bourbon-and-waters—which had too much water, he commented —his complexion began to resemble raw liver. Surprisingly though, as he carried on a discussion about the recovery the country was making, his conversation with the other guests remained cordial and restrained. Henry was a big Roosevelt booster, which Marvin said he couldn't understand. Imagine a *banker* liking Roosevelt!

Mike and Dooky were into their second beers by now, Mike having weakened and gone the way of his friend. Mike was getting a glazed look, and Dooky was cracking jokes out of the side of his mouth and guffawing loudly with some of the women. Mitch resolved to stay sober.

"Say, Mitch—this party's a little different from the one your ma gave at the Cato Shores! We didn't have nothin' but iced tea at that'n!" Dooky let out a braying laugh that everyone heard.

Mitch wanted to take the stupid cowboy hat Dooky was wearing, wad it up, and stuff it down his throat. Luckily, many of the guests were getting drunk, too, or they might have taken offense at Mike's paradiddles with the barbecue utensils and Dooky's familiarities with the women. The volume of the party noise rose steadily, ladies' giggling, deep rumbles of laughter coming from the men, who were mostly off to one side of the patio telling stories. Stuffy Byers held them enthralled with a tale Mitch couldn't hear, and when he'd finished they all let out whoops of laughter.

When Stuffy laughed, his stomach heaved up and down behind his belt like a live animal trying to free itself.

An hour and a half into the party, Mitch found that he was the only sober person there except for Mrs. McCallum. He began to wish he were enjoying himself half as much as everyone else.

Aw, what the hell, he thought, and took a swig of an el Diablo he'd made for someone else.

The taste was pleasing, and he took another and, later, another. Gradually he felt more connected to the party and less like one of the help. He waved to the piano player Grace had imported from Oklahoma City, a young man on the other side of the patio playing a medley of Ginger Rogers–Fred Astaire dance tunes. He held up a glass and nodded, and the young man nodded, too, in a friendly way. Mitch mixed a drink and took it over.

A delicious odor of spicy beef wafted over the patio, and the guests began to move in the direction of the grill, where Dooky and Mike were loading plates.

Grace approached Mitch for a drink, and as he handed it to her she said, "You're doing a fine job, Mitch—you'd think you'd been tending bar for years."

"Thanks, Mrs. Sampson," he replied. "It's pretty new to me, but I had a few years' experience jerkin' soda."

"Call me Grace. Yes, I reckon you've mixed me a cherry Coke or two in the past." As she took the glass from him, she said, "Tell the boys after they've served everyone, you three can load up your plates and go in the kitchen and eat."

"Thanks, Mrs.—uh, *thanks*. It looks pretty good, smells good, too." The rum had loosened his tongue. "We had our fill of Army chow down at Fort Sill this summer."

Grace was wearing a filmy organdy dress that dipped down to her waist in back, with a long strand of pearls falling across her bosom. Her hair was waved across her forehead and caught in a loose knot at the nape of her neck, her eyebrows plucked to a thin line. With a smile, she stepped close and patted him on the shoulder, then drifted back to her guests.

He felt his armpits dampen and his knees weaken. After she walked away, he thought how, every time he'd finished a sentence, her blue eyes stared up at him and crinkled in the corners, as if he were somebody wonderful and unusual. Her fascination with him seemed to be partly amusement, and he wondered if she only wanted to make a temporary conquest. Probably she was just trying to make a fool of him.

The next hour was devoted to the consumption of the beef, salads, black-eyed peas, and pan after pan of cornbread and Parker House rolls. The dessert table held pecan and lemon meringue pies, plus a huge birthday cake for Hal, with forty candles. Seated at long tables, the guests exchanged views on wheat and sorghum farming, beef prices, and the war in Europe. There were heated discussions about Roosevelt, the New Deal, and whether he was going to get the country into war.

After dessert, things quieted down. Most of the guests left, and the ones who stayed settled down to poker in the den. As Mitch was putting away the liquor, Dooky told him that Henry McCallum had fallen flat on his face on his way out, and had to be helped to his car by his wife and Stuffy.

Mike said, "Wonder if our folks'd keep their money in Henry's bank if they knew he was a fallin'-down drunk."

Mitch couldn't help thinking that Mike's dad didn't have any money to keep anywhere, but he kept it to himself. All those kids, and Mr. O'Herlihy hardly made anything at the grain elevator. The family was dirt poor—always had been and, barring a miracle, always would be. That time his mother had run off and come home pregnant had been a low point for the family, but the parents had stayed together, more by necessity than anything else. But any money beyond a bare subsistence would always elude them.

Dooky didn't say a word, didn't even pretend that his folks had savings.

Mike and Dooky were scouring the barbecue grill and the pans.

"I think our folks all know about Mr. McCallum," said Mitch, "but I guess he's awful smart about money; my dad says so."

Why was it that all evening he'd been thinking about what his mom would think about this and his dad would think about that, when all he was trying to do was get away from them and their opinions!

He was folding up the tablecloth when he suddenly felt dizzy. It must be the tequila—by now he'd had *two* el Diablos. The piano player had left, and it was completely dark. The only light was a yellowish glow from the Japanese paper lanterns strung all around the patio and from the gibbous moon, which had climbed directly overhead.

Barney Scruggs appeared. "You fellas're welcome t'come in and set in on some poker. I'll stake you each to five bucks." Grinning behind a huge cigar and a cloud of smoke, he reached into his back pocket to extract his wallet. Mike and Dooky grabbed the bills, but Mitch declined.

"No, thanks, Mayor. I learned up at Alva that I'm a real poor gambler; think I'll just mosey on home." His friends and Barney headed toward the den.

Grace Sampson all at once appeared at his side. Taking his arm, she looked up at him, her eyes slightly out of focus.

"Oh, you *can't*! Let's have one more little nightcap. I saw you drinking that tequila—you didn't think anyone saw, but I did. Wasn't this a won'erful party? I think my husband is off in the bushes with Sally. She thinks he's God's gift to women, and so does he, so they *should* be together, i'n't that right?"

She giggled and drew Mitch over to the drinks table, which was topped with boxes of liquor and glasses. "You wait here; I'm gonna bring out something my daddy taught me to drink. He was in *oil*—didja know that, Mitch? My daddy made lotsa money taking land away from the Osages and the Cherokees and puttin' up oil wells! You just sit here!" She walked away, her small hips swaying, her bare back a white arc in the darkness.

Mitch didn't feel like sitting. He walked around the patio, enjoying the quiet after the din of the party, sniffing the perfume of the jasmines twining around the trellis. The dim light from the lanterns softened everything, lending the place an exotic aura. He stood looking off over the Sampsons' back fence. The big elms and poplars cast their long shadows over the flat expanse behind the house. He liked the open feel of this place. The house and its grounds were seductive, but they weren't the real town. The real town was out there in the dusty Main Street, the bare stretches of land, the narrow creeks that all but dried up in summer, the scrawny, hard-bit trees and dry chaparral.

He loved all of it, but he knew he couldn't stay in Cato much longer. His father would forever be his judge and jury, and besides, there was nothing for him to do. He had to get away.

He felt his body slacken. An alien, remote feeling enveloped him like a transparent glove, making him feel he existed outside his body, looking down. It must be the drinks, but he hadn't had *that* much.

Or maybe he felt this way because he knew that he and Grace were about to be alone.

She returned just then, carrying two fat, round goblets, swishing the dark liquid around as she walked, her eyes shining in the darkness. "I bet this is the first time you ever had one of *these*!"

"I bet so, too. What is it?"

"It's a brandy sangaree. Drink it slow. You want to really savor it. There's some good ol' French brandy in it, and some sugar and nutmeg. I sorta left out the nutmeg—couldn't find it; my help's gone. D'you like it?"

"Yeah, sure." The drink burned going down, but it left a warm sensation wherever it touched, like a hot poultice applied from inside. "It's…kinda different-tasting."

"You have to '*acquiah* the taste, honey,' as my cousin in Savannah always says." She laughed. They stood without talking in the semidarkness, sipping now and again. They could hear voices and laughter from the poker players, and occasionally Sally Scruggs's shrill giggle. Then they didn't hear her anymore.

"I oughta go. Got some fence posts to put in tomorrow for Charlie Detwiler. He wants me out there right on seven o'clock in the morning."

"Oh, sure. I know you need your sleep. Just let me walk you to the door. Leave the glass there—the cook'll get it in the morning. Did Hal pay you?"

"Oh, yes, ma'am, with some extra."

Outside the front door, where white oleanders and petunias lit up the path in the moonlight, she put her hand on his bare arm and said, "I'll be seein' you. Won't I?"

"Sure." He briefly put his hand over hers, and as he walked away, looked back.

Grace stood gazing after him, her dress blowing softly in the first breeze of the night.

○

Two days after Hal Sampson's birthday party, Grace called Mitch at the O'Herlihys' to see if he had any time to work at their ranch. She said that when he'd mentioned putting in fence posts it triggered something—she remembered they needed some put in out at her ranch, the Sandy Flats.

He said he'd be finished working for Charlie by the end of Tuesday.

He worked six days at the Sampson ranch, starting on Wednesday, taking his orders from Duke Farrow, the ranch manager, who wasn't very friendly. Duke, a small, wiry man of about thirty-five, squinted at him from under shaggy black eyebrows. Evidently, Hal was in Fort Worth looking for new ranch stock.

Duke gave the impression he was wondering how a squirt like Mitch was being favored with this job. Jobs of any kind, even lowly handyman jobs, were hard to come by these days. Mitch didn't know, either, but he was willing to take the favor.

Duke didn't work alongside Mitch; he said he was too busy inoculating cattle, but he showed him the area he was to fence, gave him some tools, and pointed out the pile of posts which had already been delivered.

On the third day Duke went to Red Arrow to do some business at the courthouse —paperwork concerning the ranch that Grace told him Hal should have tended to. That was the day Grace fixed a picnic lunch and brought it out to the far corner of the ranch where Mitch was working. She drove up in her pickup truck in a swirl of dust and put the basket of food under a scrubby post oak, where there was a small irregular patch of shade. Then, coming over to where Mitch was manipulating the posthole diggers, she put her arms around him from behind. He took off his leather gloves and turned around.

"I'm awful sweaty, Grace," he said, and she replied, "That's just the way I like you." And she wriggled down on top of him in the sandy dirt and started pulling down his jeans. They rolled around for several minutes, kissing. He could barely pant out the words "Is anybody around?" and she breathed, "Not for miles!" Their clothes were half off when she stood up and led him over to the bit of shade under the oak tree. She took a tablecloth out of the lunch hamper and spread it on the ground.

The sight of Grace's naked body on the blue-checked cloth, her turquoise bracelets still on both arms, was something he would never forget. Finally to see her breasts, her flat belly, the triangle of light pubic hair— to be able to fondle all of her while she fondled him—he had never been so out of his mind with pleasure and the seeking of pleasure. It wasn't the first time for Mitch—there had been Sara Jane and one or two others. But this was the woman he would always remember. He only stopped once, to say, "I don't...have anything—with me."

"It's all right—I'm wearing something."

O

Saturday they followed the same routine—evidently she wasn't afraid of Duke's finding out, or she had banished him somewhere miles away.

Sunday Mitch rested.

Monday and Tuesday she drove out with the lunch hamper again. The only difference in their lovemaking was that each time it got better, and now Grace brought two or three blankets instead of the tablecloth.

Mitch had never lived in such a state of perpetual delirium. His senses were honed to a new sharpness, and he felt as if he were walking a foot off the ground. He told himself he was living in a fool's paradise, and to prove him right, on Wednesday Hal Sampson came home. Mitch's work was finished anyhow. He'd somehow managed to put in a heck of a lot of barbed-wire fence, three hundred feet or so. That wasn't too bad for a man working alone, and taking out all that 'rest' time with Grace.

The thought that nagged at Mitch the most, other than how much Hal knew, was how much Duke Farrow knew. He was pretty sure Duke knew something, because after that third day, when Mitch arrived early to start work, Duke seemed different. His tone had changed from merely unfriendly to sardonic, even contemptuous, and Mitch felt sure he wasn't imagining it.

Mitch was in love, no question about that, but worrisome feelings were creeping in. This could become too much for him to handle. If his parents found out about it, he could not just choose to leave town, he would *have* to leave—it wouldn't matter to them that Grace had gone after him! Lying on the little cot on the O'Herlihys' screened-in porch where he'd been sleeping all summer, he could think of nothing but Grace—her breasts, the waist he could almost fit his hands around, the way she moved under him… Thoughts of her stirred continually through his mind. It was as if he hadn't owed a body, or hadn't known it very well, before Grace came along. She'd discovered every inch of his anatomy with him, and for him. For the first time he felt within himself a vivid, powerful masculinity.

And the woman who'd made him feel that way belonged to someone else.

○

The sign outside town read:

WATONGA
pop. 2,793

Home of Roman Nose State Park
Named for Chief Henry Roman Nose
Last warrior chief of the Cheyennes
Fought at Battle of the Washita

Marvin had driven in the Plymouth over rough, dusty roads; partially graveled ones; and a few smooth patches of paved highway to get here. As he traveled southeast, through three counties, the roads followed low hills streaked white with gypsum. Abby had better appreciate how far he was coming to see her! He had passed several oil fields on the way down, with dozens of derricks and rigs, pumps pounding rhythmically away. The heat was awful, even with all the windows rolled down. He was going to have to stop at a gas station and get himself looking presentable again—didn't want to look like a sweaty farmer when he met her.

Watonga had a lot of Indians. Along the side of the road he'd seen stocky women in blankets and moccasins, huddling in twos and threes, and here on Main, men walked along wearing long braids interwoven with bright ribbons and beads.

Cassie would love to see this! He'd explained to her so many times why Cato didn't have any Indians, and here he was, driving through a town full of them. Probably mostly Cheyenne, with some Arapaho too—Abby had said the town was named for an Arapaho chief. He put Cassie out of his mind. It was hard to enjoy sinning, when thoughts of your family kept getting in the way.

Neither he nor Abby had wanted to wait another minute to see each other, but he hadn't been able to slip away until now, hadn't been able to think of a way to do it smoothly, until he came up with the dog alibi. It couldn't exactly be labeled "slipping away" when he was having to make a 150-mile round trip. Here he was, a man of forty-nine, behaving like a lovesick youth! He'd called Joe Kelly, who told him there was an

English setter breeder around Greenfield, so he'd decided to go down and take a look at what the man had. Liddy was going to be angry either way, but if he came back with a dog she couldn't suspect anything… *could she?* There wasn't enough room for one of his dog crates in the Plymouth, but he hadn't dared drive the Model A this far. Somehow he'd managed to maneuver a small crate into the backseat, hoping to take back a puppy.

Abby had said to meet her in front of the only drugstore in town. She didn't want him picking her up at home, probably didn't want her parents seeing her with an older man. They wouldn't know he was married, because he wasn't wearing his wedding ring, but he couldn't hide his gray hair so easily. He didn't want to meet them, anyway.

He got to the corner drugstore half an hour early even after stopping to freshen up, so he decided to go in and see what the store looked like. After buying a *Collier's*, he wandered back to the prescription counter and gave it the once-over. Not nearly as nice as his, although the woman who'd waited on him was quite pleasant. She'd be a help to any business. Like Liddy.

He went back out to the car and sat leafing through the magazine. Then, glancing in the rearview mirror, he saw her coming along the sidewalk in a lightweight pleated skirt that moved seductively around her legs.

His heart lurched as she got in and slid onto the seat beside him.

O

For the first time, Dan built a fire next to the grave and lit it. This was the way he wanted his communion with the Indian to be: a silent, dark vigil, lit by a small, lonely fire. He'd have to get home before too late or his mom would raise holy Nell, but he'd stay as long as he could.

He sat thinking, for the hundredth time, about whether he should tell Charlie Detwiler about the Indian, whether they should dig up the grave together. He had read in a *Rio Kid* magazine that some Indian tribes believed that unearthing their remains would interrupt their travels in the spirit world.

"Bones lying in boxes are sacrilegious," he'd read. "It is an insult to the ancestors." So he thought maybe he wouldn't do it, not now anyway.

After sitting for an hour or so in the little pool of firelight surrounded by vast, dark prairie, he doused the fire, scrambled back down the embankment, and walked through the willow and mesquite bushes along the river toward home. By now he knew every step of the way.

9

*If you bet on a horse, that's gambling. If you bet you can
make three spades, that's entertainment. If you bet cotton
will go up three points, that's business. See the difference?*
—Blackie Sherrod
Dallas Times Herald

Cassie often wondered why there were no Negroes in their town. She
had seen kindly Negroes portrayed in movies many times: Bill Robinson
dancing with Shirley Temple, Louise Beaver playing warmhearted maids,
Hattie McDaniel playing those fat kitchen roles. When she had asked
her father about it, he said there was no work for them, nothing for them
to do, so why would they *want* to live here?

And he always threw in the Indians, saying, "We don't have any of
them, either."

Those explanations had been good enough for her when she was
little, but now she was nine.

It was a broiling-hot mid-afternoon in July when a Negro man actually
walked into the drugstore. Only Cassie and her dad were there; Marvin
behind the cigar counter, composing another ad for *American Field* (Perky
was trained and ready to be sold), and Cassie coloring in a coloring book
at the front ice-cream table and sipping a Coke.

The streets had been quiet all afternoon, and they hadn't heard a
car.

The Negro man took a few steps toward them through the door.

Marvin looked up. "What can I do for you?" he asked, in a harsh
voice.

"I was wonderin', suh, just whichaway to Texas? I went and got
mahself all twisted and turned aroun', and I was wond'rin' which way
to go, outside o' this heah town."

He smiled at Marvin, looking perplexed, and turned his head and
smiled at Cassie. His hair was grizzled with gray, and he was wearing a
jacket much too large for him. His dark trousers looked as if he'd been
rolling in dust, and he held a frayed cap in his hands, twisting it around
and around as he spoke.

"Are you walkin' or drivin'?" asked her father. Cassie knew what he was thinking. Had the man dropped off a freight train? Many hobos came through on the trains these days, and some got off at Cato trying to find a meal.

"I'm drivin', suh. I been ovah to Tulsa to see my daughtah, and I'm goin' back to Fo't Wuth. It's a long way… Don' rightly know why I trah'd comin' thissaway—sho' used up a lot o' gasoline!"

"Drive out of here on the Fifteen toward Higgins." Marvin jerked his thumb toward the west. "There's signs out there'll tell you which way to go."

Her dad sounded like the conversation was costing him money.

"Oh, yessuh, I'm much obliged." The man took a few steps toward the fountain. "Suh, you wouldn't be knowin' how I could earn some mo' money fo' gas, would you? I can do mos' anything. Maybe you got somethin' needs doin'." Cassie cringed at the way the man shuffled and bowed to her dad. Marvin stiffened, putting out his cigarette with a swift, stabbing motion. "No, I don't need any work done. Now, you'd best be gettin' on out o' town. I'm sorry, but you're not allowed to spend the night here."

Cassie caught her breath. Was this *true*?

"Oh, yessuh. I undastand. Could ah maybe, then, jus' have a glass o' watah befo' I go, suh?"

He smiled, his white teeth flashing briefly.

"Cassie, give this fellow some water." Marvin made a quick, minimal motion toward the stack of paper cups on the backbar. She went behind the fountain and reached for a large paper cup, looking questioningly at Marvin. He nodded. She filled the cup with cold water and handed it over the soda fountain, and the old man took it gratefully and gulped it down. He finished and handed it back.

"Missy, that sho' was good. Could ah trouble you fo' one mo' fillin' up? Then I'll be on mah way, headed fo' Texas."

Marvin strode over to the fountain. He grabbed the paper cup from Cassie, filled it with ice, Coca Cola syrup, and carbonated water, and handed it back to the man. The gratitude on the man's face was too raw for Cassie to look at directly, and she turned her face. Her father had added the humiliation of the paper cup to the warning that the man must leave town before nightfall, then tried to wipe the insult out with a coke.

The man finished drinking and walked slowly to the door, shuffling his feet, whether because of his age, a limp, or to further abase himself—Cassie wasn't sure. He stopped, waved his cap at them, and left.

Marvin picked up the paper cup and tossed it into the trashcan behind the counter. Cassie rinsed out her own coke glass in the mixture of water and disinfectant they kept in the sink, then turned and looked directly at her father. The baleful look she directed at Marvin accused him of all the wickedness in the world.

O

Dan and Cassie had noticed a change in their mother's demeanor ever since Uncle Fred had called from Waxahachie to say that he and Aunt Bertha were coming up for the races at Red Arrow. The races were always held during the annual county fair, in August. Liddy vehemently opposed the races, which she believed should not be any part of a wholesome event like the fair. They attracted the wrong sort of people: gamblers, bookies, bootleggers, and loose-living women.

Even people who liked to *watch* horse racing were suspect—they might be tempted to gamble. Of course, the sport of horseback riding was all right; Liddy had ridden plenty of times with Rowena Richards, when she'd first moved to Cato. But horse racing was the work of the devil and his lieutenants.

But if Fred and Bertha were coming up just to go to the races, what could she do? Dan and Cassie could hear the creaking of Liddy's iron will. It seemed impossible that their mother would attend the races—wholly outside the world of reason and rationality.

Occasionally Liddy laughed at her own inconsistencies, although usually she pushed them to the back of her mind. She knew that even though she thought of herself as a stalwart Christian, she liked clothes too much, and was vain, jealous of younger women, and competitive about her children. She didn't drink, smoke, or do anything the least bit unchaste, but all the same, she admitted she was worldly and full of sin. Liddy had always been respectable. She was God-fearing and law-abiding. She and her circle of friends were muscular Christians, going to church services and attending tent meetings, religious rallies, and revivals. They believed in the goodness of God and the insidious ways of the devil, the blissful rewards of heaven and the fiery punishments of hell. Other than school, Liddy's religion and her job at a dry-goods store had been the only things to occupy her youth, and she still held to all the things she had been taught. Gambling, horse racing, drinking, and infidelity were mortal sins, and laziness and uncleanliness were not very far below them on the list. Even though Marvin didn't like it, she still said her prayers on her knees every night before she got into bed, as she had done since she was a little girl. She read a chapter in the Bible every night, although sometimes she was tired and fell asleep between verses. Living such a pure life was difficult, partly because it separated her from Marvin, who seemed to revel in a lot of things she believed truly were sins.

Sometimes she craved a bit of freedom of the kind men had. Compared to her, her brother Fred had had a great deal of independence, growing up. He could fly to the devil and back if he wanted, while she had to abide by all the unwritten rules of the community, minding her p's and q's. She could never bob her hair or shorten her skirts—not that she had wanted to, exactly, but it would have been nice to have the option—and she couldn't be seen unchaperoned with a beau until she was practically marching down the aisle! But that pattern would not be wholly repeated if she could help it. She would teach her daughter to think for herself, rear her to be independent. Marriage didn't lead to happiness; at least it hadn't for her. She planned to steer Cassie away from marriage. Depending on a man for your happiness didn't work.

O

The August afternoon was hot, not a breath of air stirring. Cassie ran out the back door, barefoot as usual, when Uncle Fred's white Cadillac swooshed into the driveway, its springs overburdened with all the big hats, purses, gold watch chains, fancy shoes, and suitcases of the Texas folks. When Uncle Fred beeped the horn, it sounded to Cassie like a cross between the bray of a donkey and the honking of an annoyed goose. Liddy ran to hug her brother as Aunt Bertha enveloped Cassie in a hug, and Grandmother McIvor gave Dan a kiss on the cheek. The greetings went on for some time until Liddy said, "For heaven's sakes, let's get out of this heat!"

"It's hotter'n this in Texas, honey," drawled Aunt Bertha as she moved her impressive weight behind Liddy, who was leading them all inside.

As they passed through the nearly empty living room, Uncle Fred picked Cassie up and swung her around. "How's my Oklahoma girl?" He ended the swing with a wet smack on Cassie's forehead, then pulled a dollar out of his pocket and stuck it into the pocket of her shirt.

"That's jus' for being a purty little gal! I see you still got those pigtails! Don't ever cut 'em, honey, and don't ever grow up!"

"I *am* goin' to grow up, Uncle Fred. And when I do, the first thing I'm gonna *do* is cut my pigtails!" They laughed together at their joke, and Cassie flopped down on the small brocade sofa and felt the bill through her pocket.

"That the only furniture Liddy's got in here? What's the matter, can't your daddy afford any more stuff than this?"

Cassie moved her hands on the worn brocade. "This was Grandmother Field's."

Shaking his head, Fred joined the others in the backyard.

Everyone knew that Liddy thought her brother could do no wrong. It had always been "Fred said this," and "Fred thinks that," prompting Marvin to say, more than once, that he could get sick of Fred without even seeing him. As a newspaper publisher in Waxahachie, Fred was not only prosperous, but according to Liddy a pillar of the community as well; a leader in the Chamber of Commerce, Rotary, Masonic Lodge, and Presbyterian Church. He wore pins or rings signifying his membership in all these organizations, and when he moved his hands the big diamond in his Masonic ring flashed like fire.

Cassie adored Uncle Fred. He always had a twinkle in his eye, and a joke. He was small like Liddy, and his brown eyes darted about the way Cassie imagined a leprechaun's would. She was in love with his cigars. He was smoking one now in the backyard, where she and Dan had started a Ping-Pong game on the old worktable Liddy had painted green and marked with white lines. Aunt Bertha and Grandmother McIvor were fanning themselves on the willow settee, with Aunt Bertha taking up most of it.

"Fred, honey, you go in and get me my purse—I wanta show Liddy a picture of mah new summer house! And get me some lemonade or *somethin'* to drink when you're in there."

Liddy jumped up. "I'll get us all something. I was just fixing to get some iced tea and cake. And then I want to see your summer house, Bertha. Do you mean that fishin' shack Fred has out on the lake? You rebuilt it?"

"Hell, no, we didn't rebuild that ol' firetrap—that'd be throwin' good money after bad! Mah new summer house is in mah backyard!"

Aunt Bertha's maiden name was Thibodeaux. It was Cajun, but she said she couldn't talk Cajun, just deep-fried South. Uncle Fred had met her when he was a young traveling salesman selling printing presses in Louisiana. One evening plump Bertha, his landlady's niece, played the piano for the boarders. She could play by ear all the ragtime tunes of the day. Cassie had heard her once on a visit to Texas, and Aunt Bertha could make a piano rock like a freight train. Now a thick layer of fat pressed at her features—even her face was fat, with those snapping brown eyes, high penciled eyebrows, and Cupid's-bow mouth painted firehouse red. Also, she was undoubtedly the bossiest human being Cassie had ever met.

As Cassie offered her cake and iced tea, Aunt Bertha asked questions. *What subject did she like in school? What were her friends' names? Did she still like the movies?* As she listened to Cassie's mumbled replies, her arched eyebrows rose and fell as if she didn't believe a word, and half expected her niece to be struck dead any minute for telling such huge fibs. Cassie was still too young to realize that this was the attitude of a confirmed liar.

Sounds of a backfiring car shattered the stillness of the afternoon, and they hurried to see an old Chevy with a house trailer pull up under the elms in front of the house. At the wheel of the Chevy sat a handsome, smiling Negro, and next to him his wife. In the back seat was their son Carlton, Cassie's Chinese-checkers playmate from Texas.

"It's about time, Jesse—I thought you got lost!" said Fred. "Good thing I gave you a map. Sister Lydia, I brought you some help."

O

"There's no more to be said about it!" said Marvin to Liddy, standing in the kitchen. Liddy had called the drugstore and told him that Fred and Bertha had arrived, and that with them was a family of coloreds, brought to put on a barbecue. Marvin had rushed home.

Jesse, at Uncle Fred's direction, had brought uncooked spareribs in a new-fangled Kelvinator freezer on the trip up. The ribs had stayed frozen all the way from Waxahachie to Cato—a modern miracle. Fred said his 'man' Jesse was an expert at barbecue, and that he made his own sauce. Jesse's wife Feemy would do everything else.

Uncle Fred had planned the thing right down to the size and shape of the pickles to be served.

"There's no more to be said about it!" said Marvin again. "You're goin' to have to get them out of here." He jerked his head toward the driveway, where the family still sat in the Chevy. As soon as he got home he had directed them to pull up behind the Cadillac, away from the prying eyes of the neighbors.

Cassie took the family iced tea, and she and Carlton exchanged shy hellos. Jesse and Feemy were sweating profusely, and Carlton had pulled off his shirt.

Feemy gave Cassie a big smile when she took the cold drinks. "Thank you so much, honey."

Feemy was pretty, with skin the color of Grandmother Field's walnut dining-room set, which was now ensconced at their house. Her crinkly hair was pulled back like Liddy's. Jesse was almost white-haired, but his arms and shoulders were muscled and strong-looking. Cassie noticed his callused hands as they rested on the steering wheel, the knuckles big and bony.

Carlton looked older than when they'd played Chinese Checkers up over Uncle Fred's garage. His neck and arms were longer, and his face was wider. Probably his legs were longer, too. He didn't thank Cassie, he just grabbed the glass through the rolled-down window. She stood by the car for a long moment, then returned to the backyard.

With his back to the kitchen sink, Marvin reached up impatiently and undid his bow tie. He wiped the sweat off his forehead, and let out a loud sigh. "Liddy, how come your brother brought all that food? Doesn't he think I'm breadwinner enough to provide it? You been cooking for days! And what the hell did he bring those colored folks up here for? Surely he knows we've got race laws here in Cato! You'll have to tell him to send them back where they came from!"

Cassie had been sent back to the kitchen for more iced tea. She slid through the screen door silently, aware that their discussion was tense and potentially explosive. She stood holding the empty pitcher in her hands.

Liddy was saying, "I just don't understand why Negras can't spend the night here in town. They could in Paul's Valley! My daddy had a colored nurse; best nurse he ever had, he said."

"Just stop it, now—*stop it!* The point is, we gotta get these folks out of town. I don't want 'em here, even if it *was* allowed! They're a goddamn nuisance."

"Marvin, could *you* tell Fred? I'm just so upset. I think he'd take it better from you—you can explain about the town and all."

"Liddy, I swear, your brother Fred is the biggest blowhard I ever knew! So he's *got* money! I wish to hell he'd stop tryin' to prove it to everyone in three states!"

The pitcher slipped in Cassie's hands and made a squeaking sound. Her parents turned. She said, "Aunt Bertha wondered if there was anything more warmin' than this."

"What does she mean by *that?*" said Liddy, frowning.

"I dunno; I guess she wants *hot* tea. An' she acts like she wants it right away. She says she's got a taste in her mouth like the bottom of a bird cage." Cassie paused. "I heard everything you said about gettin' rid of the colored family." She put the pitcher down on the counter with a loud crash. Then she opened the screen door and said, "I wish a bomb would blow up this town into a jillion pieces!"

A few minutes later Marvin took Fred behind the garage. He confessed that Cato's racial laws were backward, but he'd appreciate it if he and Liddy didn't have to be embarrassed in any way. After all, they ran a business here. Fred went inside and made a call to a politician friend in Dallas, who made a call to someone in Red Arrow. In a few minutes Fred got a call back, and permission was given for Jesse to park the trailer in the fairgrounds near the racetrack. They could stay there one night, and one night only.

"So," said Fred, waving his cigar and grinning, "we'll have our barbecue over there!"

"But, Fred, I have all this *food!*" said Liddy.

"I can eat most of it right now, and your family can eat the rest of it later on. It's settled."

Liddy prepared a box of chicken, rolls, and potato salad and took it out to the colored family to take with them. Cassie trailed behind her with a large thermos of ice water (they'd run out of tea) and paper plates and cups. By now, the family had been in the suffocating car for almost an hour, and they weren't smiling. Still, they were gracious when accepting the food, and Cassie said to Carlton, "See ya at the barbecue." Carlton took the box, put it next to him on the seat, and said, "Uh-huh." He scratched his shoulder with his hand and blinked his eyes, but he didn't smile.

Marvin finished giving Jesse directions about how to get to the Red Arrow fairgrounds, and the car and trailer backed out of the driveway. Marvin and Cassie stood watching until the car pulled out of sight. When Cassie turned to go inside, Marvin put a hand on her shoulder, but she shrugged it off.

That evening Fred and Marvin smoked in the backyard while Liddy did the dishes and Aunt Bertha unpacked. Dan went to the store, and Cassie got to be alone with Grandmother McIvor.

She was content. This was her grandmother, a woman who had been part of the children's lives since they were born. Hers was the soft, loving lap they had all nestled in, the patient, white-haired figure, plump as a mama teddy bear, whom they had taken comfort from while growing up.

Grandmother had a new riddle for Cassie:

> *"In marble walls as white as milk*
> *Lined with skin as soft as silk*
> *With a pool so crystal-clear*
> *A golden sun doth always appear.*
> *No doors there are to this stronghold*
> *Yet thieves break in and steal the gold."*

Cassie guessed it right away: an egg!

In the early days, when they'd been more cramped for space, Cassie had slept with Grandmother. She loved to snuggle up to her, deriving comfort from her soft body, and was only vaguely conscious of the faint sour smell wafting up from the bedclothes. Maybe her grandmother didn't take a bath every day, but neither did Cassie. At night the child didn't mind seeing the false teeth with the bright pink gums, floating in the glass of water by the bed; or the long trails of gray hair, let down from its knot; or the sagging breasts, indistinctly perceived through the flowered nightgown. All these things were simply Grandmother. She was undeniably the calmest person ever to occupy their home, and sometimes there was much to be said for calm.

O

Liddy had decided to go the races, and had persuaded Marvin to go, too. She said she'd feel uncomfortable without an escort, with the sort of men who tended to hang around the racetrack —a fact she didn't think she needed to point out. Marvin acquiesced, although he seldom closed the store. Grandmother McIvor didn't want to go; she said her arthritis was bothering her.

After much discussion, it was decided that Dan and Cassie could attend. But to make Aunt Bertha and Liddy more comfortable in the car in their dress-up clothes, Dan would drive Cassie over in the Model A. He was sixteen now and had a license, but this was the first time he'd been permitted to drive out of town.

Liddy decided to wear the green linen with white piqué collar and cuffs she'd made for a church convention in Enid, the only time she'd left Cato last year. As she pulled the dress over her head, she grinned to herself—now she was wearing it to the horse races! Peering into the pitted mirror that topped the chiffonier, she applied rouge to her cheeks, then reached up to a high shelf and took down the large-brimmed straw hat she had redone to go with the outfit. She had put a green taffeta ribbon around the crown that matched perfectly. As a finishing touch, she fastened on her coral beads. She emerged from the bedroom pleased with her efforts.

Then she saw her sister-in-law. Bertha was in a banana crêpe de Chine dress with a coat of brown-printed chiffon. The dress was low enough to show her ample cleavage, and she wore a coquettish straw hat with a huge brown silk flower. She looked so…rich! The pearls cascading down her bosom swung as she walked, like the queen of the Nile, down their front steps.

Fred waited near the Cadillac in a white suit with a vest and a wide-brimmed Panama hat. Marvin wore the only summer jacket he had, a polka-dot bow tie, and his straw boater. Fred, puffing on a big cigar, whistled as the women came out of the house.

Marvin nodded. "You ladies're gonna knock 'em dead."

In her white shirt and seersucker shorts, Cassie felt embarrassingly plain.

"Now, I've told you where the trailer is, Dan," said Uncle Fred. "You think you can find it?"

"Uh-huh, sure." Dan flipped his hair out of his eyes and stood on one foot and then the other.

Cassie wanted to ask Fiona, but Dan said they had to get going. He took her by the arm and pulled her over to the car, with Liddy warning them the whole time, "Don't go near the horse races—children aren't allowed there... It isn't a nice place! And Dan, you watch out for—"

Her words were lost in the car's noise.

The adults piled into the Cadillac, with Marvin in front and Bertha and Liddy in the back.

"Sis, you look too damn good for a Methodist! Only Presbyterians are entitled to look that grand!"

"I'd hate to be a Presbyterian!" she retorted. "You think you're predestined from birth, with no control over your lives, so that's supposed to give you license to do the most despicable things, like smoke smelly cigars and waste your money at the horse races!"

After three-quarters of an hour's drive, they arrived at the fairgrounds. Liddy wanted to visit the needlecraft exhibits. She was proud of her sewing ladies, and it wouldn't be right not to go see their work. She asked a man if he knew where the homemaking exhibits were, and he pointed.

Hundreds of prizes were given out every year at the fair for the wonders that women wrought with their gardens, cookstoves, and workbaskets. There were ribbons for layer cakes, loaf cakes, cookies, candy, popcorn balls, spiced apples, pickles, jellies, jams, preserved fruit, embroidery of all kinds, boys' suits made from castoff garments, afghans, pieced quilts, hand-painted cake plates, oil paintings, and a myriad of other homemade objects. It was so exciting to see all these things gathered together in one place, and it was especially exciting to see *her* ladies' things!

Rachel had won a blue ribbon for the baby quilt, and there it was, on a stand. And in the crochet division, Minna Thatcher had won a red ribbon for a lacy black stole.

But the men were impatient to get to the races, and Bertha didn't seem very interested either; most of the time she was fixing her makeup.

"Liddy, come on, now, my feet are killin' me!" On the way to the racing pavilion, the women minced along in their high heels, trying to keep up with the men. "Ah don't know why they're in such a hurry to lose their money!" she said, panting.

Liddy was certain now that her brother intended to gamble on the horses, but she hoped Marvin wouldn't succumb! As the men disappeared under the grandstand, the women found seats in the bleachers.

Bertha said, "Ah know one thang—ever since Fred got started on horses, ah always git a sound sleep at night! No more o' that midnight rasslin'!"

Liddy, embarrassed to hear anything about Fred's sex life, looked off into the crowd. "I guess I was vain to think Fred came up here to see me and my family."

"He loves ya, honey," drawled Bertha, "and he loves me, too, but sometimes I think he loves them derned ol' horses more! But ah jus' take mah little trips inta Neiman Mahcus, and it sorta eases the pain!"

The two of them were more dressed up than anyone else, except for a group down five or six rows. She realized suddenly they were from Cato: Hal and Grace Sampson, the Scruggs, Stuffy and Charlene Byers, and Henry McCallum and his mousy wife. Abby Gallagher waved; she was sitting next to Charlene; the ruffle on her white blouse framed her face like a queen. Grace looked beautiful in rose silk. Hal stood up and waved to Liddy. Liddy blushed and nodded her head, and they all turned and waved at her. She had heard a bothersome rumor from Rowena about Grace and Mitch being lovers, but she knew it couldn't be true! Mitch would never look twice at a woman that old, with three-quarters of the Cato girls after him night and day.

The men were back. "We put our bets down; you girls want us to bet anything for you? Mornin' Glory looks good in the first race," said Fred. Bertha opened her purse and handed him a ten-dollar bill, and Liddy, suddenly caught up in everyone else's reckless mood, brought out two dollars. "You wouldn't—they wouldn't bother with this, would they?"

Marvin stared at her in amazement, but Fred grabbed the bills, and the men left again.

"They want us to go to a pauper's grave with 'em!" said Bertha.

"How do they know where to place the bets?" asked Liddy.

"It's probably back where people can't see 'em. The pari-mutuels get church people riled, even though they're legal lots o' places now." Liddy felt her face go hot. It struck her that *she* was church people, and she had just bet on a race.

Morning Glory came in dead last.

O

Oh, my God, it's Abby, Marvin realized as he sat down. He thought his heart was going to leap out of his chest, not from lust this time, but from fear. *She hadn't told him she was coming back for the races!* Not once did he glance her way, even though he heard her laugh and felt her presence brushing against him. He spent the whole time talking to Fred, cheering on the horses, or studying his racing program.

For lunch, they all went up to the clubhouse overlooking the track. With their food, everyone drank iced tea. When Liddy excused herself to go freshen up, she met Charlene in the ladies' room. "How come Abby Gallagher's here, Charlene? I thought she went home to Watonga."

"I ran into her one day before school was out, and invited her to come back for the fair. She's stayin' with us for a couple of days. I'm real glad I did. Abby's kind of lonely, I think."

Liddy pinched her cheeks for color, displeased with her reflection in the mirror.

She doubted Abby was lonely; she was much too attractive for that. She remembered how the young teacher had flirted with Marvin at the picnic, but thankfully she had been able to put it all out of her mind.

Back at the table, Liddy noticed that everyone's tea was darker than hers, and Bertha's voice was even louder than it was before. A man announced over a loudspeaker that since this was the last day of the races, the trainers, owners, and pari-mutuel officials were here in the clubroom too, having a party. The room was filled with smoke, and some of the people looked downright disreputable. She avoided looking at the Cato crowd, who sat a little distance away by the window. Fred went over to visit them, acting as if he'd known everyone for years. Her brother no longer looked dapper; his tie was loose, his vest and coat unbuttoned. Marvin seemed a little tipsy too, and like a high school boy, kept putting his arm around Liddy to hug her. She was embarrassed that people should see him acting so ridiculous.

All at once Bertha sashayed over to the piano and began to play a syncopated jazz tune. A tiny jockey wearing tight green satin pants and a striped satin jacket materialized next to the piano and plunked down next to Bertha, handing her a drink. A few minutes went later Liddy couldn't believe her eyes. The grinning jockey had his arm around Bertha's broad waist and was singing the words to a tune she was pounding out, gazing up into her eyes like an infatuated child, while Bertha's body was rocking and heaving like a huge Jell-O mold. Her smokestack hairdo had tumbled down around her face. *"Won't you come home, Bill Bailey, won't you come home?"*

Now Bertha was singing along with the jockey, and their duet was raucous and earsplitting.

While Liddy watched, Fred walked over and began pulling at the fellow's sleeve. The jockey jumped to his feet, and suddenly he and Fred were trading punches. A man in a sheriff's uniform finally broke it up and Fred, pale as ashes, dragged Bertha away from the piano. Everyone in the room heard her yell, "Fred, take your hands offa me—I'm *comin'*!"

Liddy, mortified, hurried back to the ladies' room, the only sanctuary she could think of.

When they went back to the grandstand for the last two races, Fred insisted they all move down near the Cato group, where he started paying way too much attention to Grace Sampson. Bertha, her hairdo and makeup partially restored, was laughing too loudly at one of Barney Scruggs's jokes, an off-color one, Liddy could tell. She was glad Marvin was here, though he seemed distracted, and had stopped paying any attention to her.

Sitting on the hard, uncomfortable seats, she wished the day would come to an end.

O

Marvin had decided that the only way to get through the afternoon was to keep drinking with Fred, though keeping up with him would take some doing. Somehow he had maintained his pose of cool standoffishness with Abby, but when Fred had insisted they join the Cato contingent, there was nothing he could do, though he made sure he didn't sit close to her. He took Liddy's arm and propelled her to the far end of the long seat, near Henry McCallum and his wife. Only once did his and Abby's eyes meet, and he felt that familiar warmth flood through him. This time it was pure desire. He had grown tired of the betting, and got a shock when Liddy bet on a horse again. It must have been Fred and Bertha's outlandish behavior in the clubhouse that drove her to it. He saw Hal Sampson bend over Liddy and whisper something, whereupon she handed him two dollars. The next thing he knew, she was waving ten dollars! Her horse had come in first, at five-to-one odds. "Marvin, Fred! I won! *Lickity-Split won!*"

Liddy's expression was a mix of shock, exhilaration, and guilt.

○

Dan sat scowling at the road, gripping the vibrating steering wheel as they bumped along.

They had gone several miles before Cassie dared make conversation.

"It's nice of Daddy to let us have the car, huh?" she yelled, bouncing up and down on the seat. She had taken out her pigtails and run a brush through her hair, which stood out electrically in washboard waves, as if with a life of its own.

"Whaddya *mean*, nice? I have to pay for the gas myself for this piece of junk to take *you* to the fair! Think that's justice?"

Cassie sang,

"Fair, fair—we're goin' to th' fair!
Ain't we a twosome; ain't we a pair!"

Dan turned in disbelief. Would nothing daunt her?

"Fair, fair—we're goin' to th' fair!
It's taking too long, when are we there!"

She took her flyaway mane in her hands and spread it out from her head, and when Dan turned to look at her again, she crossed her eyes and stuck out her tongue. The day was a success—she'd made Dan laugh. It seemed like most of the time he was mad at her or picking on her about something. Taking everything out on her, doing the very thing he complained about his dad and Mitch doing to *him*.

They were crossing one of the many bridges that spanned Wolf Creek. Dan looked down and saw the dry, washed-out banks. Just then there was a *bang!* and they swerved sharply to the right, the front of the car sagging on its right side. Dan turned off the engine and got out. After taking a look, he slapped the fender as hard as he could, then shook his hand as if he'd hurt himself. "God damn it, we got a flat tire! I don't know if the spare's any good, neither!" He looked at Cassie and frowned. "Well, get out, Miss Princess—I can't fix it with *you* in there!" He began taking off the spare at the rear of the car and getting out the jack, using curse words the entire time.

"Mama wouldn't like it if she knew you was cussing like that in front of me."

"Who cares? You gonna tell her, you little rat? Now shut up."

She went to the side of the road and sat down in some weeds. But they made her legs itch, so she stood up again. A blue sedan slowly approached them and pulled over. It was the high school music teacher Mr. Philips and his wife. Cassie knew Mrs. Philips better, because she was the organist at the First Methodist.

"Hey, there, Dan! You got a flat?"

"Yeah, me and Cassie was on our way to the fair." Dan mustered a grin from somewhere.

"Cassie, you wanta go with us? We'll give you a ride over. Looks like Dan'll be here awhile." Cassie looked at Dan. "Yeah, sure, take her. But, Cassie, you go to the trailer and wait for me. I'll be there in about a half hour. Think you can find it?"

"Near the racetrack and the horse barns."

"I know where the track is; we'll drop her off there," said Mr. Philips.

The three of them chatted on the way about things that were interesting to Cassie, like the Pioneer Day parade and the puppies she had at home, so the time went fast. As soon as they let her out of the car, she started for the part of the racetrack that Uncle Fred had described.

"Look for a tall flag," he'd said. She found the flag, but was distracted by the sounds of music coming from a band of country fiddlers and pickers in a little clearing.

A large crowd of people had gathered around the music platform, and people were clapping their hands and tapping their feet to the music. There was a fiddler, a bass fiddler, a mandolin player, and a handsome banjo player, and there was a young man with hair falling in his face and a guitar hung by a strap around his neck. He was picking the strings with some sort of metal things on his fingers. Cassie asked a lady standing nearby what kind of guitar that was and the woman said "A Dobro—*shhhh!!*"

The banjo player's voice rang out with a twang:
How old are you, my pretty little miss?
How old are you, my honey?

A girl stepped out from the back of the podium and sang, her long hanging to her waist:

If I don't die of a broken heart
I'll be sixteen next Sunday!

When the Dobro player finished the song, he gave all the ladies a flick of his long eyelashes, and the girl next to Cassie went "*Whoosh!*" and fell into the arms of her boyfriend.

The audience stamped and cheered and whistled, and so did Cassie.

She wanted to stay and listen some more, but she knew she'd better find the trailer. Making her way through the crowd, she stopped at the Ferris wheel to look at everyone enjoying the ride and to listen to people yelling and squealing. Heck! Dan had promised to take her on the Ferris wheel.

Feemy was sweeping out the trailer.

"I'm s'posed to wait here for my brother. We had a flat tire," she told Feemy.

"Jesse and Carlton be at the horse barns, but Carlton'll be back soon. Would you like to wait inside the trailer, honey?"

Cassie nodded. She pressed her lips together, thinking of how mean Dan had been to her when he had to change the tire, calling her a rat. She could cry if she wanted to, but she didn't want to.

"Here's my Carlton. Carlton, here's Cassie! She an' her brothah was comin' over to the fair and had them a flat tire!"

Carlton sat down next to her on the bed. His skin was dark and shiny, and his enormous brown eyes looked at her; then his eyelids came down the way they had in the driveway. After a long time he said, "You still like Chinese checkers? I brought 'em."

They played for a half hour, and when it got too hot, they played outside for another long time. Cassie finally tired of the game. *Where was Dan?* It had been much more than an hour.

Suddenly she made a decision. "Let's *us* go to the fair, Carlton!"

When he went inside to ask Feemy for permission, she didn't say a word, simply took a dollar from her purse and handed it to her son. "You go over there where yo' daddy's talkin' to them hoss mens, and you tell him what you gonna do, and you go to the bathroom over there. Cassie'll wait fo' you." She grabbed a yellow shirt off the shelf. "And you change yo' shirt."

For the first time since Cassie had known him, Carlton smiled. He shucked off his shirt lickity-whoop and yanked the clean one over his head. Cassie waited for him outside the trailer while he ran to the stables, and when he got back they set out.

"What you wanna see first?" she asked him.

"I wants to ride on that big ol' wheel."

Liddy had given Cassie a dollar that morning, and it was wrapped in a handkerchief in her shorts pocket.

As they went up into the air, strapped side by side in the swinging seat, Cassie's stomach quivered—that excited kind of quivering she hadn't felt since Mabel used to drive fast over the country hills. As they rode up high above the crowd, they laughed and laughed.

"Look! There's my trailer!" Cassie's eyes followed where he pointed. A small woman stood outside the miniature caravan, her hand shading her eyes and looking in their direction.

Carlton shouted, "Mama, Mama, I'm here!" The wheel started up again, and they rocked downward, swaying in the drop until they reached the ground. Carlton tried to walk in a straight line, and Cassie leaned against a post while her stomach settled into place.

Next, Carlton wanted to shoot clay pigeons, but Cassie said they couldn't spend any more money for a while. "We don't wanna use up our cash!" she said. "Come on, there's some places where ever'thing's free!"

She pulled him toward the other exhibits across the fairgrounds. At times the crowd parted for them, people staring openly at the little white girl and the young Negro boy. They ignored the looks directed their way, and Cassie showed Carlton how to shoulder his way through. All at once they came upon a gathering in a small clearing, with a raised platform in the center. A sign read:

4-H of BLISS COUNTY
HEAD   HEART   HANDS   HEALTH
HEALTHIEST BOY & GIRL CONTEST

Standing on the platform was a group of teenagers.

"Is there gonna be some speakin' or singin'?" Cassie asked the man standing next to her.

"This here is a contest, dearie! Why don't you an' yore little nigger friend enter?"

The man guffawed and nudged a man nearby, who glanced down at Cassie and Carlton with a sour look on his face.

"Carlton isn't a nigger. He's *colored*!" said Cassie.

"He's colored, all right; he's downright sooty coal-colored!" At this, both men laughed loudly. They reminded Cassie of the town loafers in Cato.

"Do you know Sheriff Bartlett?" she asked, with her head cocked to one side.

She didn't know what had prompted her to say it, but it had the desired effect. The men stopped laughing and turned away. Carlton's expression didn't change, except that his eyelids were at half-mast again.

Cassie turned her attention to the contest, and right away ruled out two of the girls. They were too hollow-eyed and peaked to look really healthy, and their hair hung down in strings. Reminded of her own hair, Cassie put her hand up, and a thick clump flew out to meet it. She shook her head back and forth and heard a pleasant crackling. When the contest was over, Cassie's own choice for healthiest girl, the girl who had enormous muscles in her legs, had lost to a pretty girl with good posture and flashing teeth. For healthiest boy, a handsome lad who looked like a stiff breeze would flatten him took the blue ribbon.

The crowd applauded, and the children moved on.

"I think that contest was a bunch o' horsefeathers." Cassie frowned as they walked along.

"How's come?" asked Carlton.

"Well, the ones *I* picked looked like they could do lots o' stuff on a farm, an' like they wouldn't ever get sick, not even chicken pox. But the judges just picked whoever looked pretty!"

Carlton nodded, but he didn't seem as concerned as Cassie about the fairness of the contest. Life wasn't fair anyhow. "Le's us go see the fiddle contes', okay, Cassie?"

"Wait a minute. How much money you got left?"

Carlton fished out his change, spread it around on his hand, and counted. "Fo'ty-five cents."

"You like pie and cake?" she asked. His expression was all the answer she needed.

They couldn't decide between loaf cake and layer cake, so they went to the pie table and discovered even more choices. It was hard to decide, and the minutes ticked by.

"Would you please hurry up—there's others waitin'!" This was from a scowling, plumpish blonde woman in a flowered apron, who looked down at Carlton with obvious displeasure. Cassie pulled him away to where a little gray-haired lady was smiling at both of them.

While Carlton ate spice cake and Cassie had lemon chiffon, the woman said, "You children gettin' more outside than in!" Wetting paper napkins, she wiped their faces. "You kids seen the snake with two heads?" she asked. She pointed in the direction of the next tent, and the children jumped up and headed toward the huge block letters proclaiming TEMPLE OF WONDERS.

"For the price of a ticket you will im-me-jately be allowed to enter!" said a man in a striped shirt and derby. "Come one, come all—see the hairy lady, the undraped models, the thinnest man on earth, and the indescribable, the amazing Fat Lady! Enter! Enter. ENTER!"

Liddy had said not to go near the horse races, and Cassie had minded.

She gazed around at the men standing in line, who reminded her of Clink Kerry and Smiley Applebaum, two of Cato's town loafers. Also standing in line was a family of gypsies; at least they had on colorful, odd-looking clothes, and the woman wore big dangly earrings. It was not a respectable-looking crowd. *Good!* They paid their twenty-five cents and went through the flap with everyone else.

The first thing they saw was the two-headed snake in a cage. It was all alone, or as alone as a two-headed snake could be. Carlton stood in front of it so long, Cassie had to drag him away.

"Ah likes to see its two tongues come out at the same time!" he said.

"There's more—come on!" They moved on to the rear of the next group, looking at the Hairy Lady, who sat on a little stage dressed in a bare-midriff outfit like Hedy Lamaar's and a fez like Charles Boyer's in *Algiers*. This was confusing for Cassie, who'd seen the movie three times, but to add to the mystery, the creature had a black beard, bushy black eyebrows, and hands covered in dark, curly fuzz. Her midriff was so hairy Cassie couldn't see any skin. Her legs were covered, but her huge, bony feet, the toes covered with more black hair, protruded from her paisley harem pajamas. On her chest, twin protuberances of an impressive size lurked beneath the gold-embroidered top. The Hairy Lady seemed to invite their curiosity by leering back at them, smiling broadly and puffing on a big cigar, and crossing and uncrossing her legs seductively each time she took a puff. Cassie was reminded of Groucho Marx in *At the Circus*—probably it was the cigar, and the eyebrows.

The children stood rooted to the spot. No matter what they saw next, it couldn't top this.

They were finally forced to move on. Next they came to the group they'd entered the tent with. All stood mute and awestruck, because before them was The Thinnest Man On Earth.

Sitting on a high stool was a bald, emaciated fellow, so gaunt that his scalp seemed to be stretched over his skull. His skin was translucent as silk, and blue veins traced his limbs and torso like roads traced on a map. He looked so shrunken and weak that Cassie was afraid he might fall off the stool and crack his bones.

There was one more cubicle to enter, where, as they went through the flap, the children heard the exhaled breaths of their fellow gawkers. After the Thinnest Man on Earth, it was almost a relief to see The Fat Lady. She sat on a broad stool preening, combing her long red hair with a silver brush and comb while holding up an enormous silver mirror. Then she stood and moved around the podium, moving her ponderous weight in time to music from a Victrola. After a minute or two of waltzing about, she took her tiny white poodle in her arms and danced him around the stage. It suddenly occurred to Cassie that the fat lady was young.

"Carlton, that's no lady; she's a *girl!*"

"Don' make no diff'ence—she still real fat."

"But how'd she get fat so young?"

The Gypsy woman they'd seen in line stood behind them with her baby. Two other children clung to her long skirts. "Trixie ain't as young as she looks, kids. She just ain't got no wrinkles."

"You *knows* her?" asked Carlton.

"Yeah, my husband runs the merry-go-round." The woman had a trace of foreign accent, mixed in with her Oklahoma twang.

"Are you a Gypsy?" asked Cassie.

"Heck, yeah." The woman jiggled the baby in her arms and hitched up her skirts. "My folks came over from the old country a long time ago. We moved out to this godfersaken territory fifteen years ago—now we're stuck on the cow-town circuit... We better move on. They're fixin' to bring in the next bunch o' pigeons."

Cassie stared after the woman, wondering what she had meant by "pigeons."

She felt pretty sure it wasn't flattering.

Coming out into the bright sunlight, their ears picked up the strains of music from a nearby tent. It wasn't the ragtime that Aunt Bertha played, although close to it. The syncopated thumping of a drum and the clang of a cymbal underscored the sounds of a tinny piano. Cassie and Carlton stopped in their tracks and looked at the open flap of the tent a few yards away, where a long line of men stood. A big sign read:

TEN LITTLE BEAUTIES
TEN LITTLE MODELS
UNDRAPED, UNVEILED, AND UNASHAMED
HUMAN BEAUTY
IN ALL ITS SPLENDOR AND GLORY!

But the tickets were fifty cents, and they were out of money. They decided to head back to the trailer.

○

Taking his time while looking around, Dan eventually found the trailer. "I thought Cassie would be here," he said to Feemy.

"Oh, Ah'm sorry, suh. I let 'em go to the fair 'cause that little girl seem so sad and—and my Carlton, he wanted so terrible to *see* things!"

"It's okay; I'll find 'em," said Dan. He wasn't sure two kids would be all right wandering about on their own, especially when one of them was a Negro. But his sister was always talking to strangers, she'd be all right.

First he washed his hands and face at the horse barn. After that, because the day had started out so bad, he decided to reward himself. He'd heard from Sean that the Temple of Wonders was pretty exciting, so he headed that way. The crowd was mostly boys and men.

The Hairy Lady was no doubt a man. The tits were a real fooler, but you could buy those in a store. Mitch had told him Betsy Byers wore them! He wondered how Mitch knew. The Thinnest Man On Earth was a pitiful sight, and Dan couldn't look at him for more than a couple of minutes. The fair authorities should be prosecuted for putting such an obviously sick person on view for money. He might tell his dad; maybe he could put a stop to it. Dad knew all the doctors in the county.

The only "Wonder" Dan liked was the Fat Lady, who actually seemed to enjoy the crowd. She danced to "The Shadow Waltz," her lumbering movements around the stage disguised by the graceful undulations of her huge, quivering arms. She threw flower petals to the crowd, and as she blew kisses to them all and bent to give the poodle little pecking kisses, she began to seem a goddess of seduction. Dan wanted to warm his hands on those gigantic, heaving breasts. Every time she bent over the little dog, it was a challenge to gravity. Would she be able to remain upright? Would they work themselves free of her costume? *God, he hoped so!*

After her last kiss on the dog's head, she put him back in his box, and while looking directly at Dan—picked him out of the whole crowd—she put one hand to her face and fanned her fingers around one cheek, while hefting an immense breast with the other hand. Then she turned her back to the crowd and jiggled all over. Dan was mortified to discover he was getting an erection. He glanced around to see if anyone noticed. Suddenly he didn't want to be around these hordes of people. He remembered that bend of Wolf Creek when he and Cassie had crossed the bridge.

Patting his ever-present paperback *Guide to Prehistoric Artifacts*, he hightailed it out of the fairgrounds.

O

As the children walked toward the racetrack, Cassie reflected that having all the relatives visit them had been a tremendous piece of luck. As sure as God put worms in little green apples, if her mother hadn't been so distracted by the company (and if the tire hadn't gone flat), she and Carlton wouldn't be having all this fun. She breathed in deeply— the dust, the smells of popcorn and burnt sugar, the heavy odor of the oil from the big engines operating the rides. Another few hundred yards, and they spotted the Chevy and trailer; soon they were watching Jesse set out all his barbecue tools, his large hands expertly arranging tongs and brushes and long-handled forks.

Not long after that, the grownups arrived. Her dad, Uncle Fred, and even Aunt Bertha had the smell Cassie had noticed before on her dad—the smell of something stronger than beer. Her mother looked tired. The ladies had taken off their hats, and their clothing was puckered and clinging, not flowing and loose like that morning. Aunt Bertha's makeup had puddled under her eyes, and she was moaning that her feet hurt. She plopped down on one of the camp chairs and took off her high heels. Cassie looked up to see her uncle throw his arm around Jesse's shoulder and pour amber liquid into his drink. Dan arrived just as Fred finished pouring.

"Dan, where you been? You were with Cassie today, weren't you? How come you look so grimy?" asked Liddy. Dan reddened and looked quickly at Cassie, who was busy studying the glass Chinese checkers.

"You look like you been out behind the barn, Dan!" contributed Aunt Bertha.

"We saw *ever'thing* at the fair, didn't we, Dan?" asked Cassie in a loud voice. "We liked the pigs an' the horseshoe contest the best."

Dan nodded and got a paper cup of lemonade from Feemy, who was looking worried about something. Everyone went on chattering.

"You kids realize your mama won ten dollars on that nag Lickity-Split?" Uncle Fred walked over to inspect the meat, his legs wobbling slightly.

Marvin put his arm around Liddy's waist and said, "Honey, you gonna be a regular over here now? Be comin' over here all the time, spendin' my hard-earned money?"

A shocked Cassie waited for her mother to reply. She'd certainly toppled from her pedestal! No matter how preposterous the idea seemed, her mother had gone to the races, and she had *gambled*.

Jesse's soft voice cut through the family's conversation. "Food's ready!"

Fred said, "Jus' wait, ever'body; wait'll you taste these ribs! People all over Texas been tryin' to git this man's recipe for twenty years! Ain't that right, Feemy?" He took a bill out of his wallet. "See this hundred? I been tryin' to git Feemy to tell me Jesse's secret for the longest time—how 'bout it, girl!"

Fred grinned at her, wobbling on his feet as he waved the bill in the air.

"Now y'all oughtn't t'devil mah husband, Mistah McIvah—you leave this ol' Jesse alone!"

Feemy's white teeth flashed as her hands moved up and down on her apron.

The children, sitting on the steps of the trailer gnawing on ribs, watched the grownups.

After gobbling down a plateful, Dan wandered away to inspect the stables.

"How come your dad and mom don't take that hunnerd-dollar bill?" Cassie asked Carlton.

"Oh, that jes' be a kinda game they-alls play. Mistah McIvah, he know whut's in mah daddy's recipe—it jes' be ketchup an' brown sugah an' a li'l lemon juice an' some Woosershire sauce an' chili powdah th'own in. I seen that hunnud *befo'*."

The sounds of the day were changing; the noise of the crowd leaving the racing stadium had quieted down and the music of a calliope had begun. By the time they'd finished Feemy's peach cobbler (brought up with the spareribs in the Kelvinator), darkness was falling.

Dan, it had been decided, would drive the Model A home without Cassie. He hadn't mentioned the flat tire, so she didn't.

Liddy thanked Feemy and Jesse for the wonderful food. She told Feemy she should have entered her cobbler in the fair, and Jesse that he should send his sparerib recipe to the White House, because it had been reported in the newspapers that FDR didn't like Eleanor's cooking. Jesse laughed and said he'd think about it, because he sure did like that Mr. Roosevelt.

Carlton and Feemy stood at the door of the trailer. Cassie, at the bottom of the steps, asked Feemy, "You goin' to be here tomorrow?"

"No, honey, we goin' back to Texas first thing in the mornin'."

Cassie looked up at Carlton.

He came down one step. She went toward him. He came down another step.

"We had fun," said Cassie.

"Uh-huh."

"Well, I'll be seein' you. That was good barbeycue."

Feemy nodded her head at Cassie, briefly tightening her grip on Carlton's shoulder.

Carlton's eyes were wide open now, and his lips were spread in a dazzling smile.

10

When beauty fires the blood, how love exalts the mind!
—John Dryden
Cymon and Iphigenia

In August the War Department announced an order for eighty-five million dollars' worth of aircraft. The Neutrality Act that Roosevelt and Congress signed in 1935, sixteen years after the Treaty of Versailles, had been revised, so now the United States would be supplying warring nations with arms on a cash-and-carry basis. Marvin said he was right after all: Roosevelt *was* getting the country into the war, one step at a time. "He said America would help ever'body battling against Hitler but we wouldn't be gettin' into it. But we *are!*" He stormed and fumed and fussed about FDR, even though Liddy pointed out that Congress was in on all the decisions too.

O

Liddy was determined to keep working with her needlecraft ladies, and the women had been enthusiastic about her becoming their sales representative. They were pleased to have their talents discovered, and they trusted her. When she drove around the county collecting their sewing, she wanted to be as efficient as possible, wasting neither time nor gas, so she spent quite a while mapping out routes. She also spent hours making lists of all the possible outlets for the work, writing to every friend and relative she knew across the state. She had acquired an outlet in Red Arrow and another in Antelope, and she'd heard there was a new children's shop opening in Enid.

She learned from Rachel Klein that those two sweet Nichols sisters outside Arbuckle knitted lovely cap-and-mittens sets—those would be just the thing for that new shop! And she'd been corresponding with a store in Oklahoma City that sold bed and table linens. But Marvin always discouraged her from extending her area too far; he said it would be the height of folly to try to get into shops in the cities, or even the big towns.

She thought his objections were mostly about gasoline. He could drive all over creation with his dogs, or all the way down to Ardmore to see Joe Kelly, and never have to answer to a soul about it. He even made her keep a list of how much she spent when she filled the tank!

"How come you don't keep a list of *your* gasoline expenses?" she asked him one morning at breakfast when he went on about the bills she was running up. "And while we're at it, how about the cost of all the dog kibble and those expensive ads?"

He just clammed up and rustled the newspaper really loud.

It wasn't as if she didn't make any money at this, as if she were doing it as a hobby. Her commission on sales, 25%, was four times her gas bill. Some of the things she sold for double to the stores, and they marked them up double again, and everyone was happy. Sometimes she would place things on consignment. She was building her own business, helping women step out of their dreary lives, inspiring them to create beautiful things and doing them a favor by selling them to folks who appreciated them.

The only drawback was that sometimes she got involved with some of the women's family problems. She heard about Minna Thatcher's depressions, and Rachel Klein had a brother who had been thrown in jail for assault. Every time Liddy visited Jerusha Corkle, she puzzled and worried over how the poor woman could stand living with slovenly, shiftless Ezra, let alone cope with the idiot boy Harley. The poor Widow Groves had no idea of her own worth! Liddy simply *had* to talk her into charging more for her baby things.

She felt so sorry for Rachel the day Rachel confided in her about her brother. Standing in her kitchen with a bundle of her quilted hot pads to hand over to Liddy, she burst into tears, so that Liddy felt moved to say, "Timmy, you go on outside and play. Find your daddy."

Rachel was so downcast, Liddy started babbling about any old thing. She'd been having a hard time getting the store in Elk City to hand over payment for all the needlework she'd been taking to them, some of which she was sure had been sold. "I'm pretty good at collecting, though—been doing it since I was a kid, when I used to try to get folks to pay my dad for his doctoring services... Some people never *would* pay!"

Rachel sat down and blew her nose. For the moment, her mind was off her brother, so Liddy babbled on for some time about the old days with her country doctor father in Lindsay.

Driving home, Liddy thought how all the women's troubles seemed to make her own fade away a little, although she still had her share. She was worried about Mitch. How could he get involved with a married woman, especially one in her forties! When she pictured him being intimate with Grace, her stomach turned. And Dan seemed skittery and nervous, and when he wasn't being held prisoner working in the store (his phrase) he was constantly going off somewhere alone. She didn't like him spending so much time with Sean O'Herlihy, who was usually up to no good, like his entire family. Dan would be just fine if he had a better class of friends. Cassie had been quiet lately, trying to please her teachers. She and Dan didn't get along, but Liddy didn't suppose they ever would.

But her main concern was Marvin. He was smoking too much and working too hard, and he was losing weight. He seemed preoccupied, by what, she didn't know. Probably bird dogs—he kept buying *more* of the creatures! The last one he'd driven halfway across the state to get was nothing but a mangy pup—what a waste of money! His temper was short, and she didn't like being around him.

With Dan in school most of the time, she would have to find some help for the store. Liddy usually did the interviewing, so she talked to the oldest Purvis girl, Esther. But Marvin said he wouldn't have her.

Then she talked to Eula Tully, the ticket girl at the movie theater. Even though she was slow-witted and couldn't get her lipstick on straight, she could handle money. But it turned out Eula didn't want to leave her job.

Liddy first heard about Lola Mallory when she was playing bridge at Flo Schonberger's. The ladies had braved an untimely August drizzle for their monthly game. The wind blew rain into their faces as they parked their cars, all of them vying for the least muddy parking place. They laughed and yelled out to one another about the changeable weather. Two days before, it had been a sweltering ninety degrees.

Now the four of them sat in a warm corner of Flo's living room, glad to be together. Flo, who was ten or twelve years older than the other three and had no children, had devoted her life to helping her husband run the dry goods store, and she always had stories to tell. The most important news she had today was that George's sixteen-year-old niece, Lola, was coming to live with them. Lola's mother, George's sister, had been dead for five years, and her father had died just two weeks ago in

Liberal, Kansas, after a long illness. Even though Lola had nursed him until he died, she had managed to keep up her high-school classes and make excellent grades.

"And besides all that," said Flo, "she's real pretty. George and me were actually relieved when Frank died. Now she can come live with us and have a normal life. Maybe help out at our store."

"That's real nice, you getting a young girl to come live with you," said Liddy, shuffling the cards. "She'll probably seem like a daughter."

"When we gonna do another bazaar?" asked Rowena. "That was a hoot!"

"I got my feelers out for some new outlets farther away," said Liddy. "I oughta go both places, but Marvin always has a fit about gas. I'm too busy to put on an event now, anyway, even if you-all helped me."

Flo, pouring tea, said, "Hetty Saltman is makin' some embroidered napkins, but she says it takes her three weeks to do just one."

"If she wouldn't spend so much time listenin' in on phone conversations, she could do a set of eight in a week," said Liddy.

"Flo and I have a surprise comin' for you, Liddy—fer one o' your shops," said Rowena.

"What? I don't like surprises! Tell me *now*!"

"We're not ready. But in a month or two you'll see." Rowena took a sip of tea and bit into a mint, looking pleased with herself.

"Anybody goin' to the play at the school? I hear it's real funny," said Violet. Miss Thornhill was doing her annual fall production, this year forsaking drama for comedy.

"I hear there's gonna be a shakeup at school, change o' teachers," said Flo mysteriously. George was on the school board, but Flo didn't always tell them what she knew.

"What kind of shakeup?" asked Liddy.

"Oh, one of the teachers. Somebody might be let go." They waited for more information, but none came.

"Man or woman?" asked Violet.

"Never you mind," said Flo.

Minutes went by as the ladies played several hands. The room was quiet, with only the sounds of rain blowing against the windows and the occasional brush of a tree limb against the house.

"It's nice Lola's coming." Liddy lay down her cards in raggedy rows, hearts first. She'd been dummy three times already; Flo was an aggressive bidder. She let a long second go by. "But I think she ought to come work for Field's Drugs instead of for you."

"Why is that?" asked Flo, studying Liddy's cards, looking sour, like she'd expected more trump.

"Because we need someone, and she's going to be *living* with you. What if there are some things the three of you don't agree on? Lola sounds like a wonderful girl, but she *is* a teenager. Besides, she's just Dan's age. Dan could use a pretty girl around—might settle him down." She didn't mention that Dan was moodier than ever lately and his grades were horrible—way below what he was capable of!

"Stars and garters, Liddy! I haven't even *got* Lola yet, and you want to take her away!"

Flo reached out and rearranged Liddy's messy dummy. "But I s'pose we don't really need any more help right now. We've got Greta, and I'd hate to let her go."

The amber shade on the iron floor lamp lent their faces a warm glow. On the third trick, Flo used Liddy's two of hearts to trump Rowena's ace of clubs. With a grin, she said, "You better meet Lola first to be sure Marvin likes her, an' she likes him. Now I need to concentrate."

Violet winked at Liddy. They played two more hands and adjourned for a delicious lunch of salmon croquettes served on Flo's Bavarian china with rosebuds, after which they had rhubarb fool with whipped cream. Then they went back to their cards.

O

Mitch was constantly trying to figure out ways to see Grace. She'd called him twice at the O'Herlihys' (with little Maureen standing just down the hall), and they had met at some unlikely places in and out of town. Once they met late at night at the Cato Shores in the deserted dance pavilion, and another time they fucked in the cab of her pickup. And once they met in the alley between the old laundry building and Veterans Hall and did it in Mike's ancient clunker.

But Grace said she wouldn't make love in a car ever again, like some kind of pathetic, pimply teenager. She said she liked him a lot, but it wasn't her style. It began to dawn on Mitch that this couldn't go on. For one thing, people were going to find out. There was Duke Farrow (maybe), and there was Mike, whom Mitch had confided in because he had to talk to someone, and because he was always having to borrow Mike's car. He was sure Mike wouldn't tell, but you couldn't be too careful.

Mitch was still on the outs with his dad, and he hadn't seen Dan for a long time. Once Dan had come by the O'Herlihys' to see him, but he'd been gone, out working on the ranch.

He'd made good money from Grace, working out there, and he'd worked hard. But it had still been embarrassing taking money from her. Duke had been standing near the ranch house when Grace handed him the cash, and he'd had that grin on his face again. Mitch had felt a powerful urge to sock him, but he didn't do it. It would be like admitting the whole thing.

The last time he had seen Grace, she'd asked him to run away with her. They could go somewhere else and be together, she said, while they decided what they were going to do. She said her marriage with Hal was over, that she'd been unhappy with him for a long time. Mitch's arm was around her in the car, and her eyes had looked so sad. In the dim light of a streetlamp, he could see where the lines at the side of her mouth had deepened.

He took her arms from around his neck, and said he would think about it.

The next day, the Germans bombed London.

O

Dan had to make a delivery of pig salve to the Klein farm for a sow with an infected teat, and Cassie begged to go along. Coming home, it was raining and almost dark, and as they crossed the railroad tracks, they saw a train pull away from the station. Through the smoke, Cassie saw Flo and George Schonberger on the station platform hugging a slim young woman. She was bundled up in an overcoat, but her hair was uncovered, and it framed her head like a soft dark cloud. The girl looked over at Dan and Cassie, and her eyes seemed to search their faces.

Cassie thought she was pretty, but more—she looked vibrant and full of life. The Plymouth speeded up all of a sudden, and they lurched over the tracks, heading toward home.

O

London had its first air raid on Sunday, September 3, 1939, and Britain and France immediately declared war.

Mitch enlisted the next day, along with Dooky and Mike. They all went to Enid and signed up, Mitch in the Army Air Corps and Mike and Dooky in the Navy. Then they drove home to tell their folks. They got back by mid-afternoon.

Mitch didn't know which would be hardest, saying good-bye to his mother or to his dad. He decided that even though his mother would be the most upset, it would be harder to face his father, so he did that first. The timing was perfect; his dad was leafing through his prescription file with his glasses perched halfway down his nose, and there was no one else in the store.

Mitch was surprised to see that Marvin looked so old, and that his bow tie hadn't been cleaned lately.

"Dad…" He waited while Marvin slowly turned on his stool, took off his glasses, and reluctantly gave him his full attention. "I signed up."

Marvin just stared at him as though he didn't think the boy was half-bright, as if he weren't even part of the family.

Mitch didn't know what to do with his hands, so he shoved them deep into his pockets.

"This thing with the Germans—it's like Hitler wants to take over the world."

What a stupid way of expressing it! His phrasing was so childish. His dad always unnerved him, made him sound and act like a dumb-ass.

"And you're goin' to stop him, huh?"

"I think I ought to get in it. Me, Dooky, and Mike joined up together. I'm goin' to be in the Army Air Corps. Mike and Dooky are goin' in the Navy."

"Well, *they'll* sure be an asset. They'll prob'ly help 'em out a lot—them and their peckerwood families know so much about oceans and ships and all."

Mitch turned to leave, then decided against it. He turned back.

"I didn't come in here to hear my friends raked over the coals, Dad. I came to say good-bye. I'm—I'm sorry we didn't get along these last months."

"We would have, if you hadn't made your mother so miserable all the time, if you'd of been a lot more thoughtful of her."

"Dad, you know the reasons I moved out. I can't help any of that now. Like you're always sayin', it's water over the dam."

Suddenly his dad stood up, and Mitch was amazed to see tears rolling down his face. "You don't have to join up. We're not even at war—there isn't even a draft!"

"I know. But, Dad, it's comin'. You been sayin' it yourself for years—Roosevelt's goin' to get us in. And we *should* be in."

"Mitch, war is awful. Didn't I ever tell you about the blood...and the death—the arms and legs lost? And the head wounds—I've seen brains lyin' all over the place, hangin' out of young boys' heads, and limbs swelled up with gangrene. I worked with those injured soldiers... Didn't I ever *tell* you?"

Mitch looked at his father, at the obvious anguish on his face. They hadn't hugged each other in ten years or more. He wanted to put his arms around him now, but he didn't think his dad would like it. "I'm goin' to be fine. I'll keep myself safe. I'll be back in a few months on furlough, and then we'll talk some more, okay?"

They shook hands, and Marvin rested his hand briefly on Mitch's shoulder. After he left, Marvin wondered why he couldn't have hugged his son.

Mitch drove up the driveway in Mike's heap of a car, and when Liddy saw him, her heart gave a big leap. Mitch grabbed her and hugged her hard. She got to feel his strong body and look into his face—this was her beloved firstborn! He smoothed her coppery-silver hair back from her face, and kissed her on the cheek. Then he told her to sit down, and he sat with her and took her hand. He told her he'd enlisted, and that he'd already told Marvin.

She put her face in her hands, and her shoulders began to shake.

"Mom, you're gonna have to be strong, because this is what I want to do. We're all goin' to have to defend our country. Just read the papers."

"Oh, Mitch! I can't face it! Mitch…!" She began to cry, but then stood up and left the room.

She was gone long enough for him to smoke a cigarette, and when she came back her face was pink and blotched, but she helped him pack up the few things he wanted to take. There wasn't much, just some family snapshots and addresses. He said he wouldn't need any clothes.

She had to say it. "Honey, you don't know how much I'm going to miss you!"

"I know, Mom; I'm gonna miss you, too."

"No, I mean…your father—we're not—it's not going to be the same without you here!"

Mitch didn't ask what she was talking about; he knew. But he couldn't deal with his parents' marital problems right now.

Liddy started to cry again, and she didn't stop until just before he drove off. Then suddenly her expression brightened. He didn't know how she made her face change like that. Standing in the driveway, she grinned and said, "You write!" a half-dozen times, and he said, "I will!" as many times back.

School had started, so he went by to say good-bye to Dan and Cassie, going to the main office, which handled both the elementary and high school classes. He asked the secretary if he could pull his siblings out of class, and told her why.

Mitch gave Cassie a hard hug, and he and Dan shook hands. Then he hit his brother on the shoulder hard enough to make him wince.

"You're the oldest now," he said, and left.

O

In the next few weeks, the family gradually adjusted to Mitch's absence. Maybe it had been a good thing, his moving in with the O'Herlihys those last few months; it made his leaving less painful for everyone—except, of course, for Liddy.

Visions of Abby had been in Marvin's head all the time Liddy's relatives were in town, and even during his troubles with Mitch. His visit to Abby in Watonga had only served to intensify his obsession. What was a fellow supposed to do? Spend all his time worrying about his family, until the wellsprings of his manhood dried up? Now, with the start of school, Abby was back, and she'd called him at the store when no one else—*praise God*—was there.

"Marvin...It's me."

When he picked up the phone and heard her voice, something caught in his throat, and he had to swallow before he spoke. "Oh—hello, sweetheart! I'm glad you're back."

They talked for only two minutes, making plans to meet at the Antelope Tourist Court, where they had been once before. At the end of the conversation he said, "There's no one here, but don't call me at the store again, Abby. I'll call you."

The advantages of the Antelope Tourist Court were that it was away from Cato, but he could still get there in forty minutes; it was cheap (only five dollars); and the old man at the desk asked no questions when Marvin went in to pay. Abby parked at one side of the parking area and waited until he walked to the little room. When she came to the door and knocked, she seemed as excited as he was.

The room was barely furnished, with only a bed, chair, and nightstand. There weren't any table lamps, only a cheap overhead glass fixture that gave the room a glaring light. What did he expect for five dollars?

It didn't matter. They kissed over and over, undressing slowly, admiring each other's bodies as they groped their way to the bed.

In a fit of modesty, Abby wouldn't take everything off, so he made love to her while she was still wearing her slip. She moved sinuously under him, moaning softly the whole time. When the lovemaking was over, she told him how much she'd missed him. He knew that was God's truth, for she'd been as passionate as a man could wish for.

He lit a cigarette, and since there was no headboard, propped himself against the wall. Now, the bed seemed too narrow, and the mattress lumpy. They hadn't bothered to get between the sheets, and the bedspread gave off a stale, musty odor. As they lay together, Abby talked of the things she'd done at home since he'd been there, and of her parents. She said she'd spent most her time reading, except for a two-week summer course in Oklahoma City on teaching arithmetic. She mentioned that the instructor had been a young man. She was no doubt trying to make him jealous.

Marvin tried to think of a subject to bring up outside his own dull life: the store, his dogs, his family. None of these topics seemed suitable. He finally fastened on the war in Europe, and mentioned all the airplane plants opening up in Kansas. But Abby wasn't much interested in the war, so he smoked another cigarette, enjoying the look of her, caressing her body. Her mouth was pink and scraped where his moustache had rubbed, and somehow this excited him, as did the idea of competing with a younger man. They made love again—not bad for an older fellow—and lay naked afterward for a long time.

But finally he said he had to get back. He had used the excuse of the bird dogs again with Liddy, telling her he was taking a look at a dog in Antelope. He thought that was pretty cagy, in case anyone saw him over here. He told Abby that Dan was minding the store, but that he couldn't be gone all evening. Suddenly he felt exhausted, and a bit shaky. He was afraid she would notice. "Are you all right, honey? Not afraid to drive home in the dark, are you?"

He parted the blind to look out. It was almost pitch black.

"No, I'm fine. But when will we see each other again? I don't like always being the one to call."

"Put your number down on a piece of paper, sweetheart, and I'll call you real soon."

Abby's hair had come down during their lovemaking. She sat on the side of the bed and began to arrange it again on top of her head, fastening it with two tortoiseshell combs. She made a lovely picture, with her bare breasts and upraised arms.

All at once she asked, "Do you love me, Marvin?"

He stood in his undershirt and pants, suspenders drooping, looking down at her. Why hadn't he known it was coming?

"Why, sure, honey! How could you doubt it, after what we just did!"

"It's not the same as love; you know that. I don't know why I—you'll *never* leave your wife, will you?"

He put his shirt on, pulled up his suspenders, and began to tie his tie, hands trembling. There wasn't a mirror; there wasn't much of anything in this run-down room. Was he going to have to stand here and make undying declarations of love? The girl was beautiful, but he wasn't going to change his life for her. She didn't know it yet, because he had just decided.

He leaned over and kissed her on the cheek. "I love you, honey, I'll call you." He put on his hat and opened the door, putting one foot outside.

"Better not leave for about fifteen minutes," he said, and left.

O

Liddy had been smart to hire Lola the moment she stepped off the train, but no one could possibly have predicted that it would turn out so well. Putting off her needlework rounds for a couple of days, Liddy stayed around to introduce her to folks, and was discovering that she liked the girl tremendously. Lola was warm and pretty and smart, and she had a wonderful manner with the customers, always upbeat and smiling, ready to kid back if a customer wanted to banter, or to listen if someone wanted to talk in earnest. As people found out about her, the store became a more popular place. There was no question about it—Lola was helping business!

The whole town, not just the Schonbergers, had adopted her before the month was out.

Everybody knew her story and was kind to her. She was their special girl, their lovely, winsome orphan.

Marvin was pleased when Lola appeared in the drugstore every day neatly dressed, the picture of wholesome young womanhood. Any other time, he would have found himself interested in the girl, but there was too much Abby in his head, and besides, Lola treated him like he was ninety years old!

It occurred to him one day as he watched Lola and Dan making syrup together, that Dan was getting a crush on the girl. He didn't know whether she realized it or not, or whether she was encouraging him. He decided not to worry, though. Dan usually managed to muck up most everything, and he would no doubt botch this as well.

As for Cassie, she idolized Lola from the moment she saw her on the train platform. She'd never met anyone like her. And it wasn't just that smile that flashed so suddenly, or her expressive brown eyes, or her tall, curvy figure. Cassie was sure Lola's figure was the reason men came into the store more now, and stayed longer. One day her dad had to ask Perry Hicks, who ran Hicks' Feed & Grain next door, to leave. He'd been looking at magazines and Lola for two hours, and in all that time he'd bought a stamp, a box of cough drops, and asked for change for a quarter. Lola was interested in everyone around her, and her shining intelligence

190

stood out among other, more ordinary girls. Her whole being was that of a light, luminous presence.

But what Liddy told Cassie she admired most of all, what she really *respected*, was Lola's unwillingness to moan about her situation in life.

Dan kept veering away. For a couple of weeks he worked next to the new girl, training her in everything, including the soda fountain. She was a quick learner, grasping everything immediately. She seemed to appreciate his teaching her, but he wished she wasn't so effusive—smiling at him like that. He held himself aloof, refusing to be drawn in. The trouble was, she was like that with everyone. The store started swarming with people of all ages, shapes, and sizes, all wanting to meet the new girl.

Dan thought her friendliness was overdone. Even though his dad wanted his clerks to be polite, she needn't be quite *that* cordial.

In the space of three or four weeks, Lola had more friends in Cato than he did. She made several girlfriends right away, Greta Sundersson and Betsy Byers among them. Cassie wasn't allowed into the older girls' conversations, but she didn't feel left out; rather, she felt lucky just to be allowed to listen in on them. Since Mitch was gone, no one in her family laughed much anymore, and the sound of anybody's laughter was pleasing. Sometimes the girls giggled so much, though, that Marvin would walk slowly up to the front of the store and turn his head in their direction. Greta and Betsy would leave, and Lola would get back to work.

O

Liddy cried bitter tears when she told Marvin that Rowena had confirmed the rumor about Mitch and Grace.

"My son ruined by a married tramp!" she said. "Rowena said Seth Scruggs told Barney, and Barney told Herb Richards that Seth saw the two of them in Mike O'Herlihy's old car out at the Shores. Marvin, I'm never speaking to that woman again, and I don't want you speaking to her either!"

She was so worked up that he agreed to ignore Grace if she ever came in, although he didn't know how he'd do it if she wanted to buy something. What good would it do? But Grace never came in anymore anyway. Neither did Abby. He had to give his son credit, bedding a woman like Grace, even if it was a damn-fool thing to do. The fruit never fell far from the tree, they said.

But I'd never get involved with a married woman, he thought. He'd always believed if Grace wanted to kick up her heels, she'd do it somewhere else. Of course, if people knew what he'd got himself into with Abby, there'd be all kinds of hell to pay! Liddy would divorce him for sure. Then his problems wouldn't just be with his sons. He was going to have to extricate himself pretty soon.

But he didn't want to give her up. His thoughts ping-ponged back and forth: Abby…no Abby. His mind and his feelings ran hot and cold, as if he were a kid again.

A vision from last night aroused him once more: Abby naked with her hair down, embracing him from behind as he sat on the bed getting ready to leave.

O

Dan sat cross-legged, smoking by the Indian grave. It wasn't dark yet; he still had an hour or two of daylight left. He still hadn't told anyone about the Indian, but he was really beginning to want to. His two secrets, the Indian and the old nail curses, hung onto him like weird, suffocating shrouds. It seemed sometimes that he couldn't breathe, they engulfed him so.

Could he trust Cassie? She was just a little kid, so telling her wouldn't really count, and she had proved herself a good scout by not finking on him at the fair. Maybe he'd tell her someday, but not yet.

Next time he came here, maybe he'd smoke a pipe for a change. Maybe he could get hold of a peace pipe—Antelope had a curio shop full of old Indian stuff. He could strip down and rub earth colors all over his body, drink tea made out of roots, and smoke the pipe. But what kind of roots? And weren't you supposed to share the pipe with someone else?

He had come out here today because he was worried. He didn't think he could listen to any more bad news. Years ago he had thought his nail curses had caused Ben Hargraves's mother to get cancer, Mrs. O'Herlihy to get pregnant by the Singer salesman, and Dooky to be held back in school. It was ridiculous, of course, but now *more* awful things were happening.

First Ben got burned in the diner cooking hamburgers. It was a grease fire, and Reuben managed to come back and put it out, but one of Ben's hands was badly injured, and he'd had to have Doc Ledbetter treat and bandage it. Then Dooky's uncle over in Caution got caught in a threshing machine and was killed. But almost the worst thing of all was when little Maureen O'Herlihy got polio. They said they didn't know where she got it, but they'd closed the Cato Shores for a month afterward. She was going for a lot of treatments all the way to the Antelope Hospital, and the doctors said she would walk, but she'd always have to wear a brace.

He knew he should think about all the unfortunate things that happened to everybody else in town, and in the whole world, none of which could possibly be attributed to him. Still, the memory of his poisonous spitefulness lingered. He regretted the devil getting in him that time, causing him to bury the nails and wish evil things on his brother's friends—especially Ben. Ben was a sweet guy. Mitch's friends didn't tease him anymore at all, although Dooky had been rude one day last summer, ordering him around, telling him how he wanted his milkshake mixed for only thirty seconds, as if Dan hadn't been jerking soda since he was nine. Marvin was out, and when Dooky finished his milkshake, slurping it up like a hog at a trough, he insisted that Dan follow him to the back of the store and said he wanted a certain expensive brand of condoms that were "guaranteed." They didn't have that brand.

Dooky! Acting as if he was catnip to women, when everybody knew that the only girls he could get to go out with him were those two slutty Nichols sisters outside Arbuckle.

Now Dooky and Mike—and Mitch—were gone, and Ben Hargraves had grown into a heavy, slightly stooped young man whose normal expression was that of a solemn and wise dog. Although Mitch's age, his face was rough and red with acne, and he wore Coke-bottle-thick glasses, through which he gazed at the world with a kindly nature. He was one of the simple souls, content to work at the Mistletoe Café, where he and his dad, Reuben, ran the place without a woman in sight.

Just yesterday Ben had come in to buy a new accounts book. "What you heard from Mitch lately, Dan?" he asked.

"He's at Randolph Field—you know, in San Antonio?"

"Well, ain't that fine! Bet he's a real good soldier, too!" Ben smiled his puppy-dog smile, tucked the accounts book under his arm, and left.

Dan stood for a moment watching him shuffle through the door. Besides the bandage on his hand, Ben's shirttail was out, and his shoes were run down at the heel. He looked as if he could use some help putting himself together.

"Dan, what's the matter? You look like somebody died!" Lola was at his shoulder, so close he felt her warm breath on his neck.

"*What?* Nothin'." He walked back to the ice-cream carton he'd been working on and resumed scraping it out.

"I can't stand it when my friends are unhappy," she said, smiling as she peered into his face.

"I was just remembering the cave Ben and me and Mitch used to have, that's all."

"There was more than remembering an old cave in your expression!"

So he told her. He knew he'd be sorry, but he told her all about the curse.

He began, "When I was real young I got mad at my brother Mitch and his friends for…a lot of reasons. I'd read about this folk curse you could do, and I wanted to get even. *What did I know?* I was just a dumb little kid. So I got some nails and some well water from old blind Walt Zimmer, and I wrote their names thirteen times each on a piece of paper, and I buried the nails at their houses. Ben was one of 'em. Those curses were for life! And Ben's mother died of cancer not long after that!" He looked away. "And some other stuff happened."

"What? What happened?"

"Just— bad stuff." He had the sense not to tell her he'd thought the O'Herlihys' baby was his fault!

"Walt Zimmer? I've never heard about any old blind man. But you know what you ought to do? You ought to go dig up the nails! It's like they're still in your mind, like *they're* cursing *you!* We'll go out to the country, and we'll do a magic chant and wipe it all away! It'll be a… kind of a *reverse curse!*" She clapped both hands to her mouth, stifling a giggle.

"It isn't funny."

She stopped laughing and put her hand on his shoulder. "I know. But let's do it. We'll do it together. I need some exercise anyway—been eating too much ice cream. Your dad never should have told me I didn't have to pay for it!"

Dan didn't think she'd been eating too much ice cream, and he wished she wouldn't stand so close. "Okay, how about S-Sunday?"

So now he was sitting here with the Indian, thinking it all over, trying to make some sense of it, wondering if he'd done the right thing telling her.

"I swear on your grave, red man, I swear I'll atone for my sins. In the name of the Great Spirit, I renounce my evil ways!"

○

They went Sunday night under cover of darkness. Dan said he didn't want to get shot at.

Both dressed warmly for the cold night. Lola was wearing corduroy pants, a big wool jacket, and a knit cap. Walking along, she was almost as tall as he was. Dan brought a shovel, a flashlight, and a gunnysack. He said that afterward he was going to throw the stuff—nails, jars and all—into Wolf Creek.

The jars at both Ben's and Mike's were in exactly the places he remembered burying them.

At Ben's, with Lola discreetly shining the flashlight on the ground, it took no time at all to find the jar and cover the hole again. Across the street at the O'Herlihys', though, it was another matter. The lights were on and everyone was still up. They could hear roughhousing from the four boys inside, and little Maureen crying, with Mrs. O'Herlihy soothing her. But Lola stood lookout, and Dan managed to finish.

Next they hiked out into the country. It was three miles or so to the Schlanaker farm southwest of town. To keep from being seen by anyone on the road, they walked through plowed fields and thickets of heavy brush. The fields near the Schlanaker farm were bare and stubbly. Lola pulled her cap down over her ears, crossing her arms as she trudged along, her breath turning to mist. There was no sound of birds, only the crackling of brush under their feet and the sounds of small creatures foraging in the night.

"Smell that skunk?" Dan asked.

"Sure do!"

"There's fox around here, too, and possum." The sky had turned a dark cobalt blue, and a nearly full moon hung low in the sky. They came out of the brush, and there was the farm. They ducked under the barbed-wire fence, taking turns holding it for each other, then trudged over the field to the farmhouse, where there were no lights. Although it had been years, Dan found the place he thought he'd buried the nails. He dug for several minutes in the dirt, but the jar wasn't there. It was so dark now, they were operating entirely by the light of the moon. They heard the plaintive wail of a coyote, quickly answered by another.

"I know Dooky's in the service, but do his folks have any other kids?" Lola whispered.

"No. They're kind of elderly."

Finally Dan recalled the exact place he'd buried the nails; he remembered now, it was several yards away from the front porch; he'd been afraid to put them any closer. Lola shone the flashlight on the spot while he stomped the shovel over and over into the packed dirt. He knelt down and pulled out a dirt-encrusted Mason jar.

Suddenly a light went on inside. Without a word, they bolted and ran as fast as they could, Lola carrying the jar and Dan the shovel. They raced across the field, scuttling under the barbed wire and back into the brush, running until they were so winded they couldn't run any more.

Lola was laughing with excitement. At last they sank down on a fallen tree branch. After a minute or so, Dan pulled out a cigarette and offered one to Lola, but she shook her head. He lit up and sat blowing smoke into the darkness.

Lola said, "There! You feel better? Because *I* do!" She pulled off her hood. With her hair floating around her face and her strong high cheekbones, she looked like a beautiful goddess.

Dan reached over and pulled her close. "Yeah, I feel a lot better. How could I have ever done anything so nuts? Maybe I *am* nuts!"

"No, you're not. I think you're very...*fine.*"

Even though it was dark, he could see her eyes shining. They sat drinking in each other in the moonlight. He kissed her three times, pulling her closer each time, his heart pounding like internal thunder with each kiss. It was wonderful, but then she drew back and said, "Now we have to do the reverse curse, and then get rid of all this stuff!"

"I was gonna go throw it in Wolf Creek, right after I take you home."

"Oh, no, I'm going to stay with you until this is over! I brought some things to do the reverse curse with!" She stood up. "I want you to pretend you don't even know me. Close your eyes!"

She waited, then pulled a folded cloth out of her jacket pocket.

"Keep 'em closed!" she ordered. "Now!" Lola stood draped from the top of her head to her hips in a piece of thin white material that looked like surgical gauze.

"I got this from Uncle George's store. Now, put on this ring." She handed him a ring he'd noticed on her hand before. "It's amber, and it was my granny's in Arkansas. Can you see the little insect trapped in there?"

He shook his head.

"It's too dark, but there is one. Granny said amber traps the light of long-vanished days. It's a *magic* ring! Now, close your eyes again. I'm the white witch—a *good* witch—and I've made up a charm to recite."

Dan had begun to chuckle at her tomfoolery.

"Stop laughing—you've got to go along with this! I'm going to knock down the evil eye, the one that put these curses on your friends."

"But *I'm* the person with the curse—*I've* got the evil eye!" he protested.

"Never mind! Just pay attention!"

Dan decided he liked this playful side of Lola. She began to sway from side to side, then to turn around and around, with her arms held out straight. She circled slowly a half-dozen times before she stopped and began to chant:

> *Dooky, Mike, and Ben*
> *Forgive Dan for his sin.*
> *He now renounces all his hate*
> *On you and all your kin!*

Dan laughed out loud. She was *good!*

"How long did it take you to think of that?" he asked, laughing and choking on his cigarette.

"I made it up while I was sitting in church! Isn't that awful? Wait a minute—there's more!"

Lola kissed him, then again stepped a few paces away.

"You have to say the chant; then we're all through, except for throwing everything in the river! Repeat after me!"

Dooky, Mike, and Ben
Forgive Dan for his sin.
He now renounces all his hate
On you and all your kin!

Dan obediently repeated the ridiculous words in a dry, singsong voice.

"Perfect! We're finished!" She took off the gauze, wadded it up, and stuck it back in her coat pocket.

Dan said, "I do feel better. Kiss me some more, it makes me feel like the reverse curse is really working." He put his arms around her, and they tasted each other again, this time exploring with tongues.

She said, "Better stop!"

They hiked back to the bridge over Wolf Creek and threw the jars and nails into the rushing water.

11

For in and out, above, about, below,
'Tis nothing but a Magic Shadow-Show
Played in a Box whose Candle is the Sun,
Round which we Phantom Figures come and go
   —Edward Fitzgerald
   1809–83

It was sometime in late October when old Mr. Farrow died and Mabel came back to bury him. The Red Arrow Mortuary managed to hold him long enough for her to get there on the train. The only people who came to the funeral besides Liddy and Cassie were relatives: Duke Farrow and some other distant kin, who blew in and looked as if they meant to blow right back out again. Duke, standing on one booted foot then the other, seemed happy to leave as soon as the body disappeared below ground. He'd been the one who found the body and made the burial arrangements, and maybe he thought he'd done enough.

At the cemetery, Mabel's big wrists and hands protruded from the sleeves of her dark coat as she held her baby against her. Cassie thought Mabel looked just the same. Her skin was still rough and red, and her eyes still didn't track together. Watching Mabel cry, Cassie recalled how much she'd loved her years ago. Liddy could see that none of the relatives were going to be of much comfort to Mabel, so she invited her to supper. Mabel accepted gladly, and arrived with the baby before suppertime. She had taken a run out to her dad's to see what condition his property was in. Things looked awful, she said.

Cassie asked Mabel twice about Lally, and twice Mabel put her off. "We'll talk about that later, all right, honey?" she said.

Cassie loved playing with the baby. Her name was Lillian Louise, but Mabel said everyone called her Lulu. She had golden curls, fat, rosy cheeks, and a loud chuckle. While the two women visited in the kitchen, Cassie put Lulu on the couch, and the two of them bounced up and down, with Lulu chortling and crowing like a rooster. Once when she fell off, she landed with such a loud thumping noise that Liddy came running in, but Lulu just laughed. Cassie picked her up and planted her back among the cushions, and they settled down and looked at some of Cassie's scrapbooks.

Chatter poured from the kitchen. Liddy sounded like a river that had been dammed up and was suddenly free to flow. She told Mabel all about her needlework ladies, and took her into Mabel's old room and showed her the quilts and other items, including six big floppy dolls Rowena and Flo had created. Mrs. Richards had made them from a pink wool blanket she'd cut up, and Mrs. Schonberger had knitted the hats and shoes and made the gingham dresses. With their yellow-orange yarn hair and freckles, Cassie thought the dolls looked like female Fergus Kleins.

Liddy had asked her if she wanted one for Christmas but she said no, she was too old.

"Mabel, I want to give you one of these dolls for Lulu. Don't argue; it's hers!"

Mabel couldn't speak. She put the doll in Lulu's chubby arms. After that, Liddy brought out snapshots of Mitch in his uniform, and had Mabel read the letter Mitch wrote about missing Mabel's cinnamon rolls. Mabel hadn't cried since she got there, maybe not since the cemetery, but Mitch's letter made her sob a little.

Dan came home, and asked, "Mabel, you like it out there?"

"Yep, Dan, shore do. Them hills is beautiful, 'specially in the spring. The grass starts turnin' in February sometimes, sometimes even Janyary— and it's so *green*! The trees have purty pink and white blossoms, and the winters ain't even cold! Just like here, it's good when it rains— makes it better fer the farmers an' us."

Mabel asked, "I was wondrin' how Buck's folks is doin'."

"They're fine," said Liddy. "I never knew until recently that your mother-in-law was such an expert weaver! Jerusha's making lots of things for me to sell!"

"Wal, I'm goin' to see 'em tomorrah; they's dyin' to see Lulu. But I didn't want to impose on 'em fer a meal—that's why I was glad you ast me over. And when am I gonna see Mister Field? Reckon I'll go by the drugstore tomorrah—gotta see if he's still got the spare tire he swore I gave him!"

Cassie carried Lulu up to her bedroom, and the baby went right to sleep, her cheek puffing out against the pillow, round arms and legs sprawled on the quilt. Mabel came in, and it was then that she and Cassie got to have a talk. They sat on the side of the bed, and Mabel put her arm around Cassie the way she used to.

"Child, I sure don't wanta hafta tell you this, but Lally died. It was in one o' the migrant camps in the Imper'al Valley, the kind Buck and I stayed in fer a couple years, end o' 'thirty-five and 'thirty-six. The childern wasn't taken care of too good in them places...I'm glad we got out. That Verley Hoffman—I didn't like him, but he did try to see to his fam'ly. He got sick and couldn't work, and his wife never was very full o' beans. Their baby was sick fer a long time, too, but I think he's okay now. It pert near killed Josie Hoffman when she lost Lally. She went kinda crazy fer awhile! But I hear they got 'em another chile. It's a boy. Too bad—woulda been good to have another girl." She gazed down at Lulu.

Cassie's wiped her tears away with the back of her hand.

She had planned on seeing Lally again someday. Lally had never seen any of her puppies.

She remembered her in her long dress and straw hat. That was the only thing she'd ever envied Lally, that big hat. Well, that wasn't quite true. She'd been envious, too, of the black-and-white piglets the sow had been nursing that day.

She went to the whatnot shelf in the corner of her room and took down the cornhusk doll Lally had given her, handing it to Mabel, unable to speak. A great sob made her chest heave and her throat close up.

"But what did she die of? She was just *my* age!"

"Honey, like I said, things warn't none too healthy at them pickers' camps. There was lots o' typhoid—an' that's what Lally died of. She lived in a house made outta corrugated cardboard, and I remember whenever it rained that winter of 'thirty-six, the house just went all pulpy. The 'thorities tried to watch over the camps—the Cann'ry Union and the State Emergency folks. And the Cann'ry and Agricultural Workers tried to get the pickers organized to make things better, but whenever some folks'd try to fight fer things, like more doctors—or at least *some* doctors—and 'noculations and such, they'd find theirselves all at once without no steady work.

"Friend o' mine, Oly, he got fired once—his wife Rosy was a good friend o' mine; she did the cookin' o' the beans and macaroni, and I baked all the bread, and whenever we could get some leftover fruit that was goin' soft so they couldn't sell it, I'd make pies. That's how Buck and me got to be better off. They hired me away to the Brawley camp from the Calipatria camp. Buck's one o' the best irrigation men they got now."

Mabel drew herself up. "We got a little cottage, Buck and me, and we mought git to buy it someday. I know yore ma didn't think too much o' Buck way back then, but she'd be s'prised how he's settled down. He's good to me most all o' the time, and he thinks the world o' this young 'un! But Oly, he got up to his elbows in organizin' the cherry pickers, and that was the end o' him and Rosy. They just tossed 'em out in the middle of the night… We never saw 'em again."

Mabel picked up one of Cassie's braids, tightened the rubber band, and put it back on.

"Now, don't you be too sorrowful. Lally wouldn't o' wanted you to. Her and me, we used to talk about you, how you two maundered all 'round the town that Fourth o' July, seein' ever'thang! She tol' me that was the best time she ever had!"

Mabel put the doll on top of a book next to Cassie's bed, stood up, and led her from the room. They went downstairs.

Liddy was in the kitchen drying her hands.

"Miz Field, I feel terrible I didn' help you with them dishes, you bein' so good to me!"

"Mabel, I still owe you lots *more* meals!" said Liddy. "And Cassie and I are comin' out tomorrow to help you clean up your dad's place—no arguments!"

An angry, high-pitched cry was heard from upstairs, and that was the end of the evening.

Mabel looked exhausted anyway. She said the train ride from California had been restful compared to her usual workday, but Liddy said she doubted it had been too relaxing, sitting up two days and nights with a baby.

Mabel brought Lulu down, wrapping her in a blanket. "Cassie, you want any ol' magazines? My dad had three thousan' *Saturday Evenin' Posts* an' *Liberty's*—he never th'ew nothin' away!"

"I don't think so," replied Cassie. She thought for a minute. "But he had a calendar I wouldn't mind havin'. I saw it once—it was the Dionne quintuplets. Could I have that?"

"Lord's sakes! I remember that calendar on the wall—'*course* you can have it!"

Dan came downstairs and gave Mabel a powerful hug. "Goodbye, Mabel."

"I *hate* sayin' good-bye'! I don't *never* say it!" Mabel grabbed Dan around the shoulders and pulled him to her billowy chest. They all walked out with her to the pickup truck, the same one Cassie had ridden in that time they went to Lally's. Mabel tucked Lulu into a drawer which she had wedged onto the floor in front of the seat, and backed out.

The next day Liddy and Cassie went out to the farmhouse. As they drove through the countryside, Cassie again admired the scarecrow on Tom Thatcher's property. He looked jaunty and friendly to her, but maybe he looked just the opposite to the birds.

Mabel's dad's little cabin was rough, but Mabel had put up all the blinds and was raising the dust with a broom. Mabel gave Cassie the Dionne quints calendar right away, and even though it was yellowed and torn, Cassie couldn't wait to take it home. Liddy worked with Mabel for several hours, leaving once to go over to Minna Thatcher's to collect some of her crochet work, while Cassie played with Lulu on the screened porch. When they left, Mabel declined another invitation to supper. She said she wanted to get everything done, and that she had to get back to California.

They never saw Mabel again. She came by the drugstore the next morning, but Lola was the only one there, and she said Mabel was in a rush to catch the 10:05 going west. Lola quoted her saying, "Tell Mr. Field I'm sorry I didn't get to see 'im, and tell Miz Field I hate sayin' good-bye. I thought I'd lost all my mem'ries of Cato like beads off'n a string, but they all come right back while I was here!"

Homer Botsin said Mabel had only the suitcase she'd arrived with, a large box tied with rope, a rag doll, and Lulu. He said she gave him a big grin and asked, since he could get himself a discount, why didn't he come out to California on the Santa Fe like everybody else?

Cassie had pining thoughts about Mabel and Lally. She wished Mabel had said good-bye, but Liddy explained that it was hard to leave friends, and maybe it was especially hard for Mabel, since she was going so far away. Cassie tried to imagine Lally dead, and couldn't, so she tried to stop thinking about her. Instead, she concentrated on some special assignments for Miss Gallagher, who wasn't even her teacher this year but who continued to ask her for stories.

And at last *The Wizard of Oz* was coming to town! That was enough to take her mind off Lally and everything else.

O

Only two lightbulbs lit up the Cato Theater's marquee and the wooden letters displayed there, but bright lights weren't necessary, because Cassie was drawn as a tiny moth to a candle. Although she had planned to see the show with Fiona, when she saw the marquee she couldn't wait. She and her dad were the only ones at the drugstore the night it opened. They had first stopped at the Mistletoe for chili, and while she ate and her dad chatted with Reuben, Cassie read some of Reuben's spattered old placards. The one next to the cash register was from Will Rogers:

THE COUNTRY IS PROSPEROUS AS A WHOLE.
BUT HOW MUCH PROSPERITY IS THERE IN A HOLE?

Reuben had never remarried after losing his wife years ago, and some of the signs poked fun at women and marriage:

NOTHING SCARES A WOMAN AS MUCH AS LARYNGITIS.

MARRIAGE IS A LOTTERY, BUT YOU CAN'T
TEAR UP YOUR TICKET WHEN YOU LOSE.

Besides the chili Cassie ordered some raisin bread pudding, and Reuben gave her free malted milk balls for dessert.

After supper, Daddy gave her a dime and let her go alone to the movie.

Now she sat, with a medium-size crowd, in the darkened theater, impatiently watching previews and news clips. *The Lone Ranger* was coming soon, and *The Movietone News* showed a film clip of Ginger Rogers having her handprints put in wet cement at Grauman's Chinese Theater. The newsreel about the funny-looking man in Germany giving salutes and riding around in open cars with his uniformed staff was finally over, too.

Cassie squirmed in her seat, and at last the feature began. The MGM lion came on, growling, with the words *ARS GRATIA ARTS*. Cassie didn't know what it meant, but it didn't matter—the lion and his roar heralded a good time. She felt gypped when the movie opened with Dorothy and Toto running down the road, because the color was a dull brown. The sign had said *Technicolor!* But when Dorothy and Toto were in Oz, and gorgeous bright colors filled the screen, the theater filled with 'oohs' and 'ahs'! Dorothy told Toto she didn't think they were in Kansas anymore, and Cassie knew what she meant; she'd been to Kansas once, and it was just like Oklahoma.

The movie was full of fantastic things Cassie had never seen before, like the funny voices that came out of the Munchkins' mouths, and the Wicked Witch with her green and orange smoke, and the flying monkeys who looked like scary bellhops from a fancy hotel, and especially the Wizard's sorcery, which was amazing. Then, when Dorothy whirled back to Kansas and woke up, the Scarecrow, the Tin Man, and the Lion turned out to be Uncle Henry's hired men. Dorothy said, "I'm never going to leave here ever again, because I love you all and—oh! Auntie Em! There's no place like home!"

Then it was over.

Cassie floated out of the theater and across the street. Her father was waiting for her, and on the way home she asked him if he'd ever been in a tornado. He said he hadn't, but that he'd seen some terrible windstorms right here in Cato.

"Daddy, you should see *The Wizard of Oz*—it was *wonderful!* Would you like to go with me and Fiona?"

"No, honey, have to work."

Something about his voice made her look at him. He looked tired.

Going to sleep was really hard because of all the colors left over from the movie and swirling through Cassie's brain.

Her favorite character was Dorothy. She was the one who told everyone (except the witch) what to do! She knew enough to take Toto out of danger, and she knew how to take care of her friends. Of course, they took care of *her* when they carried her out of the field of poppies and when they rescued her from the wicked witch's castle.

When Cassie had heard the movie was coming, she had checked the book out of the school library. The book had a lot of things that weren't in the movie, like the Hammerheads, the Quadlings, and Boq, the rich Munchkin; also the Kalidahs, the pack of wolves, and the jolly little clown.

The movie was different from the book in lots of ways. Why did they change the Silver Slippers to the Ruby Slippers? That was easy—because red looked better in Technicolor!

But the clowning of the Cowardly Lion and the dancing of the Scarecrow were wonderful! The Tin Man's dancing, which sounded like all the milk cans in the world falling down, made up for all the word jokes in the book. If she had to choose, she would probably choose the movie. It had made her laugh, and when the Scarecrow said good-bye to Dorothy, it had made her cry.

Just before she dropped off to sleep, a revelation came: *The characters in the Wizard of Oz were like her own family.* Auntie Em reminded her of Liddy, when she stayed home building things and digging in the earth. She would put her hair back in a knot and throw on an old dress and awful shoes, and she'd put on that harsh expression just like Aunt Em's. The Cowardly Lion reminded her of Dan! Dan used to bully her. He didn't do it anymore, but she remembered. If she told Daddy, he would back off—until they were alone again. That was a *sure* sign of a coward.

Why was he like that? Grandmother McIvor had told her once she thought it was because Daddy whipped him so much. But Daddy had whipped Mitch, and Mitch wasn't a bully. Except Mitch teased Dan, which sometimes was the same thing. There was that one time, though, when Dan was brave—when he went out to Walt Zimmer's to get the well water so he could put the hex on Mike and Dooky and Ben. Dan liked to talk to her, and he shared things with her. Sometimes he acted like he needed her, and once he'd brought her a wild rabbit from one of his hikes, but the dogs ate it.

In one way the Scarecrow reminded her of Mitch. Mitch didn't think he had any brains, either, Daddy was always telling him he didn't. But the Scarecrow wasn't the least bit handsome, and Mitch was.

She didn't know who the Tin Man reminded her of. Her father? The Tin Man wanted a heart. She didn't think her father needed a heart, but maybe her brothers thought he did.

Cassie thrashed about under the covers. What about herself?

Was she like Dorothy? Dorothy was courageous. She knew when danger threatened; that was why she ran away—to protect Toto. She was always telling off people who needed it—Miss Gulch and the Wizard and the Lion. She was stubborn and opinionated. Cassie didn't think she was anything like Dorothy.

Finally her thoughts began to run down. She yawned and stretched her legs under the covers, feeling the sides of the bed with her toes. She couldn't think of anyone the wicked witch reminded her of, unless it was Winifred Weston. They had the same crabby look, the same hard black hair and long nose. All Mrs. Weston needed was the orange smoke.

She turned over in bed, feeling the softness of the pillow against her face,

The Wizard tried to help everyone, no matter how much of a fake he was. Who did she know who was like that? He gave everyone what they wanted, or some version of it, and he was even going to take Dorothy back to Kansas. It wasn't *his* fault Toto jumped out of the balloon! Of all the people in the movie, she decided, she would prefer to be like the Wizard. He got to hand out all that advice.

When Cassie finally went to sleep, she dreamed about Lally Hoffman. But Lally wasn't Lally, she was Fiona, and she wasn't dead. The dream started out in black-and-white, and Lally was living in Cato again, only with Fiona's parents. The Bannisters had a farm instead of a dry-cleaner's, so Lally-Fiona was a farm girl with pigs. She was standing near her windmill, and Cassie was way up in the sky floating above her. Then the dream changed to Technicolor, and suddenly all three of them—Lally and Fiona and Cassie— were floating in the sky. They were throwing the spotted pigs malted milk balls and chunks of raisin bread pudding with huge black raisins, then the pigs changed into puppies with black and white spots, just like the puppies Sadie had years ago.

Cassie's stomach dropped about a mile, and she made it to the bathroom in time to throw up. After that she felt better, but not good. She woke up Liddy, who mixed some bicarbonate of soda and brought it to her in bed. When Liddy asked what she'd eaten that evening, Cassie told about the chili and the raisin bread pudding, but she left out the malted milk balls.

12

Amazing grace, how sweet the sound
That saved a wretch like me
I once was lost, but now am found
Was blind, but now I see
—Rev. John Newton
Olney Hymns, 1779

As Cassie scrubbed on her knees in the vestibule of the church, a bucket of hot soapy water beside her and the sleeves of an old red sweater rolled up, her body rocked with religious fervor.

She sensed that she was caught up in something greater than herself and, scraping the dirt and mud out of the grooves in the wood floor, felt on the brink of some new knowledge of God.

Liddy came into the vestibule with a bunch of colorful fall branches, her tweed coat belted tightly around her waist. The day had brought rain. Cassie looked up, and went back to scrubbing. From the expression on her mother's face, you'd think she'd never seen her work before. "Where's Mrs. Weston?" Liddy asked.

Cassie dipped the brush in the bucket of water. "She's showin' Alice how to polish the lights by the altar."

The First Methodist Church was in debt, having oversubscribed for Reverend Brook's raise in salary, a new water heater for the parsonage, and Alvin Jonas's scholarship to the theological seminary. Mrs. Weston was chairman of the Revival Committee, and as usual she'd been telling everyone how to run things. She had even hired the revival preacher, Reverend Garret Alexander of Fort Worth, whose name she obtained from the Bishops' Board, and the revival was starting tomorrow and would last for one week.

Cassie was wary of Winifred Weston and usually stayed out of her way, but now that they were working together toward this important event, she followed her every direction. Cassie hadn't forgotten that day Mrs. Weston had chided her for whistling—which she was just learning! The bad end Mrs. Weston had warned about hadn't happened. Cassie wasn't sure she knew what a bad end was, but she hadn't given up whistling. She'd noticed that whenever Mr. and Mrs. Weston came into church,

Floyd Weston had a hangdog look. He would slink to his pew as if he neither wanted nor deserved to be there, and Mrs. Weston's eyes would dart around checking on everyone, as if she were a one-woman sin committee.

As Liddy walked down the aisle with her branches, Mrs. Weston nodded. There was something about the wary way the two women approached each other that made Alice, who was standing on a rickety ladder with a jar of glass cleaner and a rag in her hand, stop to watch.

"Oh, hello! Your daughter has been a gem. She and Alice are still working!"

"Yes, they're little marvels." Liddy didn't mention that Cassie worked best for an audience.

"Have you met Reverend Alexander yet?"

"No, he hasn't arrived," said Winifred. "I expect we'll just have to wait until the service tomorrow morning, like everyone else."

"Here are the branches I said I'd bring." Liddy laid them on a pew and started to leave, but Mrs. Weston detained her.

"I've been hearing about your sewing women. Congratulations!"

"Thank you."

"Personally, I always buy my linens and bed coverings at Sultan's in Enid; they have such lovely things." Liddy started back up the aisle, but there was more. "I feel that your time has been so...well, *taken up* lately, with all the driving around you do, that lately you haven't had time for *church* activities." Beaming a counterfeit smile, Winifred put one hand at the top of her chest, patting it with the other. Liddy wondered whether she was trying to get her circulation going or was giving herself a massage.

"I've been available for every single thing anyone has asked me to do, Winifred, and quite a few more. If you'll recall, I took care of all the publicity for this revival. And I've been telling everyone about it—my sewing ladies, and *everyone*."

"Is Mr. Field going to be attending?"

"No. Is Mr. Weston?"

"Uh—no, Floyd's crew has to do all those cattle inoculations next week."

"If Cassie's through, I'll take her home with me."

"Oh, just one moment." Mrs. Weston raised a finger in the air. "Let me check to see if she's done everything I told her to do. She's *so* conscientious!" They walked back up the aisle to where Cassie stood admiring the damp floor, a brush in one hand and the bucket in the other. "Cassie, did you get those fingerprints off the wall over there? Oh, I see you did! What did I tell you! She's a little dynamo!"

"Certainly is. Cassie, let's go. Go get Alice."

O

Sunday morning at breakfast Cassie said, "*You* should come to the revival, Daddy!"

But he wasn't much for religion. She remembered once the two of them were looking at the stars on a hot summer night. This was something they did if she was still awake when Marvin got home. Lying on cots in the backyard, they would gaze together at the black vault of sky shot through with a million blazing pinpricks. One night she shared her new theory with him. "I'm pretty sure Jesus's disciples *live* up there on the stars, aren't you, Daddy? Peter lives on that one and Matthew lives over there, and—"

"Where you gettin' these ideas? No, nothing like that. Stars and planets, that's real; that's science. Someday you'll study it in school. But Jesus and his disciples, well, that's something your mother believes in. Personally I think it's a lot of horse…just a way to get folks to abide by the rules. It isn't for me."

They stayed together on the cot, looking at the stars until she felt him carrying her up to bed.

Now he lowered his paper over his plate of eggs. "No, thanks. I got enough religion at all those old-time tent meetin's your mother used to drag me to."

"You went to *revivals?*" Cassie could scarcely believe it.

"Nobody could live in Oklahoma all these years without gettin' an earful o' that Billy Sunday—all hellfire, and sinners plungin' around in bloody fountains!" Marvin took a big sip of coffee and let the cup clink loudly back into the saucer.

"Now, Marvin," Liddy reproached, "you know we need to get the word out. The Baptists have been making all kinds of converts lately, and we've just been sittin' here!"

"Fiona's a *hardshell* Baptist," interjected Cassie.

"What's wrong with lettin' the Baptists have their way?" insisted Marvin. "You do less harm than when you go and get everybody riled up with one of these hellfire-and-brimstone preachers!"

"Winifred Weston says he isn't hellfire and brimstone; he's a very highly educated young minister who's had training at the seminary at Fort Worth." Liddy brushed furiously at a few crumbs on the tablecloth.

"Doesn't matter where they train 'em; if he's comin' here he's gonna be using every way known to God and man to get people down to that altar, get 'em on the church rolls, and then get money out of 'em. And don't tell me that's not what you're doin'! And don't let that straight-stick Winifred Weston tell me either!"

"What is the use of trying to be civil to you on a Sunday morning! You're just so loaded down with guilt you can't see the truth!" Startled, Marvin looked at her for signs that she knew something, but Liddy prattled on. "This is for the good of the souls of the people of Cato! You should see the way your daughter's been working!"

"I *been* seein' her up and down the street with that scrawny Purvis girl, passin' out flyers! I was ashamed it was my daughter, if you want to know the truth! Might just as well be the patent medicine man's daughter, beatin' the bushes to stir up trade while he sells snake oil off the back of the wagon!"

Liddy glared at him. "Cassie, let's go; we'll worry about these dishes later! Let's go to church now. Just ignore your father!" They marched away from the breakfast table, righteous and united in their battle against the heathen in their midst. Cassie glanced back at her dad, who seemed quite happy to be left alone with his newspaper and cigarette. He was probably going to burn in hell.

O

From the first moment he was seen sitting on the podium until he drove out of town almost a week later, the visiting revival preacher gave full measure. He was handsome, blond, and blue-eyed, and he exuded purity leavened with an ingratiating suavity. The congregation was used to Reverend Brooks's mousy brown suits and somber neckwear, so when they saw the young minister in his dark blue sharkskin suit, white silk shirt, and shiny patterned tie, they sat up straight. As Mrs. Philips finished playing her rollicking organ solo, "The Little Brown Church in the Vale," the young stranger rose to speak.

Silence settled over the room.

For a full minute, the only sound was the occasional creaking of a pew, but finally he began.

The voice that poured out, filling the church, was a trained, deep baritone, and the cadences were the measured and hypnotic rhythms of old-time revivalism.

There was no resisting it.

"Friends, may I repeat to you the Scriptures your minister has just read? John 11:25 and 26:

"Jesus said unto her 'I am the resurrection, and the life; he that believeth in me, though he were dead yet shall he live. And whosoever liveth and believeth in me shall never die. Believest thou this?

And I would add Romans 3: 24 and 25:

"Being justified freely by his grace through the redemption that is in Christ Jesus, whom God hath set forth to be a propitiation through faith in his blood:

"My friends, I am here today to ask you, do you *believe?* The souls within this bright and shining church—*you*"—and here he raised his hand and pointed out into the congregation—"*you must come to Jesus Christ, reconsecrated, resanctified, saved by the blood of Jesus Almighty, Son of God!* You must rededicate yourselves to him. Rededicate your bodies, rededicate your minds, and, *yes! ladies and gentlemen, boys and girls*"—and here, it seemed to Cassie, he looked directly at her—"*you must rededicate your souls!*"

By the end of the service Cassie's heart was overflowing.

She got saved the next night. The minister hit his themes hard: blood, sacrifice, sin, redemption! Jesus died on the cross—*for you!* Cassie was sobbing when he gave the call to the altar, and she when she walked down the aisle there was a whole lineup of crying and sobbing females kneeling next to her: Fernie May Applebaum, Eula Tully, and Ernestine, Esther, and Alice Purvis. Cassie was squeezed between Eula and Alice, and Eula's cheap perfume and billows of freshly permanented hair made it hard to breathe. Liddy always said Eula had lazy manners, relaxed morals, and the IQ of a pleasant day in April, but, casting her personal opinion aside, she had put pressure on her to come to the revival. Now here she was, being saved!

The next night when the minister put out the call to the altar, Liddy and Violet Shafer went down. Mrs. Shafer was a convert from the Assembly of God, but Mrs. Schonberger and Lola went to the First Christian and wouldn't switch. Liddy said Rowena Richards was a hold-out for agnosticism. Did that mean she believed in ghosts? Cassie wasn't sure.

Liddy had told her sewing ladies about the revival, but the Kleins always went to the First Christian. Minna and Tom Thatcher were here, though, and so was Jerusha Corkle. Right after Reverend Alexander laid his hands on Jerusha in a blessing, she lifted up her head and started babbling in some kind of crazy language. It went on and on for a long time, her voice getting louder and more eerie-sounding by the minute.

"Fladina...faldina—guggle—GUGGLE...galomay, gallom—y, WHAhappuna Whoo-ooo—eee—ZOO-eee! Shoo—OH! Lord—am—y Soul!" Only it went on a lot longer than that, and Jerusha's mouth was foaming with saliva the whole time.

It reminded Cassie of the witch's incantation in the *Wizard of Oz* book: "Ep-pe, pep-pe, kak-ke! Hil-lo, hol-lo, hel-lo! Ziz-zy, zuz-zy, zik!"

The minister looked somewhere else, evidently embarassed, but the congregation was spellbound. Finally Liddy led Jerusha back to her seat, trying to shush her. She didn't quiet down though, so Ezra took her away. On the way home, Liddy said, "They speak in tongues a lot over in Arkansas. I guess that's where Jerusha picked it up."

"I thought Jesus made her get carried away like that!"

At breakfast Wednesday morning, Cassie blurted out the news of her salvation to her dad, but she had to do it through the newspaper he held in front of his face. When he finally put the paper down, she told him about Liddy's, too, but she didn't mention Jerusha's babbling.

Marvin let the newspaper drop. He said he'd be damned if he knew whether he and Dan could live with all these holy Methodists, and that the two of them might have to go out on a drunken binge in order to make up for it. Dan laughed out loud, but Liddy didn't crack a smile.

Cassie soon found out that there was a catch to being saved; in fact, there were several. You had to take a pledge not to work on Sundays, dance, drink liquor, play cards, or go to the picture show. It was this last proviso which stuck in her craw.

She studied her mother's face the night Reverend Alexander mentioned the card playing. Until then, Liddy had been vigorously nodding, especially on the liquor part, but when he said cards were the work of the devil and you could never approach the throne of God with a card in your hand, whether it was a poker card, a pinochle card, or a bridge card, Liddy's expression changed.

Reverend Alexander said the ace of spades was the symbol of the devil, the queen of spades was the symbol of the devil's mistress, and all the other kings and queens and jacks of all the other suits were the devil's slaves and handmaids. *The jokers were the ace of spades's number one deputies!* He said that in European countries, cards were a plot by the royalty to let loose the devil among poor people and sap the strength of the commoners.

Over breakfast on Thursday, Cassie related to her dad all about how playing cards was a sin, and he said in his whole life he'd never heard such unadulterated balderdash.

Since she'd been saved right away, she could relax and study the crowd. It seemed to grow every night, mostly with women. She watched Mrs. Weston, who never once went down to be saved. She probably felt that in her case it would be unnecessary, since she was perfect already. But you could tell she was moved by Reverend Alexander. She sat listening to him, with her face all soft and her eyes misted over. Every now and then she would lower her head and stare at her lap, as if afraid to show too much Christian feeling.

○

There was to be a covered-dish supper at the Brookses' parsonage before the last service on Friday night, so after school on Friday Cassie baked a devil's food cake, the only thing she knew how to make. Liddy was taking lima bean surprise.

Mrs. Weston was already there. "Won't you come in?" she trilled as she met them at the door. Over her ruby silk dress she wore a see-through black apron with a red bow on the pocket, the one she'd bought at the needlework bazaar. On her head was a shiny gold hat encrusted with little fake rubies and diamonds. Liddy thought she looked like she was going to the opera.

"Evening, Winifred," said Liddy. "My, you look…" She didn't finish the sentence.

"*Elegant?*" supplied Winifred. "Well, I thought this was such an important occasion!"

Their regular minister's wife, Drucilla Brooks, smiled at Cassie. Mrs. Brooks was dressed plain as a Quaker. The thing Cassie liked best about Mrs. Brooks was her smile, as if she knew something funny about the world but she was never going to reveal it.

"I brought these tablecloths from home," said Mrs. Weston, leading them into the dining room. "They fit the tables better than Drucilla's. Put your food anywhere, Liddy. Cassie, what do you have in that big box?"

"It's a cake."

"Oh, how nice. Just take it in the kitchen, will you?" Just then Reverend Alexander came into the room, and Mrs. Weston sent Cassie on her way with a little shove.

Evidently the preacher had been staying at the parsonage all this week. Cassie hadn't thought about his sleeping anywhere; if she'd thought about it at all, she'd have supposed that he went into some other dimension until time to appear before them again on the podium. Several ladies were clustered in the kitchen, and after finding a place for her cake, she dawdled, gazing at all the food. The ladies were whispering, and it was hard to hear.

"...not really from Fort Worth—from Alabama, I think."

"Oh, is that it? I didn't *think* no Texan talked like that."

"He was engaged last year but had to break it off—his fiancey was from a rich family from Dallas, and she wanted to keep on livin' rich."

How did they hear all these juicy tidbits? Her mother sure wasn't in the know. She loitered near the refrigerator, toying with the chrome handle.

"He told Miz Weston, when she had him and Preacher Brooks an' Drucilla fer supper."

"How do you s'pose he wears such fancy clothes on a minister's salary?"

"Dunno, but he sure looks dashin.' Cassie, don't you think you better go on out with your mama?"

It was crowded in the front parlor. Suddenly Reverend Alexander entered, spreading his arms wide. For his very last appearance he was wearing the dark blue suit he had sported the first time they saw him.

His hair was slicked back, and his blue eyes sparkled. Cassie noticed his cologne, as he moved around the room like an adagio dancer.

"Ladies! Ladies and gentlemen! How nice of you to arrange this get-together. I know how you'all been cooking, and I can't wait to sample your handiwork."

They bowed their heads while he gave a long, flowery prayer of thanks; then he led the way to the dining room table, crowded with casseroles, salads, and breads. With a flourish of his gold cufflinks, he took a plate and began to serve himself. Alice, Delores, Hermie Brooks and Cassie were the only children, and Mrs. Brooks told them they could eat in the room off the kitchen. The girls sat on an old cot, balancing their plates in their laps, and Hermie sat on a large carton printed on the side with "Paper Fans, Red Arrow Mortuary, Perpetual and Permanent Interment."

They went back into the dining room to get dessert. Cassie didn't mention that the low, lopsided chocolate cake was hers. She noticed that Alice and Delores gravitated to the high fluffy-iced ones, but Hermie took a big piece of Cassie's and ate every bit.

It was at that moment that Cassie decided to use the bathroom. Mrs. Weston was standing in the hall, close to Reverend Alexander. She was speaking in a low, urgent voice, with her hand on his arm. Her body was tensed forward, mouth pulled grotesquely to one side. Cassie hadn't seen such raw pain on anyone's face since the time she kicked Dan in the shin.

"But, Garrett, dear, you could do so much more good work if you stayed another week! Look at all the souls you've saved here in just five days! Can't you—wouldn't you be able to change your schedule?"

The minister edged away, and her trembling hand fell off his arm. "Oh, no, ma'am, that's been set since last January. I'm afraid I have to be in Amarillo tomorrow."

"I was going to offer you our farm for a few days' rest. We have a comfortable guest bedroom…" Her voice trailed off. The scene reminded Cassie of *Jezebel*, when Bette Davis, like a sick cow, pleaded with Henry Fonda to marry her. She was sure any minute Mrs. Weston was going to get down on her knees just like Bette had.

By now Cassie had to pee really, really badly and was trying not to put her hand in her crotch.

Suddenly the preacher became aware that someone was listening. He turned to Cassie, standing a few feet away. "Young Miss Field!" He took two steps toward her. "Don't forget your promises to the Lord. I know you're going to make an excellent little shepherdess in His pastures. Study your Scriptures and mind the Commandments, and your life will be a shining light to others. You can make it so!"

Cassie stared up into his eyes, which were as blue as Aunt Bertha's aquamarine ring.

Alice Purvis came from the parlor and stopped as she saw the three of them. Mrs. Weston left the hallway, her shoulders rigid, the ruffles of the black apron hanging unevenly across her bony backside, and Reverend Alexander disappeared through a doorway.

"What was the matter with *her*? Looked like she was goin' to bawl!" said Alice.

"She wanted the rev'ren' to stay and keep on savin' souls, but he said he had to move on."

The last night of the revival was the most rousing of all. Everyone who had been saved was there (except for Jerusha), their souls cleansed, and faces shining. Eight new female recruits for the Lord came down the aisle: five from Red Arrow, two from Cato, and one from Caution. While Mrs. Philips played "Onward, Christian Soldiers" on the organ, moving her shoulders and her arms up, down and sideways as if she were operating a pinball machine, they had the offertory. Reverend Brooks handed out pledge cards with suggested amounts for pledging. (Tithing was strongly recommended.) In the blank after "I promise to pledge," Cassie checked "Yes," but she put a question mark for the amount.

Cassie looked all around but didn't see Mrs. Weston, and on the way home Liddy asked if Cassie knew what happened to her.

"She was tryin' to get Rev'ren' Alexander to stay another week. Alice said she was almost *cryin'*." Liddy didn't respond, so Cassie added, "Maybe Mrs. Weston wanted to get saved, but she couldn't work herself up to it in just a week. You think that was it?"

Her mother's face showed the hint of a smile. She said, "Mmm-*hmmm*, something like that."

In a few weeks the revival became an emotional but fading memory. November changed the trees to even more beautiful colors than October's. The rains started coming with the winds, then the leaves all blew away.

13

To be in on a secret is no blessing.
—Leo Rosten,
Treasury of Jewish Quotations

As the holidays approached, and Liddy's needlecraft business prospered, she spent more and more hours driving around on the rutted country roads. To save on gas, she tried to get the women to bring their things to her when they came into town to shop, or have the husbands bring them, but there were still pickup and delivery trips to the shops in Red Arrow and Antelope. She hadn't been to Enid or Oklahoma City yet, although the shop in Enid sounded like a wonderful possibility.

Seth Scruggs filled the tank one frigid November morning as she started out on one of her twice-weekly journeys. The women usually had cups of tea and homemade cake for her to munch on while she admired their sewing and chatted. Occasionally she had no time to talk, would simply dash to the door and take the things, hand over the payment, and leave, but she really didn't like to grab and run. As she had discovered when she worked for the WPA, there was more than sewing involved here. Hadn't she, too, started doing this partly out of loneliness —the loneliness of the housewife? And the rural housewife was loneliest of all.

The Corkle farm lay southwest of town, across the road and not far from the Kleins'. She turned into the Corkles' long driveway. Jerusha always seemed to need to talk. She wanted to complain about Ezra. Ezra spent most of his time in town on the bank steps, except when he was fiddling for a country dance somewhere. As far as Liddy knew, he had never worked, just whittled and fiddled, and many times the Corkles didn't have enough to eat.

"I shore drove my ducks to a pore puddle!" said Jerusha often. She said it had been easier when Buck lived with them, because he would occasionally drive cattle or work in the wheat harvest. Jerusha never mentioned Harley, so Liddy didn't, either, although she knew that raising the feeble-minded boy had to be an extra burden.

This morning, to cheer her Liddy said, "That Lulu is a corker! My, Jerusha, you have a beautiful granddaughter!"

Jerusha's wizened face beamed, the missing teeth more than evident. Then her face fell, and she said, "Don' know's we'll ever see that chile again."

Liddy handed Jerusha twenty-five dollars in cash. "You better open an account at the Cato Mortgage and Loan—you're getting rich!"

"I'll think about it, Miz Field."

Liddy apologized for being in a hurry, and rushed back to the car. Her own marriage was in such a weak state that she felt unqualified to advise Jerusha on hers. She and Marvin had had another fight, which wouldn't have been so bad except that Cassie heard the whole thing. She'd had a flat tire out near the Thatchers' farm and had to use their phone to call Seth Scruggs to come fix it. She was late getting home, so there wasn't any supper. Marvin was sitting at the table, looking impatient, and Cassie was doing her homework nearby.

When she asked him if he could go downtown for dinner, you would think she had asked him to shoe a running horse. "I've been out on the road all day," she said. "And I'm making money! I've made a hundred and thirty-seven dollars this year!"

"You *better* be makin' some money, because you're not doin' *me* any good with all this travelin' around! I been working hard all day, too! The only thing I ask you to do is get three meals a day, and you can't even take time to do that! What happened to all that religion you were expoundin' just a few weeks ago? Doesn't the Bible say to honor your husband?"

"I've been making three meals a day for twenty-two years! Don't I get any time off for good behavior?"

He swiveled toward her, mustache bristling. "That's what *I'd* like—time off! And I just might arrange to have some!"

Liddy spat out the words. "You can start right now. You can move into Mabel's bedroom."

She wheeled toward the spare room to move the sewing things, but Marvin shot out of his chair and thrust ahead of her. He picked up an armload of quilts and crocheted blankets and threw them at her. "If I'm goin' to sleep here, then get rid of all this crap!" He threw three more armloads into the hall before he stopped, out of breath, then left the house.

She cried after him, "Those things are precious! They're worth a *lot*!" She bent down to retrieve and refold everything.

O

Now the two of them were like ships that passed in the night. It seemed as though everything between them had gotten worse since she started her business. He didn't admire her for what she was doing, when everyone else did! What she was most afraid of was that he didn't think about her at all. She would have liked him to give her a pat on the behind, the way he used to. He was self-centered; that was it. He was a self-indulgent, self-absorbed man who thought only of his own happiness.

She missed Mitch with all her heart and soul, and worried about him endlessly. War was coming, and what would happen then? His last letter had been cheerful, talking mostly about San Antonio. She had read in the paper that they were turning out pilots by the hundreds down at Kelly and Brooks and Randolph Field, but thank God Mitch didn't want to be a pilot; he said he was going to attend airplane mechanics school at Chanute Field, in Illinois. Airplanes were frightening machines—she would *never* go up in one! She planned to write him tonight, no matter how tired she was, because the sooner she wrote, the sooner he'd write back.

She'd never talked to him about Grace. Liddy was sure that would blow over as soon as he met a young girl, but he was still too young to get serious about women, anyway.

She and Marvin were going to have to pay some attention to Dan. He was always going off on long hikes, and every time she asked him about school, he gave her a vacant look, then muttered something that sounded made up. Marvin, in a rare sociable mood at breakfast yesterday, had told her Dan was getting stuck on Lola. Liddy didn't see anything wrong with that; Lola was a lovely girl and would no doubt be a good influence.

She pulled onto the road going toward the county seat. At least there was one place she was appreciated: at the Home Arts & Crafts shop in Red Arrow. As she turned left from the Corkle farm, she saw Crazy Penny get down from a truck on the other side of the road. She watched in her rearview mirror as Penny lumbered, in her loose and loping gait, back toward Cato. Usually trucks let her off right on Main, but Penny must have been babbling so much the driver forgot to stop.

Please let her be gone by the time Cassie gets out of school, Liddy prayed.

O

Liddy's prayer went unanswered, and when Cassie was reading the funnies the following rainy Sunday, she was reminded of something Crazy Penny had said. That Sunday Liddy had a cold and didn't go to church, and for once she let Cassie stay home too. Cassie was sprawled on the rug while Liddy read the paper, alternately coughing and blowing her nose.

Little Orphan Annie was once again trying to leave the orphanage. Cassie owned a ceramic mug with Annie's picture on it, and sometimes she wore a big Annie pin with round, blank eyes and curly red hair. Dorothy in *The Wizard of Oz* had been an orphan, but she lived with her aunt Em and uncle Henry.

"Mama, what's an orphanage?" Cassie asked.

Liddy lowered the paper, looking blank at first. "That's where all the unwanted babies are kept."

"Why doesn't anyone want 'em? What about their own folks—why don't *they* want them?"

"Um-m," said Liddy, "sometimes the parents have died. Or they just don't want to raise the babies. They aren't married, or something like that."

"You mean you can have babies without being *married*?"

"I'm reading, Cassie. Why don't you draw a picture of Little Orphan Annie, and put in her dog."

Cassie knew she wouldn't be able to get anything more out of her.

Lately she had come to realize that there was a dimension to the relationship between the sexes other than love, hate, and exasperation. Certain ideas, and glimpses of ideas, had begun to reveal themselves to her, and she felt she was on the edge of unraveling the secret that, for a long time, had been beyond her grasp. She knew that this mysterious something seemed to have its effect on everyone, but no one would tell her what it was. No one spoke about it—no one was *proud* of it! It was something to be covered up, to turn red in the face about, like Mitch had that time he and Grace Sampson had met in the post office. Cassie had been thinking about Mitch that day as she crossed Main, about how she hadn't seen him for so long, and how she missed him. She had gone to pick up a package of medicine, but the postmaster's window wasn't open yet, so she had to wait. And there came Mitch, walking in to mail a letter. She ran over and gave him a hug, rubbing her face against his old corduroy jacket. She loved his smell, a combination of shaving lotion and the outdoors.

It was then that Grace Sampson came in. Grace smiled at both of them and mailed a letter, and after she left, Mitch's face turned crimson. He stood reading the Wanted notices on the post office wall, and finally, after awhile, he left.

Cassie was still waiting for Mr. Richards's window to open when Mrs. Billings and Mrs. Weston came in together and stood whispering just inside the door. Cassie heard "old" and "young" and "Isn't it a shame!" and "out at their ranch!"

This relationship between men and women, this whatchamacallit, was connected with love, but it *wasn't* love. She thought it was probably more like hugging real hard, a sort of intense squeezing—something you *did*. She was pretty sure it had to do with how babies got started.

Fiona had told her something about it. The baby part no one was ashamed of—everybody showed off their kids, whether it was Mabel with Lulu, or Sadie with her litter, or anybody in town with small children: the Kleins, Sheriff Bartlett, the O'Herlihys. The O'Herlihys must do a lot of squeezing and hugging, because they had Mike, Sean, Brian, Colin, Seamus, and Maureen.

The Bannisters were even proud of Aura Lee, Fiona's little sister, who was a pain in the behind. And Reverend and Mrs. Dickens had two kids, so *they* must have done whatchamacallit.

And what about her own parents! She didn't want to think about it.

Could one person want to whatchamacallit with someone and the other person not want to?

Yes! You saw it in the movies all the time, like the time Bette Davis got down on her knees to Henry Fonda. Except she wanted him to marry her, even though she'd made that big mistake and worn the red dress when she should have worn white.

It was possible, then, that only one person, not both, would get the feeling that led to the rest. Then there wouldn't be any rubbing or hugging at all, and the person who had wanted to do it would be left standing in the dust.

She had seen the dogs climbing one another and staying that way for what seemed like hours, although the reason for their being in that position remained obscure. But she wouldn't ask her father about it, not if you tied her in the blazing sun and let red ants crawl over her face. That time she'd asked him why he was always separating Tizzy from the male dogs just because she was in heat, he got mad and made her go to her room. When Cassie had a temperature, she might have to go to bed, but she sure didn't get locked in her room! Poor little Tizzy.

If only her mother would tell her something! But Liddy was too prudish to give her even a few basic hints.

Her mother's modesty about her own body was extreme. Once when the meter man had come to the back door, her mother leaped off the couch as if she'd been shot out of a cannon. And when Cassie asked why she'd bolted up like that, Liddy said, "You don't want a strange man to see me sprawled out on the sofa, do you?" Cassie didn't know. In the first place, he wasn't strange, just Clink Kerry reading the gas meter. And in the second place, it seemed as if she had made much too big a fuss. Clink Kerry wouldn't have cared if her mother was standing on her head in the corner stacking BBs.

If whatchamacallit was how people got babies, then her mother had done it, and everyone else had, too, and they were all a bunch of hypocrites pretending they hadn't!

Once, before her mother started selling sewing stuff and was working at the store, she had allowed an infinitesimal crack of light to shine in. Sheriff Bartlett's younger brother Jim, new to Cato and newly married, came in. Jim was learning to manage the icehouse. At six feet six and a half, he was even taller than the sheriff.

"Hi, Jim!" said Liddy. She was cleaning the display counters with a bottle of cleaner and a rag.

"Howdy, Miz Field. I was wond'rin' if you've got a box o' chocolates fer Peggy. It's our six-month annivers'ry today." Jim grinned, sticking both hands in his back pockets.

"Why, sure do. How's about these cherry chocolates here?" Liddy brought out the box, which had a photograph of a half-bitten chocolate oozing out of itself on the lid.

"That'd be fine."

He handed over a dollar, and Liddy rang up the sale and gave him his change. "You want it wrapped? Cassie'll do it for you. Might make it more romantic."

Jim turned the color of the cherry on the box. "No thanks, ma'am, I think she'll like it fine thisaway." He hurried out, his big shoulders filling the door as he left.

Liddy went back to wiping the counter, and Cassie went back to her spelling notebook. Her cogitations were interrupted by the sound of muffled giggling from Liddy. She looked up. Her mother was rubbing hard on the glass, and her shoulders were shaking.

"What's the matter?"

"I was just thinking what a long, tall drink o' water that young man is, and Peggy such a little bit of a thing. Wonder how they *manage*!"

Cassie stared straight ahead, her eyes locked on some lettering her dad had painted on the mirror behind the fountain: "STRAWBERRY SUNDAY — 15¢. " She couldn't believe her mother might be talking to her about whatchamacallit. She waited for her to explain, since asking directly would be futile. Like the time she'd asked her what Kotex was for, Liddy had said it was for wounds and abrasions, and Cassie knew that wasn't right; otherwise, why was it always wrapped in a plain brown wrapper, and why, when Marvin sold it to a woman customer, did they always stop chatting and look like some kind of terrible news had struck?

From what Liddy had just let slip, Cassie gathered that whatchamacallit was a size thing. A size *comparison* thing.

But size comparison of what? She remembered Dooky's proud exhibition of his sticking-out thing when she was five. She had learned what it looked like from Dooky, and its name, a year or so later, from Amos Hicks. Amos called it a "jules." He said that his dad called it "family jules" but he just called it a jules. Amos had freckles all over his face and arms and legs, but he didn't have any there. When Amos stood under the elm tree holding his jules outside his dusty shorts, Cassie had run home.

Someday she would tell someone about Dooky and Amos and ask some direct questions— though she was pretty sure Liddy wouldn't talk about it. Cassie's brain felt worn out from going around and around, with so few facts to go on. She wondered if Fiona knew more than she did. She didn't think so, because just last week Fiona had said something about her aunt buying a baby from an orphanage. At least *she* knew more than that! You couldn't buy babies, and you sure couldn't buy them from an orphanage!

When Crazy Penny came to town, Cassie learned more than she had in nine years from her mother. She loved to eavesdrop on Penny on Main Street, although you could hardly call it eavesdropping, because when Crazy Penny talked, you couldn't hear anything else. She would almost always end up on the bank steps, where she could easily collect an audience of town loafers, and the bank steps were right next to the drugstore. Crazy Penny would stand there, tall and gangly, with her hacked-off straw-colored hair, wearing a torn and tacky dress.

She would yell out to the men, "I'm wearin' my new berzier today—see?" and she'd thrust out her chest and pull down her blouse so they could see her red or purple or white brassiere. Her big teeth would shine in a crazy smile, and her dark eyebrows would bob up and down like window shades.

Or she might ask, "Didja know I'm goin' to git me a baby?" She was obsessed with this subject. "I'm lookin' to git me a daddy for 'im!" She would wave around a couple of dollars, "I brung all my money to spend today! Gonna git me some o' them hair ribbons at Schonberger's!"

"Whar you gonna wear them ribbons, Penny, on yer underwear?" The men didn't like her to veer too far off the subject. Another would join in. "Hey, Penny, you got any new B.V.D.'s?" Penny would obligingly begin a discussion of slips or panties or sanitary belts, but soon Marvin or Liddy would come out and say, "Penny, come in here and stop entertaining everyone in town. Come in here and we'll give you a Coke."

Penny's parents had moved her out of town to live with her maiden aunt in Slapout, but every few weeks she'd hitch a ride down to Cato. Upon arriving in town, she would visit her elderly parents just long enough to upset them; then she would drop by the high school until the principal chased her away. Finally she'd come down to Main. Crazy Penny wasn't bad enough to be institutionalized, though she'd once been put away for six months, but she was outrageous enough to have to be put in the care of her Christian aunt.

Liddy was the one who always tacked the word "Christian" onto Miss Durmond's name—"that Christian Miss Durmond." She said if Miss

Durmond could put up with Penny, she was the absolute personification of the teachings of Christ.

Once Cassie had seen Penny outside the grocery conversing loudly with Clyde Spokes, Mayor Scruggs, and Stuffy Byers—all respected citizens, who were not above having a laugh at Penny's expense.

"My sweetie's the schoolteacher up in that country school!" she was saying. "I wanted to go thar and learn my tables, but he said I had to stay home with my aunt. We're goin' to git married—less'n I find me somebody today! Mayor Scruggs, where's yer son Seth—is he over thar at the gas station? He useta like to wrassle me, but I could allays pin 'im down! Then he'd git on top!"

Penny, euphoric at the attention of the men, walked away waggling her hips lewdly from side to side and smiling back over her shoulder. Cassie, crossing the street at a snail's pace, heard Mr. Byers and Mr. Spokes guffawing at the mayor's expense.

Just last Friday, Penny was into conversation with a crowd of bank-step loafers when Cassie and Fiona, returning from school, came upon her.

The girls heard, "Hey, Penny, how'd you git down here today—ridin' the turnip truck?"

"Nah, that truck driver didn't have no turnips; he had a whole bunch o' fresh corn. An' he was *so-o-o* nice." She nodded her head up and down to emphasize this.

"What'd you talk about, yore garters?"

"Uh-huh. An' he liked 'em, too! We stopped by the side of the road once't so's I could show 'im!" Penny spread her legs and hiked up her skirt to show a torn, ruffled petticoat and two black garters topping her raddled stockings.

Where did she get all these items of clothing? Cassie wondered—and was this scenario true? Or was Penny just an actress, anxious to please her audience?

"You sure there wasn't no turnips on 'at truck, Penny?"

"Yep, I am. I'm only crazy when the wind's blowin' from the south, and I know turnips from corn, and it was corn."

She loomed in front of the two girls near the vacant lot next to the drugstore.

"Howdy, girls!"

She was wearing a skirt which wasn't properly fastened, so that it slid down her hips toward the ground, and a tight red taffeta blouse with a pocket half torn off. Blood-red lipstick was smeared around her mouth. "Didja hear the news? I'm gonna git married to my teacher fella! See this ring?" She held up her hand and waved it around in the air. "He got it outta th' gumball machine!"

"Really? Tell us about it!" said Cassie. She wished Crazy Penny wouldn't yell so loud—at any moment her dad might come out to put a stop to the conversation.

"We're gonna do it as soon's he gits the money together. I'm savin' my money. I got four dollars already!"

Cassie and Fiona looked at each other and giggled.

"You girls laughin', but it's true. O' course I already *had* 'im a time or two. One night he took his out, then he said you take out yers, so I did. We was goin' along like a butter churn makin' butter, and it was nice! It was better'n that time those kids had me walkin' that water wheel out to the Shores when there weren't no water in the pond. You ever done that? You girls should try some o' them things!"

The girls giggled and drew closer, Crazy Penny vigorously nodding her head up and down.

Soon her movements became even jerkier and more exaggerated. She rummaged through the big pouch she carried, fingers twitching. She looked up at the sky and all around, her head bobbing like a string puppet's. Cassie wondered if she might suddenly do something dangerous — lash out at them, or hurt herself in some way.

"I got me a baby from it, but the church ladies took it away. It was like in a dream. They was all these women around, my mother and my aunt and some others, and a awful smell o' somethin'—I don' know what, on a piece o' cotton, and then they took it. I warn't all the way asleep, so I could see it was a real cute little baby. They wouldn't tell me was it a boy or a girl. I can still hear it cryin'."

She sat down on the sidewalk bordering the vacant lot and began to weep, her legs stretching down into the weeds. She looked up at the girls as if beseeching them for help, tears running down her face, while sobs convulsed her body.

Marvin appeared around the side of the drugstore. "Cassie! Fiona! Penny—*you get on outta here*! You better tell your aunt to keep you at home for a while. Go on, now! You get on back to Slapout!"

Penny lumbered to her feet and hurried away. Seeing her father's angry face, Cassie persuaded Fiona they should skip their usual candy bars and go directly to Fiona's folks' Dry Cleaners, which had a little room in back where they could pretend to study. They had a lot of new information to sort out.

O

It was the day Jim Bartlett came in to buy the candied cherries that the revelation came to Cassie. Liddy had finished cleaning the display cases in front and was starting on the ones in back. Cassie stood up, stretched, and put her spelling notebook where she would remember to take it home. She walked to the magazine rack at the front of the store to get a movie magazine, her reward to herself for finishing her homework. As she reached for the magazine, it suddenly dawned on her: *Crazy Penny's baby must be in an orphanage!* She stood stock-still, amazed that she hadn't realized it before. She wondered if Penny had thought of going there to look for her baby. She remembered the look of anguish on Penny's face. Why did people like Penny have to endure pain like that? Why didn't God arrange things better and make it so that *no* one suffered, especially not crazy, innocent people like Penny!

She stood gazing out at a tumbleweed blowing straight down the middle of the street. She couldn't wait to tell Fiona where she thought Crazy Penny's baby might be. If it really was at the orphanage, Fiona's aunt might want to go get it. It was a relief to finally know one thing for sure about whatchamacallit—you didn't have to be married to get a baby.

She'd just have to keep working at it. Cassie was pretty sure she and Fiona still didn't know everything, even after they'd found that picture of a butter churn.

O

Drop your pennies, drop them one by one!
Drop your pennies, see what God hath done!

Collecting the offering for the entire Sunday school was the duty of the Sunday School monitor, chosen by the teachers of all the classes,

229

primary to sixth grade. For more than a year, Cassie had been their choice to do the collecting. Cassie suspected that it was because the teachers liked her mother, but she wasn't sure. She would place the quarters, dimes, nickels, and pennies in a special collection box with a lid, trudge upstairs with the box, and hand it to the head usher, Mr. Cutter.

But one Sunday something went wrong. Cassie collected the money, made her way upstairs, and handed it over, but when she got back to her classroom, Winifred Weston, principal of the Sunday School, stood in the doorway.

"I found this in back, Cassie, near the coloring books, full of your classmates' collection money." She shook the can, and it made a loud clanking noise. All the kids were watching. "Why didn't you put this in with the other money?" she said, glowering down.

Cassie tried to think why, but she couldn't. She knew she'd been eager to get out of class that morning. The lesson was about Joshua and the battle of Jericho, and she had practically skipped out of the room. But she couldn't admit this to Mrs. Weston. How *did* the can get near the coloring books?

"I guess I forgot," she said.

"That, young lady, is simply not a good enough excuse! We will have to report this."

Greta Sundersson, only a few years older than Cassie, was her teacher. She put her arm around Cassie's shoulders. "Mrs. Weston, she does a good job. This one time—"

But Mrs. Weston took her to Reverend Brooks's study before the church service. Holding the child by the arm, she said, "As *I* see it, Reverend, there is dishonesty involved!"

"This was simply a matter of a child's forgetfulness, Winifred," he said, turning away to fasten his black robe. "I don't want to hear it mentioned again. And I especially don't want the child's mother told," he said, pinning the woman with his eyes.

Later, Cassie thought about telling Liddy herself. Her mother was always saying the preacher needed to stand up 'like a man' to Mrs. Weston, and this time he had. But she didn't tell, because Liddy might get mad at her too.

After that, Cassie didn't want to be the collection monitor any more. She told Greta, and the teachers picked Ernestine Purvis. She didn't want to be in the same room with Mrs. Weston ever again, either, but there wasn't anything she could do about that.

She couldn't understand why Mrs. Weston was so mean. She hadn't even waited to hear Cassie's reason for forgetting—not that there was one. The woman couldn't be angry because she'd witnessed that scene with Reverend Alexander, could she? Liddy didn't like Mrs. Weston, either, and Cassie knew why. It came from the time Mrs. Weston said Daddy kissed Mrs. Scruggs.

O

It started raining on Thanksgiving Day and didn't stop until Saturday.

Liddy was making herself a skirt out of an old pair of Marvin's trousers, and Marvin had packed up the dogs and guns and left early Friday morning to meet Joe Kelly, which was why Liddy was so grouchy. Cassie had heard them arguing, her mom saying she wasn't going to open the store, that it would just have to sit there locked up.

Cassie put on her overalls and a heavy fleece pullover that had belonged to Mitch. Tucking it inside the overalls and rolling up the sleeves, she started out the door, but her mother yelled at her that she'd better wear galoshes and a raincoat, so she went back up to her room and looked in her closet. She wouldn't have worn the ugly rubber raincoat for anything, so she went into Dan's room and put on a pair of his boots. They were way too big, but they made her feel as if she was embarking on an adventure.

She managed to get out of the house without further interference. Trudging toward town, she spied Fergus Klein sitting on the steps of the First Christian. His mother was inside at a meeting of the Ladies' Guild, he said, the ladies were making another quilt. He looked bored.

"Where you goin', Cassie?"

"Nowhere special. Whatchu doin'?"

"Nothin'. Let's us go down to the river and catch crawdads."

Cassie hesitated. She didn't exactly know what crawdads were, but she'd heard of them. She wasn't supposed to go near the river, although her brothers had played there since they were little boys. She had never understood what could go wrong for her at the river that couldn't go wrong for them. This could be a chance to find out.

"Okay, let's go."

Fergus ran inside to tell his mom, and was back in twenty seconds. His everyday wear was overalls, and today he wore a red wool shirt tucked inside. His high-topped work boots looked as if they couldn't come to a worse fate than they already had, and his uncombed orange hair stuck out all over his head.

Cassie was pleased to see that her outfit looked a lot like Fergus's. She hadn't combed her hair today, either, just tied her two pigtails together in back with a plaid shoelace.

They trudged in the direction of Wolf Creek.

"How come you don't have to help on the farm today?"

"Daddy said I could come to town. I been workin' hard—we got a new litter o' pigs, and I been bein' mom and dad to 'em—their own ma don't like 'em much."

They hiked through brown winter grass, then scrub and leafless woods, until they reached Wolf Creek Bridge, with Fergus leading the way. Sliding down the bank, they reached the wet sand that bordered the river on both sides. Cassie had never seen the water so high, but she had never seen it this close, either. It rushed and bubbled and gurgled, loud and purposeful on its way to meet the bigger stream of the Canadian River.

"Down this way—that's where I seen a whole bunch o' crawdads last Saturday! Look, Cassie—see 'em?" The shallow pool, cut off from the river and enclosed by a jam of logs and flood-caught brush, indeed held a bounty of crayfish. The children knelt and watched the things crawling forward and swimming backward. They were about four inches long, and a muddy gray-brown color. They were all legs and shell and antennae, with funny-looking eyes sticking up on tiny stalks. There must have been two hundred or so.

"How do ya catch 'em?" asked Cassie.

"I've kinda forgot. I think we need some buckets. I can run back to town real fast. Didja know whenever you boil 'em they turn red? Bright red!"

"How's come?"

"Dunno."

Cassie stood gazing at the curious creatures, then dropped to her knees to study them more closely.

232

"I'll go to the fillin' station for some 'quipment. Or I'll go see Clink Kerry—he sells fishin' worms and crawdads for bait next door to the fillin' station. I'll be back lickety-whoop!" He left in a flash of arms and overalled legs.

Cassie was pretty sure Liddy wouldn't let her cook any of these animals at home; the only kind of fish her mother sanctioned was catfish. But she would catch the crawdads and figure out what to do with them later.

She watched them prowl around in the shallows and climb over one another for several minutes; then, bored, she stood and began to follow the bank of the rushing stream. By now the knees of her overalls were soaked, and so were her boots. Breathing deeply, she decided that since she'd never been here before, she would explore the creek side. It certainly didn't seem dangerous or threatening in any way. Just treading on the hard, wet sand was a liberating experience.

It felt good. It felt *free*.

Suddenly such a feeling of elation overwhelmed Cassie that she could hardly breathe. She was Cassie—*Cassie!* Here, *now*, walking along! She felt as if, at any moment, she might rise up and float away.

She turned and looked back the way she had come. The stream wound along in a gentle curve, but she could still see the bridge, with its weathered cross-beams and piers, a quarter mile or so around the bend. Across the creek, about fifty yards away, was a stand of tall, bare cottonwoods, and next to them a clump of smaller trees that still sported a few orange leaves.

Striding along, she saw a pair of rabbits move in the brush up above the bank, but she heard no birds. Had they deserted the area for the winter? Then she heard an unfamiliar noise. It was not a sound of nature, not the wind in the trees and not the sound of the river.

It was a human voice, a woman's voice, moaning.

She sounded hurt. Cassie turned her head in the direction of the sound. It was coming from the riverbank a few yards away, up a little road, barely more than a path, which she would not have suspected was even there. The path lay between some tall brown weeds and soggy-looking grass. With a strange foreboding, as if she were deviating from all that was right and proper in her life, she turned from the river. The path was lined with catclaw and tall, dry jimsonweeds with their thorny gourds, its surface covered in blueweed and yellow-berried nightshade. She followed it up the embankment, as the sound of rushing water grew fainter. She walked quickly, her boots making no sound on the wet, sandy track, as the moaning continued, growing louder.

Suddenly she came upon a blue sedan parked on the little path. Startled, she moved toward the car with the hurt woman inside, hoping to be of some use, possibly save a life. She peered through the steamed-up windows.

A man and a woman were writhing together in the backseat, their clothing partially on but mostly off. Cassie stared at the man's bare buttocks, which seemed whiter than any skin she had ever seen. Enthralled, she stood for an immeasurable moment.

Suddenly the man saw her and, with a cry like a sick calf, pulled away from the woman.

It was Mr. Weston. But the woman wasn't Mrs. Weston, and she wasn't hurt. She looked in perfect health, except that she was almost naked. Staring at Cassie as if she were a creature from another planet, Eula Tully raised a hand and brushed away a damp strand of hair.

Cassie didn't remember walking back to the crawdad pond.

Fergus was there with two pails, a dip net, and a pair of men's work gloves he'd gotten from Clink. The clan warning had been sent out, and now there were only fifty or so of the crustaceans left, busily propelling themselves backward all around the muddy pond, their fanlike tails roughing up the shallow water. The others had evidently found hiding places elsewhere— mudholes to slide into or rocks to crawl under.

"I'm gonna grab 'em behind their claws like Mr. Kerry says to," said Fergus, "then throw 'em in the buckets. Or if that don't work, he says for me to shoo 'em your way and you catch 'em in this net, then we'll dump 'em in the buckets."

Cassie took the net, and they both stepped into the pond. Fergus got nipped several times through the gloves, but after fifteen minutes they had a dozen or so crawdads scooting around in the bottom of the buckets. The net was by no means a perfect solution, because the crawdads' jointed legs and pincers got caught in it and then had to be disentangled and picked out.

Growing bold, Cassie tried to pick up one of the creatures and was rewarded with a painful nip. "Ow!" she yelled, but she managed to get it into the bucket with only a slightly bloodied finger. Fergus gave her the gloves, and she managed to maneuver seven or eight more in her pail, getting pinched two more times in the process. It hurt even through the gloves, and by now she was shivering with cold.

It was hard to concentrate because she kept thinking about the strange scene she had witnessed on the riverbank. Imagine, Mr. Weston and Eula together! Him married to someone else, and the two of them buck naked in the back of a car!

While she was grappling with one of the prickly crawdads, her foot slipped. At that precise moment, the creek swelled, and a small tide of water engulfed her. Flailing out with her arms, she tried to regain her footing and not only lost the crawdad she was holding but slid under the water. It was a while before she could come up for air, and she floated there for a moment, sputtering.

Fergus put down his bucket and came over. "You okay?"

"Yeah, I just…" She spat out a mouthful of creek water and managed to get to her feet. Her pulse was racing and she was gasping for breath. She remembered when she had almost drowned on the day of the picnic, and she felt like she had then. She was very cold, and her teeth began to chatter.

"Can't you swim?" Fergus asked. "My granddaddy taught me in our big water tank on the farm."

"Sure. I took lessons."

"Well," said Fergus, "you better take you some more."

Shivering with cold and wet, she thought of asking his opinion of the thing she had seen, even leading him there and showing him the car. She almost said, "Did you know that married folks sometimes get nekkid with people they aren't married to, and squirm around with 'em like…like *crawdads?*"

But then she'd have to say who it was, and something kept her from telling. She decided she wouldn't tell anyone for a while—maybe ever. She shouldn't have come to the river today, and she shouldn't have gone up on the bank, and she *sure* shouldn't have looked in that car! If her parents ever heard that she'd seen those two and what they were doing, she'd be more of a prisoner than ever!

When they had caught two dozen or so crawdads, they decided to call it a day. Cassie, still shaking with the cold, carried her bucket, and Fergus carried the net and the other bucket. They trudged back through the pasture and the patch of woods, then climbed the little hill they had slid down. When they got near the church, Cassie said, "Here, Fergus, you can have mine." She held out the bucket.

"You sure? They're real good to eat."

"Uh-huh. I'd like to watch 'em turn red, but my mom'd prob'ly make me throw 'em out."

Fergus's mother was waiting on the steps. All the other church ladies were gone. Mrs. Klein had gotten plumper since that time she'd nursed Timmy in the drugstore, but she was still fair-haired and pretty. All she said was, "You kids are a mess. I was through here half an hour ago." But she seemed happy to get the crawdads.

As Cassie walked home, her hands felt frozen from carrying the metal pail. Mitch's pullover was clammy and stuck to her chest, and her feet slipped and sloshed in Dan's boots. Her mother was lying in wait. Cassie took off her boots in the kitchen and set them on the newspapers she had laid out, taking care to keep her bloody finger out of sight.

"Cassie, where exactly have you been?"

"Just playin' with Fergus in that little stream near the gas station."

Liddy stood with her hands on her hips. "Your clothes are a mess, and you're sopping wet. Go get in a tub of hot water. You know I don't like you playing around town with boys. I'll have to speak to your father about it."

Cassie didn't like being bawled out for being with Fergus, who was as nice as any girl she knew. As she started up to her room, Liddy's nagging voice followed her up the stairs.

"I don't want you ever, ever, *ever* going down to Wolf Creek. Do you understand? You better not have been there today! People have *drowned* down there, and you can't swim well at all!

"And, Cassie, I've *told* you and *told* you—I don't care if you *are* just nine! You have to watch your reputation in a small town. People will start to talk over the slightest thing!"

○

Quail season had opened in October, and Joe Kelly wanted Marvin to drive over to the hunting camp where he and Marvin had their annual outing, running their dogs and shooting quail and pheasant. Because of the upcoming Christmas season, Kress's busiest time, Joe couldn't go any later than the last week in November.

But as the four-day Thanksgiving vacation approached, Abby started trying to get Marvin to drive down to Watonga. She knew it would be too risky for him to drive her there, and she had a car of her own anyway, an old Pontiac—but she wanted him to meet her. They were both tiring of the tourist court.

Abby was made of much finer stuff than that, he knew. She was a beautiful, cultured woman, and plunking her down and making love to her in one of those cheap rooms was like setting a diamond in pig iron.

Abby had been mentioning diamonds. She wanted to know if Liddy had a diamond ring, and when he said he'd gotten her a small one wholesale when they married, Abby turned her head on the pillow and looked at him. He knew what was in her look, and he'd changed the subject.

Marvin had to choose, and he chose Joe Kelly and the hunting camp. He didn't get that many chances to be outdoors anymore, stuck in the goddamn store all the time.

He knew she would probably break off the affair now. Maybe that was what he wanted.

14

The world is not necessarily just. Being good often does not
pay off and there is no compensation for misfortune.

—Unknown

Dan had started to feel that Lola was his girl. There was no reason
why he shouldn't feel that way. Their bodies brushed against one another
at the store, and they had little meetings at school between classes; all
the guys saw them and were envious. She was always smiling at him!
She hadn't asked for her amber ring back, which he kept in a corner of
his underwear drawer.

Everything was going fine until the day the Red Arrow football team
beat Cato, and the out-of-town team came into the drugstore. Marvin
wasn't there, and the football players got rowdy. When Lola went by
the quarterback's table, he pulled her apron string so hard her apron fell
off. Dan couldn't believe it when Lola simply laughed and tied it back
on. As she walked behind the fountain with a tray of dirty glasses, Dan
said, "How come you let him *do* that!"

"Do what?"

Dan threw a copper mug into the sink, where it made a loud clank.

"You and Cassie can finish up. I'm leavin'!" he said, and stalked out
of the store.

O

Cassie missed the slap and casino games she and Fiona used to play
before she signed the pledge at the revival, but movies were the hardest
part. Luckily, she had already seen *The Wizard of Oz*, but she had to miss
Babes in Arms, which Fiona said had Mickey Rooney and Judy Garland
dancing with about a thousand other dancers in the last scene.

It was going to be really hard, she knew, when *Gone with the Wind*
came to Red Arrow in December. It had been getting publicity for a year
now, as had the book two years before. Even Liddy bought it. Except for
a Bible concordance in 1933, it was the only book she'd ever bought.

Cassie read *Gone with the Wind*, too, leaving out the battles and the
slow parts, such as the collapse of the South.

Cassie started working on Liddy to give up their no-movies pledge. "Mama, can't we go see *Gone with the Wind*? You play cards!" she couldn't help adding in an accusing tone.

Liddy equivocated. "They were talking about gambling. We never gamble."

"I bet Mrs. Weston would say you're startin' to backslide."

"I don't live my life to please Winifred Weston," Liddy replied testily. "She's just a bitter, mean-spirited troublemaker, with nothing better to do than judge people."

"Okay, then, if we don't care what she thinks, let's us go see *Gone with the Wind*."

A few days later, Liddy went to Rowena's for the monthly bridge game. During the game, Flo said she'd fixed up her old sewing room with organdy curtains and a flowered bedspread, and that Lola slept there now.

Liddy said, "I had a sewing room, Mabel's old room downstairs, where I was storing all the ladies' sewing things, but Marvin's moved in there now." When only silence greeted her comment, she continued, "He's got a sore back, and he's so restless it keeps me awake. Besides, he snores. I don't miss that." No one said a word. Flo and Rowena wouldn't look at her. But Violet jumped in and said, "When Phil was alive I couldn't stand his snorin'. Sometimes I'd tape his mouth shut, and he wouldn't even wake up!"

O

Abby cried and cried, blowing her nose on his handkerchief and stuffing it under the pillow, then taking it out again with each fresh burst of emotion. "The school board wants me fired!" she sobbed. "Do you know how horrible that is? What will the other teachers say! And my parents! Just last year, I got a commendation for the way my kids were testing!"

Marvin didn't know what to say.

Through her tears, Abby stammered that she was going home until she could find another position. "I *love* teaching! Someone's found out about us!"

He was thinking the same thing. Someone on the school board had heard something, and maybe it was all over town! This was what he'd been most afraid of. No, it wasn't. The thing he'd been most afraid of was that *Liddy* would find out. He and Abby hadn't met in weeks, and on this freezing night in December they lay propped against the pillows on the bed. The room seemed even more miserly than the one they usually had. Thankfully the small lamp lit only a small space near the bed; the overhead fixture was too glaring to use. The management must be trying to skimp on heat, too; the room was cold.

Abby wore her slip, and he was in his underwear. He had his arm around her shoulders and was soothing her as well as he knew how, but he wasn't very good at it. Hating himself for his weakness, he felt an immense sense of relief. Abby would leave town, and he could get on with his life. The affair had become way too important. Abby was lovely, but she needed to find someone to marry her, because he wasn't going to. His prowess wasn't what it had been, either. He had come through tonight, but last time he'd been a dismal failure.

He lit up a cigarette and stared at the wall.

Abby blew her nose again, then got off the bed and walked to the window. She pulled the blind to one side and gazed out. Suddenly she turned. "I hate this room! Marvin, how come you've never taken me anywhere but here? It's so ugly!" Her tears started up again, and he got up and put his arms around her, cradling her head on his shoulder. Where did she think he could take her—New York? San Francisco? He didn't have that kind of money. He didn't have *any* money.

"If you loved me, you'd figure out how to make things nicer. We wouldn't have to be so furtive!" Her face became suddenly contorted, and all at once she put her hands on his chest and shoved him, hard. He fell back on the bed. Standing over him in her slip, she had the same look Liddy had when she was angry.

"I gave myself to you, and it's like I was *nothing*! I'll leave Cato, and your life will go exactly on the same!"

He was silent. There was nothing more to say, because she had summed it up very well.

O

As the year drew to a close, Cassie heard of changes about to occur.

Grace Sampson was moving away; there were rumors of a divorce from Hal. And Miss Gallagher was reported to be leaving after the first of the year.

Cassie heard Liddy and Mrs. Richards discussing these things, and when her mother said the names, there was always a funny inflection in her voice. She didn't seem to be upset about Miss Gallagher leaving, but Cassie was.

Why was everyone always deserting her? Mabel—Lally—and now Miss Gallagher! Always the people she loved. Miss Gallagher wasn't her teacher this year, but that didn't mean she didn't still love her.

Just before school closed for Christmas vacation, Cassie went back to the fourth-grade room carrying a combination Christmas and going-away card decorated with holly and berries. She had worked on it the evening before. Miss Gallagher pulled her over to her desk and planted a kiss on her forehead, which left a shiny red mark from her lipstick. Cassie saw it afterward when she went to the girls' room.

O

On Christmas Eve, Dan and Pauly were dropping Sean off. The three of them had been driving around for a couple of hours, smoking and joking. They were in Pauly's folks' car, and just to be funny Dan yelled, "Happy Easter!" to Sean when he was almost inside his house. Then they turned the corner by the water tower, and there was his dad.

Marvin didn't see them. Abby Gallagher was standing on her half-lit porch at the top of the steps, and Marvin was going down the steps with his shoulders hunched and his head stuck down in his overcoat collar, as if no one would recognize him that way. Even in the half-dark, the boys could see how unhappy Miss Gallagher looked. She was wearing a kind of kimono, and her hand was stretched way out in the air. Dan would never forget the sight.

Pauly turned the corner, and Dan couldn't see any more. He didn't *want* to see any more. He said, "Please don't tell anyone. You're my friend." And Pauly said, "'Course not."

That was the end of the subject between the two boys. But not between Dan and his dad.

O

The ornament-covered tree was a nice balance to Grandmother Field's gold brocade sofa at the other end of the room. The tree looked cheerful and smelled delicious. Cassie had sent Mitch some fudge, and she'd knitted Dan a green muffler on her knitting machine. Her mother told her Mrs. Schonberger had offered to teach her how to knit with needles, but Cassie preferred the machine. She'd ordered it from an ad in *Ladies' Home Journal* for $1.98 plus tax.

Cassie went to bed early, knowing that good things would happen in the morning. Dan would get a radio, and she would get the bicycle that she'd mentioned numerous times to her folks. Fiona had one; even Alice Purvis had one. Mitch had owned one, but now it belonged to Dan.

Dan was off somewhere with Pauly, and her dad was keeping the store open late, even though Liddy had tried to talk him out of it. She said the same thing every year: who would want to buy anything after eight o'clock on Christmas Eve?

Cassie had a hard time going to sleep. Much later, she heard her dad come up the stairs and go into her mother's bedroom. Their voices got so quiet she couldn't hear, and she finally dozed off. In a half-conscious state she heard the phone ring downstairs, and her dad's voice speaking and pausing, speaking and pausing, for a long time. Then it was quiet again. She had just gone to sleep when angry voices from Liddy's bedroom woke her. She heard the words "...says it's a sure thing!" from her dad.

"But we've only got three hundred and fifty dollars in the bank now!"

"I happen to know you've got almost two hundred dollars. I saw your bank book."

"You looked in my *bank book?*" Her mother's voice shook with anger. "You had no right to do that! That's my hard-earned money, and you've no cause to even *think* about using it!"

Cassie got up, tiptoed down the hall, and stood outside the door. This could affect the bicycle.

Liddy's voice went on: "Men have invested in oil fields and drilling equipment all over this state and come up dry. What makes you think you and Joe Kelly could ever hit it big?"

"Joe has all kinds of connections with drillin'—men who've made a fortune. All he wants is five hundred dollars from me—*he's* puttin' in a thousand!"

"Let him! I'm not going to let you throw *our* money away on any crazy wildcat schemes! We've worked too hard for it! It was bad enough when you took a hundred dollars to build that dog camp over at Antelope—you didn't even ask me; you just *took* it! It was like stealing from your family!"

"You're crazy! I swear, sometimes I think you're goin' off your nut— you're worse since Mitch left! It's like you think every idea I have is…is like you don't think I have good sense! Why, right down there around your home town, Paul's Valley, the Fortuna Company brought in that Seminole field, and it's bringin' in enough oil for half the world! And you think people aren't gettin' rich in this state? Even the *Indians* are rich!"

"I don't care. I'm not an Indian, and I'm not a gambler, either, and I won't be married to one. Those wildcatters, they'd mortgage their homes and auction off their *kids* to drill a hole! No, Marvin, *no!*"

Cassie heard a door squeak. She looked down the hall. Dan stood there, fully dressed. He said, "Cassie, go to bed."

She went to her room and got under the covers. She was sorry she had listened in for a lot of reasons, one of which was that the sheets were now cold as ice.

O

The next morning when Cassie went down to the living room it was still pitch dark. Presents were piled under the tinseled tree, most of them wrapped in paper from the drugstore: a big red and white Santa on a background of green. The room was warm for once; Liddy had left the door open to the rest of the house. There was no bicycle in sight, but that didn't mean anything, since there wouldn't have been any way to wrap it. It must be in the garage, but she wasn't going to go look and spoil the surprise.

She knelt down to inspect the gifts. A large box for Dan, squarish and heavy, which was probably his radio. She fingered a few of the other packages. Most of them were for her. One was a book, and the others felt like clothes.

She went in the kitchen and looked at the clock: six thirty-three! They'd *never* be up! She heard the floor squeak in the living room and hurried back. Dan was there, and she could swear he'd just been kneeling under the tree, feeling the presents like she had.

Liddy came in, nightgown trailing the floor, her hair loose and falling down her back.

"We'll wait for your dad to get up to open the presents."

No one mentioned the argument from last night.

"When will he be up?" asked Cassie.

"Soon, I expect. Let's grab a snack while he sleeps a little more."

Cassie put her head down and gripped one hand inside the other behind her back. She followed her mother and Dan into the kitchen. It was while she was standing in the kitchen, drinking cocoa and eating cinnamon toast, that she learned the truth.

"Whatever made you think we could afford a bicycle now?" asked Liddy.

"I thought I was gonna get one!" she moaned. She truly could not believe it.

Her dad came downstairs finally and stood there and said, "Times are hard, Cassie. You better grow up."

And she said, "But how about a *used* one? They don't cost much—"

"Do you think we're the Rockefellers?"

She got a set of watercolors, thirty-six little rectangles of color with a tray for holding the water; three big drawing tablets, a part-angora sweater in a soft shade of green from Aunt Hannah, and *By the Shores of Silver Lake*, by Laura Ingalls Wilder, from Aunt Bertha. Mitch sent her a check for ten dollars, and Grandmother McIvor sent a book of Katzenjammer Kids cartoons.

Dan forgot to get her a present. This made her mad as hops, because she'd spent a lot of time knitting the muffler. It reached only to just below his collarbone, but it looked good. You would think he could come up with *some* kind of present for her, even if it was only a Big Chief tablet. She went in the bathroom and cried for a long time, because of the bicycle and because Dan was such a butt, until her mother came to the door and told her to wash her face and set the table for Christmas dinner.

Her father was on the phone in the kitchen and her mother was mashing potatoes, wearing a sour expression.

Liddy had decided that Christmas or not, she was going to have to talk to Marvin.

After the gift opening—in an effort to economize, she and Marvin didn't exchange gifts—she fixed a second breakfast of hotcakes, eggs, and sausage. They all seemed contented after that. Then she read out loud Mitch's last letter from Kelly Field. He had a special Christmas greeting for everyone. You'd never know that he and his dad didn't get along, because Mitch said in the letter how much he loved them all.

When the kids had gone upstairs with their Christmas gifts, she said, "Marvin, we have to talk."

Sprawled on the couch, he groaned, "What in the world is wrong now? You said we shouldn't get each other anything!"

"It's not that. It's—it stems from our discussion from last night." At his bilious look, she added quickly, "I don't want to have another fight, Marvin. I want the kids to have a nice day." For the first time in months, she sat down close to him. "You've got to start showin' me more respect. I mean it!" She braced herself.

But he merely said in a resigned voice, "Whatever you say."

"No! That's not good enough! I want you to *notice* me! My job is going real well now—the ladies like me, and I'm *helping* them! I gave that bazaar back in May, and it was a big success, and I've placed the quilts and everything all over the county in shops. I'm making money, and it's *my* money, to invest in the next phase of this—business, or venture, or whatever you want to call it." She stopped, out of breath.

He sat up, took a cigarette out of his shirt pocket, and tapped it against the wall. "What do you want *me* to do about it? You're doin' everything your way, like usual!"

"I just want some consideration! You've been coming home later and more exhausted all the time, and you want me to wait on you just like always. When do *you* ever wait on *me*? And another thing, if I decide sometime I want to travel to some cities, maybe even Tulsa, to market the sewing, then I will! And you're not to nag me about gasoline or using up the tires, or any of that!"

She looked dead serious, he thought. She seemed angry, asserting herself like a man, and he didn't like it, but he supposed this was what he had chosen. He didn't want a divorce, and he didn't want Abby anymore. He didn't know if he could ever love Liddy the way he had loved her once, but maybe she didn't love him in the old way either.

He gave in. "Okay. You're right, I guess. I'll start tryin' to be more —cheerful. I reckon that's what you want."

She leaned over and gave him a kiss. He made it into a rough one, and his mustache scratched her face, just like the old days.

O

They had dinner around four: fried quail with the occasional Number Seven shot in it, with mashed potatoes and canned green beans. Liddy had made pumpkin pie and served it with whipped cream. It felt just like Sunday, but it was Monday, so Cassie and her dad listened to *Amos 'n' Andy* and *Burns and Allen* while Liddy and Dan cleaned up the dishes. Her mom must have felt sorry for her because of the bicycle, and she didn't have to do anything but clear the table. Dan had to dry.

Dan was silent the whole day. Her dad didn't seem as if he was really there with them, or perhaps he was there but not sure he wanted to be. Liddy kept saying things to cheer him up: that they'd finally gotten the water heater for the parsonage paid for, and that Rachel Klein's brother was out of jail—things like that.

Cassie got sleepy early because she had lain awake so long on Christmas Eve. She was in bed with her new book when Dan knocked on the door.

"Come in."

He sat down on the bed. "I just remembered," he said. "I had something I was kinda plannin' on givin' you, all along. But I forgot I had the idea. I cleaned this up with some alcohol an' a little bit o' soap. You can blow on it if you want to, or you can keep it as a souvenir."

Dan pulled his arm from behind his back, and in his hand he held a long, slender bone whistle. Dangling from it was a beautiful beaded pendant and a feather. It was made by an Indian out of an eagle's wing bone, he said, and he'd found it near Wolf Creek.

She took it in her hand, turning it all around and admiring it. Imagine Dan giving her something from one of his hikes, something he'd found out on the prairie. Sometimes Dan could surprise you; just when you had given up on him ever acting like a regular human, he'd come up with something like this. She threw her arms around his neck.

O

Cassie got her way on one thing. Liddy said they would go see *Gone with the Wind* on New Year's Eve Day. They would go to Red Arrow to the matinee. Dan and Marvin could come if they wanted to, but she and Cassie were going regardless.

Cassie was surprised by Liddy's decision to go against the pledge. Even though she'd been pestering her to go, when her mother actually gave in it was like when they played "dead man" at school and whoever was catching you would always catch you at the last minute, but while you were falling you were never really certain. When New Year's Eve came, Dan wanted to go, but Marvin didn't. He said he just wanted to stay home, put his feet up, and listen to the radio. He tried to talk Liddy out of going, since it was a freezing day and the roads were icy, but she had made up her mind. She refused to allow Dan to drive and got behind the wheel herself, then steered in a nervous, erratic manner, nearly skidding off the road on one frozen curve. The Plymouth didn't have a heater, so they were freezing by the time they got there. The Home Arts and Crafts shop, where her ladies' handiwork was displayed in the window, was next to the theater, and Liddy insisted they stop and look. The printed sign read:

CREATED BY WOMEN
OF BLISS COUNTY
Represented by Mrs. Marvin Field
Cato, Oklahoma

Liddy was delighted, but Dan barely slowed down, and Cassie kept tugging on her arm. Who cared about all that sewing stuff *now*?

At last they walked into the Red Arrow Cinema Palace. Dan was wearing the muffler Cassie had knit him, but he stuffed it in his pocket as soon as they got inside. By the time Cassie had taken in the huge theater lobby with its red carpet, gold sconces, and ornate mirrors behind the candy counter, Liddy was putting her change back in her purse. She seemed astonished.

"Ninety cents for me and fifty each for you kids! Don't tell your dad!"

The beautiful glow of the lights in the lobby, the luscious smell of popcorn, and the framed Gone With the Wind posters warmed Cassie's spirits. She breathed in deeply and let the happy feeling spread through.

Liddy bought three bags of popcorn. "These are the only treats I'm buying, so don't ask for more." Dan led the way through the heavy curtain, and they found seats, not as far down as Cassie liked to sit, but fairly close. Dan sat on the aisle, his long legs sprawled out, and Cassie sat between him and Liddy. The theater filled gradually, and at last the curtains drew back and the newsreels began. The first was about the Russian invasion of Finland, accompanied by loud music. A man announced in a nasal voice that Finnish ski troops hadn't been able to resist the Russians, even though the Finns were crack shots and superb skiers. There was a newsreel about Rockefeller Center being completed, one about a German destroyer sinking a British ship, with three hundred sailors lost; then still another about the RAF raiding a place called Wilhelmshaven in Germany and losing fifteen planes. Cassie just wanted the newsreels to be over, and finally they were. As the credits for the movie rolled and the music began to play, she felt her heart begin to expand again the way it had that time on Wolf Creek, when she was out walking and had felt so free. It felt like a big white balloon filling her up to the top of her head and all the way down to her knees. She glanced over at Dan, whose face was as glum as ever. He shoved popcorn in his mouth and said, "What're *you* lookin' at? It's just a movie, remember? Just lights and movin' shadows!"

The southern plantation scene unfolded before her eyes, and she forgot about Dan and everything else. She was astonished by Scarlett O'Hara's beauty. She had read that they'd imported Vivien Leigh from England, but that couldn't be true—she sounded just like the Deep South, like she was from Louisiana, like Aunt Bertha. She acted just like Aunt Bertha, too, as if she'd stomp you in the ground and spit on you if she didn't get her way.

When Ashley came on the screen, Cassie felt her balloon sag down to the floor. He was old and desiccated-looking, and he didn't talk like anyone else. Scarlett couldn't leave him alone, though; she was crazy about him. When she got a chance to go to Charleston, Mammy said the only reason she wanted to go was so she could jump on Ashley "like a *spidah!*"

The moment Cassie would always remember was when Melanie was going to have her baby and Scarlett went to the train yard to get the doctor. The audience in the Cinema Palace gasped as she walked through the acres of dying soldiers.

Rhett was disgusted with Scarlett because she was so crazy about someone else's husband— her best friend's, at that—but Rhett was just as bad, trying to get Scarlett to love *him*. The whole movie was about Scarlett wanting Ashley and Rhett wanting Scarlett, with nobody satisfied. The sign came on saying "End of Part One."

Liddy didn't move, but Cassie and Dan got up and walked out to the lobby with everyone else, and Dan bought two Hershey bars and gave her one.

Suddenly Dan's mouth stopped chewing and his face changed. He was staring across the lobby at a girl who had her back turned. She turned around, and it was Lola. She was with a tall boy in a football jacket with RED ARROW RATTLERS lettered on the back. Dan turned red and slithered back through the curtains into the theater. Cassie waited a few minutes and followed. She found her seat just as a harp and an organ finished "Jeanie with the Light Brown Hair" and the second half of the movie began.

An awful lot happened, and then there was a long scene with a clock ticking while Scarlett and the other women waited for the men to come back from Shantytown. The ticking of the clock seemed to go on forever. Cassie drifted off to sleep, the chocolate bar melting in her hand.

She felt Dan shaking her. "You wanted to see this thing so bad, you better stay awake." He took her hand and made her slap herself five times on each cheek.

The rest of the movie was one catastrophe on top of another. The worst was when little Bonnie got thrown off her horse and died. Cassie sneaked a look at her mother. Liddy's eyes were fastened on the screen like thumbtacks on a wall, and she was crying as much as Cassie.

Her mother rummaged around in her purse for a clean tissue and gave one to Cassie. Dan was turned away from them with his legs sticking out in the aisle, rubbing his nose with his fist.

Cassie was so caught up, she forgot to look at her mother when Rhett said, "I don't give a damn."

The music surged up, and then it was over.

Liddy and Cassie kept sitting, and so did everyone else.

Liddy must have liked the movie, because it had improved her disposition. She let Dan drive home, and she put her arm up along the seat, touching him on the shoulder as he drove. She wore a faint, faraway smile, and she hummed music from the movie under her breath.

Dan seemed different, too, but not improved. His scowl was back.

It was almost dark outside. Cassie lay on the backseat of the car huddled against the cold, her legs drawn up and wrapped in a woolen blanket. She thought about how Scarlett always got her own way. Good thing her dad hadn't come. If he thought Bette Davis was high-handed and bossy, what would he think of Scarlett O'Hara? She pulled the blanket up, and tucked her legs tight. There were lots of folks who felt unrequited love like Scarlett's for Ashley and Rhett's for Scarlett—who threw themselves at someone. Mrs. Weston at Reverend Alexander, and Dan at Lola. People were dumb, she thought, always setting themselves up for disappointment. When she got grown, she would only love someone who loved her back, otherwise no dice. And it wouldn't be for a long time, because it just caused trouble. She'd have to keep her brains above her belt, like she'd heard her mother tell Mitch and Dan to do so many times. At Wolf Creek, Eula Tully and Mr. Weston seemed to like each other about even-Steven. She guessed she'd messed up their fun pretty good! She hadn't told anyone about seeing them—not even Fiona!

Tucking the blanket more closely around her legs, she felt something hard under her hip, and pulled out the eagle bone whistle. She had decided not to mention it to her mother; Liddy would probably confiscate it for hygienic reasons. She tucked it inside her sweater, next to her ribs, letting the tiny beads of the pendant scrape against her skin.

Remembering her parents and how poorly they got along, she sat up.

What about *them*? Did they love each other equally? Did they love each other at all?

She looked out the window and saw that Dan had brought them to the outskirts of Cato. It was almost pitch dark as they crossed the railroad tracks. A train had just departed, and steam and smoke filled the air.

Part Three

1942–43

15

I had a little dog, his name was Dash.
I'd ruther be a nigger than poor white trash.
—Black folklore

In the spring of 1942 Cassie was thirteen, and tall.

She didn't like being tall. On her it was gawky, not statuesque like on Lola.

Being thirteen was the worst thing that could happen to you. Although it seemed to have a beneficial effect on her friends, on her it stank. She wanted more than anything to be grown-up, and she worried about not being one in the most significant way of all: she couldn't get her period.

She had gone through a humiliating scene with Fiona about it. She'd found some thick yellowish stains on her panties, and she'd never seen that kind of stain before. It wasn't pee; she was sure of it! They were alone in the Girls Room, so she dragged Fiona into the little cubicle.

"This is it, isn't it?" she whispered. She held out her panties by the tired elastic and showed Fiona. Fiona just looked at her and shook her head, her long bob swaying in the dim light. "Cassie, don't you know? It's *blood*! Hasn't your mother told you?"

No, she hadn't. But Cassie had been looking at Tampax and Kotex and sanitary belts for years— why couldn't she have figured it out? *So what made the stains?*

There was no one to ask. She couldn't talk to her mother about these things. Liddy was unwilling to discuss anything concerning female anatomy and its accompanying problems.

Once Cassie began, "Mama, you know, uh, Daddy sells all that, uh, Kotex at the store? When will I have to—"

"Don't be tryin' to grow up so fast! You'll be sorry when you do!"

Every bit of her mother's attention was engaged in getting Mitch back alive from the war. And now Dan was talking about enlisting as soon as he graduated from high school. Cassie heard her mother's knees thump down on the floor every night, sometimes mornings, too, as she knelt for prayers. She said getting out to see her sewing ladies and finding new outlets for their work was the only thing that kept her from going off the deep end.

Cassie couldn't wait to be grown-up, and free and independent. She'd finally gotten permission to get a permanent at Tootie's Beauty Nook, but it grew out, and her folks said they couldn't afford for her to get another one. Now she wore her hair in a long, straight bob like Fiona's, holding it back with a barrette or a bobby pin. Cassie thought her complexion was okay; she didn't have pimples. But it wasn't her face and hair that were the awful parts; it was her body.

Fiona and Alice Purvis made jokes about menstruation, like "What did the vampire say to the schoolteacher? 'See you next period!'" And a poem, which Cassie thought was disgusting but which she laughed at anyhow when she saw it penciled on the girls' bathroom wall:

> *Rosie's is red,*
> *Her two lips are, too.*
> *Try Tampax, Rosie,*
> *That's what to do.*

Cassie and Fiona found an old book in the library called *Natural History*, with some quotations from somebody named Pliny who said women's menstrual blood was "…a fatal poison, corrupting and decomposing urine, depriving seeds of their fecundity, destroying insects, blasting garden flowers and grasses, causing fruits to fall from branches, dulling razors…"

Cassie and Fiona laughed and laughed at this, but Pliny's words made them feel powerful, or in Cassie's case, potentially powerful. The library wasn't a separate room, just a small area with bookshelves and a high counter around it in one corner of study hall. There she and Fiona had discovered some juicy parts of *Anthony Adverse*. They had to hunker down, pretending to be librarians, when all they'd been doing was looking for dirty words.

The flat places where her bosoms were going to be—maybe—had been hurting since she was eleven, the buds swelling and aching so much that she couldn't sleep on her stomach. And if she accidentally bumped her chest playing basketball, she felt a stabbing pain. This had been going on for two years, but she still didn't have to wear a bra! The dark hair had started down there and under her arms, but the fact that she couldn't get "the curse," as Fiona called it, proved her backwardness. Fiona and she weren't as close, all because Cassie was still stuck in babyhood, while her best friend was on her way to a world of sanitary belts and men.

Her menstrual fluids just would not appear. They were stuck somewhere in her insides, clogging everything up. Maybe she needed some Drano.

○

It was Cassie's opinion that Dan was determined to take all the fun out of her growing up, as if she weren't worried enough already. One night when he was supposed to be studying for finals, he said there was something he wanted to talk to her about. He stood frowning in the doorway of her bedroom, arms crossed, black forelock hanging down, and said he'd noticed she was getting tall. Dan was six feet now, himself.

She was sitting cross-legged on top of her bed, pasting pictures in a photograph album. "I'm five feet six."

"You're not really bad-looking," he began, "and even though the folks are going to try to keep you hemmed in, I think you deserve some freedom."

Cassie's mood brightened.

"Boys are going to start payin' you a lot of attention," he said. "I'm goin' to be leavin' for the service, so I won't be here to watch over you anymore."

Cassie tried to look sorry.

"There's goin' to be some guys who'll want you to do things, like park in cars and neck, and...uh...more." Dan looked ill at ease. "*Don't do it.* You gotta dress like you're above all that. Don't ever wear pointed brassieres and stuff, and watch how you sit and stand. Don't sit with your arms behind your head, or wear see-through blouses. Always wear underwear, and don't sprawl like a kid; keep your knees together—that's real important. Oh, yeah, and never, *never* sit on a guy's lap!"

Cassie knees were, at the moment, covered in blue jeans. She pulled them together, spilling snapshots off her lap.

Dan dropped one arm and raised the other, propping himself in a new position against the doorjamb. He gave the impression that even though he didn't want to, he was being forced to continue.

"Don't wear dark lipstick and nail polish; those things are dead giveaways to whether a girl has loose morals or not. Keep your fingernails medium length; that's the best, not too short or too long. Freckles are okay; don't try to cover 'em up." He cleared his throat. "If you want to be popular with guys, wear long hair. We all like it. Not frizzy, though, just soft and curled."

So it was okay to *want* to be popular.

"And, Cassie, this is somethin' maybe a brother shouldn't talk about with his sister, but, for gosh sakes, keep your legs and underarms shaved. All that hair's unattractive to us men. Grooming's important."

Now she was a horse.

He was really getting warmed up now, and throwing his hands out with expressive gestures. All signs of embarrassment had disappeared. "Smoking is awful—never, *ever* smoke! Kissing a girl who smokes is like licking an ashtray. *And it's real important never to dance with another girl.*"

Cassie responded for the first time. "Dance with a *girl*! Why would I want to do *that*?"

"You'd be *surprised* what some girls wanta do. I been around, and I know."

Where had he been around *to*? Cassie wondered. He'd been right here in Cato all the time.

But she maintained a respectful silence. Dan was going away to war, and he might be gone for years. It was going to be pretty wonderful.

○

After a series of strokes, Grandmother McIvor died a peaceful death at Uncle Fred and Aunt Bertha's house in Waxahachie. The reports on her health had been bad for the past year or so, and Liddy had been meaning to go down to see her, but kept putting it off. Now she experienced the same guilt Marvin had felt with his mother—why hadn't she paid more attention?

She wanted Marvin to drive her and Cassie down to the funeral, but he said he couldn't leave. He insisted that he had to stay and see to it that Dan studied, because Dan's grades were so bad, if he didn't improve his marks in geometry and science, he might not graduate.

So Liddy and Cassie drove down alone.

Cassie chatted on the way. She told Liddy about Amos Hicks rolling marbles down the wooden stairs outside the classroom while Alice Purvis was explaining why Juliet took the poison; she told about Fergus bringing one of his little pigs to school for a science project.

Liddy's mood alternated from feeling desolated by her mother's death to a surprising cheerfulness. Cassie thought maybe she was glad to get out of Cato, like Cassie was. Liddy reminisced about how her mother and father had raised her and Uncle Fred on the sparse earnings of a horse-and-buggy doctor. Then she began to chat about finding a new sewing lady, a woman up in the panhandle who made apple-head dolls by the ton. She enthused about all the needlework she could sell in Oklahoma's big cities, and she said she was going to go soon and try to make some contacts.

"But your dad's always going on about the price of gas."

Grandmother Field's funeral in Ada had been simple and restrained. Grandmother McIvor's was more showy and expensive, paid for by Uncle Fred, of course. There was a beautiful casket, many magnificent flower sprays, and a large gathering of mourners.

At the funeral and the wake afterward at Uncle Fred's, Cassie stayed closed in on herself. She wanted to remember her own version of her grandmother, didn't want to get distracted by what everybody was saying— how Mary McIvor was such a wonderful Christian lady who knew the Bible backward and forward, and how good and charitable she was in every way. It was all true, but Cassie wanted to think her own thoughts.

Liddy cried at the cemetery and all the way back to Uncle Fred's, moaning, "I don't want to leave her!" Cassie cried, too, and was much sadder than she had been at the funeral of Grandmother Field, whom she hadn't even known. All she could remember from that occasion was the river of tears flowing down her father's face, and how impressed she'd been with Aunt Hannah.

Back at Uncle Fred's, she left the crowd of grown-ups in the living room and went into the kitchen, where she found Feemy, as always, in charge. Yesterday when they'd arrived, it was Sunday, Feemy's day off.

"My goodness, Cassie, you's almost *grown!*" drawled Feemy in her slow, musical voice, and her arms enveloped Cassie.

"You look the same, Feemy. Is Carlton goin' to be around today?"

"I *tol'* him you was gonna be askin' fo' him! He comin' over to bring me some shrimps later on. Cassie, this Milly. She heppin' me today."

"Hi," said Cassie.

"Hi," said Milly.

Milly, a teenager of eighteen or so, was busy chopping onions; tears were streaming down her face. The big table where Feemy was chopping green peppers was cluttered with pans full of tomatoes and uncooked rice, and there was a big basket of fresh okra.

"Carlton can't drive a car, can he? When will he be back?"

"Unnhh-uh. You think they lets little chillens *drive* down here in Texas, chile? He be back soon, real soon. You want anything to eat?" Feemy pointed to a pie piled high with meringue, triggering a memory of the day Cassie and Carlton had walked around the fair at Red Arrow, eating pie, riding on the Ferris wheel, and seeing all the freaks.

"No, thank you. Is Jesse still workin' for Uncle Fred too?" she asked.

"No, Carlton and me livin' over the garage still, an' Jesse down at Beaumont. He's workin' at one o' them ship-buildin' plants down there—makin' good money, too!—lots mo'n he can make here in Waxahachie!"

Feemy let out the full magnificence of her smile. She was as pretty as ever, still slim, skin like coffee with cream.

"They payin' *real* good down there. Carlton got a bicycle now—you oughts to see him ridin' on that thing! He can do hisself all kinds o' mischief an' didoes on it—oh, heah he is now!"

Carlton entered through the kitchen door carrying a huge box full of fish packed in ice.

"Looky who's here, honey! It's Cassie!"

Carlton was tall now, taller than Cassie, but he still had the sober, enigmatic look he'd had when he was nine. He put the box on the table with a loud thump. Cassie was sure he was pleased to see her, but he didn't even say hello.

"We gonna eat in 'bout an hour," announced Feemy. "You two git outta mah way, now; ah'm gonna need some elbow room." Feemy began to remove the wrapped packages of fish from the box. "Carlton, where's the oystahs?"

Carlton's face fell. Evidently he'd forgotten, because he looked blank.

"Son, you know my behind gonna be in a sling—'scuse my language, Cassie—if I don't get this gumbo made jes' the way Miz McIvah like it, like she had when she growin' up in Loosiana. Gotta have shrimps, gotta have crabs, gotta have *oystahs* in it!"

Carlton spoke at last. "I'll go get 'em. Cassie, you wanta go with me to the fish place?"

"Her mama not gonna let her go witchoo—whatchoo *thinkin'*, boy?" It was clear from Feemy's expression that she didn't approve.

"I'd like to go," said Cassie. "Wait a minute."

She went through the swinging door into the dining room and peeked into the big living room, where clouds of smoke and the babble of loud voices arose. Her mother was talking to a woman who was gesturing with both hands, and she was weeping and laughing at the same time. Aunt Bertha was smoking and flirting with a tall man next to the fireplace. Uncle Fred was telling a story, and it must have been about Grandmother McIvor, because he was crying and blowing his nose while he talked. Cassie had never heard people make this much noise. She looked over to where a young Negro waiter was mixing drinks. *There was the reason!* If her dad could see her mother now, sitting there happily surrounded by these Texas whiskey guzzlers, he'd be more shocked than she was.

She sneaked upstairs, grabbed a sweater, and slid back into the kitchen, where Feemy stood holding a crab in one hand and a huge pot in the other, looking crossly at Carlton. It looked as though she'd just given him a lecture about something.

"Let's go," said Cassie.

The spring day was sunny and pleasant. There never was any wind here. They walked along the sidewalk for a while, then turned off onto a dirt road.

"How far is it?" she asked.

"'Bout six, seven blocks thisaway."

They walked for a while in silence.

"We don't have much fish in Cato, just catfish an' crawdads. I hear you got a bike." She knew she would have to do the talking, because Carlton wouldn't.

Carlton looked almost animated. "Uh-huh. I usually rides it to the grocery store."

She added Carlton to the long list of kids she knew who had their own bikes, while she had to make do with Dan's old rusty one. "You still playin' baseball?"

He nodded. "Got the bes' hittin' record at my high school."

"Wow!"

"*Evah*," he added. He must really be good; it wasn't like Carlton to brag. They were going through colored town now. Negroes stared as they walked past street after street of faded, ramshackle dwellings. There were no sidewalks.

"Hey, there, Carlton, whatchoo doin' walkin' with that fine-lookin' little white gal?" a young man called. Carlton didn't respond. They walked another two blocks, and someone else said, "Hey, pretty mama, where you *goin'* with yo'self?"

"Nice little silk, boy! What*choo* doin' wid it?"

Cassie decided to ignore all the remarks and broad grins from the men leaning against the houses, and the stares from the women who gawked at her from windows and then withdrew. Maybe she shouldn't have come on this errand.

This was just the way it had been walking with Carlton around the fair at Red Arrow, only in reverse! But they had been little kids then, so now it was more embarrassing.

Carlton became more silent, if that was possible, and Cassie grew more talkative. She went on and on about Mitch's enlistment, Dan's poor grades, and her father's bird dogs. They crossed a wide street and came to a grocery store covered with big hand-lettered signs advertising food and drink. "Where do they get the oysters from?" she asked.

"Galveston...*think* so. That the place where they gets the shrimps, anyways."

They went into the store and waited, while a heavy black woman wrapped a big parcel containing three dozen or so oysters. Carlton told her to put it on Mrs. Fred McIvor's charge account, and they were on their way again. Going back, people didn't stare at them quite as much, and there were no remarks thrown her way.

When they got back to the kitchen, Liddy greeted her with a harsh look. She took Cassie by the arm and pulled her upstairs, and she told her everyone was *scandalized* that she had left with Carlton and traipsed all over town with him.

"I didn't *traipse*! I just went to get some oysters!"

Liddy said Cassie had embarrassed her in front of Uncle Fred and Aunt Bertha and everyone else. Her mother's biggest worry seemed to be offending the relatives, not that Cassie had committed some terrible racial offense, but she went on and on. "Grandmother McIvor would spin in her grave if she knew what you did today. And we just put her *in* there!"

After the wake was over, although Feemy had cooked and smilingly served seafood gumbo to a crowd of forty, cleaning up afterward with only Milly to help, she still got the blame for allowing Cassie and Carlton to leave together. Aunt Bertha stood with her hands on her wide hips, swathed today in three tiers of flounced black crepe, her face flushed with anger. Her penciled eyebrows skittered up and down, and her red Cupid's-bow lips, which looked like the red wax lips you get from penny machines, jerked as if they were being tugged by invisible wires.

"Ah just don't *know* what you was tryin' to get away with, Feemy. Ah'm so mad, ah could spit! What wuz you *thinkin'*! *Carlton* don't know no bettah! It's up to you to watch out for these childern!" Her harangue went on for quite a while. Although Cassie thought Uncle Fred would stand up for her and Carlton and Feemy, he didn't.

Finally Cassie went to stand between Aunt Bertha and Feemy.

"Aunt Bertha, it was *my* idea to go along!"

"You hush up, now, Cassie. Ah'm talkin' to mah help!"

Feemy ran out of the kitchen and up to the apartment over the garage, sobbing.

Upstairs in their room, Cassie cried bitter tears when Liddy told her she'd almost gotten Feemy fired. Later that evening, as she dipped a washcloth in cold water and applied it to her mottled face, it occurred to her that almost everyone had cried that day, and not only because of Grandmother McIvor.

She doubted if Carlton had cried, he never showed any emotion.

She wondered if she would ever see him again. She was leaving early tomorrow morning, and Aunt Bertha probably wouldn't let the two of them say good-bye.

16

'Tis impossible to love and be wise.
—Francis Bacon,
Essays: of Love

Marvin liked to listen to the radio and smoke. He'd made a nest for himself in Mabel's old room, with a radio, lamp, armchair, and his standing ashtray with the bronze Scottie on top.

Now he slept there, too. Cassie and he had a fine time in his room listening to the radio on Sunday nights, when Cassie would look over his dog ads and check the spelling. The most impressive ad, accompanied by pictures, was for Champ and Shinny's puppies:

SUPERB DOGS! OUT OF SHAWNEE CHIEF CHAMP
EX GEORGIA SHINNERY MAID

#1—PERKY'S SULTAN. Great shooting dog for cover; works to gun, widens in open country. Magnificent style, magnificent looker, fine disposition; white with lemon & orange ticking. Handles anything with feathers. 2 yrs. Staunch on point, backs at sight or command, steady to wing and shot, force broken, sits at command to deliver bird to hand. Experienced on quail and prairie chicken.

#2—SHAWNEE SHINNERY SUE, 2 yrs, beautiful-proportioned white & black female, square muzzle, low-hung ears, straight tail. Boys, she is a honey. Snaps her birds off, steady to wing, shot, backs at command. She will do anything; work where she is commanded to. Put in front of horse or car; she will find all the darn chicken in the country and handle them with style.

Marvin Field $250 each   P.O. Box 12, Cato, Oklahoma

Cassie reveled in these Sunday evenings, with her mom in her bedroom listening to war news, Dan off somewhere with Pauly, and just she and her dad listening to the radio.

But part of her was still mad at him about the basketball. He had stopped her playing on the girls' team last year, when she was in the eighth grade. It had been great fun; the team had traveled with the boys' team on the bus all over Bliss County, and they had won quite a few games. Cassie was a good shooter, and almost never missed a free throw. But at the end of the season her dad called her into the prescriptions area and said. "Now, Cassie, don't think you're goin' to be playin' basketball in high school, 'cause you're not. It's okay for boys, but not for girls, so that's that."

"Why *not?*" she spluttered. "Dan and Mitch played! And I'm *good!*"

"They were able to take care of themselves, out o' town."

"*I* can take care of myself out o' town just as much as *they* could! I don't understand why there's *two* sets o' rules around here, one for them and one for me!"

"Your mother and I talked about it and decided it this way, so don't ask questions."

She went to the back apartment and threw herself down on the cot, burying her face in the smelly old pillow. She cried for a half hour, but no matter how much she carried on, her dad wouldn't give in.

A few months after that she found an old scrapbook of her mother's, and along with the pictures of her mom and her girlfriends and what Liddy called their "swains" leaning against the old flivvers, there was one of Liddy and an all-girl basketball team. The girls were all wearing old-fashioned middies and knickers, and her mother was in the center of the picture, grinning and holding the ball. Behind them was a big banner lettered *PAULS VALLEY VIXENS*. She didn't understand it. If her mother had played basketball, why didn't she intercede for her with her dad?

All Liddy would say was, "Times are different now," and "This is how your father feels about it."

O

War was going full force in the spring of 1942. In Europe, the Germans continued to bomb England while General Rommel was scattering British forces in Africa.

The Japanese crushed the Allied forces on Bataan, with 36,000 killed or captured. Doolittle's flyers launched a lightning raid on Tokyo and other Japanese cities, the Japanese attacked Midway Island, suffering heavy losses, and U.S. fliers blasted six Japanese ships in the Aleutians. When Axis shells fell on the Oregon coast near Fort Stevens, everyone on the West Coast went wild. They were being invaded by the Japs!

The U.S. draft had begun in October 1940, and Pete Seeger sang *The Ballad of October 16* at the American Youth Congress in Washington, D.C.:

Oh, Franklin Roosevelt told the people how he felt
We damn near believed what he said
He said, "I hate war and so does Eleanor
But we won't be safe till everybody's dead!"

Cassie and Fiona learned how to roll cigarettes on a little contraption Fiona bought, but they didn't smoke them, just gave them away. Along with every other kid in town, they collected tin cans and aluminum foil, making astonishingly big balls of the foil, which were sent off to be turned into airplanes. Some of the older boys, swept up in the scavenging spirit, got caught stealing tractor seats and plows to sell for scrap.

At home they had to use something called oleomargarine instead of butter, and they had to color it themselves. Cassie was always given this chore. You spurted the yellow coloring into a bag of the white, lardy stuff; then you rolled and kneaded the bag until it was all the same color. After it turned yellow, it wasn't quite so bad.

Davy Schultz, the town baker, became Cato's first victim of the war. Cassie was in the drugstore when he came over to tell Marvin that his windows had been broken for a second time.

"I don't know who iss doing zis!" he wailed, wringing his pudgy hands. "I haf had to replace ze glass twice now already!"

"Sure sorry, Davy," Marvin sympathized. "Some superpatriot, no doubt."

"Ze sheriff sinks it iss roughneck boys from Red Arrow. I vill haf to leaf, Mr. Field! I haf a frient in Fairfiew. You know ziss town? He tells me zey need baker over zere. Lots Mennonites people, und zey are nice to me, alvays supportink me so good!"

A week later, he was gone.

O

With millions of soldiers being transported on the railroads, the tracks through Cato were scorching with use. Hundreds of trains came through, full of young men and equipment, and Liddy was sure Mitch would be on one of them.

At first she went to the depot just once a week; then it was every other day, if she didn't have pickups or deliveries. Homer Botsin, who was married now to a widow from Tangier with a daughter Cassie's age, would call to tell Liddy that a troop train was coming through, or sometimes, with a kind of intuition, she would just know. Most passenger trains were now canceled, and for security reasons, the troop trains were unscheduled.

The trains would sound their whistles long before they reached the station, warning everyone off the track, and Liddy had her ear cocked for that long, far-off note. She would fly to the station in time for the sudden rush of noise: first the whistle, then the deep rumbling of the train— the railroad platform and the earth around it shaking and reverberating with sound, finally the ear-splitting racket of wheels on the rails as the train barreled through.

Liddy would stand sometimes for an hour on the platform, her dress whipping around her in the wind, hair blowing, ginger-and-gray tendrils floating around her face.

Watching for Mitch…waiting for Mitch.

Suddenly hundreds of young faces would flash by in a blur of khaki or navy caps and sleeves, all of the boys framed in the windows of the train. Then they were gone, so quickly it seemed they had never even been there.

Marvin would joke to Stuffy and others about Liddy's obsession.

"My wife's had some fool notions in her time," he would say, "but this beats 'em all!" Or "Someday she's gonna see someone she thinks looks like Mitch, an' she's gonna jump on that train like a hobo!"

All he said to Cassie was, "She's got a bee in her bonnet… We better just stay out of her way."

Some days Cassie went with her mother to wave at the soldiers. It felt patriotic, and she liked the attention she got from the young uniformed men, who never yelled anything too bawdy or flirtatious, since her mother was right there.

"Hi, kiddo!" they yelled, and "Hello, little girl!" One soldier, bolder than the others, called out, "How about a date after the war?"

Liddy always seemed nervous and jumpy, trying to see if Mitch was among them. One day, after the second train had gone through, Cassie was alarmed to see a distracted, almost haunted expression on Liddy's face, and when Cassie spoke, her mother seemed to look right through her. Cassie shook her arm. "Mama, why do you come here? It's silly! You're never gonna see Mitch!"

Liddy's eyes narrowed to focus on her daughter, and her voice was harsh. "You take care of your business and I'll watch mine. Go on home, Cassie."

Cassie turned and started home, walking backward for a few paces, staring at her mother as she dragged her saddle oxfords in the dirt.

O

Dan intended to enlist in the Army Air Corps just as Mitch had, lest his number come up and he find himself in the regular Army. But when he graduated from high school and started talking about it, Liddy put up such a fuss that he stayed around. For once, Marvin sided with Liddy, and discouraged him from going.

Dan didn't care what his dad wanted him to do—ever since that Christmas Eve three years ago, he didn't give a rolling goddam about his father or his wishes. To think how he used to get beaten by the old goat, when all the time he was poking Cassie's teacher! Dan had carried the knowledge silently, but it ate at his insides until finally, a few weeks after seeing Marvin that night with Abby Gallagher, Dan confronted him.

It was a Sunday morning. His dad had asked him to help dip the dogs for fleas, and to avoid a scene in front of Liddy, who hadn't left yet for church, he said okay. But once they were alone in the backyard, he came out with it. "Dad..." He choked getting the words out. "Dad, I saw you and—and *her*."

The worst part of the whole thing was that his emotions betrayed him, and he started to *bawl*!

"How could you *do* that to Mom?" Dan put his hands up to his face and brushed at his eyes.

"Where?" asked Marvin finally.

"Christmas Eve. P-Pauly and I saw you come out o' her h-house." Dan's knees gave way, and he sat down on a pile of boards.

Marvin walked a few paces away toward the kennel gate, then slowly turned and came back. He crossed his arms and looked off in the distance, as if studying the treetops on the rise a mile away.

"Son, that was somethin' I got into, and then I had a hard time gettin' out. You're too young to understand, so just forget all about it. It isn't goin' on now—believe me, it isn't."

"Yeah—because she *moved away!*"

"I said you'll have to believe me—and, damn it, you just will."

"Well, it better be true." Dan stood up. "Otherwise—and just so you understand how I feel—if it *isn't* true, I'm leavin' home, and I'm never speaking to you again."

He walked back into the house, and Marvin didn't get any help with the dogs that Sunday, or ever again.

Now it was three years later, and Dan still harbored a few grievances against his father.

Abby Gallagher aside, the old man still thought he was irresistible to women. Just last week Dan had witnessed him lapping up the flattery of a female—this time Tootie Hicks. It was early one Saturday morning, and Tootie evidently didn't know Dan was making root beer syrup in back. He could hear her and Marvin chatting, getting chummier by the minute.

Dan poked his head out from the back. Marvin was writing in the charge book, and Tootie was saying, "You was always gonna come into the Beauty Nook, Marvin, and let me give you a haircut and trim that mustache. I need to start gettin' me a discount on some o' this stuff! Why am I always runnin' out o' shampoo and peroxide, anyway?" she whined, in a kittenish voice. "The salesman came through last month and took my order, an' the stuff still hasn't come!"

"Tootie, I don't have enough hair on my head to make it an even trade. Besides, Heck wouldn't like you takin' away his business."

"Well, Heck Purvis ain't no hair sylist like me!"

Tootie smoothed her dress over her hips with both hands and moved her pelvis around in a bargain-basement imitation of Mae West. And his dad seemed to enjoy watching her do it.

Dan wondered if Marvin knew that Tootie was flirting with him just so she could get a cut rate. Probably not; he probably still thought of himself as catnip to women. The whole thing was disgusting.

As much as he might try, Dan couldn't fault Marvin about the way he treated Lola. He was always polite and chivalrous with her. Lola was forever kidding his dad about how he loved his dogs and how he always had to have everything on his prescription counter just so. And Marvin joshed back about the way she caused their men customers to hang around without buying anything. Marvin knew that she was perfectly capable of dealing with this category of males, so there was no seriousness in his tone when he said, "Lola, when you gonna start attractin' some *rich* trade? Perry Hicks an' Clink Kerry never buy anything bigger'n a stamp!"

"I can't help it if this town is full of moony good-for-nothings, Mr. Field! Don't blame that on me!"

Watching these exchanges, Dan felt his temperature rise. If Lola knew his old man better, she wouldn't think he was so great. If she knew about his personal life, and how he used to beat up on him and his brother, she wouldn't give him the time of day.

And Dan resented his father's favoritism toward Cassie. He'd made Mitch and him work so hard, and his sister always got a free ride! He never made her sweep out, or open up in the morning —never gave her any responsibility. Always bragging about her grades to the customers. He'd kept that county spelling award she'd won sitting on the back bar for months! When Marvin compared Cassie's school marks with Mitch's and his, it really burned him up. She was a real little toady at school, and if Mr. Schnauben, the science teacher, hadn't taken such a dislike to him, he'd have a good grade average, too. His mom was always saying, "Dan, if you tried half as hard to get good grades as you try to irritate your teachers, you'd be way ahead!" But he had never tried, and now it was too late. He'd made it through school, and he couldn't wait to get out of Cato. Getting away from his father was one of the main reasons. One way or another, he would leave, and soon.

O

At fifty, Marvin enjoyed the outdoors more than ever. Hunting was still a real pleasure, and so was training his dogs. He liked the affection he got back from the dumb four-legged critters.

Life had calmed down in his middle age, and so had he.

Liddy, however, seemed more frenetic than ever, more desperate to achieve some far-off goal, the meaning of which eluded him. It was just as well that he slept downstairs; he got more real rest when he was alone, anyway. It was hard to live with a woman like her. He wished she were calmer, and not so cussedly temperamental. He wished she would attend to *his* needs more. She certainly was feeling her oats about her little sewing sideline. He still thought of Abby with an old lover's longing, but was relieved she was out of his life. He was too old to keep up a steamy affair, and way too old to divorce and remarry. Abby would have wanted children; he was smart enough to know that, even if she'd never mentioned it, and he couldn't just drop one family and start another—it would be too much of an upheaval.

It had been a terrible jolt when Dan told him he knew about Abby. He hadn't wanted Liddy to know, and he certainly hadn't wanted his children to find out. He wondered if Dan had told Mitch. But Marvin and Dan were all right now—he had worked at it. Got him an expensive watch when he graduated from high school, and bought him some nice clothes, all of which he seemed to appreciate.

Yes, business was good, and he and Liddy and the kids were all healthy.

Keep it simple. Keep things settled down.

O

A friend of Stuffy Byers, one of the head engineers in the State Department of Transportation, offered Dan a job building roads all over northwestern Oklahoma. The money tempted him to stay around for a couple more months, so Dan's part in the war was postponed. He put off deciding about everything—no use starting college when the draft was going to get you, no use enlisting until just before your number came up. He was a walking grab-bag of indecision. But he wouldn't be staying much longer—he wouldn't be able to live with himself. Just the other day out on Wolf Creek, he'd stopped to watch a pair of red-tailed hawks soaring above his head, gliding on the early morning breeze. They were beautiful, the embodiment of freedom. Maybe he could be a flier—it was the only exciting thing in modern warfare! Mitch had written Liddy that he'd passed the tests to be pilot material, but that he wanted to stay with the friends he'd made in basic training. Dan couldn't believe that his brother had turned down the chance to fly airplanes, and had chosen instead to be a mechanic!

He'd written Mitch to say, "Are you nuts? Why don't you train to be a pilot?" But he never heard back.

Most of Mitch's friends and one or two of Dan's were already in the service. Mike O'Herlihy and Dooky Schlanaker were on a carrier in the Pacific; they'd been shipped out soon after Pearl Harbor. Sean, emulating his older brother, had signed up for the Navy, and was in San Diego.

Pauly Spokes, on the fence like Dan, had started college in Alva, and Ben Hargraves, 4-F because of his eyes, was still helping his dad run the Mistletoe Café. The two of them plastered new signs on top of the old ones: posters with silhouettes of soldiers and Nazis. All of them said things like: "THIS IS THE ENEMY!" and "GIVE 'EM BOTH BARRELS!"

O

After school was out that spring, Lola Mallory began working full-time in the drugstore, planning to work all summer and save her money for college in the fall. The Schonbergers would pay for most of it, of course.

Cassie listened to Lola and her friends chattering about their plans. All the talk made her think college would be the most exciting thing that could happen! Lola planned to go to OU, and Fernie May Applebaum would take a stenography course in Oklahoma City. Blond, buxom Greta Sundersson wasn't going to college. She was semi-engaged to Sean O'Herlihy, and was busy sewing on her trousseau. She had a job at Schonberger's Dry Goods, and she had to help out at home too, because Inga worked as housekeeper for the Scruggses.

Everyone was amazed when Barney Scruggs bought the big Sampson house after Hal and Grace separated. Grace had moved to Tulsa, and Hal still lived out at the ranch. Liddy's bridge group agreed that living in the big mansion had made Sally's head swell up three sizes too large.

Lola's and Dan's work hours were separate, and Cassie noticed how, when they changed shifts, they passed each other like ships in the night.

Cassie asked her mother why Dan and Lola's courtship had lasted such a short time.

"I don't think Dan's nearly mature enough for Lola."

"But they're the same age!"

"Yes, but Dan still doesn't know if he wants to be a doctor, lawyer, or Indian chief! He's so busy worrying about himself, he can't stop to think about anyone else!"

Cassie approached her dad with the same question, and he said, "I think Lola got to know your brother, and that was the end of everything in the romance department," he answered. That was what Cassie thought, too! All you had to do was be around Dan for a little while to want to be somewhere else. It was Cassie's conviction that Dan couldn't be nice for very long to anyone, and especially not to her.

But one day Dan said, "Since I'm leaving soon for the paving job, maybe we could do something together. How'd you like to go for a hike?"

Dan had never asked her to go on one of his hikes before, and Cassie couldn't help being flattered. She put on her oldest jeans, her flannel shirt, and some high-top tennis shoes she'd scrounged from the attic. Dan was wearing his usual hiking clothes: torn khakis and a beat-up windbreaker. They started out. Dan's route to Wolf Creek was different from the way she and Fergus went to catch crawdads, a lot farther east. They walked for half an hour before they got to the creek, then crossed over on some flat boulders.

"This is great!" Cassie yelled, carefully choosing which rocks to step on over the rushing water. "I've never seen this part o' the creek before!"

"Come on. I got somethin' to show you!"

Once on dry land, she had to work to keep up, because Dan didn't slow down. They hiked through what seemed like miles of dry sagebrush mixed with scrub oaks, mesquite, and small trees. She was panting when they came to a sandstone hill, which Dan immediately started up, not even looking back to see if she could follow.

She scrambled up after him. The tennis shoes had no tread at all, and she slipped and slid on the grainy, lichen-encrusted rock all the way up, grabbing outcroppings and knobby roots in order to keep from sliding back down. Once she had reached the top, she trudged a few more yards to a cluster of large boulders, where Dan had stopped.

"Cassie, this is somethin' I been knowin' about for a long, long time, but I never told anyone. I kinda hinted about it to Charlie Detwiler, but I never brought him here. You're the first one."

His expression seemed to say, "*And you should appreciate it.*"

"Oh," she said.

"Is that all you got to say, *oh?* Listen, this is something important, and I want you to realize it!" He took her arm and gave it a shake.

"What is it?"

"Under these rocks is the burial place of an Indian. He's nothin' but bones now. I dug him up once and looked at 'im, and I think he was a warrior, because he's got the outfittings of one."

"What kind of outfittings?"

"A bow and some arrows, and what's left of a quiver. And there's different-colored beads that used to be on his clothes, so if I wanted to I could prob'ly write to O.U. and find out what tribe he is. But I never have. I think he's Kiowa."

"How come you haven't written 'em?"

Dan dropped to the ground like a marionette released from its strings, settling himself among rocks and pebbles. He gestured for her to sit, too, so she sat down cross-legged, facing him.

"It's like he's my own special Indian, you know? I guess that's why."

They were quiet for a long time. The sun was going down, and Cassie shivered in the late afternoon chill. So this was where Dan disappeared to all the time. Why he seemed to love the outdoors so much.

Dan fished out a cigarette and lit up, taking a long puff.

"Can I have one?" Cassie asked.

"What do you think?"

She sat staring at the boulders. Finally she spoke. "Why're you showin' this to *me?*"

"I don't know. I just had to tell somebody about him before I leave. Maybe I'll be leavin' for good; you never know." He drew deeply on his cigarette, and they gazed at one another. Cassie didn't say any more. She tried to let the Indian feeling soak into her bones—the feeling that Dan must experience here on this lonely hill.

After awhile, they hiked back to town in the near darkness.

O

In typical Dan fashion, it was only a few days before he changed again.

This was the other side of Dan, the mean, dark side.

He was responsible for the fact that she didn't get to see *For Whom the Bell Tolls*, with Ingrid Bergman and Gary Cooper, which played for a week, because he ratted to Liddy that it contained a scene Cassie shouldn't see. She didn't know what the scene was, something about a sleeping bag, but after he blabbed about it to Liddy, Cassie refused to speak to him for a week. She had wanted to see Ingrid's short hair!

A week later, ricocheting back to the nice Dan, he offered to take her to Red Arrow to see *The Song of Bernadette*, which Cassie had been reading about in *Photoplay* for months.

Cassie asked Fiona to go along. Fiona had nursed a crush on Dan for years, and Dan had once mentioned that he thought Fiona was pretty. Prettier than *her*, he probably meant. Fiona was always saying she wished she had a brother. Every time she said it, Cassie said only somebody who didn't have one would say something like that.

Dan drove the girls in the Plymouth, saying he wasn't going to go to the movie; he thought he'd just hang out at the local pool hall. But at the last minute he bought a ticket and went in, seating himself a few rows behind them.

The movie was about a young girl in France who saw a vision of a lady with a glow all around her. She told everyone in town about it, but no one believed her, and from then on she fought with everyone: her family, the community, even the local priests. She was the laughingstock of Lourdes, but then the miracles started happening—water came out of the ground, a little baby was cured of illness, and lots more. Businessmen started making tons of money from people who came to see the spring welling up out of the ground. Later she went away to a convent, where she got sick with tuberculosis of the knee. Just before Bernadette died, she had a vision of the lady again. She asked a priest, "Why don't they believe me?" and the priest read from the Bible, and bells rang.

Cassie and Fiona both cried buckets.

On the way home, Cassie sat between Dan and Fiona in the front seat.

"Jennifer Jones is so beautiful!" breathed Fiona.

"And so saintly!" Cassie added.

All at once Dan started frowning and driving really fast. Evidently taking his kid sister and her friend to the movies had set off a negative reaction.

"Cassie, *you* were kind of like Bernadette back when they had that revival, seein' visions and all, weren't you?"

"Was not!" She didn't like the sarcastic tone to his voice.

"Didn't you tell me you were talkin' in tongues back then? Gobbledy-gobbledy-*gobbledy*!"

She reached over and scratched the back of his neck with her fingernails, and he grabbed her arm and twisted it. The car swerved wildly back and forth on the dark road.

"Hey, you two, *cut it out!*" yelled Fiona.

They reached Cato, dropped Fiona off, and went home. Dan's neck was bleeding, and he had to hold his handkerchief to the wound. "That's the last time you'll get taken to a movie by *me!*"

When they got out of the car, she stuck out her tongue.

But maybe since he'd taken her to the Indian grave, she shouldn't have scratched him.

O

At nineteen, Dan had some experience with girls. He was pretty sure that was part of the frustration he was feeling—that and his indecision about enlisting. After things had blown up between him and Lola, he'd gone out with two other girls. One was a feisty little cheerleader from Antelope, and the other was a willowy blonde from Woodward. The girl from Woodward had made Dan nervous. He was sure his clothes were pathetically shabby compared to those of the guys she was used to, and he couldn't afford the gas to drive over there all the time. The other girl, the cheerleader, he had just stopped calling. These were both "nice" girls, which is to say, they liked to neck—they even seemed to love it—but that was it; they would go no further.

His relationship with Lola was peculiar—bizarre, almost. He'd fallen for her the day he saw her arrive in town, but when she made it plain she didn't want to be his exclusive property, it hadn't seemed worth the bother. She was an unattainable goal, part of some knight-and-fair-lady scenario in which he didn't want to compete.

He'd been on the road job for two weeks, then came home for the weekend. Sitting at the soda fountain like any ordinary customer, he was thanking Stuffy one more time for the job.

"I like the work," he said. "Sure appreciate you recommendin' me." Stuffy was slurping a root beer, so he went on. "It's good pay, and I like being outside. Except on some real hot days, and there's been quite a few of those lately." Dan's shirtsleeves were rolled up, exposing the new hard sinews of his arms.

"They must really be workin' ya pretty good, Dan. Looks like ya got a new muscle!" Stuffy took hold of his upper arm and gave it a squeeze.

"And your skin is so *brown!*" said Lola from behind the fountain.

Dan sat up a little straighter. A direct compliment from her was something new.

He asked her to make him a strawberry milkshake, and when she bent over to dip out the ice cream, he noticed her breasts pressing against the neckline of her blouse. That had always been one of the best things about working with Lola, but he'd never had this view before. Right now he would have liked to get behind the fountain so they could rub shoulders and arms the way they used to, but he couldn't think how to manage it. When she set the shake in front of him, she smiled, and he couldn't be sure, but he thought her eyes held his for an extra moment. He felt something go through him. Stuffy left, saying he needed to look after his broomcorn business, and they were alone.

"Dan, have you seen the new refrigerator your dad bought?" she asked.

"You mean he actually replaced the one with the shotgun hole in the door?"

"Yes. Come on back, I'll show it to you!"

He followed her, pulse racing. When they got to the back apartment she pointed.

"There! What do you think of *that?*" A shiny white refrigerator stood in place of the old one.

A long moment passed while they stood side by side, gazing at the white box. Then he turned to her. "I don't think it's near as pretty as *you.*"

When their lips met, it was as if they'd been waiting forever, and the longer they held the kiss, the longer Dan wanted it to last. He put both arms around her and pressed her against him, his hands roaming all over. He pressed his knee between her legs, hard, because it seemed as if he couldn't get close enough without actually being inside her.

"Oh, my gosh!" Lola panted. "What if your dad comes back?" She left Dan and hurried to the front of the store, where Perry Hicks stood waiting to buy chewing tobacco.

There was no way to see her that night, because when her shift ended she had to drive her aunt to some kind of church meeting in Red Arrow. She would get back late, she said, and he had to leave at five the next morning.

Back on the road gang, he spent most of his time thinking about her. The crew had to finish a road near Cheyenne, and they were kept over the weekend.

When he came back the second week in June, he called her at home. "Can you go to a movie in Antelope tomorrow night?" He hoped she couldn't hear his thumping heart.

When she said, "Sure, what time?" it speeded his heart up even more.

He'd been kidded a lot when Lola first came to Cato—folks expecting something that never did happen. This time he was determined to keep everyone else out of it. He didn't know how to convey this to Lola without sounding as if he was ashamed to be seen with her, so all he said was, "Can we keep this kind of quiet?"

She laughed. "Good idea. I have to work until eight. Why don't I meet you behind the grain elevator near that old falling-down shed? It's on the way out of town."

He took a bath, but the day was a scorcher, so an hour later he took another, then applied cologne. He wore his newest white shirt, and polished his shoes. He didn't have a car, so he had to ask Liddy if he could borrow the Plymouth, lying about going to see the girl in Antelope.

"I thought you dropped that one!" said Liddy.

"Not quite."

Lola stood hidden behind the shed, in a white dress with a low V-neck. Her long brown hair was pulled back in a ponytail, and her eyes looked darker than he'd ever seen them. How could she look like that after working all day? Driving along, he was so aware of her closeness he felt light in the head. The bare skin of her arm touched his shirtsleeve, electrifying his body, and she smelled heavenly.

The movie was *Mrs. Miniver*. They held hands for the first time since the night they'd dug up the nails. Lola grabbed his arm when Greer Garson and Walter Pidgeon were enduring the air raids, and she burrowed her head into his shoulder when the young girl died.

On the way home he told her about Mitch, who had been shipped to California for more intensive training. It was a word used often in the news now: "intensive bombing," "intensive troop concentrations," "intensive air strikes."

"He's going to be shippin' out, I just know it! And if I wait any longer, the war'll be over! Even if my folks never speak to me again, I'm leavin'."

"But you just turned nineteen!"

"Doesn't matter. Mitch was my age when he signed up."

She moved so close to him then that they seemed to breathe each other's breath, and when she started kissing his neck, he drove to the road he knew like the back of his hand, down near Wolf Creek. It veered off through a locust grove, and was dark and private.

In his wildest dreams Dan hadn't supposed Lola would let him make love to her, but as her lips and thighs opened and their tongues began to melt together, it seemed the most natural thing in the world. He wasn't prepared for it, in any way save one. They climbed into the backseat and began fumbling at each other's clothes. She let him go inside her, both of them half-naked and shameless, moaning and sweating together.

It was not a gentlemanly thing to do, making love in the backseat of a car. It was depraved and degrading, and ridiculously uncomfortable... It was heaven on earth.

O

When Pauly came to the house the next day and said he'd left college and was going to Red Arrow to sign up, Dan said he was going too. His road job had wound itself up, and Marvin and Liddy knew there was no dissuading him.

"You don't have the slightest idea what you're doing. I tried to tell Mitch—" was all Marvin said.

The next morning, while Dan packed, Liddy gazed at him with reproachful eyes. "I guess you think you have to do this."

"Mom, the whole *world's* at war. You don't want a yellow-bellied coward for a son, do you?"

"Yes, I do! Now I'll have twice the worry!"

She sat down heavily on Dan's bed. This was just like when she'd said goodbye to Mitch.

He closed his suitcase and sat down next to her. "Mom, you can be brave, can't you? Lots of other guys have gone—whole *families* of brothers!"

"That doesn't make it right." Her voice was muffled, her face covered by her fingers. He put his arm around her and squeezed, placing her head on his shoulder with his other hand. She lifted her head, managing a weak smile. "You better write. Mitch hasn't written much."

"I will, I promise."

"Mitch promised, too."

"You're gonna keep busy with your sewing ladies, and with church and stuff—you won't have time to worry about us."

"Is that right!"

He pulled her to her feet, and they embraced.

Cassie was standing in the kitchen, looking a little sad. He kissed her good-bye, rubbing his scratchy cheek against hers, and told her that he and Mitch would be back, but that no matter what happened to them, she should do something with her life.

Cassie had never heard Dan talk in these solemn and lofty tones before. She couldn't think of a response. He had talked of leaving when they were at the Indian grave, but neither of them had thought of his dying until this moment.

Clyde Spokes was planning to drive both boys to the enlistment office in Red Arrow. As soon as they pulled away, Liddy put on her oldest clothes and went into the backyard, determined to vent her anger at all men who made war. She stomped on the shovel, spading up dirt furiously, her energy fueled by sorrow and rage, and she didn't stop until all the dirt in one corner of the yard was turned over. Finally, breathing hard, she took off her gardening gloves and stood surveying what she had done. She wanted to burst into tears again, but instead she went inside and had a long, hot bath.

Tomorrow she would plant a victory garden. Everybody was supposed to have one.

17

Fán shì bì yu yin
(Everything has a beginning)
—Chinese proverb

One afternoon in October Marvin left to run his dogs, leaving Lola and Cassie in charge of the store. Cassie had just finished selling two large boxes of bandages to an out-of-sorts Coach Lansford, who remarked that either he'd miscounted last year's order, or this year's football players were a bunch of splay-footed jugheads.

Cassie decided that this was a good time to talk to Lola about her coming-of-age problems. She had to talk to somebody, and when she'd approached the subject, her mother had rebuffed her again. Something had changed about Lola, but Cassie couldn't put her finger on it. She seemed moody and withdrawn, but Cassie didn't want to worry about that right now. She needed advice. Lola sat on a stool at the soda fountain, hand cupped on her chin, staring dreamily into space, as Cassie began. "Would you believe it? My mother used to tell me Kotex was for bandages!" She peered sideways at the older girl, hoping to segué into her series of questions.

Did Lola think she'd ever get bosoms? Or bleed real blood?

In the old days Lola would have said, "Your mother's a caution, but things could be worse." That was what she'd said the time Cassie complained about Liddy making her a skirt with the zipper down the front, which all your friends would know was made from your brother's old tweed trousers. Later Cassie remembered that Lola didn't have a mother to complain about.

Now all she said was, "Guess your mom didn't want you asking questions."

Cassie sat down on a stool, too, and opened a package of crackers.

"I'd...like to ask you something, Lola. It's kinda personal. It's just that I can't...can't get my period. And all my friends have!" Her voice came out in a Jean Arthur whine.

To her surprise, Lola's eyes filled with tears. She ran crying back to the apartment, and stayed there. Cassie sat listening to the humming of the ice-cream freezer and Lola's muffled sobbing. How could talking about her problem make Lola go to pieces! She waited a few minutes, then went to see what was wrong.

Lola sat huddled in the old upholstered chair. She had a box of tissues in her lap and several soggy ones in her hand, and her face was flushed and swollen.

"Cassie, I'm sorry. I had a fight with Aunt Flo this morning. I'm afraid I may have to go out of town for a while. I wonder, d'you think your dad would hold my job, if I did?" She leaned back against the chair, her hair spread out like a beautiful brown fan. She looked so sad, Cassie had to try to keep from crying, too.

"He'd better!" Cassie said.

Lola smiled. "I—I might have to ask you a really big favor one of these days. Would you do it?"

"Anything. Anything at all you need, you just *ask!*"

That night Cassie heard her father and mother talking in her mother's bedroom. The door was shut, and their tones were hushed like when she was little, when they would start out murmuring in low voices about Mitch or Dan or money or the dogs, and get louder until they were shouting. Now their voices stayed so quiet that Cassie had to plant her ear right up against the door.

"This morning, and yesterday, and the day before," said her dad.

Murmurs from Liddy.

"She just goes in the bathroom and heaves; I can hear her. Then she comes out white as a sheet. I hate to make her do any work, and I feel sorry for her, but I think I'm goin' to have to let her go."

"Should I talk to Flo?" asked Liddy, loud enough to hear.

"I wish you would."

Cassie hurried back to her room. She wondered why she hadn't realized it before. That had to be what the crying and throwing up was about. She may not have known that menstrual fluids were blood, but she knew that pregnant women threw up. Poor Lola—not married, and puking every morning with a baby! No wonder she'd stopped talking about college!

In the days following her parents' conversation, it seemed to Cassie as if everything was on hold. It was like they were floating, anticipating some action or event over which they had no control. She realized she missed Dan. Maybe if he were here, he could do something.

○

Liddy and Flo sat at the dinette in Flo's kitchen, chatting about the next bridge game and where it would be held. Then, after a little interval, Liddy spoke. "Flo, dear, Marvin doesn't think Lola looks very— good —right now. She isn't working as hard as she used to." She waited, to soften what was coming. "As a matter of fact, dear, he thinks maybe Lola is pregnant."

Flo began to sob, unleashing a torrent of words. "Oh, Liddy, I think so, too! I asked her, and she didn't deny it! And she's always been such a good girl!"

"I know, Flo. She's been a real asset to our store, an angel to the whole community!"

"And wouldn't you know, the boy would run off and join the Army Air Corps! Lola finally admitted it was a boy from over at Kingfisher. She wouldn't tell us his name or how she met him, except it was at a dance. He's stationed in Georgia or somewhere, not likely to be back until the war's over. She says he doesn't write very often. Imagine, getting her pregnant, then not even *writing*!"

"What's she going to do?"

Flo put a handkerchief up to her face. "I told her she could go away and have the baby, and give it up for adoption. I don't think there's anyone she can marry."

There was a long silence. Liddy knew Flo was thinking about Dan.

Oh, no.

It was out of the question. Dan couldn't marry anyone, just because *Lola* had been sinful and careless!

"Liddy, does Marvin know any doctors to do an—an abortion?"

"I know Doc Ledbetter won't! Two years ago that Stevens girl in Arbuckle got in the family way, and she was only fourteen. They called Marvin, and Marvin talked to Doc, but he wouldn't do it, said he could be prosecuted. 'Course, if it was *his* daughter or granddaughter or niece, you can bet it'd be a different story!" She reached out and covered Flo's hand with her own. They sat quietly sipping tea, unable to come up with a solution to one of the world's oldest problems, an unwanted life.

O

It was several days before Cassie learned how Lola wanted her to help.

She said she'd talked to Marvin, and he'd agreed to give her some time off. She wanted to go up to see her father's doctor in Liberal, Kansas, the one who'd seen him through his long illness. She left the reason for the trip unexplained, although she hinted at the need to get some of her medical records.

But she didn't want to go up to Kansas alone; would Cassie come with her? The reason she didn't ask Greta was that Greta got on her nerves right now. She said she wanted Cassie for company, because Cassie cheered her up.

She was going to drive the Schonbergers' old Buick, and they would leave Friday. They'd be gone just over the weekend, so Cassie wouldn't miss any school.

"Did you ask my dad about lettin' me go along?"

"No. Don't you think he'll let you?"

Cassie was pretty sure he wouldn't; he would never let her do anything. She wasn't allowed to have a bicycle or wear lipstick or play on the basketball team, so why should a trip out of town be any different?

She wondered if Lola thought her parents were unaware of her pregnancy. If she knew they knew, she would realize they wouldn't want Cassie being friendly with her right now!

"When do we leave?" she asked.

Cassie began hatching a plan, one which had many intricate and interwoven parts. First, she told Liddy that she and Fiona were going to study all weekend for an algebra exam, and she asked her mother not to call and bother them—she said she and Fiona would be studying like a house afire! She told Fiona that she was going to Kansas with Lola, but her folks didn't know, and she told her not to tell anyone and not to show her face downtown. She made Lola swear not to mention to her parents that Cassie was going with her, and told her about the made-up algebra exam. Lola looked at her strangely, holding the root beer glass she was drying in midair, as if trying to sort out what was right and what was wrong. Finally she nodded her head.

It was then Cassie realized that Lola was desperate for company.

Cassie's plan almost blew up. Friday morning at breakfast Marvin said, "Cassie, I'm goin' to need you to work this weekend. Lola's leavin' town for a couple days."

Cassie stopped pouring milk on her cereal. "But, Daddy, I have to study with Fiona! I told Mom all about it, how we have this big algebra test on Monday!"

She put on a serious face, personifying the image of a female Einstein.

Liddy spoke up from the kitchen. "Marvin, *I'll* work for Lola. I'm all caught up with everything, and I don't have to go pick up any sewing for a few days. I want Cassie to do well in math. Lord knows *I* never did."

Cassie knew she was taking a giant step toward her own independence. Too bad she had to make up stories to do it, but it was their fault, not hers. If they would give her some breathing room, she wouldn't have to lie and sneak around.

Friday afternoon Lola picked her up near the bridge, and as they rounded the curve on their way out of town, Cassie began to whistle. They went north, past the farms she knew so well from accompanying her father or Dan on deliveries. A few miles out, they passed the thriving Weston place on their left, with its two towering elm trees flanking the lane in, and the white pergola with its climbing vine. The signpost with the name "WESTON" stood out in the late-afternoon light. Another mile further was the Thatcher farm, and three more miles out they came to old blind Walt Zimmer's. They passed the road going into old Mr. Farrow's cabin, still sitting unsold and abandoned. Cassie had heard her dad say that Mabel hadn't earned a cent on the place, and old man Farrow dead now for three years.

The fields got more prosperous-looking as they drove through the northern reaches of Cato's farmland. There was Charlie Detwiler's spread to the east of the road, and the Sampsons' ranch to the west.

They joined the highway that turned north to Arbuckle, and on up to Liberal. Occasionally a car would pass, its lights amber in the fast-growing darkness, but mostly they were alone on the road. The radio was broken, so while Lola drove, Cassie began to hum; then, having heard no objection, she began to sing. Lola joined in on a chorus of "Deep Purple" then left the singing to Cassie, who eventually tired of trying to remember the words and quieted down. Her head began to nod, and she was asleep by the time they turned north at Balko. She didn't wake up until Lola nudged her at two in the morning, outside a coffee shop in Liberal. They ate hamburgers, then got back in the Buick and slept for several hours, Lola in the front seat, Cassie sprawled in back.

The next morning Lola looked swollen and puffy-eyed. She sat in the coffee shop until Cassie's pancakes came; then she said she wasn't feeling well, and went back out to the car. Cassie didn't ask why they hadn't spent the night with some of Lola's old friends. She knew why.

Lola knew her way around town, and they reached the doctor's office around nine. They parked and went up a few steps into a modern office building, where the nurse at the reception desk gave Lola a hug and gushed, "Lola, darlin', you just go right in; Doctor Bond's waitin' for you!" She pointed Cassie to a corner of the reception area. "You sit over there, honey."

On the walls were three large labeled pictures of a salmon, a trout, and a largemouth bass.

The small black letters on the single closed door read, "ROBERT BOND, M.D." The office was quiet except for the nurse's typing. Cassie sat leafing through an old *Life* magazine and became absorbed in an article about a Victory Caravan train going all over the country with Jimmy Cagney, Pat O'Brien, Groucho Marx, Bob Hope, Frances Langford, seventy musicians, and a bunch of other Hollywood stars and starlets. They were raising money for Army-Navy relief, and they had made the incredible sum of six hundred thousand dollars!

She was brought back to the real world by the sound of weeping. It had to be Lola. The reception nurse stopped typing momentarily; then once more her fingers set up a rhythmic clattering. The crying went on, accompanied by a male voice talking in a low monotone. Then there was no sound at all. A buzzer buzzed, and the nurse went into the doctor's office.

More time passed.

A very pregnant woman with a small child came into the waiting area and smiled at Cassie. She heaved her body into a chair, then opened a bag and began to knit. The little girl stared at Cassie, took her thumb out of her mouth, and pronounced loudly, "Docker. Mama. Bye-bye," and put her thumb back in her mouth.

"Would you come in here, young lady?" A balding young man wearing a white coat was standing in the doorway. This couldn't be the doctor; she'd imagined someone old and gray-haired. She went in, and he closed the door and motioned her to a chair next to Lola's. Lola wasn't crying now, but her eyes were downcast, and she didn't look happy.

Dr. Bond perched on the edge of his desk, one twitching foot crossed over his knee. He looked to be brimming with vitality, as if his body couldn't contain all his energy. He glanced from one girl to the other, smiling. "Cassie, I'm really glad you made the trip up here with Lola. She needs a friend right now. I understand your folks have employed her since she moved to Cato, that right?"

Cassie nodded, and pulled up her socks.

"She wants to tell you something," said the doctor.

Lola looked down at her clasped hands, then directly at Cassie. "I'm pregnant, Cassie. I—I guess you might have known already."

Cassie gazed at the medical school diploma on the wall. It was from St. Louis.

"Uh, yeah."

"Okay, *that's* over with! No going back!" He grinned. "Cassie, Lola wants to have this baby. I told her I couldn't give her an abortion. It's not that she's too far along—she's three and a half months—but it's just that *no* doctor can do it legally. I'd get sent to the state pen. And I'm afraid I wouldn't do that even for Lola here, although I think she's a mighty fine gal!"

He got up from the desk, patted Lola's shoulder, and paced around the office. "I could send her to a guy here in town who would do it, but I think too much of her for that." He sat down, this time in his squeaky desk chair, leaned back, and let a long moment go by. "She has two choices. She can have the baby up in Wichita, where the nuns of the Cathedral of the Immaculate Conception have a big home for girls like Lola. She would get very good care, and she would have her baby in the hospital there. The mothers almost all give their babies up for adoption. Or she's welcome to stay in Liberal with me and my wife, have her baby here, where she grew up."

There wasn't a sound.

Finally Lola spoke, ad her words were slow and deliberate. "Cassie, this is what I want to do. While I'm trying to decide where to have this baby, I'll take you home. We can stay at Dr. Bond's tonight, and we'll drive back tomorrow. I'm sorry I had to make you go through all this, but I—I needed a friend."

Cassie said, "That's okay. Nothing was happening in Cato, anyway."

They laughed, and Cassie, not realizing she had said something amusing, joined in.

After that, Lola drove Cassie around Liberal for a while, showing her the schools she had attended, but they were both tired. Around four o'clock Dr. Bond took them to his house, and Mrs. Bond gave them supper. They went to bed when it was barely dark outside, sleeping in the four-poster bed in the guest room. Cassie wanted to ask Lola who was the father of the baby, sneaking up on the subject, but before she could ask, Lola was asleep.

Just after daylight the next day, they headed back to Cato.

On the road, driving, crying, and fumbling in her purse for tissues, Lola began to talk. She said she'd been sure the father of the baby loved her; otherwise she never would have let him make love to her. "We just got carried away. I loved him so much right then!"

Cassie knew what "carried away" meant. It meant you weren't thinking with your brain, and would do anything at all, no matter how outlandish, with someone of the opposite sex. But she still didn't know why people got so steamed up about each other's bodies. It probably had to do with the thing that had happened to her at *Days of Glory* last week, when Gregory Peck had kissed Tamara Tamanouva with his juicy lips, and something moved all around inside her.

She opened her mouth to ask who the father of the baby was, then closed it. Being a Nosy Parker didn't usually bother her, but for once it did. As if she wanted to tell, Lola said that she had received two letters from the baby's father since he'd been gone.

That opened the door, so Cassie asked, and Lola paused a long minute and then said the boy's name was Bobby, he was from Kingfisher, and he'd joined the Army Air Corps. She said she hadn't told him about the baby; she couldn't get up the nerve. Then she started to cry again.

"I don't want to *force* him to marry me! And I don't want his folks mad at me for gettin' pregnant!"

It sounded like Lola knew the boy's folks. Cassie stayed quiet. It must be because she was only thirteen that she didn't understand Lola's reasoning. The boy probably loved Lola, so why did she think she would be forcing him?

The car's tires whooshed along. Cassie looked out the window, wishing she'd worn warmer clothes, maybe her heavy red sweater. Just then they passed a grove of tall trees with the most beautiful saw-toothed orange leaves she'd ever seen. She thought the trees might be maples or persimmons—Liddy had planted some of those last year— but she wasn't sure. The trees were so lovely she wanted to get out and climb them, grab hold of them, somehow make them part of her drab existence.

She forced herself back to Lola's problem.

She asked, "Does Bobby like the Air Corps? Mitch does! He fixes airplane engines and stuff." She was trying to make some sort of helpful comment, but the sentence lay there like a dead snake. She squirmed down in the seat, stretching out her legs and studying the black hairs. They reminded her of Crazy Penny's shins. Liddy wouldn't let her start shaving her legs; she maintained that the hair would grow back stubby and blacker than ever, and she'd have to keep on doing it. But Cassie *wanted* to keep doing it. Wasn't that the point, to keep shaving, so you wouldn't have the ugly hairs?

They were going through Slapout now, where Crazy Penny lived with her aunt. Cassie glanced at the gas station on one side of the road, and the general store on the other, the only places of business. It didn't seem possible, but this town was even smaller than Cato. She remembered how Penny had cried when she told about the church women taking her baby away. No doubt she wouldn't have made a real good mother, but Cassie would never forget how miserable she'd looked that day. *Would Lola have to give her baby away, too—have it carried off by a bunch of nuns for someone else to adopt?*

Three-quarters of an hour later, when they'd turned off the main highway and were about to pass the Farrow farm, Cassie was struck with an idea. "Lola, *turn!* Turn in here!"

Cassie's barked command made Lola steer the car down the long dirt driveway, then stop. Cassie beckoned her to get out, and Lola followed her onto the wooden porch of the little cabin. Resting her foot on the first splintery step, she asked, "Cassie, why are we stopping?"

The doorknob rattled as Cassie turned it both ways, but it wouldn't budge, so she went around the house through the overgrown yard and found a high window that looked as if it could be pried open. Pulling a fallen limb over, she stood on it and managed to push the window open enough to squeeze through. She walked through the kitchen and into the front room, unlocked the door, and pulled Lola inside. She said triumphantly, "You can stay here and have your baby! Mabel would think it was a fine idea!"

"Who's Mabel?"

"She used to work for us, when my mom worked all the time at the store. She shook us hard when we didn't behave... Well, not me, my brothers. And she made cinnamon rolls, and braided my hair real tight. Then she went to California to pick fruit, her and Buck."

"Cassie, whose place *is* this? Is it Mabel's? Is that what you mean?"

"Yeah. Ol' Mr. Farrow died, and she got it. Nobody's wants to buy it, I don't think." She looked around in the dim shadowy light. There was no furniture, only a few packing crates with a moth-eaten blanket thrown over them, and one chair with a missing rung.

But they could scrounge some things from somewhere.

"She was the nicest, warmest-hearted person I ever knew. She would love *you*. And she would want you to keep your baby. She finally got one—her name's Lulu."

Lola walked to the middle of the room. Her legs buckled under her suddenly, and she sat down on the floor with a thud. A cloud of dust flew up. The light was fading fast, and it was cold.

"I don't know what to say! You mean you think I could stay here in *secret*? What about the neighbors? What if Aunt Flo and Uncle George found out? What about food? And I don't think I can have a baby without a doctor. Cassie, you're nuts!"

"I know, I know... I'm thinking!" She plopped down next to Lola, and another puff of dirt rose. They sat side by side in the stillness, Cassie cross-legged, hands grasping her ankles; Lola with her weight balanced on one hip, one arm supporting her. Motes of the cabin's unsettled dust caught magically, beautifully, in a wide ray of light slanting through a west window.

"There's a sink in the kitchen you can use to wash up, and there's an outhouse; I used it once. I could bring you food twice a week in the basket on my bicycle. It belongs to Dan, but I can borrow it. If only I was older I could drive! And if we called Dr. Bond long-distance he could talk to Doc Ledbetter about you, and Doc could come out here on visits! My mom says he isn't a goin' doctor, but I bet he'd come!"

Another long silence. She could hear Lola thinking.

"What'll I tell Aunt Flo and Uncle George? Where will they think I am? And what about a car? Even if they lend me the Buick, like they did for this trip, I can't be seen driving around here!"

"Can't you tell them you're going back to Liberal?"

"I don't think so. I don't think Dr. Bond will lie to my aunt and uncle."

This was the thorniest knot of all. How could people around them, mainly the two doctors, remain honorable if she and Lola were going to concoct a total fabrication?

"Cassie, there is *no way* I can stay here in Cato and have this baby." Lola got up, dusting herself from her shoulders down to her ankles. "Thanks for trying, though. Let's go."

"But wouldn't you *like* to? Wouldn't you like to be here, near everybody and yet not near 'em? You know what I mean! Wouldn't you feel more at home here than anywhere else?"

She stood up and moved close, peering into Lola's face.

"Give it up, Cassie. I'll meet you out front."

Still racking her brain, Cassie locked the front door, then climbed out the kitchen window, reaching up to close it after her. She got into the front seat and closed the door as softly as she could.

"Don't start the car yet," she said. "I think I know how to do it. But you have to *want* to do it this way; that is, have the baby in Cato. *Do you?*"

Lola crossed her arms on the steering wheel. "It's just that I don't want to be obliged to Dr. Bond any more than I am already! He was so good to my dad. He didn't charge hardly anything during Daddy's illness; then he gave me money when I left! I bet he's so disappointed!"

She began to cry again, speaking between sobs. "I want to be grown up about this! I don't know a soul in Wichita; they'd all be strangers! Catholics are...*different,* aren't they? All those crucifixes and rosary beads and long black robes! Maybe they'd try to get *me* to be a Catholic!"

"Well, if you stay here you won't have to turn Catholic—there aren't any of 'em around for miles!" That got a small grin. She continued. "There's someone here in town who'll help us —he'll have to. We won't tell Doc Ledbetter or Dr. Bond a thing. We'll get this man to take you to a doctor over in Red Arrow or Antelope or somewhere."

"*What* man? Cassie, what are you talkin' about?"

293

"Let's us both go home now. You tell your aunt and uncle you've decided to go to this Immaculate Conception place up in Wichita. And tell 'em you need the Buick. But in the morning, you take all your stuff and light out for here. I'll meet you right after I get out of school."

She pointed. "And be sure and hide the car in back of the house, in those big bushes." She didn't tell Lola anything more about Floyd Weston just then. Although Lola had gotten herself in trouble, Cassie knew she was a thoroughly moral person, and she might have scruples about blackmail. Cassie, on the other hand, had none.

As they neared her house, Cassie began to worry about her own predicament. By now her parents had probably found out that she'd been nowhere near the Bannisters' this weekend. And her clothes were a mess.

Her mother was in bed with the door closed and the war news on, and her dad was out in the dog run. It looked as if she was going to have smooth sailing. But just as she started to tiptoe into her room, Liddy came out and started giving her the third degree.

"How come your clothes are so dusty?" she asked. "And you've got cobwebs in your hair! Weren't you studying the whole time?"

"Me and Fiona helped Mr. Bannister clean out his garage. But only at the end of the day; we were cramming the rest of the time!" She should win a prize for coming up with that one.

Liddy turned and went back into her room.

Cassie cleaned herself up and made supper. Liddy said she wasn't hungry, and instead of listening to Charlie McCarthy with her dad, she took a bath and went to bed. Before she went to sleep, she offered up thanks that there was no algebra exam tomorrow.

She'd gotten away with the whole thing.

O

The next day Fiona questioned her about the trip, and acted as if she was entitled to an answer. All Cassie would say was that Lola wanted her to go away with her to get some medical records. Fiona raised an eyebrow. "I stayed out of sight like you told me to, and I was really bored!" she huffed.

Later that day, as Cassie and Fergus sat in study hall working on an assignment about the Axis powers, her mind wandered onto Lola. She would have to talk to Floyd Weston right away.

She thought about how she never had told a soul about seeing him and Eula Tully that day down at the creek. For months and months after that, every time Cassie bought a movie ticket, Eula Tully's eyes would open wide like a jackrabbit's. She seemed to be waiting for some sort of retribution, some leak of the scandal, but Cassie would merely look back at her with a deadpan expression and saunter slowly into the theater.

Once Cassie had waited on Eula in the drugstore, ringing up a sale of bath powder, and not once did Eula look her in the eye! Another time they'd ended up sitting next to each other at a basketball game, because the people between them left. That time Cassie wouldn't let Eula ignore her. She purposely chattered away about the home team and the visiting team, and who might win and who might lose. Then she couldn't help herself; she got in a zinger about how she'd been crawdadding just last week down on Wolf Creek and had only caught two crawdads!

None of it was true, of course. Eula left a few seconds before the game was over, when the score was tied.

It had been three years, and still she kept the dirty deed to herself. She wondered if they were still doing it, and she wondered if she was the only person in town who knew. If she wasn't, if *everybody* knew, her plan wouldn't work. For years now, when she saw Floyd Weston at church he averted his eyes, no doubt hoping that she would forget her special knowledge, that it would evaporate into the ether. Was it her imagination, or had he changed from the timid, plodding farmer he had once been? Lately he sported a mustache, not a thick gray one like her dad's, but a thin, brown scraggly thing that reminded her of a caterpillar. And he wore plaid suits—to church! Maybe his fooling around with Eula was giving him confidence, because now when he followed Winifred like a flunky down the church aisle, his step had more of a spring to it.

"Cassie, how many sources are we s'posed to use for this dumb report?" Fergus whispered, bringing her back to study hall.

She shook her head, trying to clear her brain.

"Two. I got a lot of *Daily Oklahomans* at home. Want me to bring you some?"

"Yeah, I'd 'preciate that! I done looked from stem to gudgeon in this liberry, and there ain't *nuthin'* about no Mussolini!"

At her desk by the door, Miss Thornhill raised her eyebrows at them for talking during study hall. Cassie lowered her head. She'd never noticed it before, but Fergus's hair was the exact color of the apricot ticking on her dad's dog Perky's Sultan. Fergus would have been the logical one to tell about Mr. Weston and Eula. She never would have seen them if Fergus hadn't suggested going crawdadding that day. But she wasn't going to tell him. Why hadn't she told Fiona? She could hardly believe she hadn't; up to now, the two of them told each other everything!

She needed to rustle up some food and get it out to Lola, along with blankets, but first she'd have to see if there was air in the bicycle tires. She packed up her books, got permission to leave, then went to the school office to make a phone call.

She'd decided on a different approach from the one she'd first hinted to Lola about. If this plan worked, she wouldn't have to resort to blackmail. She picked up the phone and asked Hetty to ring the First Methodist Church. Reverend Dickens said yes, he could see her now, even though he was working on his Sunday sermon. Last year, church higher-ups had replaced the kindly Reverend Brooks with this new man, the rather stiff Reverend Dickens, who had an elderly wrinkled wife and no children. Cassie missed Drucilla, Hermie, and Delores, who had moved to Anadarko.

After school, without explaining where she was going, she gave Fiona a quick wave and hurried away. As she walked along in the fall afternoon, kicking through piles of fallen leaves on the gravel road, she thought about the chance she was taking, talking to the preacher. Winifred Weston was chairman of the board of deacons now and ran things the way she wanted to, but that had no bearing on this situation, because Mrs. Weston wasn't going to be involved.

She walked across the railroad tracks, skirting Main to avoid running into her dad, and made her way to the little white church with its graceful pointed steeple. She knocked at the side door and heard Reverend Dickens call, "Come in." He was seated at a big desk strewn with sheets of lined paper, no doubt notes for the sermon.

"How nice to see you, young lady! How can I help you?" He stood up, and motioned her to a chair.

Cassie wished she'd been more attentive to her grooming this morning. Her old yellow sweater was balled and fuzzy, the shirt collar under it was as wrinkled as a wad of paper, and the pleats in her gray skirt had long ago lost their sharpness. She put her knees together, placed her hands in her lap, and began. She'd been worrying at the problem so long that any preliminaries were beyond her.

"I was wondering, Reverend, whether we could keep this talk...uh, confidential." She tried to sound businesslike, but her voice trembled.

"Of course." He pivoted further toward her in his swivel chair, which gave out a series of squeaking sounds. Where had she heard a chair like that recently?

"I was wondering, sir, if a girl is...going to have a baby, and she wants to *have* the baby, and she isn't married, who could help her? I know someone over in a nearby town who is—like that." The words either tumbled out in a rush or got clogged up, sticking in her throat and dribbling out slow as molasses.

Reverend Dickens didn't say anything for a few minutes. He was in shirtsleeves without a tie, and his thinning hair wasn't carefully combed. "Well, I can't say exactly who would help her, but probably the church ladies in her town could deliver food. Does she have a doctor? Our church doesn't have any funds for that kind of thing. She should go to her church, in her town."

"She doesn't have a church." This was the very first lie Cassie told about Lola, who was an upstanding member of the First Christian.

He didn't say anything, and during the quiet, Cassie looked around. On the wall was a calendar with a picture of a handsome long-haired Jesus holding a baby on his lap. Surrounding him were several beautiful children, all of them looking up adoringly at the Christ. They wore tunics of bright colors, as did He, and belts with tasseled golden cords. Around Jesus's head was an incandescent halo.

They sat on in silence. Cassie bent down and scratched her knee, then reached up and reclasped the barrette in her hair. Finally Reverend Dickens spoke. "Cassie, you weren't at church last night. Are you in any trouble?"

"Oh, no, it's not *me*!" She'd never even been out with a boy, for gosh sakes! She squirmed in her chair, and turned bright red. How could she keep from volunteering any more information and still achieve the desired results?

"I was just wonderin' whether this person…this girl—uh, woman— could count on help from the church, like whether there's a doctor around that you could get, and whether ladies could give her baby clothes and diapers and a baby bed an' stuff like that." *There!* It was all out.

"Our church certainly doesn't condone unwed motherhood, Cassie. You must know that. She should talk to the father and try to get him to marry her, for the sake of the child if nothing else."

"She doesn't know *who* the father is. It's got her stumped."

Now it was the preacher's turn to go bright red. He looked away, gazing out the window next to his desk. "Well, does she have parents to confide in, or other relatives who could help her? That, of course, would be best."

Cassie's shoulders drooped. Why would she be here if Lola had family she could confide in?

She stood up. "Well, thank you, Reverend. I'll tell her all you've told me." Which was exactly nothing.

He walked her to the door, and they stepped together out into the October sunshine. "I'm glad you came to me about this, Cassie," he said, not sounding glad at all. In fact, he seemed relieved that she was leaving.

O

The night before Lola left, Aunt Flo wept when the girl told them of her decision, that she was going to Wichita to the nuns. She insisted that she didn't need money, she had some saved up, but that she would appreciate it if she could keep the old Buick.

"Of course!" said Aunt Flo, and Uncle George added, "Keep it as long as you need it; we've got the Chevy. I just hope the thing holds up till you get all the way up to Wichita." His voice broke, and he hurried out of the room. "I'll look for a map—got one o' Kansas somewhere."

She felt like the lowest of the low for lying to them, but she didn't think they'd be happy with the truth, either—that she was moving into an old abandoned cabin outside of town.

Aunt Flo helped Lola pack, bringing out a few blouses of her own, two loose-fitting skirts, and a corduroy jacket. "I'm big," she said, "and these things'll help until you can get some clothes from the nuns. But

I'm goin' to order some maternity clothes and send 'em up. I'll order some nice things—the store's been needin' to stock more of that kind of thing, anyway."

Every few minutes, Flo stopped to embrace Lola or stroke her hair. "We'll be coming up real soon to see you, honey."

Lola's back was turned as she bent over the suitcase. Listening to her aunt's expressions of affection, she was suddenly filled with doubt. Maybe this was going to be impossible to carry out. But she shoved the thought aside. She would have to go through with it—it was already underway, and Cassie seemed to think it was going to run smooth as silk.

The next morning they were together in the kitchen. She'd told them she wanted to make an early start, and it wasn't daylight yet. Uncle George, as always, kept his feelings hidden. He sat at the dinette table, stirring his coffee with a repeated circular gesture, but not bothering to drink it. He looked gloomy. Looking at him was worse than seeing her aunt cry, and Lola kept her eyes averted.

At last she screwed up her courage to mention the final part of her deception.

"I'm going to be out of touch with both of you until I've had the baby. I've thought about it, and I think it will be much better that way."

"Oh, no!" exclaimed Flo. "The nuns wouldn't want you to cut off from us like that—we're practically your only living relatives!" She became so agitated that finally Lola agreed, deciding that she would have to figure out later how to handle that aspect of the plot.

It was still dark as the three of them walked out to the car. Uncle George put the suitcase, a box of food, and Lola's willow basket full of odds and ends into the trunk. Then he stuck something in her jacket pocket, four fifty-dollar bills. She hugged and thanked him, and after she was behind the wheel, one at a time they put their heads through the open window to give her a final kiss. Her last view was of the two of them standing side by side, Aunt Flo still in her robe, Uncle George fully dressed and ramrod straight beside her. His sober face was a blur of white, but she could see that Aunt Flo was smiling.

○

After her talk with Reverend Dickens, Cassie biked out to the cabin with a few supplies, but she had time for only a brief visit and look-around with Lola.

It wasn't until Saturday that she had time for a longer visit. Dan's bicycle was working fine, although when she stopped at the gas station for air, Clink Kerry found and patched a slow leak. For her second trip she wore corduroy pants, which were much more practical than a skirt. She took some of her savings, which had totaled sixty-five dollars but were shrinking fast, from an old billfold of Mitch's in her dresser drawer, and as soon as Shafer's Grocery opened Saturday morning, she bought two loaves of bread, a block of cheese, a package of tea, dried apricots, apples, raisins, a pound of bacon, and a dozen eggs. Milk bottles were too heavy and might break if she hit a rut, so she skipped milk. It took some doing to get all of it arranged in the bicycle basket, and the full load made the bike heavy and unwieldy, but finally she got started.

It was a crisp fall morning, so quiet that the sounds of the bike tires on the dirt road and her own heavy breathing were loud in her ears. The cold air awakened all her senses, which was good, because there were a lot of cow flops in the road, which she had to swerve to avoid skidding on. The glorious scent of fresh-cut alfalfa was all around her, and a mother quail, disturbed by the sound of the bicycle, flushed out of some Johnson grass by the barbed-wire fence, her five babies scuttling along behind her.

No one passed her, and no one was in sight when she turned off the road to the cabin. After pedaling down the long dirt drive, she got off and walked the bike around back, sweating and breathing hard.

Lola stood by the sink in the kitchen, looking out the window. She ran to pull open the door, excitedly embracing Cassie and thanking her for the food.

"I want to repay you for all of it!" she said. "Uncle George gave me tons of money, but it's all big bills—could you get them changed for me, so I can pay you back? You give me that grocery receipt." Cassie had stuck it away in her pocket. but handed it over, and Lola smoothed it out and stored it in an old coffee can on the counter.

"My gosh!" Cassie breathed, looking around her. "I can't believe the way you've cleaned up this place!"

"I found a broom." She pointed to where it leaned against the wall. Cassie remembered that broom; Mabel had been sweeping with it the day she gave her the Dionne quintuplets calendar.

"You need a table and some chairs," she said.

"Don't worry. I've got that old chair and the crates in the front room to sit on, and I found another chair and a cot in the shed out back. I beat the bejeebers out of the cot to get out the dust. I wear all my clothes to bed, and with the blankets you brought and the one I took from home, I'm fine. It seems like the baby's keepin' me warm!" She laughed.

Her cheeks were flushed from the cold weather, the baby, or both, and she'd lost the worried look she had on the trip down from Liberal.

Lola nodded in the direction of the black potbellied stove against the kitchen wall. "There's a stack of wood next to the shed, but I'm afraid to burn any of it, afraid someone'll see the smoke. And can you believe this? The gas stove works! Somebody forgot to unhook the service. I'll probably stay in here on cold days." She heated water in a battered, lidless pan, and made tea, and they sat on the floor in a patch of morning sun coming through the kitchen window.

"I'll have to use the pump outside, since the water's been cut off, and of course there's no electricity. But using lights would be dangerous, even if I had 'em. I found a lamp in the closet behind a box of magazines, and it's got a smidgen of kerosene. I'm hoping with the shade pulled down on the bedroom window, nobody'll notice a thing!"

This set up a warning in Cassie's head, but she didn't say anything. Lola seemed to be so positive about her situation, who would want to ruin it?

No wonder Mabel had been able to leave town so fast three years ago, Cassie thought. She'd just stashed things away without really disposing of them.

"Cassie, could you bring me some kerosene next time you come out, if it isn't too much trouble?"

The more Lola talked about the things she lacked and the ways she planned to overcome the deprivation, the more Cassie's heart sank. It seemed there were more disadvantages to this plan than they'd bargained for, and winter was coming, with night temperatures already down in the forties.

"I'm gonna see what I can do about getting you a doctor in another town," said Cassie. "We can forget Doc Ledbetter."

"You mentioned somebody would help us, but you didn't say who it was... Cassie, I'd hate it if you got in trouble because of me! Please, *please* tell me what you're considering doing—if it's for me and the baby, I have a right to know."

So, for the first time, Cassie told the secret, relating the story from start to finish. Lola held her teacup halfway to her lips the entire time, and when Cassie was through, she set it down and grinned. She seemed delighted by the story.

"Mrs. Weston's husband! Why do I feel it's what that old biddy deserves? She's never done anything to me, except one time in the drugstore she looked me up and down and made a sour face. She wouldn't let me wait on her—she went and found your dad, just for some bath powder! I was wearing my hair in an updo and I had on a red dress, and she made me feel like something was wrong with me."

"She brings it out in everyone," declared Cassie. "Makes me wanna puke frogs. Daddy says she acts like she's got a poker up her behind." They giggled.

"I never have gotten to know Eula," said Lola, "just waited on her when she came in for a Coke, but it wasn't very often."

"I think she's pure-dee scared of what I know and what I saw. She used to come in more... My folks even talked about hirin' her once, but they decided she wasn't real bright."

"Must *not* be, if she..." Lola stopped, as tears welled up and spilled over. She brushed them away with her hand. As Cassie watched Lola fight to keep control, doubt flooded her mind again about whether she should have talked her into this lonely existence. Not only did her friend not have a toilet, running water, or electric lights or, most importantly, heat, but she was so isolated! Maybe this was a terrible mistake.

Lola spoke, echoing Cassie's thoughts. Wiping her eyes on the hem of her shirt, she said, "I think maybe I'm going to feel a little bit cut off out here, but I've got an idea for something to keep me busy."

"What?"

"You'll see, once I get started. You're not the only one who can keep a secret! Now, you better go home. Your folks'll guess you're up to no good if you're gone too much! Besides, aren't you supposed to be helping out in the store? Who's your dad gonna replace me with?"

"I go to work at noon. He'll prob'ly find someone; he usually does."

"How's your mom?"

"Still listenin' to the radio and worryin' about Mitch and Dan, and drivin' around the country seein' farmers' wives."

"Would you tell your parents I said a fond good-bye? Tell them you saw me somewhere and especially mentioned them."

"Okay." She didn't know where she could say she saw Lola. She stood up and set her teacup on the sink. Her friend hugged her and gave her a radiant smile, reminding Cassie of the time she first saw her on the train platform.

○

Before the service Sunday morning, after waiting around for fifteen minutes, Cassie cornered Floyd Weston outside the church. Mrs. Weston had gone inside and was talking to Reverend Dickens's wife about the church's leaky roof, telling her who to call to get it repaired, that they'd better do it before the rainy season set in, and on and on. Cassie had one ear cocked in their direction, and it was now or never.

She stepped close to Mr. Weston. "I'd like to talk to you. Could you meet me somewhere?"

His face froze, and he swallowed. She thought he was going to explode right out of his tight collar, but finally he managed one strangled word. "Where?"

"How 'bout Wolf Creek Bridge, north side, tomorrow morning at seven?"

He nodded, looked around furtively, and scurried inside. Cassie went around to the side door, grabbed her choir robe off the rack, and ran up the steps into the choir loft, arriving in time to stand and sing the first hymn with the congregation. The interior of the church rang with "Shall We Gather at the River?" and when her glance locked with Winifred Weston's disapproving glower, she had a hard time keeping a straight face.

Cassie was at the bridge the next morning promptly at seven. She got off the bicycle and stood holding on to the handlebars, well off the road and standing between two scrub oaks. It was cold, and she wore a jacket and her corduroy pants, with a long striped muffler wrapped around her neck. She didn't have to wait for Floyd Weston. Suddenly he appeared an arm's length away, wearing a John Deere cap. He looked sour and mean.

"You gotta believe me," Cassie began immediately, "I haven't told anyone."

Floyd Weston slowly turned to one side and looked off in the distance, pretending he wasn't really here, as if it were some other man wearing his clothes. His mustache twitched like something alive.

"All right. I believe you. What d'you want?" His tone was vaguely threatening.

"I got a favor to ask."

"Yeah?"

"A friend of mine is goin' to have a baby, and she isn't married. She's living in the old Farrow place not far from you, and nobody knows about it." She waited for it all to sink in. "We need an out-of-town doctor to take care of her, and transportation to and from his office. She can't drive herself in her car, 'cause it'd be recognized."

"What about *my* car being reco'nized? And who's your friend?"

It was quiet except for the birds starting up in the trees and brush. "It's Lola, from our store. I reckon she musta done what you and Eula were doin'." She couldn't believe her own ears—had she really said that? But she sensed that the bluntest talk would get the quickest results.

Floyd Weston looked at her with narrowed eyes. She was positive he was going to try to make her back down, but she readjusted her hands on the handlebars and stared straight back at him.

With a hand upraised, he took a step toward her. He opened his mouth, but she never found out what he was going to say, because he closed it and stepped back. "You'll have to make all the doctor's appointments; I can't call from my house."

Cassie let out her breath, unaware until now that she had been holding it.

All at once his tone changed from menacing to soft and cajoling. "And if I help you out, do I have your word neither one of you'll never tell? *Never?*" He sounded now like the old meek Floyd Weston, the little man who trailed obediently behind his wife at church.

"As long as you help us—and *keep* helpin' us—there ain't any reason why your wife or nobody else has to know." Listening to herself, she wondered why she was imitating Marjorie Main in *Ma and Pa Kettle*.

She threw her leg over the bike and pedaled away.

After school that day, she was on her way to see Lola and was almost to the bridge, when she remembered the kerosene. She pedaled back to the lumberyard and bought a can from Barney Scruggs. He wanted to know why she was buying kerosene, and even though she didn't think it was any of his business, she told him her mother needed it for an old lamp she kept in case the power went out.

"Well, you better bring me in some stamps. This stuff's rationed, y'know," declared Barney.

She nodded, and finally was back on the road.

18

And on through crummy continents and days
Deliberate, grimy, slightly drunk we crawl
The good-bad boys of circumstance and chance
Whose bucket-helmets bang the empty wall
 —Karl Shapiro, "Troop Train"
 Articles of War: A Collection

Liddy stood at the train station on a freezing day in early November, the wind whistling through the open platform area and all around her. She was wearing only a dress, coat, stockings and scarf, but she was determined to be here. Marvin and Cassie—maybe the whole town— thought she was crazy, but if this was what she wanted to do, she was going to do it! She loved seeing all the fresh, youthful faces so much like Mitch's and Dan's, loved seeing them smile and wave as if they were having a good time going off to war. They would stand packed in the aisles, shouting and whooping it up. She didn't think they were drinking; they were in uniform, after all. It was all just youthful exuberance, and she wondered if any of them realized what they were going off to.

They seemed to like seeing her as much as she enjoyed greeting them.

Sometimes Rowena would wait with her, or Mrs. O'Herlihy or Mrs. Spokes, who also had sons in the service. Once in a while Homer Botsin's new wife, Connie, came down to bring Homer his lunch and keep her company, but usually Liddy was alone. Today Connie came out on the platform and started chatting; Liddy liked the woman's plainspokenness and warmth. She knit beautifully, too, and had been turning out lovely sweater sets for Liddy to sell. The best thing about her was that she didn't think waving at troop trains was the act of a crazy woman.

Homer had called Liddy to say there'd be trains going through all day. She'd been here all afternoon, and sure enough, three trains loaded with soldiers had come through already.

Now they heard the whistle of a train coming from the west, and in a few minutes the giant locomotive bore down on them. The baggage cars hurtled past, then ten or twelve flatcars loaded with Army equipment covered in olive-drab tarpaulins. Next came the passenger cars of the same color, with soldiers squeezing out of the windows.

Liddy and Connie waved, and the boys leaned out, fluttering their caps in the air and yelling out the name of the town.

"*Whoo-whooo— Ca-a-a—to-oh!*"

Did they do this at all the towns they passed through, all the way across America? The passenger cars had all gone through, and as Liddy turned to go down the hill she heard a single voice yelling above the racketing train wheels.

"*Mom... Mom!*"

She turned and looked—looked hard—and there, hanging off the little red caboose, swaying far out over the edge of the railing, was Mitch!

It was her son!

Next to him stood a stocky man with sergeant's stripes, waving and grinning as broadly as Mitch. Both of them had time to give her a "V" for "victory" before they went past.

She waved back, yelling, "*Mitch! My Lord, Mitch!*" She ran after him, not stopping until she had stumbled off the wooden platform and onto the gravel, falling and skinning both knees. She got up and stood waving until the two boys were mere specks. Then they were gone.

Fiona and Cassie were at a table in the drugstore eating candy bars and reading *Screen World*. They hadn't yet begun their homework because they were busy debating the charms of Van Johnson versus Peter Lawford. Cassie thought Lawford's British accent beat Van's freckles hands down, but Fiona was stubborn; she loved those freckles.

Jim Bartlett's petite wife Peggy, Marvin's new salesgirl and soda jerk, was working behind the soda fountain stacking glassware. Suddenly Liddy and Connie rushed in. Liddy wore a rapturous expression, and her knees were skinned and bleeding.

"Cassie, Peggy—girls—*I saw Mitch!*"

"You did?" Cassie's voice was flat and unbelieving, as if her mother had said she'd flown to the moon and back.

"I took Homer his lunch like I do," Connie said, "and I was there with your mama watchin' all the boys come through! We waved at all of 'em on that last train, and there was your ma's boy standin' on the caboose, yellin' at her!"

Mrs. Botsin's broad face beamed. This was *truth*; Liddy had not imagined it.

Cassie exclaimed, "Mama, that's wonderful!" and Fiona said, "Miz Field, that's terrific!"

Liddy sank down at the table. "It *was* him!" She paused, then said, "I think I'll call Marvin!" He was at home, supposedly napping but probably working with his dogs. She got Hetty at the switchboard, told her the news, and asked to be connected. There was a long wait... No one in the store spoke.

"Marvin, I saw Mitch! Coming through on the troop train! Yes! It was *him!* He yelled at me from the caboose!" She waited while Marvin spoke. "I couldn't believe it, either! Yes, he looked fine! I think that must have been his sergeant with him—he was waving, too! They both gave me the 'V' for 'victory' sign! Yes, come on down!"

News had spread, and people started drifting in from all over. Liddy held court at the front table, with Mrs. Botsin, Fiona, and Cassie playing her attendants. In a few minutes Marvin came in from the back, dressed in his old clothes. He leaned over and kissed Liddy in front of everyone, and for a fleeting moment Cassie wished Dan were there.

Stuffy was one of the first to arrive. "Thought your wife was crazy, thinkin' she was gonna see Mitch on one o' them trains! Guess she proved me wrong!"

People filed into the store from all the other places of business on Main. They stood three-deep at the fountain, chatting and exchanging stories about soldiers they knew—their sons, brothers, cousins, friends. Marvin, in a rare moment of largesse, told Peggy to give everyone a free Coke, then he got some merthiolate and bandages and knelt down to tend to Liddy's knees.

Connie Botsin's roly-poly daughter Margie, who was a year behind Cassie and Fiona in school, asked Marvin if she could have a lime phosphate instead. He said no, he was just giving out Cokes. She said she'd take it, and came over to the marble table and tried to horn in on Cassie and Fiona's good time.

Liddy's seeing Mitch on the troop train was a topic of conversation for days. Billy Saltman put a picture of him, and a story about Liddy seeing him, on the front page of the *Cato Enquirer*. For a while, Mitch was elevated to the status of local war hero.

O

Yes, Marvin thought, there definitely was an upside to your kids leaving home. Ever since Pauly and Dan left, Iris had allowed Clyde Spokes to hold weekly poker games at the Cato Hotel. They could smoke as much as they wanted, even cigars, and cuss and cheat at cards, and nobody ever got mad. Marvin, Stuffy, Barney Scruggs, Harold Cutter, and Clyde were the regulars. Clyde had fixed up a small room behind the lobby where no one bothered them, and they brought their own sandwiches, bourbon, and beer. Harold Cutter was the best player and almost always ended up with the pot, but Marvin still remembered one night in October when he'd won four dollars.

Tonight Harold and Marvin walked past the depot on their way to the game, carrying two bags of food they'd picked up at the Mistletoe.

"You ever miss working for the WPA?" Marvin asked Harold.

"Yeah, kinda miss that reg'lar salary. But I'm glad folks're better off now and not needin' so much government assistance. Incidentally, Marvin, you okay for insurance? I'm workin' for Hartford now, got some good deals on home and business policies."

This was goddamned annoying, Marvin thought; it was the kind of thing that could ruin the whole evening. But he liked Harold, and had long since put aside any jealousy he had felt when Liddy worked for him. He was a lot older, but he was in good shape and still had a full head of silvery hair—more hair than Marvin, in fact—and he still walked several miles a week. Liddy had told Marvin she had seen Harold walking on the road almost all the way to Arbuckle. She'd offered him a ride, but he just yelled, "No, Liddy, I'm enjoying the clouds and the birds!"

"I'm fine for insurance," Marvin said. "Got taken care of a few years ago through a friend of mine down in Ardmore."

He snapped it off, so Harold wouldn't keep pestering him. And that reminded him: he had to send Joe Kelly the money. He sent some every month. Even though Liddy had objected to his going in on that oil investment, he had gone ahead with a plan he came up with when discussing it with Joe. "I haven't got any extra cash," he'd told his buddy after his big fight with Liddy that Christmas Eve. "All the extra I make goes for insurance on the house and store."

"Well," Joe had argued in his smooth, persuasive way, "'stead o' sendin' all that money for insurance for the drugstore, why don't you just cut back on the policy and send it to me? Your store's doin' good, and it'll keep on doin' good, what can happen to it? An' that drillin' hole down near the Arbuckle Mountains is goin' to pay off real big in no time at all. Those guys know where to look!"

Marvin had decided Liddy would never know about it; and when they got rich, she'd be sorry she ever advised different. They were almost to the hotel, and Harold was jogging his arm. "You and Liddy doin' okay, Marvin?"

Now the man *was* going too far! What right did he have to pry into their marriage?

"Sure. No problems." This was no way to start an evening, and he felt his temper rising.

"Just checkin'," said Harold. "Y'know, sometimes things come along that're not helpful to a marriage. I know; I was married for twenty years. Things like, oh, maybe temptation in the form of another woman."

Marvin swiveled toward the older man, looking at him incredulously as they stepped onto the sidewalk. Was Harold trying to say he knew about Abby?

Just before they entered the lobby, Harold remarked, "Yes, it was a shame how ever'body back in the early thirties thought we oughta give all the best jobs to men, so they could support their families. Then the war came, and that wasn't the case anymore. But when I was on the school board with George Schonberger, well, we kinda thought Abby Gallagher was *too* good for our little town, so we had to let her go. We thought maybe since she was such a fine teacher, she could find a better job in another part of the state, and I reckon she has."

Harold turned and looked Marvin directly in the eye. Marvin dropped his gaze, and they went into the hotel and through the lobby to the poker room.

O

Two weeks after Liddy saw Mitch come through on the train, a letter came from her, written in her jagged penmanship on six sheets of hotel stationery:

Lee Huckins Hotel
Oklahoma City
Nov. 12, 1942

Dear Cassie & Marvin,

I got here three days ago. Am planning to leave for Tulsa tomorrow. Sorry I haven't written sooner, but been busy. Stopped in Enid—found a real nice shop there. Enid has grown so much, but Oklahoma City has gotten huge! The stores have given me lots of encouragement. They said they'd take everything that was quilted & crocheted, and all 3 shops (2 here in O.C.!) want baby & children's things. One of the shop owners is so nice—we jabbered about our sons in the service, and she gave me a contact in Tulsa, so I'm going to go there. Looks like I'll be gone from home longer than planned, but I think I'll be back Friday.

Waiting for trains isn't any fun, but I've met some nice folks. The soldiers have first priority, so we sit around waiting a lot & makes everything extra tiring. Met a young woman in the Enid station & we talked. She wanted to go meet her beau in New Orleans he's at an Army base there. I felt sorry for her, she cried & showed me his picture; told me her mother had died & she wanted to go down & marry this young man. Also the cutest little girl with her mama waiting to go to Lincoln Nebraska; the husband is a colonel up there. The little girl reminded me of Mabel's Lulu.

The woman who gave me the contact in Tulsa says there's lots of money floating around there because of Douglas Aircraft. Hope so. All my love,

Liddy

P.S. Cassie, call Mrs. Klein & Mrs. Thatcher & tell them all this good news. I'm bringing you & Peggy something nice.

P.P.S. Don't worry, Marvin, I always get the cheapest rooms. I'm glad I decided to take this trip. If I hadn't seen Mitch, I wouldn't have got spurred on to do it. Seeing all these soldiers makes me feel closer to my boys, but I can't explain why that is. Now my hand is tired from writing. Good night. xoxox

19

Be thou as chaste as ice, as pure as snow,
thou shalt not escape calumny.
— William Shakespeare
The Comedy of Errors

Cassie tugged and pulled at the rope, struggling to secure the big, rolled-up braided rag rug to her bicycle. She'd found it in the attic and stashed it in her closet until Liddy was gone. It wasn't easy to balance it and still keep the bike upright, but she managed. She made a stop at Shafer's Grocery, hiding her bike in the alley so Mrs. Shafer wouldn't see the rug.

In the cabin's kitchen, Cassie helped Lola put away the groceries. Then she untied and brought in the rug, and when they rolled it out in the tiny bedroom, Lola smiled with happiness. It looked so cheerful with its faded colors, covering almost half the floor. They lolled upon it, leaning back on their elbows.

Cassie thought Lola looked wonderful. The rich fullness to her figure was very becoming, and her skin seemed more glowing than ever.

"I been worryin' about you all alone out here," said Cassie. "Are you okay?"

"Yes! I know this was your idea, Cassie, but now I think of it as mine, too, and I take full responsibility! The only bad thing is, I haven't been able to think how to write Aunt Flo and Uncle George! They think I'm in Wichita havin' this baby!"

This was the big stumper, and had been from the beginning. They'd solved the problem of the doctor. Floyd Weston drove Lola back and forth to a clinic in Antelope, with Cassie making appointments over the phone when Liddy was gone. When talking to the nurse, she pretended to be Lola and gave the name "Lily Bond," the only thing she could come up with at the moment. If the long-distance calls were noticed later on by her parents, as she was sure they would be, she'd just have to lie and say she knew nothing about them.

Lola told her Mr. Weston always picked her up in plenty of time, but that it was difficult making conversation with him while she was lying on the floor of the backseat, so she didn't try. She said he was distant but polite, and always warned her before they rounded a curve. Lola said he asked how come she didn't go somewhere else to have the baby, because that's what most girls did, and all she could think to answer was, "I'm not most girls."

It was frigid in the house on this late November day, and Cassie kept her coat on. Lola admitted that once or twice she'd given in and burned wood in the potbellied stove, though never in the daytime. Making tea was a regular ritual now; she went into the kitchen and soon returned with two steaming unmatched cups.

"Lola, did you know Mitch is overseas now? He's in England!"

"I bet your mom's worried about her boys. How's she doing?"

"She's okay, long as she keeps hearin' from 'em—'specially Mitch, since he's overseas. Peggy Bartlett works at the store now."

"No kidding!" Lola smiled. "I'd like to float in like a ghost and watch how she waits on customers, she's so little and peppy! But I thought your dad was makin' *you* the main help."

"He says he wants someone who doesn't read magazines all the time."

Lola got up slowly, supporting her back with a hand. "There's somethin' I want to show you. Come out here."

Cassie followed her onto the screened-in porch off the kitchen, which she'd forgotten all about. A long table covered with long, curving switches was there, and sitting on it was a bucket filled with more branches. At one end of the table sat a woven bassinet, finished except for the hood. Strands of greenish-gold wands were partially threaded in.

"Is that a baby bassinet? And what is this stuff?" asked Cassie, fingering the branches.

"It's willow. There's tons of it growin' around here. I have to soak it for a few days, then peel it. I been usin' my sewin' scissors to cut it. My—Aunt Flo's—skirts are gettin' kind of torn." She held out her scratched hands.

"It's real pretty, Lola! Where'd you learn to *do* this!" Cassie ran her hand over it admiringly.

"My grandma in Arkansas was a basket maker. I used to visit her when I was little, before my dad got sick. Once I stayed with her all summer, and she taught me to weave willow. That's one of mine." In a corner of the porch sat the large basket Cassie had seen before, filled with kindling.

"I didn't know you made that."

"It's funny," said Lola. "When I'm gatherin' branches, and peelin' 'em, and doin' the actual weaving, I feel great! It's only when I don't have anything to do that I get lonely."

There was a disconsolate note to her voice, but then she brightened. "You know what I'm going to do next? I'm going to weave a honeysuckle-vine basket for Aunt Flo! There's lots of that around here, too, and dogwood and snowberry. Granny used all of 'em."

An hour later Cassie biked away. She felt a little better about Lola's solitude now. If her friend could keep busy making things, maybe everything was going to be all right.

Suddenly Cassie felt so tired she didn't think she could manage the rest of the distance home. Her legs felt like lead, and her arms and shoulders ached. She knew that her father was out running the dogs, so she took the risk of showing up at the drugstore in her corduroy pants.

Brothers Jim and Ed Bartlett, involved in one of their cold-weather checker games, sat in the back of the store next to the black potbellied stove. They had a lot of free time now that Jim didn't have anything to do at the icehouse, and Sheriff Ed's usefulness to the town was nothing if not spasmodic.

Cassie walked back to join them. Peggy was standing behind Jim, observing the game while massaging her husband's broad shoulders. She was about as tall standing up as her husband was sitting down. Cassie had heard Stuffy say to her dad, "Jim's kind of a awkward size: too big for a man and not big enough for a horse." Liddy had told Cassie about Peggy's desire to have a child, "Isn't it a shame Peggy and Jim haven't been able to start a family? She's so anxious for a baby! Maybe that's the trouble, maybe she's too anxious. And they'd both make the best kind of parents..." Cassie had thought at the time how ironic it was: Lola expecting without wanting to be, and Peggy with a nice husband and house, wanting kids like anything, unable to get pregnant.

When Peggy was new working at the drugstore and Cassie was there, Fiona's mom had come in. She whispered something to Peggy, who hurried back to the Personals Section and returned with a large pink tube. Mrs. Bannister paid cash and hurried on her way.

"What *is* that stuff?" asked Cassie.

"Let's put it this way, Cassie," Peggy laughed, "it's somethin' neither one of us needs!"

The next time she got a chance, Cassie looked on the tube: *Contraceptive Jelly. Use to prevent conception before, during and after conterminous activity.*

Now Sheriff Bartlett said, "Cassie, looky here! My brother thinks he's got me in some kinda tight spot." He looked up and winked. "But all I have to do is this." He took a black king and made three jumps over Jim's red checkers. "You see? It just takes a little professional know-how!" He raised his eyes, looking Cassie up and down. "Where you been in this freezin' weather, Cassie? And where you off to on that bike o' yours all the time? I see you goin' over the bridge, nights and days an' all in-between! You in any kinda trouble?"

"Leave her alone," said Jim. "That girl's okay! And fer Granny's sake, make a move!"

"I'm going to fix you a cup o' hot chocolate, Cassie," said Peggy. "Jim, you better stoke up that fire; it's cold enough in here to freeze the tail off a brass monkey. I think it's gonna snow."

Jim put on the asbestos glove they kept on the side of the stove, grabbed the shaker, and shook down the coals. He threw in a couple more shovelfuls and slammed the door with a metallic clang. Cassie sat as close to the stove as she could and put her feet up, and before she'd finished her cocoa, dozed off. Free from all responsibility, lulled by the sound of male laughter and the crackling and popping of the fire, she dozed.

The next morning at home Cassie woke with something warm oozing between her legs. She sat up, and there it was: blood, all over the bed.

This was it! She rushed into Liddy's room. "Mama, I need to borrow some of your Kotex!"

Liddy was half asleep. "What?"

"I need some sanitary pads and a belt."

Her mother moaned. "All right. Look in my closet in back of the hatboxes. I don't have a belt; use safety pins."

"And, Mama, the bed's all messed up."

"That's why you have to keep track. Get yourself a calendar and keep track of the days, and next month you won't mess up the bed. Soak the sheets in cold water; then wash out the stain with laundry soap. After that, hang them up to dry; then when they're dry, put them in the dirty clothes hamper. You know that much, don't you?" Her mother suddenly seemed out of sorts.

No, she didn't know. How *could* she? From that day on, Cassie was a neophyte in the exotic world of cramps and Kotex, the blissful sisterhood of Midol, the thrilling ritual of blood-soaked panties. In the weeks ahead, after avoiding the subject for years, Liddy did a complete turnaround. Now she was a treasure trove of stories connected to traumas relating to menstruation. Cassie should never get too close to water during *those days*, Liddy warned. One unlucky female she knew about had gone into galloping convulsions right after washing her hair. And she'd once heard of a girl who went swimming that time of the month, and her legs swelled up with elephantitis.

But this was what Cassie had wanted, to be on the way to female adulthood. *Wasn't it?*

O

Duke Farrow had waited for years for Mabel to deed her dad's cabin over to him. After all, he was the only blood relative she had around here. But it had slowly dawned on him over the years, maybe he was going to have to *buy* the property if he was going to get it. He planned to talk to Harold Cutter about it one of these days. He was tired of living in the Sampson ranch bunkhouse, and Naomi Nichols over in Arbuckle had said she'd think about marrying him if he'd get her a house.

One day on the way back from picking up cattle feed in town, he decided to drive in and have a look at the cabin. He drove down the long driveway, got out of his pickup, and walked onto the porch. He tried the doorknob, but it was locked, as he'd expected. Then he heard a noise inside.

What was this? The noise subsided, and nothing happened. He knocked, waited for a long time, then pounded again.

Lola opened the door a crack and peered through.

"What are *you* doin' here?" Duke demanded. "This is my cousin Mabel's place."

"I know," Lola breathed. She was frightened by the sudden appearance of this small, muscular man, and berated herself for answering his knock. Why hadn't she hidden under the bed?

"Ain't you the gal that worked at the drugstore?" he demanded.

"I'm Lola, Lola Mallory." She knew this man. The drugstore supplied the Sandy Flats with cattle medicine, and Mr. Field had told her he didn't like the manager Duke Farrow, said he always seemed to have a chip on his shoulder. "I remember you, too," she said. "You used to come in for cattle serum." She stood with her arms crossed, still barring entry.

Duke pushed back his beat-up Stetson. "Well, answer my question, girl," he demanded, glowering. "How come you're here?"

"Well, I...I got permission—and one day I just decided to move in." Lola dropped her arms and looked at Duke in a confiding way, as if she'd decided to be friendly after all.

"Permission from *who*?"

"Uh..." Years of working in the drugstore had provided Lola with a great deal of experience in using charm. She gave him a dimpled smile and twirled a long lock of hair. "One of the real estate men in town wrote your cousin and got permission."

Duke was sure she was lying. He knew there was only one real estate man in Cato: Harold Cutter. He could ask him. As if it had suddenly dawned on her what he was thinking, Lola reluctantly opened the door. He walked inside. Once there, he lounged against a wall, patting the Bull Durham sack in his shirt pocket. His eyes raked Lola's body up and down. He'd always thought the girl was a looker, but she'd never bothered to be more than barely polite. She wasn't fixed up now, and she'd gained some weight, but she was still very pretty. Prickles of desire stabbed his belly and groin. He moved a step toward her.

She smiled again, more brightly than before. She would have to make this man an ally if she wanted to remain here, because where else could she go? She was like an animal caught in a trap.

"Let me make you a cup of tea. There's a couple of chairs in here." Lola led him toward the kitchen, feeling his eyes on her hips and legs.

While the tea brewed she chatted about the bare accommodations of the little cabin, and the little ways she had improved it, conscious all the while of the way he was sizing up her body. After she poured the tea, Duke took out a flask and poured whiskey in his.

"Only way I can abide the stuff," he snorted, propping his boots on the box of kindling nearby. "Now, why don't you tell me more about how long you been here and how long you think yer gonna stay." He leaned back and took a long sip. "If you treat me nice enough, I might think about not tellin' Mabel."

Half an hour later, after she finally closed the door behind Duke, it took Lola twenty minutes to stop shaking.

O

A big box from Aunt Hannah, filled with her step-daughter Nell's cast-off clothes, arrived for Cassie one day in late November.

Liddy put the box, already opened, on Cassie's bed. In it was a two-piece blue wool-gabardine suit, and a hat to match, a few skirts and blouses that looked as if they'd never been worn, a pair of high-heeled silver slippers, and a long bright red chiffon dress, with silver trim.

These were the most exciting clothes Aunt Hannah'd ever sent her!

Cassie tried the long dress on first. Looked like it was for dancing, but where in the world would *she* ever wear it? Was she supposed to wear underwear underneath? She had only one brassiere, so cotton-crisp it showed through all her sweaters like a fabric fortress with nothing to defend, so she took it off, leaving on only her panties. She stepped into the dress and zipped it up. It was tight, but it looked good. She put on the silver shoes with their tiny straps, marveling at how well they fit, and swished into the bedroom to see herself in the closet mirror.

She couldn't believe what she saw. She didn't have much to fill out the low-cut bodice, but her shoulders looked pretty. And her hair against the red was so dark! She twirled around, trying to look at her back. The silver trim went all the way around the neckline in front, and the back showed even more skin. Why had Nell sent her this beautiful dress? Didn't she want it anymore? She was bending forward in front of the mirror to see if there was any sign of cleavage, when Liddy walked into the room.

"I don't believe it—you trying on that dress!"

Cassie gave her a puzzled look. "Didn't Aunt Hannah send it to me?"

"I suppose so, to wear when you're twenty-one! Get out of it this minute. I meant to put it away."

Why was her mother so angry? Because the dress was from Aunt Hannah? Because it was so worldly-looking? Or was it because her daughter was growing up?

Liddy was like this a lot lately, taking her worries about her sons out on *her*! Cassie knew that Liddy's nervousness and irritability had to do with Mitch being overseas and Dan being halfway across the United States, but that didn't make her easier to live with.

Cassie didn't argue. She took off the dress and handed it over, but she stashed the silver shoes in the back of her closet, hoping they hadn't been noticed.

O

Liddy lived for Mitch's letters from England, in their pale blue air-mail envelopes with the blue and red striping around the edges, but evidently they weren't enough to reassure her. Her mood would brighten for a couple of days, but soon she'd be down-in-the-dumps again. She would say, "We don't know what it's like for him! All those planes being shot down all the time. The Germans could blow up the airfield and all of them be *killed*! And now Dan wants to be a pilot!"

One day Marvin got something through the mail he thought would cheer her up. Their twenty-fifth anniversary was in three days, and Marvin had a surprise ready. Not exactly a gift, but a surprise. He asked Reuben if they could have the round table in the corner at the Mistletoe Friday night, and told him why.

Liddy was elated not to have to cook dinner. She got dressed in her new green paisley dress, and Marvin wore his yellow and purple polka-dot bow tie. When they got to the café, the corner table was covered with a clean checked tablecloth, and in the center were a new white candle and some little silver bells that Reuben said were left over from last Christmas. Just behind them on the wall was a sign Marvin didn't remember noticing before: *If ignorance is bliss, why aren't more people happy?*

The diner had a few other customers, but not so many that it felt crowded.

Liddy got so quiet, he could hardly believe it was Liddy, and when Ben handed them the fly-specked menu, she took it from his hand as if she were a duchess receiving a message from a royal ambassador. They ordered chicken-fried steak with mashed potatoes and gravy, and Liddy started the meal with the congealed gelatin salad with bananas and marshmallows. Marvin started with a bowl of chili. For a vegetable, they had canned peas, but the fresh rolls were delicious.

Just before their cherry pie à la mode arrived, Marvin unloaded his surprise. He took out a brochure from Renfrow Furniture Manufacturing in Topeka, Kansas and laid it on the table. He told her Mr. Renfrow would be coming down in a few days to pick up his trained pup, and in trade Liddy was to get a sofa, one chair, a lamp, and a set of drapes.

Liddy kissed him on the cheek in front of the whole diner.

She sat poring over the brochure much of the next day, thinking she never would be able to decide. Pictured in the catalogue were several styles: Early American, Victorian, and a set of squared-off blond furniture called Art Deco that Liddy declared was the ugliest stuff she'd ever seen. The style she finally chose was pretty modern, but with curved lines. She picked out a big wine-colored plush sofa and two dark green chairs with tufted buttons and rolled arms like those on the sofa. From a sample book she picked out yardage for drapes: big pink and maroon flowers and large green leaves that looked embroidered. Finally, she chose a shiny brass floor lamp with a pleated shade.

"Allow two months for delivery" was printed on the brochure. *Two months!* Still, Liddy was so excited after she sent off the order form that she could scarcely sleep for three nights.

Cassie was apprehensive for her mother's sake. She supposed she should take her father's word that at last there would be furniture in the house; if her mother believed it, she should try to believe it, too.

They waited for the furniture to arrive, and for Mr. Renfrow to come get his dog.

Cassie could tell things were a lot better between her folks, because all at once her mom was cooking nice meals and her dad was sleeping in their bedroom again.

○

Though life at home was much pleasanter, there was still no getting away from the war. It was in the newsreels and on the radio. Everyone was learning about the suffering of the English, the French, and even the Russians. Already there had been casualties, boys that local folks knew.

Sally Scruggs and Charlene Byers proclaimed they had been deputized by some doctors' wives in Red Arrow, socially prominent members of society like themselves, to start a Red Cross chapter in Cato. There were articles with pictures about the Red Cross in magazines every week, showing how it helped soldiers and civilians all over the world.

Sally and Charlene were organizing a Christmas party at Veterans Hall to benefit the Red Cross. It would cost two dollars just to get in, and there would be all kinds of booths, raffles, and other gimmicks to part citizens from their cash. Liddy supported it as a worthy cause; she and Rachel Klein were putting together a needlework booth. Even Marvin said maybe he would go.

Cassie had been planning to wear her navy blue jumper and the blouse Liddy had made from the silk parachute Mitch sent from England. It had full, billowing sleeves, and embroidery that Liddy had worked into the collar. But at the last minute Fiona said she was going to wear a long dress, so on a reckless impulse, Cassie decided to find the red dress from Aunt Hannah, the one her mother said she couldn't wear until she was twenty-one—*eight years from now!*

She tiptoed up to the attic in her bare feet, sneaked the dress back down into her room, and slid into it, once more enjoying the sensuous feel of the material on her skin. She strapped on the silver slippers, and just before putting on her coat, went into the bathroom and took the bobby pin out and pulled her hair down until it drooped over one eye. She looked like a brunette Veronica Lake, which was exactly her aim.

Fleeting thoughts of Lola, trapped alone in the cabin, darted through her mind, but tonight she determined to have a good time. She had done a lot for Lola already, and she planned to do much more, anything her friend needed.

She changed back into the navy jumper and parachute blouse, pinned her hair back with the bobby pin, and went into her mother's bedroom. Liddy had come down with flu and was running a temperature.

"Is there anything you want before I leave for the hall?" Cassie's tone was warm and solicitous.

"No, I just want to lie here—go on!" Liddy coughed, and blew her nose. Wads of Kleenex covered the bed.

Back in her room, Cassie put on the long dress again, plus her winter coat. She took the bobby pin out of her hair and tiptoed down the stairs, carrying the shoes.

Marvin had announced he wasn't going to the hall if Liddy wasn't, so now he was working in the back yard with Chauncey II, the smartest of Tizzy and Perky's puppies, using his whistle and choke collar. All the other pups from their litter had been sold, but he had kept the beloved parents and this one black-and-tan-ticked two-year-old.

Cassie stuck her head out the back door and yelled, "I'm goin'!"

She rushed out and down the street, fingering in her coat pocket a bright red lipstick she'd been hiding for months in the toe of an old sneaker.

Lately her dad had been watching her closer than ever. One day she'd gotten up courage and posed the question to him: If a boy should ask her to go to a picture show, "like they're already asking Fiona," she said, could she go? He said no, not until she was sixteen. She was going to be cut off from the world for years! The universe would go on spinning, and she would be stuck like a bug on flypaper.

She reached Main and walked around the block to Veterans Hall. The high heels were already hurting her feet. Cars were parked all around the place, and she could hear music. Climbing the granite steps, she looked up to see an enormous white flag with a big red cross draped across the building's front.

Fiona met her inside, wearing a long azure dress with lace sleeves and a high collar. She looked like a pretty teenaged grandmother. Cassie kept her coat buttoned up to her chin.

Apparently, Charlene and Sally hadn't consulted the churches about whether they could be permitted to stage a dance, because it was going full blast. Loud swing music blared from two big speakers on the stage, and people were slinging each other around the floor or jiggling their arms and legs and nodding their heads to "Pistol Packin' Mama." While teens and young married couples danced, Cassie and Fiona sauntered arm in arm around the edge of the floor, tripping on their skirts. They wanted to see everything at once, and they had already decided they didn't want to dance with anyone who would want to dance with them. Greta Sundersson was raking in the dollars, selling kisses from a kissing booth; she was wearing a Christmas stocking cap. At another booth Charlene Byers, in a turban and dangly gold earrings, was telling fortunes, looking a bit like a Gypsy Cassie had seen once somewhere.

Mrs. Klein and Mrs. Thatcher were running the needlework booth. Most of the things they were selling were Christmassy, like hot pads with Santas and aprons appliquéd with Christmas trees. Mrs. Klein was laughing and smiling with everyone, but Minna Thatcher looked as though she'd rather be home. Tootie Hicks had a concession doing hair and makeup. She had set up a little table on rollers, with brushes and pots of color, and was busy puttying up the cracks on Mrs. Curtiss Billings' face. Cassie was amazed to see Mrs. Billings submit to anyone's efforts to beautify her, but Tootie had let out all the stops and was painting her up like a china doll.

Thank goodness that old witch Mrs. Weston wouldn't be here tonight, not with all this music and dancing. Cassie still hadn't broken her pledge not to dance, although she'd relented on the movies and cards years ago. Truth be told, she hadn't really had any opportunities yet to test her convictions. And it didn't look as if tonight would be any different.

Just then Fiona giggled, and she looked up to see Mr. and Mrs. O'Herlihy pumping their arms up and down and whirling around the floor in a fast waltz to "Mister Five by Five."

They decided to go to the ladies' room. Once they got inside, Cassie took off her coat and showed Fiona the dress. Fiona's jaw dropped. "You look *beautiful!*" They stayed in the powder room fifteen minutes, fooling with makeup. Fiona wore Tangee to school, so lipstick was nothing new to her, but Cassie couldn't stop putting hers on and taking it off.

"You gotta show my folks that dress!" commanded Fiona, so Cassie hung up her coat at the coatrack up front and went to find the Bannisters. Mr. Bannister didn't say a word, but Mrs. Bannister shook her head from side to side. "My, Cassie, don't you look grown up!"

"How come you're not wearin' any underwear?" asked Aura Lee, Fiona's pain of a little sister.

"Am too!" Cassie replied. Giving Aura Lee a mean look, she grabbed Fiona's arm and walked her away. Whyever would anyone bring an eight-year-old to a dance!

She realized she was walking with a kind of lurching movement. These shoes were ruining her! She'd rolled her ankle three times already.

They found Stuffy Byers selling soda from a big washtub filled with ice.

"Well, well, now, here comes the two purtiest gals in this town, and I'd swear it on a stack o' Bibles eight foot high!" He chuckled and leaned toward them, opening an RC and a Nehi orange with broad gestures. "Where's yer folks tonight, Cassie?" he asked, looking her up and down.

"Mama's got the flu, and Daddy's tired."

"That's some dress." To Fiona he said, "And you're lookin' purty as a pitcher, like usual, sweetie." He asked Mayor Scruggs, standing nearby with a cigar clamped between his teeth. "Ain't these two somethin'?"

Barney Scruggs removed the cigar. "Sure are. Cassie, where'd you git that dress?"

Cassie didn't think she had to answer; she figured he was just making conversation. They left the men and made another tour around the dance floor. All at once, from out of nowhere, a vision of Lola standing next to the baby basket entered Cassie's consciousness, and as the realization dawned that she was enjoying herself like an empty-headed fool while her friend languished all alone, with no light and barely any heat, through the entrance sailed Winifred Weston with her nephew, Alvin Jonas.

Cassie dragged Fiona past the door and over to an area below the stage, where they sank down on two folding chairs. "I thought we were gonna look at the Christmas tree!" said Fiona.

Then came the biggest shock of the evening. Sean O'Herlihy, home on leave in his Navy blues, stood in front of Cassie, holding out his hand. Wasn't he engaged to Greta? She looked over at the kissing booth, where Smiley Applebaum was forking over a dollar to kiss Greta. She couldn't help thinking that for kissing Smiley, you should get paid at least ten dollars.

Standing next to Sean and presenting himself to Fiona was Seth Scruggs. Seth, like Ben Hargraves, was 4-F.

Marvin said that Seth had managed to weasel out of the service because his dad was on the county draft board, but Cassie had heard he was flat-footed. Stuffy Byers said Seth enjoyed being one of the few young men left in town. He put it like this, "That Seth sure loves to strut his okra fer the town girls!"

"You want to…to *dance?*" asked Cassie, tentatively putting her hand in Sean's.

"Yeah, that's usually what you do at these things, ain't it?" He grabbed her and whirled her onto the floor, holding her tightly around the waist, with Cassie protesting all the while that she didn't know how. "Moonlight Cocktail" was playing. It was sort of slow, and that was good.

"That's okay," said Sean. "I'm just learnin', too.

Why wasn't he with Greta? They must have had a fight. He looked handsome in his sailor uniform. All the O'Herlihy boys had curly hair, but Sean's was trimmed now in a crew cut. He still had his dimples and dark eyelashes, though, and he was smiling down at her and looking into her eyes. She didn't believe for a second that he was just learning to dance. The way he moved her around, dipping and swaying and moving his hand along her bare back, he didn't seem like a novice.

"Sean…" She tilted her head back and batted her eyelashes, the way she'd seen it done in the movies but had only practiced in front of a mirror. "These shoes are *killin'* me! Could we sit down, d'ya think?"

Just then the beat of the music speeded up, and all the couples around them started to jitterbug. Sean pulled her close, twisting her arm behind her, then throwing her out and reeling her in again like a fish. She managed to stay on top of her shoes until they got to the edge of the dance floor, where she protested, "I gotta stop!" She flopped down on a folding chair, and Sean sat down next to her. "Why don't you take off your shoes? That's what some girls do." He brought his face close to hers, smiling as if she were the only other person on earth.

She swallowed, unable to think of anything to say.

"Let me put 'em with your coat, so they don't get lost," he said. She took off the shoes and handed them over, then watched him walk across the dance floor. Sean's shoulders were broad, and they narrowed in a nice way down to his hips. Her arms and legs felt sort of rubbery, as if her muscles had turned to liquid. She closed her eyes briefly, then opened them and looked out on the dance floor, where Fiona and Seth were whirling around. Seth didn't dance like he had flat feet, and Fiona was giggling and tossing her hair around, happy as a pig in sunshine.

Sean came back and started to talk about his training at the naval base at San Diego. She couldn't keep her mind on what he was saying, because his arm lay behind her on her chair, and his hand was stroking

326

her bare back. She asked him about his brother Mike, and he said Mike and Dooky were together in the Pacific, somewhere near the Solomon Islands.

She told him about Mitch being in England, and that Dan was training to be a pilot. He wanted her to give Dan his address when she wrote to him, and went to find a piece of paper.

Sally Scruggs was on the stage near Marvin's spotted piano, holding a microphone and announcing that they were selling lottery tickets for a phonograph. Her voice kept fading in and out, and the PA system squeaked and screeched and then went off entirely.

Greta wasn't at the kissing booth anymore; she'd evidently handed the baton to Snooky Ledbetter, Doc Ledbetter's homely daughter. With the change, business had fallen off considerably, and Snooky sat with her chin in her hand, glowering at the crowd. Cassie had heard Mitch say that Snooky was so homely she could make a freight train jump the tracks, but the only thing Cassie could see wrong was her nose, which would have looked fine on a very large man.

When Sean came back she asked, "Why aren't you and Greta together—have you two broken up?"

"Yeah," he said. So that was it! He was trying to make Greta jealous—it wasn't Cassie's hairdo or the lipstick or the dress. The song starting up was a slow one, and they danced to "Sentimental Journey." Sean held her very close, and he started nuzzling her neck.

"I think I'm goin' to have to get on home—it's gettin' late," said Cassie, in a husky voice she didn't recognize.

"You want me to take you home? I got a car, and anyhow I don't see anybody here I know."

That was a bald-faced lie. Everywhere around were people he knew, people who had known him since he was a tadpole. But she supposed he didn't feel as much at home now as he had before the war.

"Uh… Fiona's folks were goin' to give me a ride. I'll see when they're gonna leave."

"Okay." The look on his face reminded her of a kicked dog, but she wasn't sure it was genuine. She limped away to the ladies' room. Halfway there she encountered Alvin Jonas, who stood blocking her way.

"Hi, Cassie." Alvin's skin hadn't cleared up, and he still didn't have any chin to speak of.

"How you been?"

Trying to edge around, she said, "Fine, how 'bout you? You still studyin' at the seminary?"

"Uh, no, I decided the life of a minister was too regimented, and, uh…too restrictive." He threw back his head and fumbled at his flowered tie. The one thing Alvin had was good hair, but he had too much of it. It sat on top of his head like a big brown cabbage.

"I'm working in the medical field now over at Antelope, and living temporarily with Aunt Winifred. My folks moved away. Aunt Winifred brought me tonight because I haven't been getting out much since I moved back. I was thinking about learning how to dance." He leaned toward Cassie and smirked, his Adam's apple moving up and down as if it had a life of its own.

So that was why Mrs. Weston was here, to broaden Alvin's horizons. Didn't she think dancing was sinful for *him*?

"Maybe you'd like to give it a whirl later on?"

"Uh…maybe."

Not on your life. Alvin belonged in the category she and Fiona had created earlier. She wondered where Floyd Weston was.

"Well, see you later." She padded away and went into the empty bathroom, where she gazed at herself in the mirror. She looked different from the way she had forty-five minutes ago, she thought. Older, and more sensual and exotic. Her features seemed hazy, blurred—not just her lipsticked mouth, but her cheeks and eyes. Her hair was a mess, and all the blood seemed to have left her head and was coursing through the rest of her body. Sitting on the toilet with the lid down and the door closed, she tried to decide what to do.

Fiona came in, saving her the decision. "Cassie, we're leavin,' " she said.

So that was that. Cassie came out of the booth, and they went to get their coats.

Fiona and her parents had already gone out the door when Sean came up behind her near the coatrack. She started to say she was going home with the Bannisters, when all of a sudden he pulled her over to a dark corner and crushed his mouth onto hers. He had his hands around her waist, and when he finished kissing her he looked into her eyes, just like he'd been doing all night.

Cassie heard a sound. Staring at them through the coatrack with little beady eyes was Mrs. Weston. Her mouth was turned down in disapproval, and she seemed ready to fly over the hangers and yank her and Sean apart. Cassie jumped away and finished putting on her coat.

Mrs. Weston waggled Cassie's silver shoes in the air. "Are these yours?" she asked, holding them high over the coats as if they were the very symbol of depravity and corruption. Cassie reached across for the shoes, put them on, and stumbled down the steps.

She reached the Bannisters' car and slid in back with Fiona and Aura Lee. On the way home, when Fiona began to giggle about Seth and Sean (whispering so her parents couldn't hear), Cassie complained that her feet hurt so much she couldn't talk. Closing her eyes and leaning back against the car seat, she wondered if she'd gotten her period right there at the dance, because her panties felt wet.

When she got home she discovered it wasn't blood. It was something else, but she didn't have any idea what it might be.

O

It occurred to Duke Farrow to tell his employer about Lola staying in the nearby cabin, but he quickly discarded the idea. Being one up on handsome, self-indulgent Hal Sampson in the goings-on around Cato appealed to him. Hal wasn't even on the ranch most of the time; he was usually off partying in New Orleans. Or should he tell Harold Cutter, who had been trying to sell the cabin all these years with no takers? No. Cutter would no doubt evict Lola, and Duke wasn't ready for that; his visit to her had pumped up his spirits. And after the baby came, she might really have to start depending on him. He remembered how beautiful she was. He remembered, and bided his time.

O

A cloud hung over Cassie all week. Someone had ratted on her, but she didn't know who. It could be any of several people. Stories had reached Marvin about Cassie at the dance.

"I don't know how I'm gonna hold my head up, you goin' to a party dressed up like a tart. All those dirty old men looking you over, and all the young men looking for the main chance."

329

His face got so red she thought he was going to have a stroke.

Cassie didn't know what the "main chance" was, but it sounded stimulating. She tried to defend herself by saying that Aunt Hannah had sent her the dress, but that only made things worse.

"Cassie, you deliberately disobeyed me," Liddy said, "and you're going to have to be punished." Liddy was over the flu. She was out of bed, but still run-down.

So far, the punishment hadn't been decided on. They couldn't forbid her to do anything, because she didn't get to do anything now, but there had been hints about a no-movies edict. They knew she often rode off somewhere on Dan's bicycle, and they were forever quizzing her about where she went. She hoped they didn't take away the bike. How would she see Lola then? How would Lola get food?

One day during Christmas vacation, she was about to leave for the cabin. She was wearing her corduroy pants and heavy sweater, when all at once Liddy blocked her way. "Cassie, your biking privileges have been revoked. Marvin and I talked it over, and this is to be your punishment. Your father says he doesn't like you out gallivanting all over God's creation, anyway."

Cassie put forth all her best arguments, but Liddy won.

Her parents didn't know that Sean had come by the day after the dance. He had thrown a pebble at her window, and she'd looked down and there he was. He told her he'd be on the corner of the pasture at the end of her street every day at four o'clock. Would she meet him? He had looked strong and handsome in his sailor uniform, running his hand over his crew cut and looking up at her with that pitiful half-smile, as if pining away for her company. But so far she hadn't gone.

To make things even worse, a week after the dance Winifred Weston paid the Fields a visit. She had never darkened their door before, so when she called and said she'd like to drop by, neither Liddy nor Cassie had any idea what it was about. After standing her umbrella in a corner—there was a light sprinkle of rain—Mrs. Weston and Liddy sat down on the brocade sofa in the bare living room; Cassie brought in a chair. Mrs. Weston wore a suit, and a felt hat with a tall, leaning crown. It had an even taller feather quivering from the hatband.

She held out a wrapped package to Cassie. "Don't open it now, my dear; wait until I'm gone. It was something I had as a girl. My, Mrs. Field, you have the loveliest…" Mrs. Weston looked around, searching for something to compliment Liddy on. It took her forever to come up with it. "...view!"

Cassie and Liddy turned and looked out the dirty window to where the woman was gazing. Could she be talking about the dried-up grass, or perhaps the old elm with its bare limbs?

Liddy served tea and stale cookies, and they talked about church matters and the weather, while Cassie sat munching on a limp gingersnap. The two women's dislike for each other was obvious. When Mrs. Weston asked how Liddy's sewing business was going, Liddy started telling about all the things the women were making. Mrs. Weston said, "I always feel it is more fitting and proper, somehow, when a person can do the work themselves rather than profiting from the work of others."

Liddy stiffened. "If it wasn't for me, no one would ever see those things, and the ladies like to make money—they tell me all the time!"

"Please don't take take it wrong, Mrs. Field. I was merely voicing my poor opinion. But are you sure they wouldn't like to keep the lovely things they've worked on, to hand down to their children and grandchildren?"

Liddy snatched up the teapot and left the room.

Cassie decided to take the offensive before she herself became the subject of conversation. No telling what the old harridan would start questioning her about: Sean O'Herlihy, the red dress, the sin of dancing, or all three. "I hear Alvin didn't finish at the seminary," she said. "Too bad."

"Alvin is destined for even higher things," said the woman.

"What's higher than a minister?" This was fun.

"You never know. And he doesn't know yet, either. But he's looking into other professions."

Liddy came back. and instead of sitting down, stood at the end of the sofa.

Mrs. Weston got the message. She stood up to leave. "I hope you are enlightened by my gift, Miss Field. Good day to you both."

After she was gone, Liddy pointed to the package. "Well, open it."

Cassie unwrapped a brown volume that looked as if it had been around for decades. She read the title aloud: "*Instruction and Hints on Social Purity, Heredity, Physical Manhood and Womanhood*, by Professor T. W. Shannon, Lecturer, Editor, *Uplift Magazine*"

It sounded awful, and dull. She leafed further through the book and found a few other passages: "In every assortment of post cards can be found pictures of young men and women engaged in suggestive acts of spooning." And: "Is it surprising that young people fall? Can teachers, minister and parents remain silent, permitting children and youths to receive information and ideas of social relations from impure pictures, books, shows and theaters, the ignorant and the vicious elements of society?"

This was too much! Cassie threw the book on the floor and ran upstairs. Liddy waited a few minutes before taking the book up to Cassie's room, where she was sprawled face down on her bed. Liddy opened the book and quickly scanned a few pages.

"Never mind, Winifred Weston is impossible. I'm goin' to have to tell that—*woman*—to keep her nose out of our family business. I dread telling your father about this; he's going to want to boot her from here to kingdom come! But what I want to know is, what happened at the dance that would make her bring you that book?"

She waited, sitting on the bed.

Cassie just sobbed louder. There were so many things she wanted to tell, and they had nothing to do with the dance! About Lola's baby, and how she was living all alone in Mr. Farrow's deserted cabin, and how it was Cassie's fault she was so lonely! She wanted to tell the whole story about Mr. Weston and Eula, too. There was so much she could barely hold it back!

Finally she stopped crying, blew her nose, and began to talk. She told about Sean dancing with her instead of with Greta, and she said Fiona had danced with Seth Scruggs, so it wasn't as if she was the only one dancing with an older boy. She didn't tell about the kiss, or Sean wanting to take her home, or about his wanting to meet her at the pasture.

Liddy stopped asking questions. She got to her feet and warned from the doorway, "Of course, you won't have anything to do with Sean O'Herlihy; he's much too old for you. That whole family isn't much," she added, "and even though Mitch and Dan have been friendly with those boys, I don't want *you* to be."

She sounded a lot like Winifred Weston.

When Marvin came home he didn't say anything about Cassie's tear-stained face. The three of them listened to the radio together, and by the time they went to bed, Cassie didn't think she was as deep in trouble as she'd thought. She didn't know what to do about Sean; just because her mother thought his family wasn't good enough was no reason to shun him. Of course, it would be a lot simpler if he'd go back to Greta.

Cassie was only thirteen and a half, for gosh sakes!

That night she thought about Sean's kiss and how he'd held her so tight when they danced. She'd been thinking about those things quite a lot. She tried burying her face in her pillow and kissing it, but it wasn't the same.

O

Two days later Liddy reinstated Cassie's biking privileges, so she went out right away to take food to Lola. Then, having little else to do during Christmas vacation, she decided to meet Sean. She walked to the pasture at five minutes to four and stood waiting under the bare cottonwoods near the fence for half an hour, but he didn't come.

O

Lola brought out mixed feelings in Duke Farrow. Besides the lust she aroused in him, he liked her fresh looks and her spirit of resourcefulness. He began to make unexpected visits to the cabin.

Lola never knew when he would turn up. Although she had never admitted her pregnancy to him, by the third visit he figured it out, putting a hand on her waist—she was wearing a long, loose dress—and feeling the thickness there. She shrugged off his hand and led him into the kitchen for one of her endless cups of tea. He had started bringing her gifts of food: slabs of bacon, baskets of eggs, a big crock of real butter from the ranch—sneaking everything past Hal's housekeeper. Once he even brought over a woolen scarf, which at first Lola refused. But that seemed to anger him, so she took it.

Keeping Duke pacified as well as neutralized was uppermost in Lola's mind. One day she took him out on the side porch to see the cradle she was weaving.

"So you're one o' them twiggers! And this here's a baby carrier, ain't it?"

She laughed. "Don't tell me you haven't noticed!"

He snorted. "I noticed. I noticed a long time ago. I was wonderin' when you was gonna mention it. Who's the daddy?" He looked sideways, rocking on his heels.

"Someone you don't know, someone a long way off. I kinda got..." She paused and stroked the willow carrier with a lingering hand. "But I'm very happy I'm going to have this baby—and I'm so grateful for this place!" She put her hand to his arm. "I don't have anywhere else to go! Duke, please don't tell anyone! I'm at your mercy." She stepped away from him, lifted her arms to gather her long hair behind her, and gave him a helpless look.

Duke grinned and slowly rubbed a hand over his unshaven chin. This was the way he wanted her: compliant and dependent. He grinned.

Lola was desperate, but ashamed, too. Cassie had mentioned her guilt about lying to everyone. Lola had felt awful; it was her fault Cassie had to falsify. Now she was doing the same thing, only worse: using her body to manipulate a man, which was much more wicked and reprehensible than the way Cassie managed Floyd Weston.

Duke stayed for hours that day, observing her as she went about her work. He watched as she did her weaving and her tidying up, finally leaving when she yawned and told him that for the sake of the baby she had to take a nap. It was not a lie; she truly was exhausted. *Thank God he didn't drop by every day!* Besides being anxious that his pickup would be seen from the road, she had to walk the fine line between friendliness and subservience that Duke seemed to demand, and it wasn't easy! Not too warm, or he would make advances, but not too cool, or he might report her.

O

On Winifred Weston's way home from the First Methodist, where she'd been conferring with the minister about having the church windows washed, she met Marvin Field driving like a wild man. They nearly collided at the end of Main, where she was getting on the bridge and he was coming off. Indignant, she motioned him to pull over. He jerked to a stop, and since he just sat there, she had to get out and walk over to him. "Mr. Field, really! You almost ran into me! Don't you think you're going too fast in an automobile of this...*vintage?*"

He pushed his battered old fedora back on his head. "Yeah, ain't it a shame Ed Bartlett's not here to read me the riot act. Now, looky here, Mrs. Weston. I know you think you got a right to give ever'body in God's creation all kinds of advice, but I'm tellin' you here and now, you better stop directin' it at my family! I didn't appreciate you comin' over to my house and gettin' my wife and child riled up over some book you read back when Hector was a pup! You got that, *ma'am?*"

Mrs. Weston backed away toward her car as his dogs set up a ferocious barking. When she turned to look back, Marvin Field was bent over—laughing! One minute he'd been practically foaming at the mouth in anger and the next, acting most inappropriately amused. Winifred sat in her car thinking how the world was becoming more difficult all the time. Not only did she have trouble running things at the church, but some of the less civilized citizens of Cato (and there were very few, perhaps none, who truly *were* civilized) seemed bent on disturbing her existence.

For instance, Tootie Hicks. She glanced in the car mirror, patting her hair—hair Tootie had tried to burn off her head. Only now was the permanent wave solution losing its stench, and she was positive she had paid for the more expensive brand! Chattering ceaselessly the whole time about her family and anything else that came to mind, Tootie had rolled up the curls on the narrow rollers, and Winifred had sat there for twenty-five minutes with the smelly stuff running down her neck. Then, when the strumpet unwrapped everything, her hair had come out, still wrapped around the curlers! She had given Tootie a piece of her mind about it, and refused to pay. Later she wrote to the Better Business Bureau in Oklahoma City, reporting Tootie's ineptitude and recommending the Beauty Nook be closed down. She was still practically bald on one side, and had been forced to wear a hat or scarf for months!

Finally, she started the car and began the drive back to the farm. She couldn't wait to find Floyd and tell him how she'd been insulted yet again by one of Cato's inhabitants, this time the ill-mannered Marvin Field.

20

What a strange power there is in clothing.
—Isaac Bashevis Singer,
Yentl the Yeshiva Boy

Mr. Renfrow came to Cato from Topeka in February, and young Chauncey was ready. Marvin had been working with him for months, training him to do everything a hunting dog should do: pointing, backing, and retrieving. Joe Kelly came at the same time, and Liddy was sure Marvin had arranged their visits to coincide. "I didn't plan this; don't jump on me!" Marvin said in an injured tone. "Joe said he was comin' up to hunt quail, but I didn't know it'd be when Mr. Renfrow was showin' up!"

"Well, I can't cook for them or have them sleeping here; they'll have to go to the hotel."

"Have you forgotten that he's the man gettin' you the furniture. and that it's *my* dog he's tradin' it for? But don't trouble yourself one little bit!"

Mr. Renfrow arrived on Friday evening. He was tall and well-dressed, with pockmarked skin, and red hair. Joe Kelly arrived the next morning. Marvin announced that he'd "earned this vacation, goddammit," so Cassie and Liddy took turns working in the store along with Peggy. The three men spent the weekend together hunting, Marvin leading the way in the Model A with the hunting dogs. Mr. Renfrow must have been happy with Chauncey, because every time Cassie saw him, he was smiling. He came into the drugstore to meet Liddy and said, "I hope you're going to be happy with the furniture, Mrs. Field."

"I'm counting the days!" said Liddy, positively beaming. Cassie thought her mother looked nice today. She was wearing her two-piece beige linen, and her coppery-gray hair was pulled up high on her head. She had even applied a little rouge.

"Great to see you again, Liddy!" enthused Joe Kelly, standing behind Mr. Renfrow. Joe was a heavy man with blue eyes, a red face (from the booze, Liddy said), and a part that ran straight as a ruler through his brilliantined hair. "It's been a long time, hasn't it?" Getting little more than a nod and an "Uh-huh" from Liddy, he turned to Cassie.

"Cassie, I swear you're purtier'n a speckled pup!"

Cassie darted a glance at Liddy, wishing he'd used some other comparison for her mother's sake. She liked Mr. Kelly, even though he'd been the cause of more marital arguments than she could count.

The three men had a final get-together in their hotel room on Sunday night. Exaggerated hunting yarns were exchanged, and a considerable amount of whiskey imbibed. The party started out stag but ended up including a female, and it was probably due to proximity alone that the evening took this interesting turn. Tootie's Beauty Nook was next door to the hotel, and Sunday night Tootie was chatting at the desk with Iris Spokes about how business had fallen off because of the new salon in Red Arrow. Tootie was wearing a tight black and yellow polka-dot rayon blouse and a shortish black skirt, and her blond ringlets bounced like little springs when she moved. She had acquired a cocker spaniel of almost the same color as her hair, and in the hotel lobby, she and Joe Kelly struck up a conversation about how to house-break dogs. An hour later she appeared outside Joe's door with Butterscotch, "to get some expert advice." The men, who had been drinking for some time, welcomed Tootie with loud greetings and open arms.

"*Sh-h-h-h!*" cautioned Tootie. "I don't think Iris saw me come up. She doesn't like me visitin' her hotel guests." She carried Butterscotch into the room and shared a drink with the men while Butterscotch, who seemed pretty well trained already, snoozed quietly on the bed. Marvin and Mr. Renfrow continued to chat about dogs and field trials, and Tootie and Joe got comfortable in an adjoining room.

Liddy didn't find out, although she smelled the whiskey on Marvin when he got home in the middle of the night, and was annoyed when he stayed home next day. "Well, what kind of crazy scheme did Joe try to get you to invest in *this* time?" she asked.

Marvin stayed in bed. He had a bad hangover, and pains in his legs from walking so much. They must have covered about fourteen miles, and drunk three bottles of whiskey! He and Wayne Renfrow were now on a first-name basis, and Marvin thought the man was a real gent, even if he was rich. And it was great seeing Joe again. When Marvin had brought up the drilling investment, Joe said the wildcatters had gone down four hundred feet, and estimated they had only five hundred more to go before they hit. He wanted Marvin to drive down and see the rig and meet the men, but Marvin said he didn't know about that. While they were on the subject, Joe said the drillers were running a little short of cash, so Marvin wrote out a check for a hundred dollars. He'd have to figure out later on some way to explain it to Liddy. It was only fair that Liddy take over the store today. He ran it, day in day out, seven days a week, on that hard concrete floor. She liked to fume and fuss at him, but life was pretty good now. They'd been getting along better. Probably the sewing business was a positive thing, since it kept Liddy's mind off her worries about their sons, and off of nagging him. He fixed himself a sandwich, poured a glass of milk, and brought a tray back to bed.

Soon his thoughts turned to his youngest child. Cassie seemed skittery and nervous these days, not nearly as cute as she used to be. Why couldn't kids stay little, especially girls? Why'd they have to grow up at all? He hadn't liked hearing Stuffy and Barney say she looked like a grown-up young woman at that dance. He didn't want her to be a grown-up young woman. What men tried to do to pretty young women wasn't nice to think about. That reminded him—he guessed he owed Harold Cutter a favor for getting Abby out of town like that. She'd written him two months ago that she was marrying the principal of the school in Guthrie where she taught, and she sounded happy.

Liddy never banished him from the bedroom anymore for various trumped-up reasons.

It was probably the worry about Mitch and Dan that drew them together. One morning he'd been awakened by Liddy's weeping. She had covered her head with her pillow, but he could feel the bed shaking, and he put his arm over her. "What is it, honey? What's wrong?"

She turned her wet face toward him. "Mitch—he's so far away. And Dan's so afraid of being called a coward, I'm afraid he'll volunteer for something really dangerous. It'd be just like him!"

He had pulled her onto his chest and said again what he had said before, so many times it had begun to sound like a nursery rhyme. "They'll be fine. They're both strong and smart; they can take care of themselves. *I* came back, didn't I? You gotta have faith. I thought you were the one that had all the faith!"

"Yes, but I'm not stupid. I hear about the casualties."

She wept some more, and he stroked her hair, and finally she got quiet. He didn't think the Army Air Corps was any more dangerous than any other branch, as long as Dan didn't end up a pilot. But the pilot washout rate was high, he was sure Dan wouldn't finish the course. He knew his sons thought the Air Corps was glamorous. *Horse pucky!* Maybe the uniforms looked better —although he'd always thought he looked pretty good in his, and so had Liddy—but it wasn't glamorous. It was *war*, drummed up by men in power to keep their country's economy going, or to get more land, or to try out their fancy new killing machines.

But the news about Germany and Adolf Hitler was so incriminating, maybe he was wrong. Maybe Roosevelt was right to get us into this one. The public probably didn't even know the worst of it yet, wouldn't till it was over.

His hand had wandered down from Liddy's hair, over those familiar, enticing warm curves, but Liddy turned away and lay still. With Cassie in the house, Liddy wouldn't let him make the least noise in the bedroom. He wondered whether, by the time Cassie left home, he might be too old to care anymore.

Now, alone in bed, he pulled the covers over his head to shut out the late-winter light, and went back to sleep.

O

By now Duke knew that someone was bringing Lola food, but he didn't guess who it was until he saw Cassie on the road with her bicycle basket full of groceries. *So Marvin Field's daughter was in on it!* Lola had been Marvin's employee, so maybe he was the father of her baby, or maybe one of his sons was. Not the older one—he'd been gone too long. It would have to be the other one, Dan. The next time he dropped in on Lola, he sat down in the kitchen, pushed back his hat, and said, "Saw yer little Field friend… So *that's* how you been gittin' yer food!"

"Yes. Cassie's been wonderful," Lola said, sitting across from him. She bent over and let her head drop, the big mound of the baby resting between her open thighs. She was wearing a dark skirt rucked up above her knees, and the white skin of her legs, showing between where her skirt had pulled up and her red knee socks began, caused a stirring in his groin. The whiskey he imbibed with his tea on these visits only made him hornier.

"Well, what about her?" he demanded. "How's come *she's* takin' keer o' you?"

A stricken look crossed Lola's face. "She went to Liberal with me to see a doctor, but he wouldn't—get rid of it, and I confided in her about

340

bein' pregnant, so she wanted to help me. She's the one who told me about this place. She's been so good to me!"

Duke sat tilted back in his chair, pondering. Lola had said he didn't know the father, but what was the connection to the Fields, anyway? He lowered the rickety chair to the floor. "Just how long do you think I'm gonna let you stay here, honeybunch?" His voice was soft, but with a threatening undercurrent.

"I don't know. I was hoping until I have the baby, at least." She sighed, looking at him pleadingly, and wiped her eyes with the back of her hand.

"Well..." Duke had never held such power over anyone before. He took another long gulp from the teacup and stared at her bare leg. Leaning forward, he rested his hand on her thigh. "We'll see. Long as you're nice to me..."

Lola yanked down her skirt. How could he think of her that way! She looked and felt like a cow ready to calve! She got up and went to the sink, trembling all over.

"You know I like you, Duke..." That was a lie. She wished with all her being that she could get away from here, away from this man who was preying on her. She turned her back, reaching for another tea bag to put in the pan of hot water.

Duke came up close behind her. He wasn't much taller than she, and she felt every inch of his stringy thighs and his erection as he pushed against her. His hands came around and caressed the bulge that was the baby. Then he reached higher and cupped her breasts. She gripped the pan, using every bit of control she had to keep from throwing the scalding water over him.

"Duke, I'm not feeling too well. I've got one *terrible* backache today. I think I worked too long with the willow. I just gotta go lie down, and I'm afraid you'll have to leave."

Her voice was as steady as she could make it. She eased away from him and crossed to the kitchen door.

His boots made a grating sound on the floor. "Wal, you better be feelin' better next time, honey."

As she heard his truck drive off, Lola sank to the floor. She rolled to her side and pulled her knees up, hugging her middle with her arms, as if to protect the baby from some still unspeakable danger.

O

Fiona was going to be fourteen on February 13, and she had decided to have a slumber party.

She was only inviting a few girls, and they were to come in costume, so Cassie climbed up to the attic and tried on her mother's old dresses, shawls, and hats, running down to look in the mirror with each outfit, glad that Liddy wasn't home. Nothing looked right until she found a big cardboard box labeled "BOYS CLOTHES." She dug into the pile of wool suits, knickers, sweaters, and caps. Finding a pair of knickers that fit— if she wore Mitch's suspenders— she grabbed a striped shirt from her own closet, and pulled on Dan's old argyle sweater and long woolen socks. In a box of old shoes she found a pair of brown leather oxfords that almost fit. Then she pinned her hair up under one of the boys' old caps, took a box of valentine chocolates she'd brought from the store and a knapsack containing her pajamas, and went across the street to knock on the Purvises' door. Alice came out dressed like a scarecrow.

Why hadn't she thought of that!

"You look just like a boy, Cassie," said Alice. "'Cept when your hair falls outta that cap!"

When they got to Fiona's, she greeted them dressed as Alice in Wonderland. Delores Dickens was a bunny rabbit, and Margie Botsin was a clown, which seemed about right. Aura Lee said she was a fairy queen, and pranced around wearing a long nightgown and a rhinestone tiara. They played records, ate fudge, and drank soda pop. Fiona liked all her gifts, but she didn't open Cassie's chocolates, so no one got to have any.

Fiona said everyone had to perform. She started off by doing a jitterbug routine to "The Jersey Bounce"; then Margie Botsin did the splits. Alice and Delores didn't know how do anything, so they had to be the audience. All Cassie could think of was cartwheels, but after knocking over a lamp, which didn't break, and a figurine, which did, she decided to stop.

By midnight they were all tired, although Margie never did shut up. They were lying around in their pajamas when they heard some boys outside, whistling and making catcalls. They turned off all the lights and piled on top of one another on the sofa to look out. In the darkness they could make out a pickup surrounded by boys.

"Looky here, girls—look what *Harley* kin do!" Standing in the glare of the headlights, Harley Corkle was peeing. He grinned in their direction, his big teeth flashing in the light, both hands holding his pecker in full spurt. They could tell who the boys were; Amos Hicks and Colin and Brian O'Herlihy. What a moron Harley was!

Suddenly Cassie had a revelation: Harley *was*, in fact, a moron! She had read somewhere in *Reader's Digest* about IQ. Moron was real low on the scale, and idiots came below that. It was just that the other boys didn't act that much smarter, so you didn't notice any big difference. Brian O'Herlihy started to do a jig in the headlights, when suddenly Mr. Bannister, awake at last, ran out yelling bloody murder. The pickup took off, wheels screeching.

An hour later, Cassie awoke to the sound of a squeaking door, and opened one eye to see Fiona tiptoe outside. She pulled the window shade aside to see her friend climb into Seth Scruggs's pickup. Maybe, she thought, I'm not the only one keeping secrets.

O

Once or twice Cassie questioned Lola about Bobby from Kingfisher, the father of her baby, who was serving in the Air Corps like Mitch and Dan. But it seemed like Lola never wanted to talk about him. She would get that guilty look on her face and say, "The only thing that matters is this baby, Cass. Let's us keep that in mind."

Months had gone by since Lola had moved to the Farrow cabin, and as far as Cassie knew, no word had leaked out. But she had an uneasy feeling that sooner or later they would be discovered. Mrs. Shafer was starting to give her funny looks when she came in to buy food. And there was always the possibility that someone would see Lola crouched in the back of Mr. Weston's sedan on the way to or from the doctor.

One day Cassie turned into the cabin's long driveway just as Duke Farrow drove by on the main road in his pickup. She didn't know if Duke noticed her, but it seemed reasonable to assume that he had. And once Tom Thatcher passed her on the way to town. Cassie didn't stop pedaling, not even when Tom braked to a stop. "Hi, Mr. Thatcher!" she called over her shoulder.

"Cassie, what you doin' way out here?"

She pumped past, calling back, "Just lookin' for a place for a picnic!" She glanced back and saw him gawking. Well, let him gawk.

Unfortunately, she encountered another neighbor of Lola's, though he didn't see her. He couldn't have, because it was old blind Walt Zimmer. Evidently he had followed his wire fence all the way out to the road, because there he was in his filthy overalls, with his straggly gray hair and beard, his clouded eyes staring like opaque marbles into space. He must have heard her bicycle wheels in the dirt, because he stopped short, cocked his ear in her direction, and yelled, "*Hey?*"

Cassie didn't reply, just kept pumping.

"Hey, there! *You!*"

Goose bumps popped up through the sweat on her arms and legs. He couldn't possibly see her! She pedaled even faster, and was still shivering with fright when she got to the cabin. When she told Lola, Lola said, "Try not to worry."

"Aren't you worried?" Cassie asked. "I think Duke Farrow saw me the other day, too!"

This would have been the time to tell Cassie about Duke's visits, but Lola couldn't bring herself to do it. He made her uneasy, but she was handling it, confident she could control the situation. So far, she'd hidden from Cassie his gifts of food and the woolen scarf.

The day she saw Walt Zimmer was the day Cassie brought Lola another letter from Dan.

Cassie was glad Dan and Lola were in touch, because if ever Lola needed a friend, it was now. But she did wonder about it; didn't Dan know that Lola was involved with Bobby, and was going to have his baby?

The correspondence between Lola and Dan was a complicated business. Lola had instructed Dan to enclose letters to her in envelopes addressed to Cassie, which Cassie then delivered, unopened, to her.

Liddy asked once, "How come Dan's writing *you* so much, Cassie? You two used to get along like cats and dogs!"

"We've gotten kinda close."

She didn't offer to let Liddy read any of the letters, although she knew that was what her mother wanted, and she worried that Liddy might take it upon herself to open one and find a letter to Lola inside.

In order to keep Aunt Flo and Uncle George from being troubled any more than they already were, the girls worked out another scheme. The plan was simple, maybe *too* simple. Cassie bought stamps at the P.O., and Lola would write a letter, stamp it, and print "*CATHEDRAL OF THE IMMACULATE CONCEPTION HOME FOR GIRLS, WICHITA, KANSAS*" at the top of the envelope. Cassie would put it in the Schonbergers' mailbox late at night or early in the morning, making sure there was no one around. The only flaw was that these letters never had postmarks.

Once, handing over a heavy letter from Dan, Cassie asked Lola why she never heard from Bobby. Didn't she care that maybe he'd been killed? Lola sat twisting her amber ring, the one she wore on her left hand. She mumbled that as far as she knew, Bobby was fine, and she didn't say another word about him. It was strange. It was beyond strange, it was bizarre.

When reading Dan's letters, Lola always got excited, but she never shared any of Dan's thoughts with Cassie. Her hands would tremble, holding the paper. Why would hearing from Dan excite anybody? Cassie wondered. That was another big mystery.

Lola was big now, and she shambled and lurched awkwardly about. Her dark hair, no longer streaked with gold, was pulled back in a limp ponytail. There were patches of brown skin on her forehead and on the lower part of one cheek, but her eyes glowed when she talked of the baby and when showing Cassie her basket creations. She said being pregnant made her feel more energetic than she'd ever felt in her life, and she was pouring all this energy into weaving baskets. By now she had created eight. Cassie told her they were fine-looking, and she meant it. Lola was a superb craftsman.

"Well, you better start pickin' one out, 'cause the ones you like best will be yours when this is all over! I can't think of any other way to thank you!"

"I like this one," said Cassie, holding an intricately woven two-colored one, which Lola said she'd used both willow and redbud strands to make.

The weather was freezing; this was one of the days Lola put caution aside and started a wood fire in the stove. The warmth reached the bedroom, so they went in and sat down with their tea on the bed. "I wonder if the baby will remember bein' here," Lola mused. "Hey, guess what! I can't see my feet anymore, and when I catch my reflection in the window glass, I can't believe how big I am! I feel so ugly, and so beautiful at the same time. *I don't know how that can be!* I've decided to name the baby after my real parents: Cyril if it's a boy, Delphine if it's a girl."

Cassie hoped it would be a girl. Imagine a baby boy named Cyril! At least you could shorten Delphine to Della.

They talked about old wives' tales of pregnancy and babies. Lola recalled her granny telling her you could get pregnant from eating a pumpkin seed. And if you broke a teacup, you and your baby would end up separated. She giggled. "Here's another one she told me: if a child is born on a stormy night, it'll have a stormy disposition, and if a young girl holds a newborn baby in her arms on her first visit, she'll become a mother! Granny told me that once, and when we visited someone with a new baby, I stayed all the way across the room!"

Cassie turned to look out the scratched and smudged window. This was going to take courage, but she'd been thinking a lot about it, and she felt compelled to say it. "Lola, I've been thinking— shouldn't you let Bobby or his parents know about the baby? Maybe they'd want to know! They'd know you were, well…in this fix…because you loved their son! All you hear about now in newspapers and newsreels is how soldiers and their girlfriends are gettin' married and startin' families. It's something to do with the war, and how nobody knows who's coming back. Everybody's doin' it!"

Cassie could tell she shouldn't have stuck her two cents in. But now it was too late, and she had to sit and watch Lola's face break into a million pieces.

She vowed for the umpteenth time to keep her mouth shut.

O

To Liddy's great horror, because of the intensive training they were giving him, Dan had been sent to March Air Force Base in California. He'd written his folks about all the flying classes he was taking; he said the classes were really difficult, but that he was loving it.

On a bitterly cold Friday, when the radio was forecasting snow, a letter from him came for Lola, and Cassie took it out the next morning. She wore all her warm clothes, including earmuffs. The road was icy and she skidded, even took a couple of spills, but she was unhurt. Lola grabbed the letter and lowered herself to the rug, opened it, and began to read.

She dropped the sheet of paper and put her hands up to her face, then took them away and gazed at Cassie. Putting a hand on one of her swollen breasts, and the other hand on the huge mound of her belly, she inhaled deeply and let out her breath. The mound moved up and down.

Cassie frowned. Why did Lola always get so emotional when she brought letters from Dan? If only *Bobby* would write!

All at once Lola's smile flashed out. She picked up the letter and handed it to Cassie. "Read it. Go ahead." Cassie took the letter and read:

> *March Field*
> *Riverside, Calif.*
> *Feb. 3, 1943*

Dear Honey,

When you get this letter, I'll be through with my flight training. I'll be getting my wings very soon. It's been one long battle learning all this stuff. I still don't know how I did it, but the guys that are teaching us are good. I came in 25th in my class, and there are 450 of us in the flight group! I was as dumfounded as you must be. Most of the flight class are nice guys, except for a couple from the east who think they're hot stuff— I had to let them know they couldn't mess with me. Some of these guys have their own little closed society, but I don't let it bother me.

How are you feeling? And how is our baby?

Cassie sat up. "How is *our* baby?" She looked from the letter to Lola. "He doesn't mean 'our baby,' does he?"

Lola's voice broke. "Yes. I lied to you, Cassie... I'm sorry. But at first I—I wasn't ready to tell you everything. I didn't know if you'd tell your folks, I wasn't ready for them to know!"

It didn't add up. Her brother, the father of Lola's child? How could Lola have deceived her like this? Incredulous, Cassie bent her head to the letter again.

I think of you night and day, and only hope that my sister is able to help. Who is this guy she's getting to drive you to the doctor? Did you say it was someone there in Cato? I don't know anybody who can help you, if you still want to keep this a secret, and I guess you do. I guess I do, too. My dad and mom will accept it someday—they'll have to. But I want to be there, and we'll get married, and tell everyone. Are you warm enough in that place? I worry! I'm so glad you're healthy, honey-bunch, and I'm glad you like the doctor that Mr. Whoever-It-Is takes you to. Tell Cassie I'm glad she's getting some use out of my bike. To tell the truth, I'd give anything if she didn't know, but maybe she'll have to substitute for me for a while. I can't write more right now, we have to put in flight hours today. Flying is the most exciting thing I've ever done!

All my love, Dan

There wasn't any Bobby. Cassie had to keep saying it over and over in her head. *There isn't any Bobby. There isn't any Bobby. It's Dan. Dan is the father.*

She stared straight ahead, repeating the litany to herself, as Lola started to bawl.

○

Back in her room that evening, Cassie felt the full impact of her new knowledge. Did it matter? Yes…it *did* matter. It mattered tremendously—to her, to Dan, and it would matter quite a lot to her parents. Her emotions veered this way and that. At first when she'd heard the truth, she'd felt a sullen resentment that Lola hadn't trusted her enough to tell her—after all she'd done!

Then she began to feel pleased, pleased that she had been instrumental in keeping Lola nearby, had helped her to keep her baby—Dan's baby! She'd been trying all along to be sure the baby arrived healthy and whole, but now it seemed of critical importance, overshadowing everything else. She supposed it was because she didn't know enough about love that it amazed her so much: Lola and Dan, the two of them so crazy about each other. Now it was clear—it happened between the most unlikely people!

Before she went to sleep, after having fussed over the matter from every angle, she decided she was proud to do this for Dan. If things turned out all right, she would be Dan's and Lola's and the baby's savior.

Now Dan would be forever in her debt.

O

That night, instead of doing homework, she wrote a letter to Carlton.

"*Dear Carlton,*

I hope you are still doing as well with baseball as you were last time I saw you. I've been thinking about you, and thinking I wish I could tell you some things, since you are my friend. I have stuck my neck out up here, and I am involved in something a little bit precarious. My parents might not be in full aprovel if they knew about it, so I better not even tell you, in case your mom found this and then blabbed to Aunt Bertha, who would of course blab to my folks.

This thing involves someone who is my pal, like you are and like Fiona is, who is my best friend. It even involves my brother Dan. You see—"

And that was when Cassie tore the letter up. What if Feemy did find the letter, or Aunt Bertha intercepted it? She would have to send the letter *in care of* Uncle Fred and Aunt Bertha; she didn't know Carlton's address at the garage. She wadded up the paper, then un-wadded it and tore it in tiny pieces. It was late; nine-thirty, and dark, and her folks had been asleep for awhile, so she felt safe carrying the incriminating bits out to the trash can.

She felt a lot better, even if she didn't send it; eased somehow of her weighty and never-ending burden of secrecy. Just before she went to sleep, she pictured Carlton hitting the baseball out of the ballpark, then running all around the bases to make a home run! She had seen Mitch do that once. Almost the whole town was there, and everyone clapped and whistled and yelled. She made a wish that this would happen to Carlton, and she went to sleep with her fingers crossed.

O

One day in March Lola reminded her, "We'd better see if the car will start." They went out to try it. It made a funny grinding sound, but the engine didn't catch.

"You think it's the battery?" asked Cassie.

"I don't know; maybe it's out of gas." They checked the gauge, which showed half full. "Good. We don't have to worry about *that*, anyway," Lola sighed.

"I'll think of some way to get the battery charged," Cassie said, patting her on the shoulder.

They racked their brains about how to communicate with each other and with Floyd Weston on the big day coming, but they couldn't come up with a solution.

Call Cassie on the phone? No, Lola had no phone. *Put up a flag?* Cassie lived too far away. *Send a messenger?* But who?

Twice before, when Cassie had called to let Mr. Weston know about Lola's doctor appointments, Mrs. Weston had picked up. Cassie had hung up and called again until Mr. Weston answered. But the third time when Mrs. Weston answered, "Hello? *Hello! Who is this?*" Cassie hung on, breathing heavily into the mouthpiece. Let her think some woman was after her husband—let the old biddy stew about that!

○

Lola went into labor on a dark, rainy afternoon in March. They were standing in the kitchen, and Lola was spooning sugar into a teacup and saying, "I think this baby is actually an elephant, Cassie! I don't have any energy anymore, and I can't sleep except when I'm sitting up." She stirred the spoon around, leaning on the counter. "I have to pee all the time, and I've had this terrible backache!"

Cassie was thinking it wasn't like her friend to complain so much, when suddenly Lola yelled, "*Oh…!*"

She stood there, openmouthed, while clear liquid ran all over the floor. She grabbed for the edge of the sink, letting the teacup fall. They both looked down as Lola's water and the tea ran together, shards of the broken cup forming little islands in a growing sea.

Lola turned to her with wide, frightened eyes. "I think I'm going to have the baby *now!*"

Cassie yelled, "Okay! I'll be back as soon as I can!" She ran outside, jumped on her bicycle, and started to town.

As she admitted to herself later, she wasn't thinking clearly. If she had been, she would have put aside all considerations of secrecy. She would have biked right away to Tom Thatcher's farm or the Weston place. Lola's and the baby's health should have been the most important thing! But what Winifred Weston and everyone else thought still had her upset and panicky, so she pedaled like a fiend all the way home to make the phone call, trying to avoid mud puddles in the road and getting soaked to the bone.

A big storm was breaking. As she pumped away, thunder smashed and rumbled across the fields, and lightning flashed in big jagged streaks. If only she could drive, because the Schonbergers' car was still hidden back there in the thicket! Then she remembered, she'd never fixed the battery!

After being nearly blown off the road more than once, she eventually got home. She peeled off her soaked jacket and was tiptoeing toward the phone when Liddy intercepted her.

"Cassie, the phones are out! I want you to go down to Hetty's switchboard and—"

"I can't!" she yelled, and ran upstairs. She had to get out of her wet clothes. Reaching into the closet to find something to wear, she spied the outfit she'd worn to the slumber party, lying in a heap on the closet floor.

She threw on the knickers, shirt, and sweater and went into the bathroom. She pulled open a drawer and got out the scissors. Taking her long mane of hair in her hands, she cut if off with three or four whacks, then cut it some more, close around her head. She went back into her room, stuck the boy's cap on her head, and ran back downstairs.

Liddy stood at the bottom, holding a wooden spoon in midair. "Surely you're not going out in this gullywasher! And what have you done to your hair!"

Cassie didn't answer. She ran out, jumped on the bike again, and headed for the Weston place. May God not strike her dead for all her deception, but with all this lightning He was going to have lots of opportunity! Biking across Wolf Creek Bridge for the second time, she saw several men below her working with sandbags.

She ducked her head, speeded up, and kept going.

The rain kept coming down in sheets. It was hard to keep the bicycle moving at all, and what was worse, it felt as though the rear tire was going flat.

Finally she saw the Westons' white pergola shining dimly through the rain. She had to get to Floyd! The skies were dark, and tree branches whipped about like mops shaken by an angry giant. She turned into the driveway and came to a stop next to the barn. Inside, a horse whinnied. Exhausted, she leaned the bike against the side. She took a deep breath and sloshed through mud to the back of the farmhouse. Peering through the kitchen window, she saw the Westons eating.

She had never attempted anything like this before, but there was a first time for everything. She knocked, pulled the cap down low over her face, and began whistling the "Pennsylvania Polka."

Mrs. Weston answered her knock. "Yes?"

Cassie stopped whistling and moved the toe of her shoe around in the mud, squinting under the cap. "Uh, ma'am, is Mr. Weston here?" For once, her voice obeyed her brain; it came out husky and low.

"Yes, but we're eating. Can I help you, young man?"

"I need to talk to him 'bout gittin' some work."

Mrs. Weston put a hand on her hip and cocked an eyebrow.

"I lost my other job," Cassie added, "Uh...sloppin' hogs."

"I don't remember seeing you in Cato before—are you from around here?"

"No, I'm from—*Antelope!*" She spoke loudly in the direction of Mr. Weston, who was cutting up meat and shoving it in his mouth as if he hadn't seen food in a month. Raising his head, he saw her, jumped up, and made a beeline for the door. "Dear—uh, dear, I'll talk to the—boy. I *have* been needin' some help."

"What do you mean? You haven't—"

He closed the door on his wife and took Cassie's arm, drawing her outside the pool of light from the kitchen. "What are *you* doin' here! I've done everything you wanted—I swear, you're tryin' to *ruin* me!"

"I didn't know what else to do—the phones are out, and Lola's goin' to have her baby—you gotta take her to the hospital!"

He just stood there, hitching up his pants. "All right, all right! Go on, I'll pick you up on the road!"

When he reached her, a few minutes later, Cassie threw her bike into some bushes and got in his car.

Lola was sprawled on the rag rug, panting and perspiring in pain. They managed to get her into the backseat, and Cassie covered her with a blanket. She looked up and smiled. "I'm glad you got here!"

Cassie murmured a silent prayer. "Dear God, please keep helping us. Amen."

Lola moaned most of the way. "I think it's comin'! Oh...*oh!* This baby wants to get *out!*"

Cassie didn't know which to worry about more, the car going off the road, or Lola having the baby inside it. After what seemed like hours, they came to the town's edge, and as they turned onto the slick main thoroughfare that would take them to the hospital, Lola began to scream. At last they got to the hospital entrance, and Mr. Weston parked in front.

Cassie ran in. While the attendants put Lola on a stretcher and took her inside, Floyd Weston averted his head, and soon Cassie saw the sedan drive off. How would she get home? For the very first time, it dawned on Cassie that he was afraid people would think this was *his* baby.

Lola wouldn't answer any questions at the registration desk except to name her doctor. As she was wheeled away, the nurse at the desk turned and raked her eyes over Cassie as if she smelled a dead rat.

"You're the next of kin?"

Cassie had forgotten about her clothes. She followed the nurse's eyes, looking down. Her knickers were torn and stained with mud from the wild bike ride, her shirt was hanging below the sweater, and her face was no doubt as grubby as her hands.

Should she be a boy or a girl now? It would be easier not to explain.

"Yes'm. I'm her brother."

"Why didn't your sister start for the hospital sooner—she's Dr. Lowe's patient?"

"Yeah, but we live a long way off, and the phones went out—it's a long story."

"Go into the waiting room—we'll keep you posted. Do you know how your sister's goin' to pay?" Looking grimly efficient, the nurse pulled out a form and cocked her head to one side.

"Not for *sure*. You'll have to ask her—she keeps all her f'nancial plans to herself."

"Just so she *has* some. Financial plans, I mean." The nurse glared at her.

Cassie stumbled toward the waiting room. Lola had been expecting a money order from Dan, but it hadn't come yet. He'd probably forgotten, like all the times he'd forgotten to get Cassie a Christmas present. But she was too tired now to worry about it. She found the waiting room, flopped onto the one sofa, and pulled her cap down over her eyes.

The next thing she knew, someone in a white uniform was shaking her shoulder. She rubbed her eyes. It couldn't be, but it was—Alvin Jonas!

"You came in with your sister last night, didn't you? Do you want to see the baby?"

Her cap was still pulled down over her eyes. She sat up slowly. Didn't he know who she was? "What time is it?" She was too sleepy to do her imitation of a boy, but luckily her voice came out hoarse anyway.

Alvin thrust out his wrist. "It's one- fifteen. Come along! Your sister wants to see you."

She followed his mincing steps down the hall, thinking that Alvin still walked like he was leading a parade. Through her jumbled thoughts came the realization that he had been away for several years at the seminary, so it might be possible he didn't know Lola at all. But soon enough he would recognize her, Cassie; she was sure of it. She stuck her hands in the pockets of her trousers, and when they got to Lola's room she kept her head down until he left.

At the sound of her footsteps, Lola opened her eyes and tried to sit up in bed. She reached out to touch Cassie on the arm. "It's a little girl! I never knew it'd be like this—*it hurt so much*— but…it's a miracle, too! I feel so blessed, like I know all the secrets of the universe, all at once!" She giggled. "The doctor gave me gas—I think it's made me a little silly! The baby's real healthy, Cassie—isn't that wonderful!"

"Where *is* the baby? And how're *you* feeling?"

"I'm great, just great. After I've been here a day or two, I want to go back to the cabin. Do you think Mr. Weston could come and get me? Tell him it's the last thing I'll ever ask him to do! Have you seen the baby? I've decided to call her Dulcie instead of Delphine—it's almost the same. She was born on a stormy night, so I wonder if she'll have a stormy disposition… I hope not! Oh—here she is!"

A smiling young nurse came into the room carrying a bundle made up of a white blanket and the tiniest human being Cassie had ever seen. She had a thatch of black hair sticking straight out from her head, and her eyes were squeezed shut, with a little horizontal crease running between them. Forgetting the old wives' tale Lola had told her, and forgetting also that she was filthy from head to foot, Cassie held out her arms for the bundle. Awestruck, she cradled Dulcie, feeling the lightness of her, and gazing down at the little face.

"She looks just like *Dan*!" Her knees felt weak all of a sudden, and she had to sit down in the chair next to Lola's bed. So this was what the past few months had been all about—this tiny bundle! This baby, red as a mulberry. As Cassie watched, her tiny mouth yawned, then closed again. "Her mouth is so dainty!"

"Yes, and every now and then she opens her eyes!"

She handed Dulcie back to Lola, who placed the baby close and then reached up and pulled Cassie down, giving her a powerful hug. "You got so dirty— doin' all this for me!"

"I know. I had to pretend I was your brother to the nurse."

"Well, *bubba,* you better get yourself a bath!" Lola grinned, then closed her eyes.

A few minutes later when Alvin came by, Cassie stepped boldly out into the hall. "I can't help thinkin' you look like somebody I met onc't before," she twanged, looking down at his shoes. The light in the corridor was blessedly dim.

"Izzat so? You don't really ring a bell with me, I'm afraid." He smiled an inane smile.

"You don't by any chance live anywheres around Cato, do ya?" she asked. "I gotta git back there—got a new job over thataways."

"I do live there," Alvin simpered. "Out in the country, with my Aunt Winifred. I can give you a ride back when my shift ends at two."

The ride home with Alvin was almost as worrisome as the ride over had been, even though there was no danger of a new life coming into the world. She had gone into the restroom intending to wash up, but decided to leave the dirt on as part of her disguise. The grime didn't seem to matter to Alvin. He quivered like a fish in a bucket, acting as if he wanted to be close friends. He kept putting his scaly, fish-white hand on the seat between them and grinning like a fool in her direction. Was she supposed to put her grimy paw on top of it? This was pathetic! Didn't he know she was a boy? She edged farther away on the seat, booming in her new, masculine voice, "How long's it usually take you to drive to Antelope? Do ya have a hard time gettin' gas?"

"No, since I work for a hospital, I get plenty of coupons. What's your new job, anyhow? And what's your name?"

"Uh, Billy—uh—*Bob*. It ain't fer sure I'll git it, but I'm tryin'!"

"Well, Billy Bob, sure hope we can get together. Let me know where you end up. Since you're new around here, I could probably show you the sights."

"That might be…interestin'."

"Folks around here are okay; most of 'em mind their own business." He turned in her direction and blinked his watery eyes a couple of times, reminding her of some sort of pale amphibian she'd seen in a science book about reptiles.

Mind their own business, indeed! Have you met your own aunt?

She couldn't think any more about Alvin right now, because they had almost reached Cato.

At the flagpole on Main she said, "I'll get out here and walk the rest of the way. Thanks a million."

"Who're you staying with? You sure you don't mind walking in the dark?"

"Folks you prob'ly wouldn't know—see ya 'round!"

She turned and tipped her cap—almost too jauntily for three in the morning. The rain had finally let up, and for the next few minutes she walked along in the dark with only the moon to guide her, familiar with every crack, rock, and tree root along the way, able to guess where deep puddles had formed.

A car pulled up next to her, and Sheriff Bartlett rolled down the window.

"Get in, Cassie—your folks're kinda worried about you."

○

It would have been better if she hadn't come home at all. Her parents were up, and all the lights were on. The sheriff went in with her, which was a good thing, because her folks were real mad. Her dad sat fuming in his striped pajamas, and her mother was pacing around the room in her old chenille robe.

"Where have you *been!*" Liddy exclaimed. "We've been wild with worry!"

"How can you get your mother upset like this!" bellowed her dad.

It was the sex thing again. She knew her parents thought she'd been off with some boy, doing who knew what sort of disgusting things, but how could she look like this if she had!

She didn't have any idea what she was going to say, but she began anyway. "I got caught in the rain on my bike."

"On the way to *where?*" her dad rumbled.

"Uh…on the way to tell some country folks about the telephone lines being down."

"*What* country folks?" asked Liddy.

"Uh…the Thatchers and, uh, the Detwilers. Then the bicycle got a flat tire. Then I saw these men sandbagging Wolf Creek, and I stopped to watch and see if I could help."

"*Help!*" they gasped in unison.

"Yes, and they wouldn't let me, so I just watched, and I guess the time kinda got away from me. Then I ran into, *of all people,* Alvin Jonas, and we rode around for a while. Did you know he's studyin' to be a minister?" She composed her face into the most innocent choir girl look she could muster.

Liddy's mouth dropped open, and she seemed incapable of closing it again.

"But he isn't going to be a minister anymore—says it's too regimented and restrictive," Cassie went on, shifting from one foot to another. He works…uh…someplace near here. Then we saw this kitten stuck up in a tree—"

"Cassie, why'd you cut off your *hair!*" This was from Marvin.

"It keeps fallin' in my eyes, and with bobby pins being rationed—"

She wouldn't have believed all this stuff, either, if she'd been them.

Sheriff Bartlett interrupted. "Folks, ain't it good Cassie's safe? And if she just takes three baths and two showers, I think she'll be fine. Now maybe we should all turn in!"

She loved Sheriff Bartlett. Her folks stopped the grilling, and the sheriff left. In the bathroom she dropped her mud-spattered clothes on the floor and stood under warm water from the shower, then she dried off, put on her pajamas, and fell into bed.

She was punished by not being allowed to do anything or see anyone for a week. The no-bicycle punishment after the dance had been nothing compared to this. She had to come straight home after school and go to her room right after she did the supper dishes. She couldn't work in the store, and she wasn't allowed to go to the picture show. They even kept her home from church, which was a big disappointment—she'd been looking forward to seeing the Westons.

Her dad took her to the barbershop instead of letting her go to Tootie's Beauty Nook to get her hair evened up. He said if she was going to try to look like a boy, he'd save money by getting her a boy's haircut. He walked her to the barbershop himself and stayed with her while Heck Purvis evened up her hair, and she had to listen to Heck's dead-by-the-side-of-the-road music on the radio the whole time.

While she was in the barber chair, Marvin read the newspaper. The other customers must have been intimidated by Marvin's manner, because no one spoke to either of them. She ended up looking just like Tyrone Power in *The Mark of Zorro*.

Her dad didn't look at her again for a long time after that. Back at the drugstore he told her he couldn't stand the way she'd hacked off her hair, and that, along with being thoughtless and disobedient, he was pretty sure she was nuts. After that he gave her the silent treatment.

She wondered if Aunt Hannah had ever done anything this bad.

She managed to call Floyd Weston from school—she finally got him, not Winifred—and she told him she had to stay home as punishment, and that he would have to go to the hospital to get Lola and the baby to take back to the cabin.

"Maybe you could pay the bill while you're there," she added. When he started to splutter, she hung up.

It worried her that she couldn't see Lola. She needed to keep her friend's spirits up, and help her with the baby. The bicycle was still out on the road somewhere, so she would have to walk, but she didn't care.

The second time she called Mr. Weston, he whispered hoarsely, "They're back in the house."

"Have you taken food?" Cassie asked.

"Yes, but I'm gittin' real tired of all this! This is it, girl! *This is it!* I don't care anymore about what happens to her—I want this over!"

"Well, someone has to care," said Cassie, and hung up.

She wrote a long letter to Dan telling him everything. She tried to make things sound as positive as she could, only telling the good things, about how cute the baby was, and how happy Lola seemed to be with things. After that she tried to lose herself in her schoolwork. The best part of her life now was doing an illustrated book report for English class on *The Human Comedy*, by William Saroyan. She hoped to see the movie someday, if it ever came to town.

21

If your mother tells you to do a thing, it is wrong to reply that you won't. It is better and more becoming to intimate that you will do as she bids you, and then afterward act quietly in the matter according to the dictates of your best judgment.

—Mark Twain
"Advice to Little Girls"

Dulcie was eight days old, and Cassie couldn't wait to see her. She felt terribly righteous as she rang up a sale of one dollar thirty-nine cents, stuck the five dollars she'd earned last week under the bills in the cash register, and removed change. Her dad was at the Mistletoe and Peggy was in the back of the store, and although she could have stolen the baby oil, ointment, and talcum, she paid for everything. She might be a liar and a blackmailer, but she wasn't a thief.

She had bought diapers at Schonberger's, but she did it when neither Flo nor George was there. Greta waited on her, and Cassie told her she needed the diapers because the First Methodist was helping out a poor family in the country. She didn't ask about Sean, though she couldn't fail to notice the engagement ring that Greta managed to put under her nose at every opportunity. Ever since the Red Cross dance, Greta didn't seem as friendly.

Cassie wrapped the baby things and took them home without Peggy or her dad noticing a thing. After school the next day, she threw on her brother's clothes and cap, plus a new addition to her disguise, a pair of her dad's old sunglasses. She put the baby supplies in the bike basket, and headed off to Shafer's Grocery. By now half the townsfolk had seen her like this, wearing shorn hair and her brother's knickers. The kids at school had gotten used to the hair, although she had to endure being called "Caspar" and "Cassius."

Fiona was the only person who came right out and said she didn't like it.

After paying for the food, she started for the cabin. The wind had come up, but she made good time, pedaling with all her might.

Lola looked exhausted. She was much slimmer now, of course, and had deep shadows under her eyes. She had just finished nursing the baby when Cassie arrived.

"I got in trouble at home," Cassie said, "and couldn't leave. I'm sorry! Things have been in a big muddle!"

Lola said, "Just a minute—here!" and handed her Dulcie, all pink and rosy. Cassie kissed the top of the baby's head and cooed to her. Holding her as she sat on one of the kitchen chairs, she described how Floyd Weston had left her at the hospital that night, how her parents had waited up, and how she'd invented one ridiculous excuse after another.

"I'm sorry I got you into all that trouble! How'd you get home?"

"With Alvin Jonas."

"Who's he?"

"The orderly at the hospital, Mrs. Weston's nephew. He's kinda weird. He tried to hold my hand all the way back to Cato, and that was the night I was a *boy!*"

"No wonder he's weird, if he's *that* woman's kin!"

They chatted about news of the war, and some of what Dan said in the letter Cassie brought.

Cassie wanted to talk to Lola about coming out of hiding and bringing Dulcie into town. She was wearying of all the deception, but she hesitated to bring it up. How could she mention the fish-eye Mrs. Shafer turned on her every time she bought food? She put it off; maybe her next visit would be the right time.

○

The weather turned warm, and Liddy put on her oldest housedress and most run-down shoes and went out to the backyard. She wanted to transplant one of her lilac bushes; if she could get it established in the sun, maybe next year it would reward her with beautiful, fragrant flowers. While she dug at the bush, she thought about Mitch's last letter from North Africa, and Dan's from California. With her hands occupied, she could let her mind wander freely over the tangled and multitudinous worries she felt for each of them, and over the people and institutions on whom she needed to fasten blame. The politicians and generals were taking all the young men, offering up their lives to war. They were going to kill all the brightest young hopes of the country.

She began working hard with the shovel, loosening dirt. Today was the first day the wind hadn't blustered like a cyclone; it made you glad to be outdoors.

Finally she had the bush out of the ground, and now she had to put it in a bucket and carry it to the new sunny spot she'd chosen. She walked around the front of the house on her way to the garage to get the bucket, stopping once again to admire the house's new coat of white paint. Last fall she had spent her WPA earnings and needlecraft commissions for Sven Sundersson to paint the place from top to bottom and put in a downstairs bathroom. The house sparkled in the sun, and the best part was the blue shutters; Sven had performed a miracle adding those.

She glanced at the serviceman's flag in the front window, with its two blue stars and red border. The flag was supposed to show how proud she was of her sons in the service, but it made her angry every time she looked at it.

What was Mitch doing today, this very minute? Was he in danger? She kept reading about the American Flying Fortresses and Liberators bombing German docks, trying to get at their U-boats. The radio and newspapers were full of North Africa. The Germans had finally been defeated at the Kasserine Pass—it was all you heard about—and now Rommel's army was in retreat.

Was Mitch part of all that? His letters were censored, so you never knew. Was he still in one piece? Mike O'Herlihy wasn't; he and Dooky Schlanaker had been reported killed in the Pacific. She wasn't going to write Mitch or Dan about that; they could learn about it after the war.

Now Dan was training to be a pilot, which was even scarier. She didn't know why he couldn't serve on the ground; there were plenty of those jobs! If only he weren't so headstrong, so in need of proving himself a man!

She missed her afternoons of bridge, where she could get some of her troubles off her chest. Rowena had tried to get the group together, but Flo wouldn't come, and since they couldn't think of anybody else for a fourth, they dropped the whole idea.

Liddy grinned to herself. The last time they'd met, they had kidded Violet about her budding romance with Reuben Hargraves. Reuben had been after Violet to go to the movies, but she said she hadn't gone yet. "What do I want with a leaky old man?" she said.

Ever since Lola'd moved away, Flo had acted as though she didn't want to see anyone. *Why?* It wasn't Flo's fault the girl had strayed from the straight and narrow! Nobody held her or George responsible; they hadn't raised Lola, so how could they be blamed? But she supposed she would feel the same way.

She'd soaked the spot for the lilac bush; now she would dig the hole. She stomped on the shovel, methodically lifting out giant clods of dirt.

But there was more to Flo's standoffishness. Liddy had barely seen her since their talk about Lola's being pregnant. There had been that long silence, when she felt as if Flo was wanting Liddy to say, "*Dan* will marry her." In January Flo and George had driven up to Kansas, but they never said where or why they went.

She lifted the bush out of the bucket, dropped it in the hole, and shoveled in dirt, then filled in the original hole. Hearing the noise of an engine, she walked around the house.

There sat a big truck with "RENFROW FURNITURE DELIVERY" painted on the side. The driver climbed down from the cab, tipped his hat, and said, "You Miz Field?"

The next hour was one of the most exciting times of her life.

She took off her shoes and went inside, barefoot, watching them unload. The men got a little impatient when she kept changing her mind about how to arrange it all, but when they finally finished she thanked them profusely and gave them each two dollars. After walking around in her beautiful room for a full ten minutes, she went outside again. The lilac she had moved sat in its new spot, full of the promise of spring. Standing in the warmth of the late afternoon and gazing at her blooming snowball bush, she felt more content than she had felt in ages. A little wren flitted back and forth from the wooden trellis, building a nest, and Liddy walked around sniffing the scent of flowering spirea.

She went back into the house and started supper.

O

The next day Liddy drove out to Minna Thatcher's to pick up two crocheted afghans, the kind that were selling so well in Enid. While she was there, Tom came in and poured himself a glass of lemonade.

"Howdy, Miz Field. Don't know how Minna has the time to make all these blankets, but I guess it's when me and the kids are sawin' logs." He took a long drink and said, "I seen Cassie out here the other day goin' full tilt on that bicycle, said she was lookin' fer a place t' have a picnic. Mighty cold day for a picnic, if you ask me!"

Liddy gathered up the throws from Minna and asked, "Was Cassie wearin' those awful trousers she's had on lately?"

"I didn't take any notice, but she looked all worked up, pumpin' along like a house afire!"

Tom smiled his toothy smile. Not for the first time, Liddy noticed his heavily-muscled upper arms.

"I'll be seein' you both next month," she said, and with a kiss on Minna's cheek, she was off.

As if she didn't have enough to worry about with her sons, now Cassie was giving her fits! Coming home in the middle of the night, chopping off her hair. Liddy wasn't nearly as upset about that as Marvin was, since it might keep the boys off a little longer. The thing that upset her most was the lying. Cassie seemed to make up whoppers right and left, each one bigger than the last. That night the sheriff brought her home, it all sounded like a pack of lies! That was the thing about having children: if you fretted too much about one, another one would pop up to drive you crazy— doing something you hadn't even thought to worry about.

To try and set her mind at ease, she drove north a couple of miles past the Farrow farm and Walt Zimmer's, and out as far as the Detwiler and Sampson ranches. She couldn't imagine Cassie going on a picnic all the way out here.

So who was she meeting? What was she up to, with all the smoke and subterfuge?

O

Winifred Weston was on her way to her weekly discussion on church finances with Reverend Dickens when she met Tom Thatcher heading in the opposite direction. This would be the perfect time to have that talk with Minna. It was the least she could do as a friend, neighbor, and happily married woman. She'd been reminded of her duty only yesterday, when she'd seen one of Minna's throws on display at the post office, along with a sign that read *"Crocheted by Mrs. Thomas Thatcher."* No doubt this was the work of Liddy Field. How she had managed to finagle the post office as a showroom was more than Winifred could imagine.

Winifred had stepped back out onto Main, where she saw Tom Thatcher and Liddy engaged in conversation in front of the newspaper office. Winifred walked right by them, and they barely spoke to her! As she turned into the dry cleaner's she heard Liddy say, "I'll be out soon." None of it would have been suspicious, but Tom was holding Liddy's hand, and they were looking straight into each other's eyes! Maybe they were only shaking hands, but it looked like more than that.

Winifred sat in the road for a long moment, then backed up and turned into the Thatchers' drive. After a long wait, Minna came to the door wearing a faded housedress and holding her baby boy. "Why, Miz Weston! You caught me changin' the baby. Come in," she said, stepping back.

Winifred followed. "I'm so sorry for dropping in like this!" Her own appearance contrasted strongly with Minna's. She was wearing her brown silk with the peplum jacket.

"Oh, that's all right," said Minna. "Lands, I don't see *no* one anymore 'cept Mis Field—jus' take care of the kids and crochet. Tom's even been doin' most of the cookin'. Would you like to go into the parlor?"

"Oh, no, this is fine." Winifred settled into a kitchen chair and put her purse on the table. She spent a few minutes discussing the weather, then got to the point of her visit.

"Uhm-m-m, I saw one of your lovely coverlets at the post office yesterday. I was *so* impressed! But there was something else I saw that... well, *disturbed* me. I'm so sensitive to these things, and it's because I care so much for you that I..."

Minna's mouth had dropped halfway open.

"The thing is, my dear, I think perhaps you had better keep an eye on your husband. Oh, yes, I know you think he's without sin, but you remember he was too friendly with that other woman, and you know where *she* ended up!"

"What're you talkin' about? I don't know 'bout no other woman!" Minna jostled the baby in her arms.

"You mean you haven't heard the rumors? Oh, that's right; you're not from around here! It concerns one of your neighbors. There are

366

some things it's better to be aware of. *'Be sober, be vigilant; because your adversary the devil, as a roaring lion, walketh about seeking whom he may devour!'* First Peter, chapter five, verse eight."

Minna's face registered anguish, and the baby began to cry, squalls which escalated to howls, then to screams. "Let me put Jaky down," she stammered, her lip quivering. She left the room and returned in a few minutes. "I gave him his bottle. Now, what were you sayin'? About Tom and some woman?" She crossed her arms close to her body, as if to ward off some indefinable menace.

"You know that our neighbor Walt Zimmer is blind, don't you?"

Minna nodded.

"And did you know he once had a wife?"

Minna shook her head.

"The thing is, your husband and Mrs. Zimmer got to be very friendly a long time ago, and I heard it was more than just friendship. *Don't tell Tom I told you any of this.* And later on, the woman disappeared! Just up and vanished! And everybody thinks Walt killed her and buried her under his barn!" Winifred removed a lace-edged handkerchief from her purse and dabbed at the gathering saliva in the corners of her mouth.

Minna seemed to have gone into a catatonic trance. She shifted her gaze from Winifred to the wallpaper, staring at it for a length of time. Finally Winifred turned to study the wallpaper, too, but it was nothing but daisies on a beige background.

She waited. "Minna? Dear…?"

Winifred gave her a little shake, but it didn't seem to register.

Winifred let herself out.

O

Alvin Jonas was still living with the Westons, working nights and underfoot every afternoon, and Floyd was getting more than a little sick of him. Winifred wouldn't let Alvin do any farm chores; she said he wasn't strong, and he worked so hard at the hospital. So while Floyd was out on the tractor checking irrigation troughs or inoculating cattle or doing the million and one things he had to do, Alvin was either sleeping or lazing about the house. The only time Floyd saw him was when he was sprawled on the sofa or feeding his pimply face.

Yesterday, Floyd had told Winifred in no uncertain terms that she would have to tell Alvin to leave. She pleaded with him, but Floyd wouldn't budge, saying he couldn't stand another day of the boy, and if she wouldn't get rid of him, he would.

Floyd barely had time to sneak off to see Eula these days, and she was getting testy about it. Not only wasn't he getting a divorce like he'd promised, but she said he wasn't paying her enough attention. She wasn't his special Eula anymore: wide-eyed, heavy-breathing, compliant as a child. He hadn't wanted her to change from that juicy, innocent young thing, but she had. Well, what did he expect? He had been stringing her along for years. Last week, they'd taken a chance and met at the deserted dance hall at the Shores. There hadn't been a soul around, and they'd had the whole hall to themselves, but she hadn't let him do it. Kissing and feeling was as far as he could get, and she'd said, "Things is going to change, Floyd. You ain't been givin' me no *regard*."

He'd seen her at church the following Sunday, and she wouldn't look at him, which was just as well. He'd been uncomfortable since Eula took up religion. Why couldn't she have joined the Baptists, for Christ's sake?

O

Liddy and Marvin began to compare notes about Cassie: that suspicious late-night escapade, the bike trips, the groceries that Violet told them she was buying, Tom Thatcher's mention of seeing her north of town. Cassie was up to something, and it was more than just chopping her hair off! The scariest thing was that she might be meeting a boy. For her to get in the kind of trouble Lola had got in would be the worst thing they could imagine. But *what* boy? Sean O'Herlihy was away in the war, and Fergus Klein lived nowhere near that part of town.

"Marvin, *do* something! Talk to her! She pays more attention to you."

Marvin didn't think this was true, but he said he would. That evening, as he and Harold Cutter walked to the hotel for their poker game, he decided to confide in the older man.

"I swear, Harold, not only does Liddy have to worry about Dan and Mitch all the time, but now Cassie's turned rebellious!" And even though he was ashamed of it, he told Harold about her staying out half the night.

"Oh, I don't think you have anything to worry about with Cassie," said Harold. "Though she does seem a little…well, *changeable*. Every time I see her, she's either giggling with that Bannister girl or lookin' real serious. How old is she now?"

"Thirteen," said Marvin, hoisting whiskey bottles higher on his hip.

"Well, that pretty much explains everything," said Harold.

O

When Smiley Applebaum collected the trash from the alleys of Cato, he drove slowly and carefully behind every residence, every business, with scrupulous regard for the rules. Liddy Field had never caught on that he took those drugs from the store; he hadn't got caught stealing anything lately. The best part of being the trash man wasn't the status; it was the stuff he could sell off for a profit. A secondary advantage was that, along with the garbage, he sometimes gathered useful information.

One day in late March Smiley had delivered his last load to the dump when he decided to drive into the Cato Shores. There never was much trash when the place wasn't open, but sometimes teenage boys left pop bottles—worth two cents each—cluttering up the area, and since he'd just emptied his truck, he turned in. He'd driven a little way toward the Snack Shack when his attention was diverted to a blue sedan parked some distance ahead, off the road. There was no driver. It was a car he'd seen plenty of times before, but he couldn't think right away whose it was. He pulled off, turned off his engine, and walked over to check for signs of ownership.

The windows were all steamed up. He peered first into the front window, then the back, and that was when Floyd Weston and Eula Tully craned their necks up from their topsy-turvy position and looked up at him. Smiley stared back, taking the spectacle in. Then, with a grin, he doffed his John Deere cap in greeting, ambled back to his truck, and left quietly—as quietly as anyone driving a garbage truck could leave.

This information could come in handy.

○

Lola and Cassie were almost home free. The baby had been born and was healthy, and no one had discovered them.

But Greta told Flo Schonberger about Cassie's buying the diapers, so Flo asked Liddy who the poor Methodist family was that Cassie was helping out. "Not that it's any of my business," she hastened to add.

"Cassie, helping out somebody with *diapers?*" snorted Liddy. "I don't think so!"

But after stewing about it a day or so, Liddy called the minister on the phone and said, "Reverend Dickens, did you ask some of our young people to take care of a poor family around here?"

When he said no, she told him the whole story, hoping Hetty Saltman wasn't listening in.

"Cassie is imbued with an admirable spirit of public service," the preacher said. "She was talking to me a few months ago about something very similar to this."

"She *was?* What was it, or who was it? Please tell me."

"I can't do that, Mrs. Field. It was a personal meeting we had."

That evening as she and Cassie did the supper dishes, Liddy asked, "What's this about you buying diapers for poor folks and saying they were from the church! Greta told Flo."

Startled, Cassie dropped a plate on the floor, but it didn't break. "Well—uh—"

"I asked him, and Reverend Dickens said there isn't any such family, so how come you told Greta a cock-and-bull story like that?"

"It was just between me and the…the mother. *She* asked me to buy 'em."

If she hadn't lied so much lately, maybe Liddy would have dropped it. "*Who?* Who is the mother?"

"It's a personal thing," Cassie replied self-righteously, her voice suddenly strong. "You shouldn't be askin'—it's a violation of privacy, an' that's one of the Four Freedoms President Roosevelt's always talkin' about. I gotta do homework." She peeled off her apron and clambered up the stairs.

Despite Cassie's bravado, Liddy called Reverend Dickens and asked him to please come to her house tomorrow after school; she would see that Cassie was there too. The next afternoon they met in the newly furnished living room. Liddy couldn't help thinking it was a shame her new room should be used for an inquisition.

Reverend Dickens was seated on the wine-colored sofa, and Cassie sat on one of the new green chairs with her arms folded, trying to look unconcerned.

Liddy said, "We want you to tell us about this needy family you told the whole town about."

"I didn't tell the whole town! I was tryin' to keep it *from* the town!"

Oops.

"I mean I wanted to help someone who needs help—and now you're all trying to make me sorry I did!" She put her hands up to her face and burst into tears.

"Cassie, I can't abide liars. If you won't tell us, you'll *show* us. You are going to take us to this family *now*." With a grim face, she took Cassie by the arm and stood her up. Cassie pulled her arm away, but made no further protest. Reverend Dickens got slowly to his feet, wondering why he had to be involved in this test of wills. It seemed to be more a family quarrel than anything else. Of course the child shouldn't be allowed to get away with a lie.

Cassie followed her mother out to Reverend Dickens's car, and obediently slid in between him and Liddy.

○

Winifred went into the den, where Alvin was flicking through the pages of a body-building magazine.

"Alvin, dear, I have to talk to you." She let a few seconds pass, in order to cushion the blow. "I'm so sorry, but Floyd needs your bedroom for an office. If it were left up to *me*, you could stay forever, but…"

Alvin stood up, then sank slowly back onto the couch. He blinked back tears, biting his thumbnail, but after a minute collected himself. There was no point in telling her the hospital had been encouraging him to move closer, so they didn't have to give him so many gas stamps.

He decided now was the time. Walking around the room, and turning at chosen moments to look her directly in the eye, he said, "I didn't want to have to tell you this, Auntie, but I saw Uncle Floyd driving away from the hospital one night—real late—and he had driven a girl there…a girl about to have a baby!"

"You saw *what?*" said Winifred. "You saw Floyd at the Antelope hospital?"

"Yes, and there was a young boy with the girl. He was wearing a cap, so I didn't see him very well." Alvin paused; he wanted to wring as much drama as possible from this. His voice dropped to a loud whisper. "And a few days later, I saw him there again."

Winifred gasped, waiting.

"He had on an overcoat, and a hat pulled down over his ears, but I recognized him. He was paying a bill at the desk, and he didn't see me. And then he helped that same girl with her baby into his car! I didn't tell you because I didn't want to worry you, but I decided you ought to know. I didn't check the records for the girl's name, but I had a feeling the name on her chart was made up."

Winifred went into her bedroom, closed the door, and sat on the edge of the four-poster bed, mulling over certain facts. She had felt unsure about Floyd at other times during the past couple of years, when he would drive off saying he had to get supplies or cattle feed, then come home without them. Once she'd followed him on foot up the road, staying out of sight by dodging along behind the trees. He'd said he was going to the Feed & Grain, but his car turned left instead of right.

She paid the bills, and Hicks Feed & Grain in Cato was the only bill she ever paid for cattle feed.

A repressed memory swam into her consciousness. Right after she and Minna Thatcher had had that little chat, she was at the church conferring with Reverend Dickens about finances. She'd finished advising him and was about to cross over to the parsonage when she was accosted by Smiley Applebaum carrying a barrel of trash.

"Hey there, Miz Weston," he said.

"Hello, Smiley." She made a point of being friendly to the town's less presentable characters, and Smiley was certainly one of those.

"How're yew today, ma'am?" Smiley put down the barrel and hiked up his overalls. A large cud of chewing tobacco filled one cheek; he looked as if he were about to spit.

"Fine, just fine." She'd been trapped by Smiley before; he could waste half your day.

"Saw yer husband t'other day, whenever I was out t' the Shores."

"Oh?" Something about his tone of voice kept her rooted to the spot.

"Yep. Looked like he had *comp'ny*." He smiled, exposing a snaggletoothed grin and a black wad of tobacco.

Was he insinuating something about Floyd?

She waited, but Smiley just grinned like a weasel in a henhouse and turned away. She thought about that encounter now, alternately stroking the chenille bedspread and plucking at the little cotton puffs. What had Smiley been hinting at? And she wondered again about the young boy who had come to the farm looking for work. Not only was it a silly time to apply for work—after dark and raining like the Second Flood, but Floyd had left, saying he was taking the boy to find a place to stay in town. And he didn't return for two hours, while she sat alone in the storm!

Winifred sat picking at the bedspread, trying to figure things out, and when she heard Alvin leave for work, she didn't even bother to say good-bye.

O

Reverend Dickens drove across Wolf Creek Bridge, following Cassie's instructions. They drove past the Westons' pasture, then past Tom Thatcher's farm, with its sprightly new scarecrow, the only colorful thing for miles around. The skies were overcast, the day dreary.

Cassie's brain was seething as they drove farther and farther into the countryside. Her hands were clasped on her knees, her body rigid as a fence board. After all these months of plotting and dodging and lying for Lola, she would go down fighting—she would never betray her! The closer they got to the Farrow place, the more panicked she became. They drove past the turnoff to the cabin, then went on another mile, past Grace Sampson's Sandy Flats ranch. They'd been driving for half an hour.

Suddenly she said, "Reverend Dickens, you can turn around now. I—I'll show you. Just turn around anywhere."

He turned at a wide place in the road, and when they reached the Thatcher place, Cassie ordered, "Turn in here."

Liddy gave her a disbelieving look. The minister drove a little way in, stopped, and turned off the ignition. They were twenty feet or so from the Thatchers' front door when Cassie burst into tears. It wasn't hard to do—she was under a lot of pressure. "She didn't want me to tell anyone—please, *please* keep it a secret! Mrs. Thatcher said they been havin' such a rough time f'nancially since Jaky came, and she didn't want anyone to know, 'specially *you*, Mama—you helpin' her out with sewin' money and all. Please, *please* don't either of you ever mention this to them. Let's just go home!"

There wasn't a sound from Liddy, so Reverend Dickens started the car and backed all the way out.

"Well, I'll be!" marveled Liddy at last. "Imagine Minna confiding in *you*, Cassie. Guess we never know what's goin' on with people, and that's God's truth." Embarrassed about taking the Lord's name in vain in front of Reverend Dickens, she bit her lip.

"I feel most regretful that the Thatcher's needs were not more evident to me," said Reverend, shaking his head. Still, he thought, there was something amiss. When Cassie had visited him last fall she had mentioned an unmarried girl, not a married one. But he didn't say a word. Stirring Liddy Field up again was something he was loath to do.

O

A few days after he'd ratted on Floyd to his aunt, Alvin was surprised to see a boyish figure biking toward him on the road. He slowed, then stopped, waiting for the cyclist to reach his car. He put his head out and waved his arm up and down.

With one hand, Cassie pulled down her cap and adjusted her dark glasses. She stopped pedaling and put both feet on the ground.

"*Billy Bob!*" exclaimed Alvin. "What are *you* doin' out here? I been thinkin' about you. Where you been since I brought you to Cato that night?" He stuck his arm farther out of the window, as if trying to touch her, and he had that silly look on his face again.

Cassie's mind darted this way and that. He couldn't force her to answer him. She mumbled something unintelligible, and pedalled on.

Alvin felt insulted. He had done this ruffian a big favor that night, giving him a free ride. He drove farther, turned the car around, and drove until he caught sight of the boy turning into the Farrow place. He wanted to follow, but he was afraid Billy Bob wouldn't like it, so he turned back and drove to his job.

The next day over a late breakfast, Alvin told his aunt he had seen the boy again, and that he'd turned into the place down the way. Her expression was impassive at first, but he thought he saw a flicker of anger. "A young boy like that in knickers came here one night, told Floyd a ridiculous story, and got him to leave," she said. "I'd never seen him before, and I haven't seen him since. Why don't you slip over to that cabin and see if there's anything...*questionable*."

Alvin was gone for an hour. When he returned, his clothes were snagged with twigs and leaves, and he was breathing hard. "Aunt Winifred, you won't believe it. The girl and baby from the hospital— they're in that cabin!"

"But it's been deserted for years!"

"Come with me, Auntie!" They set off through the Weston pasture. Alvin helped a panting Winifred under barbed wire and onto the Farrow property, where the two crouched behind a thicket, watching the house. They didn't have long to wait. Almost at once they glimpsed Lola come to stand by the window in the kitchen. She was crooning to the baby, holding it close and kissing its cheek.

"That's the girl who worked at Field's Drugs!" hissed Winifred. They continued to stare at the mother and child. Then slowly, very slowly, they turned toward each other, realization dawning. "Cassie Field!" they breathed together.

"*She's* the connection!" exclaimed Alvin. "I *thought* he—she—looked like someone I knew!" A deep flush began at his neck and rose all the way to his hairline.

"It was *her* putting on a show that night," Winifred muttered, "making a laughingstock of me and Floyd!"

But maybe not Floyd. What if he knew who the boy was? He could have been in on it, playing his own wife for a fool! The baby started to cry, and they watched as Lola retraced her steps through the house and out of sight. They ducked under the barbed wire and headed back across the pasture.

Several days followed, with Winifred keeping her new knowledge— and lack of knowledge—to herself.

Floyd didn't again bring up Alvin's moving out. He felt something in the air, some new, brassy self-confidence emanating from the boy. One day when Floyd saw him lolling on the parlor sofa, eating chocolates out of a box and drinking raspberry soda through a straw, he knew he was beaten.

He sensed something different about Winifred, too, but he didn't know what it was, and he didn't want to think about it.

22

Three may keep a secret if two of them are dead.
—Benjamin Franklin
Poor Richard's Almanac

Clink Kerry worked part-time reading meters for the gas company, and the day he saw smoke coming from the Farrow cabin, he tried to remember if he had ever disconnected the place. Old man Farrow had been dead now for years! Staring at the spire of smoke, he stopped his truck and sat in the road, hitting his forehead with the heel of his hand. He hadn't had to unhook Verley Hoffman's place when they left for California—they burned coal and butane, like Walt Zimmer—but old Mr. Farrow had used gas. When they first brought the lines out to the Sampson and Detwiler ranches, Mabel Farrow had insisted that they hook up her dad, too, even though the old man hated change of any kind.

Clink prayed that nobody at the gas company found out about this. He'd come close to being fired several times by the OG&E man in Antelope—sometimes he wrote the numbers down wrong—but it seemed nobody else wanted the job.

His tank was almost empty, so Clink decided to park on the road and walk in the forty yards or so. Reaching the cabin, he went around the side to look for the meter. Startled to see a young woman moving around on the screened-in side porch, he ducked down behind some bushes. She looked like the girl who used to work at Field's Drugs, only heavier! Didn't she move away someplace? She seemed to have made herself at home, and was weaving some kind of basket. As he watched from behind the mesquite and scrub oaks, the girl sat down and put her chin in one hand—it looked as if she was crying. Then she must have heard a noise, because she left the porch and came back carrying a tiny baby wrapped in a blanket.

Clink decided he wouldn't read the meter today. Cautiously, not even swinging his arms, he walked back to the truck and sat there, picking his nose and thinking. Maybe he ought to talk to someone about this. He was pretty sure the girl wasn't supposed to be here. It looked as though she had herself a woods colt, too.

O

Lola was nursing Dulcie. The baby's straight black hair had thickened; now it grew all over her head, not just on top. Cassie loved to see mother and child cuddling; the joy Lola and the baby drew from each other was a wonder to behold. But she noticed an uneasiness about her friend. Lola seemed downright jumpy. She dropped things and didn't even bother combing her hair. The baby clothes and blankets, at first so nicely kept, were all a-jumble, thrown on the cot and stuffed into the orange crates she used for storage.

Cassie took a deep breath. "Lola, don't you think you can come into town now and bring Dulcie? You could show her to Aunt Flo and Uncle George, and my folks. Just *show* her to 'em and say, 'Look at this baby—it belongs to *all* of you!' You can't stay here until the war's over and Dan comes home!"

Her friend's eyes welled up with tears, and Cassie dropped the subject, wondering if Lola was worried they would take Dulcie away from her.

Evidently Lola had something *she* needed to relate. She stared at Cassie with round, frightened eyes, and twice she started sentences and didn't finish them.

"Cassie, yesterday I…" But she stopped. Later during the same visit, she blurted out, "Yesterday Duke Farrow…"

"Don't tell me *he's* been around!"

"Oh, no, nothing—never mind." And that was the end of that. Cassie couldn't get another word out of her.

It was obvious the girl hadn't gotten her energy back. She walked slowly, like a much older woman. Cassie worried that there still wasn't a decent chair in the place, or a real bed. Lola nursed while sitting on the cot and leaning against the wall, with folded blankets behind her for a cushion. And when the baby cried or needed burping, Lola stood swaying back and forth, jiggling the child in her arms. It would be nice if Lola had a rocking chair.

For a long time now, Cassie had thought about confiding in someone. She at last realized that Lola needed more help than she could provide, and after weeks of soul-searching, she decided to unburden herself to Peggy Bartlett, who she was sure wouldn't break a confidence.

One evening she and Peggy were alone in the store, and Cassie had finished drying the last Coke glass and stacking it on the pyramid of glasses on the backbar. She turned toward Peggy, cleared her throat, and was about to speak, when Eula Tully walked in.

Rats! For some reason known only to their maker and themselves, Eula and Peggy had become friends. The two chatted often, usually in the evening before Eula went to work at the theater.

Cassie picked up a magazine and walked to a back table.

The visit turned out to be a lucky one. Cassie's ears pricked up as she heard Eula tell Peggy she'd found a complete set of outdoor furniture, a gas stove, an air conditioner, a croquet set, and a rocking chair at the Cato dump. She'd bought all these things from Smiley Applebaum for fifteen dollars, and she said Smiley was going to deliver everything to her home free of charge.

The next day Cassie confronted Eula near the flagpole as she crossed Main. Eula tried to ignore her, but Cassie held her by one of her sleeves. "I guess you know all about Lola. I'd like to have that rocking chair for her, the one you were talkin' about to Peggy."

"*What?* Why should I give *you* a rockin' chair? An' I don't know nothin' about Lola—she left town!" Eula jerked away.

"You mean Floyd didn't tell you?" Cassie gasped. This was a shock. Despite his promise not to breathe a word, Cassie had been sure he would tell Eula everything. "Well, she's livin' outside of town, and you better be quiet about it or I'll tell what I saw, an' there'll be a new face in hell tomorrow." She'd heard the boys at school use that one. She waited, letting her silence speak loudly on the empty street.

"Lola's livin' outside o' town?"

"Yes, and she's got a baby."

"You want the rockin' chair for *Lola?*" Eula had never been really quick.

"I'll come by and pick it up tomorrow afternoon."

This was like taking candy away from a baby. But she hadn't worked out yet who she'd get to deliver the rocker. Eula didn't have a car. She might have to confide in Peggy after all.

○

Duke Farrow knew that Lola had been away, because for days he'd checked for signs, and she wasn't there. He was sure she'd left to have the baby. When a full week had passed, he decided he'd waited long enough, so when he drove down the driveway one evening and saw a light, he knocked.

After several long minutes, she appeared. She looked pale but she'd gotten back her shape.

"Hello, Duke." Her voice was expressionless.

"Hey, there! You got yer baby, huh? I kin hear it cryin'!"

"Yes."

She'd never sounded this unfriendly before, even those times when she'd acted unhappy and nervous about his visits.

"What'd you have, boy or girl?" He pushed past her and went in, and that was when she smelled liquor.

"A girl." Lola smiled a taut smile and left the room. She came back carrying a little bundle, and peeled back the blanket a couple of inches so he could see the baby's face.

"Well, *how 'bout that!*" He grinned at her, revealing his tobacco-stained front teeth. Without pretending more interest, he turned his gaze back to Lola. "What's yer plans now, sweetheart?" He headed for the kitchen, walking with a slight wobble, the bow in his short legs more obvious than ever. "Le's us set down."

"I don't have any lights in there. Can we stay here?"

There was nothing to sit on but a couple of packing crates. He swiveled in his cowboy boots and gazed at Lola as if sizing her up for the first time.

Suddenly he was tired of the game. He had waited and waited, and waited some more. He'd gone the extra mile to be nice to her while she was expecting her baby, had been generous to a fault while she was getting too big for her clothes. He'd brought her butter and eggs more than once, and had told no one about her being here. But he'd never done what he wanted to do, when everyone knew that a slice off a cut loaf would never be missed.

"I'd jes' as soon set down. I been on a horse all day, roundin' up calves. Le's go in there." He headed for the bedroom, where the kerosene lamp was lit.

Lola stood uncertainly, holding Dulcie; then, swaying on her feet, she followed. He tossed his cowboy hat on the floor and sat at one end of the little cot, giving her several feet of space.

Lola, too, was exhausted. She was still worn out from childbirth, she hadn't had much sleep, and she wasn't feeling well. Every time she urinated it burned like fire, and she knew she must have an infection of some kind. Slowly, grasping the baby, she lowered herself onto the cot.

Duke pulled out a sack of loose tobacco and packet of papers, rolled a cigarette and licked the paper to seal it, then lit up. "You're lookin' real purty, hon." His eyes narrowed behind the smoke, and he grinned foolishly at her again. He'd never smoked in the cabin before, but he was jumpy tonight, and determined to collect his reward.

Lola was glad to be holding the sleeping baby; otherwise he would see how bad she was trembling. Now the several feet of space between them had shrunk to only a foot.

His free hand, the one without the cigarette, crept behind her back. He kept up a running patter of conversation. "Yeah, me and two other wranglers was awful busy today. There wasn't no rain, so we could git out an' start roundin' up calves for brandin'. Them little dogies, you shoulda seen 'em run!" He leaned toward her, lowering his voice to a hoarse whisper. "Now, sweetie, I know you don't want me knowin' who this baby belongs to, and you know what? I don't even care."

Slowly his hand began to move, methodically massaging all the way from her neck down to the bottom of her spine. It felt like a hot iron on the rigid board of her back. He dropped his cigarette to the floor and ground it under his boot.

She felt him tugging at her blouse.

"Duke, *what are you up to?*" Her voice sounded shrill and frightened. She tried to get herself under control—mustn't show fear. "I have to get some sleep—the baby keeps me up all night! You're goin' to have to go!" She placed the baby on the bed between them and slid all the way to her end of the cot.

"Now, wait a minute, honey. I never have tol' you how I *feel.*"

"I'm sorry, Duke; you'll have to try to understand. I—I'm still in love with the father of my baby! I'm sorry!" Duke reached over the baby, grabbed her by the shoulders and kissed her, pushing his tongue into her mouth.

She struggled, freed herself, and leaped to her feet. "You get out of here! Can't you see I have to take care of my baby? Get *out!*" He turned slightly away from her, and she began to pound him on the back as hard as she could.

Duke hunched his shoulders and ducked his head, backing out of the room. "I guess you ain't been hearin' me all these months, lady-girl! I kin git you throwed out o' here in a minute— with just a snap o' my fingers!"

She heard the door slam.

After that, Lola jammed her few bits of furniture against the doors every night before she went to bed, and she decided not to light the lamp again at all. She worried that the windows didn't have locks, so she started sleeping with a brick by the cot.

O

The next time Cassie came out, Lola looked terrible—pale as ivory, and gaunt.

"Are you eating enough?" Cassie asked her. "I gotta bring you more meat!" Meat and the rocker, which was going to be a surprise. And which she'd told Eula to hold for her, because she hadn't figured out yet how to deliver it.

Lola put Dulcie down, took Cassie into the kitchen, and told her to sit. "You know, last time you were out, I said something about Duke Farrow?"

"Yeah—what is it?" Cassie began to pace around the floor. Something had happened, or was going to.

"He's been comin' here bothering me ever since…well, a long time ago. An' he's *still* coming, even with the baby here and all! I didn't want to worry you, so I didn't say anything!"

"He saw me once on the road. Did he come down here and find you?" asked Cassie.

"Yes. And he's been…*awful*. He's been tryin' to get me to…*like* him—and I *hate* him! He keeps bringin' me food—I was ashamed to show you."

"What do you mean, trying to get you to like him?"

"Threatenin' me if I don't let him kiss me and stuff—sayin' he's going to tell about me in town!"

"Well, that's another reason to come in, don't you see? What's he want you to do? I hope you *weren't* nice to him!"

"Well, I was kinda nice at first—tryin' to hold him off so he wouldn't kick me out of here! He acts like this is *his* place!"

Cassie sat down again and tried to think. Duke thought the cabin was his because he was Mabel's cousin. The way Lola had been handling this wasn't the way she would have done it, at all. She would have booted him out on his bony butt! But she wasn't Lola, and she'd never had to deal with anyone like Duke, who had a reputation for being mean. If only Mabel were here! She would put Duke in his place, and she'd keep him away from Lola.

The squalls of a hungry baby came to their ears. Lola jumped up, and Cassie had to leave to work at the store. They didn't talk anymore about Duke that day.

○

Lola woke just after dawn to loud, creaking sounds from the roof. She'd heard squirrels up there before scurrying about, and the occasional bluejay working on a nut, or sometimes a flicker drumming away in search of elm beetles. But this sounded like footsteps. She ran in her nightgown to the porch and all the way outside.

Duke was up on the roof.

"What are you doing up there!"

"Just checkin' fer leaks, missy," he said, looking down. "You think this ol' house is gonna take keer of itself?"

"Why didn't you tell me you were goin' up there, Duke? You scared me half to death!"

Then, for the usual reasons, she changed her tone. "Would you like to come in and have some—some tea, and toast?"

"Tired o' tea. Brought coffee and a coffeepot—out on the front step. You git that and fix it, an' I'll come down."

She went inside, threw on some clothes, and picked up the fussing Dulcie. After changing her, she managed to percolate coffee, jostling the baby on her shoulder the entire time.

Instead of settling himself in the kitchen as he usually did, Duke paced around the house, picking up this, moving that, drinking his coffee (which he fortified the same as his tea), and throwing piercing looks in Lola's direction. After several such malignant glances, Lola refused to meet his gaze. Something was stuck in his craw, but she wasn't going to ask. She crooned softly to the hungry baby and rocked her in her arms, but finally decided she had to feed the child. In a kitchen chair, covering her shoulder and breast with a clean diaper—she was afraid to go in the bedroom because he might follow her in there—she began to nurse Dulcie.

Duke's footsteps echoed loudly as he strode back and forth across the loose floorboards. At last he went outside again, and a few minutes later she heard loud whooshing sounds. Maybe he was going to set fire to everything—*he was crazy and mean enough!* When she'd finished nursing and had put Dulcie down, she crept out to see. Duke was swinging a scythe in big circular motions, clearing off underbrush.

She mustn't anger him. Timidly she asked, "Why are you doing that, Duke?"

"Same reason I told you before. Things hafta git *done* aroun' here. You ain't done nothin' but set in there takin' keer o' that chile. Need a man watchin' out fer things, lady-girl!"

"Oh, I see. I hadn't thought—hadn't thought of doing any maintenance."

"You have any rain leakin' this winter?"

"Only one place, on the porch. I put an old bucket under it."

"Well, you're lucky that's the only place, but you shoulda tol' me about it. I'll git some'un out here to fix it."

She knew she didn't have to tell him why she didn't want a repairman around. She was pretty sure this whole display was a threat.

"Couldn't *you* fix it?"

He didn't reply, so she went inside.

An hour later Duke came back in, sweating. He used half a bucket of well water to wash up in the kitchen sink, while she sat holding the sleeping baby and watching him.

He turned to her and said, "Last time I was here, you wasn't very nice, remember that?"

"Duke, I remember you were...drinking...and I had just had my baby. I—I didn't know what you wanted."

"Oh, yeah, you knew what I wanted. Why'd you think I let you stay all this time?"

"But the baby—"

"*To hell with the baby!* I'll show you the baby!" Duke grabbed Dulcie out of her arms.

"No! Please don't—*please!*" Lola screamed. She began to cry hysterically.

Duke held the child in the air over his head, her blankets dangling halfway off. Then he lowered her and walked into the front room, Lola following. "I'm a-gonna put this baby somewheres you aren't gonna be thinkin' 'bout her all the time." He strode toward the bedroom and dropped the shrieking infant onto the cot.

"Please, Duke, *please don't hurt her.* Duke, okay—*okay!*" Lola forced herself to speak in a low, carefully modulated voice. "Not now, though, Duke—tonight would be so much better. Tonight I'll have everything all nice, and it'll be dark, and she'll be asleep. I promise. I can't feel very...loving right now. If you come back later, I'll thank you for everything—I'll thank you *so much!* For lettin' me stay here, and for the food, and for comin' here checkin' on things. You'll feel more romantic tonight, and I will, too."

He stepped back and looked at her, his expression a mix of disbelief and longing. "That's better. I didn't wanta make things nasty. You got the picture now." He hitched up his jeans. "Okay. I'll be here 'bout eight tonight, and you better be ready."

He shoved his hat on his head, and left.

O

For weeks after Clink Kerry saw Lola in the cabin, he puzzled about what to do. He thought about telling Sheriff Bartlett, but he didn't want to get the girl in trouble with the law. Then he considered telling the mayor. But Clink didn't like Barney Scruggs, who would no doubt use the situation to throw his weight around. He sure could tell Marvin

Field—the girl used to work for him, after all—and he pondered this possibility for a long time. Every time he saw Mr. Field on Main Street, which was nearly every day, he came close to blurting it out. Finally Clink thought of Harold Cutter. Mr. Cutter was a nice man, and he knew every house around Cato. Clink knew he'd tried to sell that cabin ever since old man Farrow died, but trying to sell houses around Cato was like trying to cut a big hog with a little knife.

O

Duke arrived at the cabin at eight o'clock sharp, boots polished and jeans freshly washed. His hair glistened with pomade. He rapped on the door. Tonight things would go his way, or tomorrow he would throw her out.

With a tense smile, Lola opened the door. Duke walked in and looked around; the baby was nowhere in sight.

"I—I promised you I'd get Dulcie to sleep, and I did," she said.

It looked as though she had gotten herself dolled up, too. She was wearing a white blouse and a dark skirt, and her hair was brushed out loose. As usual, she wore no makeup.

Duke attempted a grin, but his upper lip lifted on only one side, and the effect was a lopsided leer. "She better not be nowhere near us, where she kin git in the middle o' things," he said.

"Oh, no. I put her in a big box between the two chairs in the kitchen. She's out of the way for sure." She led him toward the bedroom, where the cot was made with a fresh sheet and blanket.

Moving toward her fate, Lola wondered how she had managed to sink this far. Cassie had been urging her to move into town, and she'd been so stubborn about it, so fearful of the laughing and jeering of the townsfolk. But she would have been better off believing Cassie, when she said Aunt Flo and Uncle George would forgive her! Anything would be better than the mess she'd gotten into with this horrible, mean-spirited man.

She stumbled, and reached for the wall to steady herself.

As soon as he was in the room, Duke pulled her to him and began to move his wet mouth over her face, licking and smothering her with animal-like movements of his tongue and mouth. He pressed his groin against hers, grinding himself into her while gripping her around the shoulders with his arms.

Lola submitted to all this, reasoning that it would be impossible to escape. He pulled her down on the cot, but the cot, unequal to the burden, broke, and they bumped heavily to the floor, Duke moving his hands over her all the while, groping her breasts. When he slid his hands under her skirt, she didn't resist. He began to unbutton his jeans.

She had meant to ask if he was wearing protection, but she was afraid to anger him. All at once, Lola felt her breath desert her. She couldn't suck any air into her lungs, and her skin felt as if he were scraping it with metal fingers.

"No!" she cried. "No, Duke, I *can't!*"

Duke ignored her. He tore at her skirt, ripping away the hooks holding the waistband, shucking her panties down until they were crumpled about her feet, and she was uncovered except for her blouse. She struggled more fiercely, managing to stumble to her feet.

"Duke, stop! I can't!"

He slapped her then, hard, across the mouth. "Wha'dja think, that I was jus' playin'?"

He wrestled her down to the floor again, clasped one hand tight around her neck, and shoved himself inside her, where she was still so raw and sore. When he had finished, he stood looking down at her motionless body and torn, disheveled clothing. Slowly he pulled on his jeans, methodically rebuttoning them while considering what had taken place. He was calm now, and by the time he left, his breathing was regular, his sweat already beginning to dry.

Climbing into his pickup, he had already begun to feel a little sorry for the girl. But she had asked for it, asked for it over and over, every time she let him into the house. And if she ever went to town and accused him of anything, all he had to do was lie. Everybody would see what kind of girl she was.

O

Lola lay for a long time on the floor. She didn't cry, just lay there faceup, staring at the cobwebs that hung from the ceiling beams. She considered the spiders and their intricate work for a long time, until she came back to full consciousness and realized that she was cold. Hurting all over, she got up and went into the kitchen, where Dulcie was sleeping soundly with two fingers in her mouth.

Lola washed herself with soap and water from the bucket. She knew she should heat the water, but she was too exhausted, and her neck hurt terribly where Duke had choked her. She carried Dulcie back to the bedroom, removed her torn blouse and brassiere, and put on her nightgown. Then, arranging the bedding as best she could on the hard floor, she huddled with the baby tight against her.

○

Cassie got up that morning with a sense of foreboding. What could be causing this sinking, heavy feeling in the pit of her stomach? Was it because she was worried about her friend? Or the dogs' barking? They had started at dawn, making enough noise to waken the dead. Maybe it was the wind rustling and whistling in the trees. Or maybe it was that the calendar said her period was about to strike.

Her dad was outdoors feeding the dogs; his *Daily Oklahoman* sat unfolded on the table. Cassie ate a bowl of cereal, barely speaking to Liddy, who didn't seem in a mood to talk, either. She decided to take her bike to school; she would go directly from there to see Lola. The bike would be safe parked under the bleachers near the football field; it was too old to awaken greed in anyone. She threw her pants, cap and shirt into a heavy paper bag, along with her schoolbooks, and went outside to talk to her dad. Passing herself off as a scholar had been successful before, so she told him that after school, instead of working at the store, she'd promised to study with Fiona for a science test. She said Fiona was about to fail, and was desperate for help. "And after that, she asked me to have supper, an' then we might go see a movie."

"Well, you're not gettin' paid," was all he said.

She mounted her bike and started out. The wind had modulated to a soft breeze, so maybe the day wasn't going to be so terrible after all. But she got so antsy in class that she cut last period and, after changing in the bathroom, grabbed her bike and pedaled out to the cabin. She found Lola with one of Dulcie's blankets wrapped around her neck. Under her eyes were dark purple stains, and she was burning up with fever. Dulcie was crying, untended, so Cassie found the sugar tit that Lola had made for emergencies and stuck it her mouth, then biked over to find Floyd Weston. He was out in the fields baling hay, and when she told him how bad off Lola was, he said, "Go stand in the road; I'll pick you up."

Winifred was nowhere in sight. "Thank God for small favors!" Cassie breathed.

She threw her bike into the bushes at the side of the road, no time to put it in his car.

They got Lola and Dulcie, and soon were on their way to Antelope; Lola in the back seat, Dulcie at her breast. Cassie was amazed when Floyd said he would come in the doctor's office too. They waited together, taking turns walking the baby.

O

Harold Cutter got a visit in his office from Clink Kerry around five-thirty, just as he was locking the door. Soon afterward he drove, alone, across Wolf Creek Bridge. The wind had come up, and the trees whipped about, with dirt blowing thick and dark against the windshield.

O

When Lola came out of the doctor's office she looked better, although her face was still flushed, and she walked with a halting, careful step, as if avoiding some obstruction in front of her. She smiled, held up a pill bottle, and said, "Doctor Lowe gave me these tablets to take, Sulfa-something. Your daddy was getting some in the pharmacy before I had to quit, and he told me they're usin' them for soldiers in the war. I have to take one three times a day."

They headed back, and after Lola and Dulcie were back in the cabin, Floyd said, "I'll drive you back to your bicycle."

Cassie realized suddenly that his voice sounded different; it didn't have his usual resentful, carping tone. He sounded, if not amiable, at least resigned. Could it be that he was beginning to enjoy the role of good Samaritan?

They heard the sounds of a motor, and looked up to see another automobile coming down the drive. They froze in place, as Harold Cutter got out and came walking toward them. Floyd couldn't leave fast enough. Driving into and over bushes and barely missing several trees, he managed to turn his car around and was gone.

Harold, with a severe expression, took Cassie by the arm. Cassie had always thought Mr. Cutter was handsome, but today he looked bothered and anxious. They went into the cabin, and after looking around and peering into the sleeping baby's face, he began to speak.

"Lola, I'm not going to tell you how I found out about all of this, but you can't stay out here another day. It's way past time for you and that pretty little baby to come into town!"

He turned to look at Cassie. He was angry with her, she was sure, and she felt shamed and guilty. He turned to Lola again. "You should go to your aunt and uncle's. They'll welcome you with open arms. Blood's thicker than water, and they love you, child! They're probably out of their minds with worry! You girls can't know what it's like to worry about your children, I think that's pretty obvious. And Lola, you don't look well."

Cassie lifted her head. "I think Mr. Cutter's right," she said, dragging it out like it was the last line in a play. "I think it's time for you to come into town."

Lola reached over and touched Harold's arm. "I think so, too. I'll come."

Just like that, Lola had changed her mind! It didn't matter why; the only thing that mattered was she was leaving the cabin.

Right after that, they started loading Harold's car.

23

Soon the storm was over; the people gathered round,
And there the dead and dying lay prostrate on the ground.
To render their assistance so quickly they began
To remove them from their struggle; soon all were taken in.
   —"The Sherman Cyclone,"
   Folk Song

The wind had been blowing all spring, and no one had thought anything about it—wind was ordinary. There had been some rain, the crops were growing, and people were feeling more prosperous as a result of the war economy. Things weren't wonderful, but they weren't nearly as bad as in the thirties. The real worry was not about money but rather about their young men, off getting killed or maimed in the war.

But on a spring Thursday in early April, a warm, wet air mass from the Gulf of Mexico met a mass of cold air blowing east from the Rocky Mountains. The warm air mass tried to rise, and the cold air tried to drop, and the result was much worse than the usual thunderstorm and hail. When the warm air started to poke through the cold, the two swirling, tumbling masses spawned a tornado.

The twister screwed down from the sky at 4:42 p.m. in the Texas panhandle, at the town of Mule Deer, then roared on its way northeast through Boydsville and Cedar Grove, crossing into Oklahoma, where it plowed through south of Red Arrow and right through Cato to Antelope, where it did the most damage. Finally, having all but spent itself, it moved into Kansas and pulled itself back up into the sky. Some of the time it had hit wind speeds of four hundred miles an hour, cutting a swath approximately a hundred miles long. The newspapers called it, then and later, "one of the widest trails of destruction ever recorded by a twister!"

After that day it was referred to as the Antelope tornado, but it was the Cato tornado, too.

When it slammed into town that early evening, some died and many more were injured, and the physical and emotional damage it left wouldn't be healed for many years.

O

It was 7:07 p.m. when the black funnel hit.

Road to Morocco was opening at the Cato Theater, and the crowd was watching previews of coming attractions when the lights went out. There was a sound like a locomotive rushing, only louder, and someone shouted, "*Get down! Blower!*" Then came the loud crashing sounds, and everyone tried to dive under their seats. They felt the roof peel off over their heads with a loud *WHOOSH!* and a wall fell in at the back, where several people were sitting.

Peggy Bartlett was working late at the drugstore. A shipment of cosmetics had come in that day, and she was trying to finish pricing them. Her husband Jim was there too, and he was able to cover her with his body just before the store's front light fixture dropped.

Marvin and Stuffy Byers were having a smoke back in the prescription area, discussing whether the Cardinals and the Yankees would go to the World Series again. The twister picked up Stuffy— along with a wall— and blew him out to the back alley, where he landed against the fire whistle pole. Stuffy outweighed Marvin by ninety pounds, and Marvin would have been carried farther, but the marble-topped prescription counter fell on top of him, pinning him beneath it and cutting and bruising him in a hundred places. Bleeding profusely from the head, he managed to get out from under and crawl over to find bandages, all the while calling weakly to Peggy.

She was screaming over and over, "*He's dead! Jim's dead! Oh, my God—he's dead!*" But he was only unconscious.

Liddy had been driving all over the county that day, and was exhausted. She had decided to have tea and toast and go to bed early. Standing in the kitchen in her nightgown, she heard the loudest noise she'd ever heard in her life—as loud as all the troop trains she had ever waved at put together —and she dropped to the floor and began to pray. She was close to a stove leg, that was what she held on to. After four or five minutes of utter terror, the noise lessened and the house began to settle with much creaking and groaning.

Then the hail came.

Nothing was disturbed in the kitchen, nor was anything moved in the breakfast room. The front of the house was gone, but the bowl full of wax apples, pears, and oranges was still in its place. The ravaging, howling current of air had taken off part of the roof and thrown all her new living room furniture to the winds.

She ran into the backyard, screaming for help. The dogs were barking wildly. Had they been quiet until now? Why hadn't they warned her? Banishing this ridiculous thought, she ran into the front yard. It looked as though the Purvises' house had been demolished, and the Bannisters, like the Fields, had lost part of their roof. The Applebaums' house had vanished entirely, and she didn't know yet about old Mrs. Pinkerton.

Cassie and Marvin!

She ran back inside, ignoring the cries of Heck Purvis, who was wandering out in the street. His head was bleeding, and his eyes looked vacant. He was probably in shock, but so was she! She had to get dressed, but she didn't dare go up the stairs, which were half torn away and dangling surreally from what was left of the house. On the back porch, she grabbed some gardening shoes and an old housedress hanging on a hook. Pulling it on over her nightgown, she sat down on the floor to put on the shoes, but she was shaking so much, she couldn't control her fingers. She got up and managed to walk outside again.

Marvin had taken the Plymouth to work, and with the house in pieces, she knew she would never find the keys to the Model A. It took her twenty minutes to walk downtown. She usually made it in ten, but she had to walk around boards, roofing, bricks and broken glass— at the same time resolutely refusing to stop to help anyone. Her own family might need her, and she had to go on. Pearl Purvis was sitting in her front yard, sobbing, blood covering her arms and legs, but Liddy didn't stop, nor did she slow down for Ernestine, who was running around holding on to a cat and screaming at the top of her lungs. The Bannister's roof looked as if it had been lifted up, turned halfway, and dropped back down, but she didn't linger to listen for sounds of distress. It was the same for three more blocks before she got to Main—people on all sides, calling for help. There were cars jammed into trees and stacked atop one another all the way into town, twisted metal bent in astonishing ways. Now rain was coming down, soaking her to the skin.

She turned the corner onto Main, where the street looked as if it had been bombed. When she got to the drugstore, she was barely conscious of the debris outside, the huge hot-water bottle and the giant thermometer shattered into red, pink and white shards. She climbed over rubble and stumbled inside, past Peggy, who was kneeling next to Jim. The big man lay crumpled on the floor, broken glass all around. She hurried to the back, where she found Marvin alive. He smiled. "I'm okay. Glad to see you." As she knelt next to him, he reached up and grasped her arm with surprising strength. "Don't know about Cassie... Can you go check at the..." He groaned. "...at the theater?"

"Yes. You sure you're all right?" She touched his head where the bandage was soaked through with blood.

"Yeah. I'm okay. Go on. Stuffy got blown out back—but go check on Cassie."

Liddy got up, pushing her way through fallen shelves and scattered and jumbled merchandise. This time she stopped to kneel by Jim. His eyes were open. She patted Peggy's shoulder and said, "I'll be back—got to find Cassie." She made her way across the street, picking her way around barrels and torn-open grain sacks from the feed store, and bricks and glass which had exploded out of every storefront on Main. Here were six or eight more smashed cars. A few frightened- looking people huddled by a cavernous hole that had once been the entrance to the Cato theater. The marquee was splintered; some of the big wooden letters were strewn about on the ground.

Fiona and Margie Botsin were outside the theater. Both girls looked distraught, but Fiona seemed the calmer of the two.

"Where's Cassie?" Liddy cried.

Fiona looked blank. "I don't know—she didn't come with us. Was she s'posed to? I'm sorry... I don't know."

"All right." For once Liddy was glad Cassie wasn't where she was supposed to be. But where *was* she?

Mr. Gruber was lying on the sidewalk, after being either sucked or blasted out of the projectionist's booth, and Reuben Hargraves and Violet were kneeling next to him. He was whiter than anyone should be and still be alive, but he was breathing.

Eula Tully leaned against what was left of the theater front.

"You okay, Eula?" Liddy asked.

"I think so." Eula had been hit in the head. One eye was swelling shut, and her face was smeared with blood.

Liddy heard a deep masculine voice. "You all get out of here now. We'll search for the folks left in there." It was Sheriff Bartlett, with

Seth Scruggs. Both Ed and Seth were unscathed and looked strong and capable. Liddy had never been so glad to see any two men in her life.

Liddy touched Ed's arm. "Do you know about Jim?"

"Yeah, but Peggy's gonna have to take care of him. I got my job to do. The depot wasn't touched—Homer's gettin' Billy Saltman to get on his ham radio to Red Arrow. This probably hit some other towns, so we may or may not be gettin' any help. Reuben, your café bought it, but can you find someone to help carry Mr. Gruber someplace safe? Ben or Coach Lansford at the café—go get one o' them. Try to find a board to carry him on—might be spinal damage. Seth and me are goin' into the theater. Miz Field, can you take Margie up to her dad at the depot?"

Ed looked at her over Margie's head, jerking his head in the direction of the café and warning her with his eyes. Liddy hated to guess at the reason, so she merely nodded, and as he stepped through the hole into the theater, she took the stunned child by the hand and led her away.

O

It was a few minutes before the cyclone hit. Dusk was falling on the already storm-darkened landscape, and outside the cabin, dry leaves, dirt, and rolling tumbleweeds were blowing faster than a person could run. Buffeted by the gale, the little house made eerie groaning noises and seemed to move on its foundation.

"Hurry!" yelled Mr. Cutter, starting to run, and Lola ran with Dulcie in the cradle and climbed into the backseat. Cassie jumped in front, slamming the door against the wind.

Crossing the bridge back into Cato, and wrestling with the steering wheel against monstrous gusts, Harold thought that if they could keep going they would be safe—safer in the car than outside it, or so he'd heard. But he'd heard other theories, too, all of them conflicting. He kept driving while the car took a series of thumping broadsides from flying branches and rocks.

They were two-thirds of the way across the bridge when they felt the car being pulled sharply to the left. Lola and Cassie screamed as the car was sucked inexorably toward the side of the bridge, and they screamed again as it crashed through the wood railing and fell twenty feet into the water.

Miraculously, they landed right side up. But the shock was so powerful they were stunned, both by the impact and by the ear-shattering sound. Then water began to boil up through the floorboard.

A strong current, fed by torrential rains upstream, nudged the big Chrysler downstream as Mr. Cutter cranked frantically to roll down his window. Simultaneously buoyed and weighed down by the water, he somehow managed to get out the window. He knew he wouldn't be able to swim in his waterlogged suit, so he pulled off his shoes and shucked out of his jacket and trousers, hooking one leg inside the door to keep from being swept downstream.

The car was filling fast, and Lola was screaming, "I can't swim!" Cassie had managed to get out through her window and pull herself around to the back door, wrenching it open. Lola handed out the baby, and Cassie took her and began sidestroking toward shore.

"Help Lola! I got the baby!" she yelled to Mr. Cutter, who was working against the current to pull Lola free.

The baby wore only a shirt and diaper. Cassie tried to swim with her the way she'd been taught in lifesaving class, scissor-kicking on her side while holding Dulcie as high as she could, but the baby was swallowing water and choking. Cassie struggled to hold her out of the water while stroking at right angles to the current, but her legs felt like lead. Her water-logged clothing dragged her down, impeding her kicks. For the forty or fifty feet to shore, she alternated between holding Dulcie out of the creek and balancing her on her chest. Stroking furiously, she at last reached the edge and pulled up onto a level sandy area. Dulcie was bawling angrily, but she was fine. Cassie shoved her farther up onto shore, then got to her feet to try to sight Lola and Mr. Cutter. The old man was treading water and trying to grab hold of Lola, who floundered and flopped about, gesturing as if she wanted him to leave her. Cassie stood for a split second, dreading to reenter the water, but seeing no alternative, she tore off her soaked skirt and dove again into the freezing creek. Lola had broken away from Harold and was grabbing at cattails on the creek's edge, but they kept breaking off, and the surging current was sweeping her away. Her head disappeared into the brown churn, and all they could see was one feebly groping arm and hand.

Cassie and the old man treaded water, yards apart, until he shouted, "Cassie, she's gone—get to shore!" Gasping for air, Cassie did an awkward, unsteady dog-paddle until she could haul herself out by grabbing onto a cottonwood sapling lying horizontal to the creek edge. Gazing at the rushing water, numb with horror and grief, she suddenly registered the sound of the baby squalling several yards away.

Lola, drowned! It couldn't be—*it just couldn't be!*

Mr. Cutter, wearing only his underwear and torn shirt, pulled up beside her, breathing hard. She looked at him for confirmation. Was this real, or some horrible nightmare? He sat up, crawled over, and put his arm around her. There was only a faint wind now, and it had started to hail.

◯

Outside the ruined movie theater, Liddy decided to overrule the sheriff.

"Fiona, you take Margie up to the depot. I'll doctor Eula." She helped Eula stand up, and together they started across the street. It was then that Liddy heard Cassie yelling. Looking toward the north end of Main, she saw her daughter walking along in her underwear with, of all people, Harold Cutter. She was crying, and appeared to be carrying a doll. As they all met outside the drugstore, it was difficult to say who looked worse: Liddy in her nightgown and muddy dress, Eula, half covered with blood, or Cassie, Harold, and the baby, all soaking wet and half-naked.

Liddy grabbed Cassie and held her tight, baby and all.

"This is Lola's baby, Mama," Cassie sobbed, "but—but, Mama, Lola's *dead*! She *drowned!*"

Liddy began to cry too. All these tragedies crashing down at the same time!

"But, Mama, this is *Dan's* baby!"

Liddy's eyes focused for a split second on the baby, then on Cassie, then back on the baby.

"Oh, dear God," moaned Liddy. She took the baby from Cassie's arms. Her knees buckled, and she swayed, holding the child. Then she rallied. "Come inside—Daddy's hurt. *Oh*, it's a girl." Dulcie no longer wore her diaper.

"Her name's Dulcie."

"Isn't she beautiful! We have to get her warm and dry, you too."

"Liddy...it was awful!" Harold groaned.

"Harold, we'll get you some whiskey. Marvin has some inside, if it isn't broken! He has some old trousers, too, and maybe I can find a shirt or jacket. Come on."

They stepped over more debris and entered the store. Jim had regained consciousness and had some color. Liddy handed the unhappy baby over to Peggy, and she quickly undressed the infant and wrapped fountain towels around her. Cassie went to find Marvin.

"Cassie, where have you been?" Marvin gasped.

After a desperate search, Liddy handed her a blanket.

"Is Daddy gonna be okay? He looks awful!"

"I think so. Stuffy got thrown out the back. I told someone to find him…" She reached into a doorless closet, found some clothes for Harold, and took them to him. One or two drug cabinets were lying on their sides; scattered near them were a few supplies. Liddy dipped a cotton ball in merthiolate and dabbed it on Eula's scalp wound, then applied a bandage. Moving fallen shelves to make room on the floor, she made Eula lie down, but there weren't any more blankets.

She found whiskey and walked up to the soda fountain. The fountain and refrigerator were undamaged, and she located a few pieces of unbroken glassware as well. She poured whiskey an inch deep in two Coke glasses, handed one to Harold, and propped up Marvin's head, holding the glass to his lips.

"Liddy, you givin' me *whiskey?*"

"Sh-h-h! Try to rest, and just thank the Lord we still have most of the roof on the store." She let his head sink back on a folded towel, and he closed his eyes. Eula got a shot of whiskey, too, and to Cassie's incredulity, her mother poured a tablespoon and handed the glass to her.

Sheriff Bartlett and Ben Hargraves came in carrying long boards for stretchers. "We'll take Jim and Marvin… Where's Stuffy?" asked the sheriff.

O

An hour after the twister hit, Barney and Sally Scruggs and Charlene Byers had arrived downtown and started herding people into Veterans Hall, which sat a little way off Main. It was built entirely of stone and was undamaged, so it immediately became a temporary hospital. Amazingly, because the twister had roared through town at an angle, the southeast part of the downtown area was left unhurt; this included Veterans Hall, the train depot, the hotel, Schonberger's Dry Goods, the grain elevator, and the First Baptist Church. But there were no telephone or telegraph lines working.

There were no lights anywhere in town, so Sally, Charlene, and Doc Ledbetter worked by any kerosene lanterns and candles they could round up. Everyone was thankful that Sally and Charlene had inspired several women to take Red Cross first aid training. Two of these women were Liddy's bridge friends, Violet and Rowena. These ladies ran everything at the Hall in the coming days, and ran it well.

But they didn't run Doc Ledbetter. Doc was an old man now, white-haired, stooped, and stubborn, and he did things his own way, wasting little time on bedside manner. But he knew how to practice medicine, and the town was grateful.

The Mistletoe Café had been less occupied than usual that evening, which was a blessing, because the front half of it now rested on top of the bank. Ben Hargraves, alone at the café while his dad took Violet to the movies, had survived by hunkering down under the bolted-down lunch counter. Billy Saltman and Coach Lansford were there, heard the tornado, and felt the café shake. The coach yelled, "Hit the deck!" and the two managed to get under a table, also bolted to the floor. But Connie Botsin, who had come downtown to deliver coffee to Homer at the depot, was less fortunate. She was chatting with Billy, and Coach Lansford told how Ben reached around the counter to grab her, but she was blasted outside and thrown against an awning pole, breaking her neck.

Southwest of town, the twister missed the Klein farm and all its pigs, but Grandpa Klein and eight-year-old Timmy were half a mile from home, walking back from fishing. Chester Klein and Fergus went out together, found them buried under piles of debris and mud, and brought them in. When the rescue workers got there hours later, the two were laid out on the porch.

Checking farms and ranches north of town was delayed when rescuers found Wolf Creek Bridge down, one of its supporting trusses lying on its side in the rushing creek. (Harold Cutter's car was found a quarter mile downstream.) Luckily, there was a tiny wooden bridge a mile west. It had been barely used for the past thirty years, but it was still intact. The delay meant that no one could get to the blown-out farms to the north until morning.

Hardest hit were the Zimmer and Thatcher farms and the Detwiler ranch. Tom and Minna's baby Jaky had been ripped from Minna's arms and dashed against a tree, shattering his tiny skull. The other children had only cuts and bruises, but Minna had a broken arm, and Tom a broken back. All the outbuildings were strewn across three acres, and half the house was gone.

Rescuers found Walt Zimmer dead under his house, his skin full of broken glass, his head all but severed.

Charlie Detwiler and his wife were eerily lucky, and long after other stories about the tornado were forgotten, their story was the one everyone repeated. The twister tore through their ranch, killing horses and cattle, but what happened to Charlie and Louise was one for the books. Before the storm hit, they had been standing together between the barn and the house, staring at the approaching black funnel, not nearly frightened enough of what was coming. Later Charlie said, "That wind come runnin', carryin' buildin's and trees and ever'thang else, and we just couldn't git out o' the way in time!" In the space of a second, they were picked up and lifted into the air, held there, then wafted over a windbreak of tall cottonwood trees and deposited, upright, on the other side. According to Louise, the worst thing about it was the dirt and mud that flew into their mouths and eyes; they had to claw it out right away or they would have choked to death.

Grace Sampson wasn't at Sandy Flats, but Hal Sampson and Duke Farrow were, and they were plenty frightened. They headed for the storm cellar, and neither got a scratch. The next day Hal found his horse trailer three miles away and nearby, a tractor turned over on its side. "Takes a lot to blow over a tractor," Hal said.

The Westons' barn was nearly destroyed, and Floyd lost some cattle. The pergola and sign were blown away, but the elms stood, and the house was unharmed. Alvin was in Antelope at his job, and Floyd, driving like a crazy man, had reached home in time to shelter with Winifred in the cellar.

Lola's body wasn't recovered for another thirty-six hours, and it was Ben and Coach Lansford who found her. Badly battered and twisted, with all clothing stripped away, her body had been carried two miles from the bridge.

O

Veterans Hall was filling up with the dead and wounded, and stories began filterering in. By a fluke of circumstance, Clink Kerry was dead. Seth Scruggs had asked him to watch the gas station for a few minutes while he went across the tracks to his folks' house for supper; Seth was coming back downtown when the tornado hit Main. Sitting in his truck, he watched the huge black cone come whirling through the air, closer and closer. His pickup rocked on its wheels, pulled in all directions by what felt like strong magnets. He was sure that any minute he was going to be sucked into the churning funnel; when the moment passed, he was shaking and limp with relief. He went to check on Clink, driving around Main because there was no way he could drive through it, and found the gas station demolished. Clink's body lay crumpled against a concrete abutment at the bridge twenty-five yards away.

Now Liddy was standing in the rain, asking Seth for a ride to the Schonbergers' house. She couldn't take the Plymouth, which Marvin had parked in the alley behind the store and which lay buried under debris. Seth had just finished helping Sven Sundersson carry the bodies of Miss Thornhill and Hank Jenkins out of the theater and into Veterans Hall. He was standing there smoking a cigarette, looking pretty shook up. Liddy walked over to him and asked, "Was the Schonberger house hit, do you know?" she asked.

Seth shook his head. "No, ma'am; they're near my folks. Everybody around there's okay."

"Good. We have to go there. This is Lola's baby, and Lola's drowned. I need somebody to take us there." She waited a moment for the information to register.

Seth piled them into his pickup and drove over the railroad tracks. Flo and George were out on the street in the rain, talking to neighbors. They all looked dazed, and when Seth pulled up with everyone crowded inside his truck, they were even more dumfounded.

Harold climbed down first, followed by Liddy, still in her nightgown and housedress and carrying a paper bag. Cassie was wrapped in a blanket and cradling Dulcie in her arms.

"Liddy, what are *you* doin' here?" said Flo.

"Flo, dear, George, I think we'd better go inside. Cassie has something to tell you."

George looked at Harold's ashen face and pale ankles and wrists, sticking out conspicuously from Marvin's clothes. George took him by the arm, and they went inside.

In the Schonbergers' living room, Cassie told them everything. She had to start with Lola's drowning. Harold helped her with that part.

"Oh, no. No, no!" Flo repeated, over and over. "This is her baby?" She moved close to George, burying her face in his shoulder as he patted and smoothed her back.

"It was my idea for Lola to stay in the Farrow cabin." Cassie could barely get out the words, but kept going. "She went to a doctor in Antelope, and she had Dulcie in the hospital there—real safe and... smooth."

She had to stop.

Flo was crying, too, and Liddy said, "Flo, George, the baby is Dan's. I didn't know until just a few minutes ago."

"What? But where *is* Lola? Where is she now?" Flo wailed. "Maybe she's *all right*—maybe she could—maybe she grabbed onto some weeds!"

Cassie and Harold shook their heads. "I'm sorry," Harold said. "I saw her go down— and stay down."

"Mr. Cutter tried to save her! He tried *so hard!*" Cassie sobbed.

"I didn't know Dan and Lola had gone out together, Flo," said Liddy.

Flo turned to her, and for a moment no one spoke. Flo looked a hundred years old, as if suddenly aged by the grief of the past few minutes. She left the room, and in a few seconds returned with clothing for Cassie and a wool shawl for the baby.

"These are Lola's, honey. You go in the bathroom and put them on."

On her way out of the room, Cassie passed George Schonberger, and she impulsively bent and kissed him on the cheek. At first he didn't react; then he lifted his head and gave her a weak smile.

Flo had given her a blouse and skirt, plus a red sweater she remembered Lola wearing. She put them on and stood looking at herself in the mirror. She felt light-headed, as if she were watching herself from somewhere high above. Wearing Lola's clothes emphasized the strange feeling. Maybe *she* had died and this was *Lola* standing here! She wished like anything it *was* that way. She grabbed a washcloth and washed her face, and the dizziness abated a little.

When she got back to the living room, Dulcie was making her presence known, whimpering and sucking voraciously on anything put in front of her. Liddy had brought bottles, nipples, and powdered formula from the store, and now was in the kitchen, struggling to remember how to mix formula and sterilize bottles in one of Flo's big stewpots. At last Flo held the baby, wrapped in the shawl and sucking greedily at a bottle.

Flo began to talk.

"We would get these letters from Lola from the Catholic home up in Wichita—we thought they were from there, anyway—but they never had a postmark or looked like they'd been through the mail. We wrote back, but our letters came back marked 'No one here by this name.'"

Liddy looked at Cassie, who cast her eyes down and rubbed at her chin.

"Finally, we got so desperate at not hearing from her, not knowing, we called Dr. Bond up in Liberal, and he told us he, too, thought Lola was at the home. We told him she wasn't! Oh, I tell you, we've been worried out of our heads, haven't we, George? And I ordered all those pretty maternity clothes—I never told anyone about that!"

George spoke, and his voice trembled. "We drove up to Wichita in January, to find out. The nuns were nice, but they didn't know anything about Lola."

Dulcie had finished the bottle and was asleep. Liddy took her, put a dish towel on her shoulder and cradled the infant against it, patting her back. She was rewarded with a loud burp.

Flo smiled. "So that's how you do it!" She walked around the room, alternately wiping her eyes and blowing her nose. "So then we decided we'd call the Bureau of Missing Persons in Oklahoma City. We didn't want to tell Ed Bartlett, somehow."

Liddy said, "Flo, why didn't you tell me about Lola being in Wichita? I knew she went somewhere to have the baby, but…"

"I was ashamed—and I thought we'd find her. Lola was so anxious to have this baby—I knew she'd keep herself safe."

She did, thought Liddy, *with Cassie's help.*

Cassie had fallen asleep. Harold had dropped off too, his body slumped sideways, looking every one of his sixty-odd years. Holding Dulcie, Liddy dropped down on the couch next to her daughter. An occasional sob came from Flo, but the room was quiet.

O

Someone had driven to Red Arrow and brought back two dozen cots for the temporary hospital. Marvin got through that first night, but he told Liddy it was hard to sleep with all the groans and cries of pain. He was awake enough in the middle of the night, even with medication, to know that Doc Ledbetter had used up his supplies of Demerol, codeine, and sulfa. Mr. Gruber needed morphine, so Marvin told Charlene what to look for, and she went to the drugstore with a flashlight.

The water tower had toppled. There was still a small supply of water, but no one knew what they were going to do when it ran out, so they had to start rationing right away. That first night, a lot of the injured went thirsty.

The water tower had fallen on a corner of the O'Herlihys' house, but young Seamus O'Herlihy was the only one hurt—knocked cold by a flying board. All the other O'Herlihys were fine, but after the storm little Maureen went missing. Hours later, with the whole family out searching, she was found three blocks away with a kitten clasped to her chest.

Stuffy was incredibly lucky, and knew it—he had only a concussion and broken shoulder. Flat on his back, peering out from his head bandage, he told Marvin, (also heavily bandaged) "Y'know, ever'thing was all jumbled up inside my head *before* this, so I don't feel no different!"

Stuffy kept everyone's spirits up, joking, and they gathered around his bed to hear him carry on. He said the reason he got knocked into the fire whistle pole was because he'd been trying to set it off; he wanted to be the first one to broadcast the bad news! Stuffy liked to repeat what Reuben told him, that he'd leaned over to kiss Violet at the movie the very second the tornado hit. Reuben said any woman who could kiss like that, he had to marry, and he proposed the next day.

Liddy thought she or Cassie should help out with nursing at the Hall, so since Liddy didn't want to leave Dulcie, Cassie went.

But she wasn't really there. She was still in the water trying to save Lola. She would catch herself reliving the whole thing, staring into space, making up happy endings—first *she* brought Lola safely to shore; then

Mr. Cutter did. She replayed the whole thing in her mind a hundred times, and every time, one of them managed to save Lola.

Search parties went out that first night, looking for bodies, but it took them a day and a half to bring in all the people who needed attention. They brought in Louise and Charlie Detwiler, who were in shock, with four sprained ankles. Neither would be able to talk or walk for a week.

Sally Scruggs told Cassie they were laying out the dead in the basement, and covering them with as many tarpaulins as they could find. "Don't go down there! Just stay up here and help."

But Cassie didn't have to be told. People she had known since she was a little child were down there.

Maybe Lola was down there!

O

The weekend was incredibly clear and sunny, making things easier for searching and cleaning up. Red Cross vans began to arrive from Enid and Oklahoma City with cots, blankets, and medical and blood supplies. Men came from the Army Corps of Engineers, all the way from Fort Sill. Cassie had never seen so much activity in their town before—so many vans and ambulances, so many strangers who all seemed to know what to do. Mobile feeding canteens were brought in, and one time or another, all the rescuers came to the front of the Hall for food and hot coffee.

The day after the storm, Liddy walked over to the train depot.

"Homer, I feel awful guilty asking you to do this, when you've just lost Connie, and you're so overburdened with work. But can you try to get through to Dan at March Field? We have to let him know what's happened!" Homer was one of those town fixtures who didn't have a replacement, like Doc Ledbetter and Sheriff Bartlett.

"That's awright, Miz Field," he said with a sad smile. "Other folks is watchin' over Margie. I'm just doin' my job, an' I'll keep on doin' it."

Two days later, when she went to check a second time, Homer told her he knew how to contact the Army Air Corps in Oklahoma City, and they would do the rest—but even though Cato's telephone and telegraph lines had been repaired by emergency crews, there were just too many messages going out and coming in. Besides the cataclysmic situation in town, troop trains were still going through at all hours, and special trains filled with medical teams were going back and forth to Antelope.

"Miz Field, I heard of situations like this, but I never been through it myself, and I don't want to ever go through it again!"

O

Liddy had told Marvin that Lola had been killed by the cyclone, but she didn't think he had quite comprehended it. And she'd told him the baby Cassie rescued from drowning was Lola's, but she hadn't told him the baby was Dan's, too. She was afraid the shock would set him back.

He was worried about his dogs, so Cassie went home to check. They hadn't been fed since the morning before the storm, and were putting up a terrible racket. Old Sadie, her muzzle completely gray, lay quietly at one edge of the pen. Next to her was her daughter Tizzy, barking for attention with the others. The supply of kibble in the shed was miraculously intact, so Cassie fed them and gave them water. She patted each one and spoke to them, telling them they'd have to be patient like everybody else. Then she went back to town to reassure her dad.

That afternoon, Liddy and Cassie took Dulcie to meet Marvin. He lay propped up on his cot, battered and bruised, the dressing on his head of a startling size and whiteness. His eyes had blackened, giving him a pitiful, haunted look. Liddy stood near his bed, jostling the baby in her arms. "Marvin, isn't she darling?"

She waited a few seconds. "Dear, get ready for a shock. This is Dan's baby."

She put Dulcie in his arms.

"What? What do you mean, Dan's baby? Dan's *gone!*" With an impatient movement, he handed the baby back.

She turned to Cassie, who in halting phrases began to tell her father the story, purposely leaving out Floyd Weston. She pleaded for her father's understanding, gesturing with turned-out hands. "I went up to Liberal with Lola to see Dr. Bond, and he wouldn't do anything about it—her bein' pregnant. He said he couldn't, and anyway, Lola wanted to have the baby."

"Wait a minute! *You* went with Lola up there?"

"Yes. She needed someone, and she picked me."

Liddy and Marvin looked at each other, acknowledging something between them.

"Then I saw the Farrow cabin on the way home, and I thought it might be a good thing for Lola to move in there."

Marvin spoke in such a weak voice, they could barely hear him. "Did you know, Cassie, the baby was Dan's?"

"No. Lola didn't tell me for a long time. I think she was afraid I'd tell, and she didn't want to hurt you and Mama. But I *wouldn't* have told!" She told them how the baby was born the night of the big rainstorm, when she hadn't come home until late. Liddy and Marvin exchanged another look.

All at once Liddy let out a little chuckle. It was the first time Cassie had heard her laugh since the storm.

"So *that's* why all the lying!" Her mother looked almost happy. "How did you *get* to the hospital?"

Cassie went off on another aspect of the tale: how Dan sent Lola letters through her, and how she delivered them. Maybe they'd forget to ask again about transportation.

"My God, Cassie!" Marvin shook his head from side to side. "You sure been kickin' up the dust!" He closed his eyes. "I can't talk anymore."

"Let's go," said Liddy. "Your dad's worn out. I'll come back later."

They went to Peggy's house, where they'd been sleeping since the storm.

The next day Liddy came back alone. Marvin was asleep, so she waited until he woke up, then leaned over to kiss him. "Marvin, I know you don't believe me, but you're going to feel a lot better soon. We have a grandchild now, and it's Dan's baby, and we'll have to love and care for her. We may even have to raise her."

"Poor Lola!" was all he said. He reached out, and they sat holding hands.

Sally, Charlene, and their helpers were bustling about tending people, and Liddy felt guilty sitting there holding hands with her husband. She should at least be helping Peggy at the drugstore, where all the front windows were broken and the back was gone altogether. She said she'd be back, and went to say a brief word to Violet and Rowena, who were busy emptying bedpans and rolling bandages; then she left.

When she returned Sunday morning, Marvin was sitting up. He refused to stay at the Hall any longer—he said it reminded him too much of the field hospitals in Europe during the war. He told her he felt as if he'd been kicked by a team of mules, but was able to walk. He wanted to help doctor people, but Doc Ledbetter wouldn't let him, so he was determined to go home. The Plymouth's top was caved in, but someone had cleared off the rubble, and it ran. If Liddy slid way down in the seat, she could drive it. She put Marvin in the back with Cassie and the baby and drove them home to three walls and part of a roof.

The weather was warm, and after Cassie climbed upstairs on a ladder and tossed down several piles of bedding, they were able to sleep on the main floor. Marvin slept in the spare room, and Liddy, Cassie, and Dulcie took the breakfast room, with Cassie on the floor, Liddy on the couch, and the baby in a laundry basket plumped up with pillows and towels.

When Flo came over the next day, she gazed around in horror. "Liddy, you ought to come to my house! Leave Marvin with Cassie, and bring the baby. We can take care of her together."

"We'll be fine as long as the weather stays warm. The good Lord must have told me to put in that new bathroom. I'm going to try to find some of my new furniture before someone else does. My new brass lamp got smashed into a tree. And I saw one of my chairs lying on its side in the Applebaums' yard. Don't know where the sofa flew to…but I can't think about that now. The refrigerator and stove are working; we'll manage."

With a resigned shake of her head, Flo said, "I'll bring you food, but Liddy, you're too stubborn to live."

Liddy thought Flo was probably relieved she'd rejected her offer. Random thoughts flitted through her mind. They'd have to get the roof fixed, and soon. She hoped Sven Sundersson remembered how much carpentry work she had given him through the years, so they'd get priority. And if Flo thought she was going to let go of this baby for one second, she was mistaken. She didn't think her friend would put up much of a fight; she'd mentioned that George was hinting he was too old to raise a baby. On her way out, Flo said, "I don't know why our neighborhood didn't get damaged. You and the Bannisters both losin' your roofs, and the Purvis's and Applebaums' houses practically gone!"

"Smiley Applebaum's house *is* gone," said Liddy, "and so are him and his wife—both of them mashed like bread dough. Old Mrs. Pinkerton and the Hickses went to their cellars. Their houses got wrecked, but they're fine."

"I hear Fernie May Applebaum's comin' home," said Flo.

O

The day after they moved back into the house, Fiona came over, and she and Cassie went outside and sat on the short, dried-up grass between their houses. There were splintered trees and rubble everywhere, but it was a lovely spring day. Fiona said that on the night of the storm, her mother had been dashed against a wall while washing supper dishes, cutting her arm on a plate, and her dad had grabbed her and Aura Lee and they all dived under the kitchen table. They'd been scared out of their wits, but as soon as the twister left they drove downtown to find Fiona at the movie. Doc Ledbetter put thirteen stitches in Mrs. Bannister's arm.

Fiona seemed a little cool at first, holding a grudge because Cassie had kept Lola's secret from her for all those months. "I thought you *trusted* me!" she said.

"I couldn't take any chances. You would have wanted to go out and visit her, and we were attracting too much attention already." Remembering the months of secrecy, the lying, and the tragedy of Lola's death, her tears started up again.

"It was all *my* fault! It's my fault Lola's dead! I shouldn't have talked her into staying in Cato— I should have let her go to the nuns!"

"But the tornado wasn't your fault—it wasn't anyone's fault!" Fiona put her arms around Cassie and hugged her. Her warm breath felt good on Cassie's neck.

O

Working at the Hall, Cassie saw more black eyes than she would see the rest of her life.

One day she stood by Alice Purvis's bed holding an IV. Alice had a broken leg, and was covered in cuts and bruises. Her pale skin almost faded into the white pillow, except where purple and yellow-green bruises circled her eyes. She looked like a small, hollow-eyed ghost. Her stringy hair, still tangled with clumps of mud, lay lank along the side of her face.

Cassie remembered Alice in her scarecrow costume at Fiona's party. She had seemed so sprightly then, hopping around doing her Ray Bolger dance.

Weak as she was, Alice wanted to talk about her sister's death. "Esther couldn't get to shelter! She was in the backyard hangin' up clothes, and she was jes' picked up an' tossed around in the air—like a big hand picked her up and threw her down! An' it *killed* her, Cassie! *It killed her!*" Alice dissolved into sobs, and all Cassie could do was pat her on the shoulder.

She looked around at the cots and pallets of all descriptions lined against the walls, then glanced over at the spotted piano, still sitting in its rightful place on the stage. The top of the little upright and the bench were being used to hold boxes of medications and bandages.

Cassie was glad the piano was there. It somehow gave her the feeling that this sad and dreary tragedy would pass.

24

True courage is in facing danger when you are afraid,
and that kind of courage you have in plenty.

—The Wizard
The Wizard of Oz

The cleanup continued, and there were funerals all day Monday and Tuesday. For the next few days, men came from lifting and hauling wreckage straight to the services, without even bothering to change clothes. Liddy said that she and Cassie should go to as many funerals as they could; these were their friends and neighbors, after all. Peggy and Flo went to some too, but there was always someone available to tend the baby.

Walt Zimmer, the Applebaums, Hank Jenkins, and Clink Kerry were put in coffins and buried in Cato without much fanfare, but Fernie May Applebaum came home to oversee her parents' burial. Everyone agreed the transformation was amazing. She'd earned the money to have her eyes straightened, and she was lovely now. Liddy thought it showed how little faith you could put in heredity, Fernie May coming from Smiley.

All the bodies except Miss Thornhill's were interred at the Cato cemetery; her family sent a hearse to take her home. Funerals were held at the First Baptist or the Church of Christ, the only two churches in town that weren't damaged. The First Methodist's steeple had fallen, landing in the church cemetery.

Minna Thatcher's mother came to take care of burying little Jaky, since Tom and Minna, injured and grief-stricken, couldn't seem to make decisions. Minna attended the funeral, but Tom had to stay flat on his back. Minna moaned and cried during the entire service, then at the end jumped up and ran out.

Liddy and Cassie held tight to each other's hands during the rites for Connie Botsin, then stayed on for Esther Purvis's funeral. Cassie remembered Heck cutting her hair—was that just a month ago? He had seemed fine then, but today he didn't act right. He spoke to no one, and didn't even help Pearl or Ernestine as they limped down the aisle. Doc Ledbetter wouldn't allow Alice to attend.

The service for Grandpa and Timmy Klein was at the Church of Christ, and they were put together in one big casket. Fergus sat between his parents in the front pew. He turned around once and saw Cassie, and she was glad she had come.

○

Floyd and Winifred Weston felt lucky to be alive. Floyd had heard that Eula was injured, but what should he do? What *could* he do?

Winifred heard about Lola's death, then learned from Main Street gossip more of the details, like who the father of her baby was. What a relief to find it wasn't Floyd's! Why had Alvin and Smiley tried to rouse her suspicions? Now Smiley was dead. It wasn't Christian to think it, but good riddance!

But Floyd must have been up to something, else why would Alvin have put those ideas in her head about him and the Mallory girl? She would have to sit Alvin down and question him, and soon, otherwise this unsettled feeling in the pit of her stomach would never go away. Alvin was still over at the Antelope hospital, working; lots more injuries there than here, she'd heard.

The Westons went to Jaky Thatcher's funeral, of course, they were neighbors—and the next day, after breakfast, Winifred asked Floyd if he thought they should attend the services for Lola.

"I didn't know the girl," she said, "except for seeing her once or twice in the drugstore, but I'm sure of one thing, she had *very* loose morals! Did you know her, Floyd?" She watched his face, waiting for the answer.

"Nope."

"Someone told me she was staying right next door to us at the Farrow place! The effrontery of it! And did you hear how Cassie Field and Harold Cutter saved the baby?"

"Yup, I heard." Floyd took his cap off the wall hook and slapped it on his head. "Got to git to work—lots to do."

"Well, are we going to that girl's funeral or not? It might look funny if we don't!"

"When is it?"

"This afternoon."

"Up to you," said Floyd. "Don't see why we have to, but it's up to you."

"I think we'd better," sniffed Winifred.

O

Even though Lola's body was to be taken to Liberal to be buried with her parents, the service was held in Cato. Lola's was the last funeral Cassie went to that week. It was held at the Baptist church, and everyone in town came, including every single survivor who could walk.

The casket was kept closed. Sheriff Bartlett told Liddy that Lola's body was in terrible condition when they found it, having been beaten about in the water for two and a half days, and he asked if they should remove Lola's ring before they put her in the coffin. They'd have to have someone cut the finger off to get it, he said.

Liddy mentioned the ring to Cassie, without discussing how they'd have to remove it.

"Yes!" Cassie said. "Someday Dulcie can have it!" So Liddy told them to do what they had to, that Cassie wanted the ring for Dulcie.

Marvin insisted on attending Lola's funeral. He walked into church with a cane, Liddy and Cassie on either side, helping him walk.

Even though the church was packed, the only sounds were the rustle of clothing and the organ music. Cassie thought she had done all the crying for Lola she could do, but seeing the casket and the flowers heaped on top made her start up again. Mr. and Mrs. Schonberger were in the front pew, and the organ music was slow and sad. When Mr. Philips sang "Abide with Me," Cassie had to clamp her eyes shut and push her hand hard against her mouth.

The minister said, "This young woman was called too soon to the other side of the river, called in the prime of her life!"

He went on for a long time, but Cassie thought he left out the most important event in Lola's life, Dulcie. Dan wasn't mentioned, either. Maybe people hadn't found out yet about that part. Probably they had, but you'd never know from listening to the preacher that until a few days ago, Lola had been living just outside Cato with her baby. You wouldn't have gotten an inkling that her baby even existed, much less was at the Field's house this very minute.

When Cassie walked up the aisle after the service, people stared, and she was sure they were blaming her for everything. Outside the church,

Winifred Weston stood to one side, whispering to Mrs. McCallum and Mrs. Curtiss Billings, and all of them looked in Cassie's direction and raised their eyebrows.

Floyd Weston stood some distance away, studying the clouds.

Cassie wasn't as shocked at Floyd's presence—after all, he was there with Winifred—as she was at Duke Farrow's. Duke stood apart from everyone else, rotating his cowboy hat and looking at the ground. Once it looked like he was about to approach Cassie to say something, but he turned away.

She watched, sobbing, as the pallbearers put Lola's coffin in the black hearse. She wanted to throw herself into the hearse with Lola. She wanted to go to Liberal once more with her friend.

O

Cassie never heard Marvin's reaction to Dan's fathering an illegitimate child, and neither did Dan, but they were not kind words. "That's the last thing I ever expected a son of *mine* to do! I feel like disownin' 'im!" he sputtered to Liddy. To himself, he admitted that his life had not been entirely devoted to proper conduct, but goddammit, he had always used birth control, or made sure the woman did. Marvin worried that every man in town would laugh at Dan, consider him a fool. They would think it of Dan, getting caught like that, but they'd think it of him, too. After all, he was the only one in town who sold condoms!

He was glad he had to stay home and recuperate from his injuries.

"Lola and Dan were irresponsible, him more than her," he told Liddy. "He should've known better!"

"Why? It's usually the girl's fault!" Liddy answered. "They're supposed to have control over themselves!"

Outwardly Liddy was brave, but inside she wasn't. It would be hard to face people because of Dan's lack of forethought, his outright sin. The evidence, all eleven pounds of it, was there for the world to see, crying or giggling or waiting to be fed. Liddy had tried to be a community leader and pillar of the church. Now people would laugh at her behind their hands, make sport of her and Marvin. When Liddy mentioned the family's loss of respectability to Cassie, her daughter looked at her incredulously and said, "You're kidding, aren't you?"

Dulcie was a beautiful baby. She hardly ever cried, but that was because someone picked her up at the first whimper. The more Marvin held her, the more he was hooked. She had a face like the cherubs in those Italian paintings, the softest, most beautiful skin, and impossibly delicate hands and feet. So helpless, so completely at everyone's mercy! One day she reached up and encircled his thumb with her tiny hand, and when he tried pulling his thumb away, she held on and pulled, pulling on his heartstrings.

So that was that, and respectability be damned. Dulcie was a Field, and as a Field she would have the best upbringing they could give her.

Of course Marvin wanted Dan to raise his own child; that was how things should be. For the first time in forty years, he offered up a prayer. He prayed that Dan would come back from the war, and while he had the Almighty's attention, he prayed that Mitch would too.

O

Liddy thought it was wonderful, the way Cato was getting back on its feet. You could hear hammers and saws wherever you went, people repairing and rebuilding.

But the psychic damage was another thing. She was worried about Minna Thatcher, who wasn't recovering from Jaky's death. Minna would leave the other children alone at home, with Tom unable to care for them. Finally her mother had to come take over. Minna wandered up and down Main with her arm in a cast, asking, "Did you see my little baby in his casket? He looked *so pretty!*" She would laugh, and her laughter would turn to crying. She would find some other passerby and repeat the question, with the same hysterical reaction.

Heck Purvis roamed up and down Main, too, unable to deal with all the loss—his home, his barber shop, and his daughter. Occasionally he would collapse on the curb and put his head down in his arms.

People started avoiding Minna and Heck, and Liddy went to see Doc Ledbetter.

"Doc, can't you give those two some kind of sedation?" she asked. "Put them in a hospital?"

"I don't have time for treating people's minds, Liddy," he snapped. "It's only bodies I know how to do. Heck and Minna'll just have to heal with the tincture of time."

415

There were still a few remaining patients at Veterans Hall. Cassie worked there late one day, folding sheets. When she left, since there was still some daylight, she decided to walk around the familiar streets. She walked to the church, where one of the stained-glass windows was broken—her favorite one, Jesus holding the lamb. The desolation everywhere made Cassie's heart sink. She was already depressed, and thoughts of Lola's death were never far away. She woke at night with terrible dreams. Pictures flashed in front of her eyes whether she was asleep or awake—images of Lola fighting to stay above the water, and of her struggle to save Dulcie. She could feel the icy water, the inexorable pull of the current. In her dreams, she couldn't move her legs and arms fast enough to save the baby, and would awake screaming.

"Cassie! Wake up!" Liddy would shake her until she was fully conscious, then lie with her until she went to sleep again. The next morning she would ache all over, as if her body had actually been going through the struggles in the dream.

More than once she flashed back to the last time she'd gone out, the day of the tornado. Lola's face had looked bruised, and she'd had her neck covered. Had Duke done that? Lola said he'd wanted her to kiss him—what else had he wanted her to do? Lola told Cassie she'd gone along with some of it, that she was nice to him so he wouldn't blow the whistle on her.

But if Lola had done what Duke wanted, why the bruises?

O

Cassie didn't know how her mother could act so cheerful. She seemed to carry on with good spirits in the face of all this destruction and death.

Cassie watched her father softening toward the baby. She wished Mitch and Dan could see him now. They had always thought he was so hard-hearted, that he had no feelings. She remembered how, after he whipped Dan that time, she'd thought he was like the Tin Man. The Wizard told the Tin Man, "You are wrong to want a heart—it makes most people unhappy." But the Tin Man wanted one anyway.

Maybe her dad had finally gotten a heart, whether he wanted one or not.

O

Amazingly, the engineers from the Army Corps had the bridge in operation in under a week.

The bridge repair coincided with the arrival of several visitors. As if Cato didn't have enough problems, Crazy Penny showed up. She came into the drugstore, jabbering and gesturing, and walking a mangy cat on a leash. Her bangs were cut up to the hairline like a monk's, the sides trimmed in jagged stair steps against her zinnia-rouged cheeks. She wore a long flowing white wedding dress, with a train, and black army boots.

Liddy happened to be there. *"Stars and garters!"* she exclaimed.

Crazy Penny's comment on the storm was the most succinct of anyone's: "Whar'd Cato go?"

Two weeks after the storm, a small, neatly dressed woman walked into Field's Drugs. She had dark hair done in a crimped permanent wave, sad brown eyes, and a nervous, pinched smile.

Peggy was busy throwing useless merchandise into a trash barrel.

"Excuse me, Miss," the woman said, "I was wonderin' how I could get out to Tom Thatcher's farm."

"Well, ma'am, they're out there, but Minna isn't doin' too good, what with losin' little Jaky. And Tom's back was hurt bad in the twister. But go down the street—here, I'll show you." Peggy took her outside and pointed to Seth's wrecked filling station. "Seth Scruggs is Cato's unofficial taxi service," Peggy explained. "He'll prob'ly take you out."

An hour after the woman arrived at the Thatcher farm, Tom called and asked Sheriff Bartlett to come out, and after Tom and the woman told him the story, the sheriff took her to the bank, where Henry McCallum took down her deposition.

This was Walt Zimmer's wife.

Over the next few days, Liddy heard most of the story. Walt's wife wasn't buried out under the cowshed after all. The town had gotten carried away with the rumor years ago and had kept it going, stoking it like a dying fire, blowing on the embers with breaths of salacious delight. They'd smacked their lips over the horror of it, actually enjoying the possibility of an old blind man hacking up his wife and burying her under the manure and dirt of the farmyard. The rumor was so strong that after the tornado, Sheriff Bartlett had directed rescuers to dig around Walt's cowshed. They hadn't come up with a body, and now here she was.

Liddy told Marvin what she'd heard from Ed Bartlett. "Walt abused her. She told Ed the first years of their marriage had been peaceable, and she thought they could make a go of it, even though she was a lot younger than Walt. But after he went blind he started beating her—that's what she swore to the sheriff. Finally, she just left."

"What about that connection to Tom?" asked Marvin.

"Tom said he helped her because his farm was nearby, and she didn't know who else to turn to. This was all before Tom got married. After the worst and last beating, she limped over to Tom's farm carrying a suitcase and asked him to drive her to Red Arrow to the train. She didn't want to leave from the Cato station; she thought it might get back to Walt."

"Where'd she go?"

"New Mexico, she has a sister there. She's been there ever since, working as a housekeeper for a rich rancher."

"Didn't get married again?"

"No, she never wanted to divorce Walt. She was still afraid of him, afraid he'd find out where she was. Isn't that amazing? Afraid of an old blind man, hundreds of miles away."

According to Henry McCallum, Walt's property would go to her. With Tom to sign as witness to her abuse, she would get the forty acres. But she wanted to sell it right away and return to New Mexico; Cato held no happiness for her.

The town didn't like this version of the story nearly as much as the other one, but it played well as a topic for discussion for several months. Everyone had a comment or question about the Zimmers:

Why hadn't Walt told anybody his wife had left? Did he know everyone thought he'd killed her? And if he hadn't buried her under the shed, why didn't he say so?

Besides Crazy Penny and Walt's wife, Grace Sampson returned. Liddy had driven out to talk to Tom Thatcher and Minna's mother about Minna. Someone had seen Minna standing on the bridge looking as though she might jump. Liddy was determined to get Minna some help; the sight of Crazy Penny had given her the shove she needed. Those children needed a mother, and Tom needed a wife. She decided to take matters into her own hands and try to get Minna committed to the mental facility in Antelope for a few weeks, or however long it took.

She turned into the Thatchers' farmyard at the very moment Grace Sampson came out of the house. So, the green convertible was hers.

Grace wasn't beautiful anymore. Small, almost imperceptible lines were etched around her eyes and the sides of her mouth, and one eyelid drooped. Her hair wasn't blond now, but light brown, and it hung unstyled on her shoulders. She was dressed beautifully, though, wearing a pair of tailored pants and a long-sleeved white shirt.

It was amazing to Liddy that none of the old loathing rose in her. No envy for the stylish clothes, no anger at her for spoiling, in the Biblical sense, her beloved Mitch. In the midst of the ruined countryside, she even felt a kind of benign warmth for this woman who had loved her son. Or maybe what she felt was pity.

"Hello, Grace."

"Hi, Mrs. Field. I've just been talking to Tom. I'm so sorry about little Jaky! I was over here the night he was born. Tom didn't want to leave his children, so I went to get Doc Ledbetter."

"I'm worried about Minna," said Liddy. "She needs a head doctor, and Doc Ledbetter sure isn't one."

"I know. She's out walking around in the pasture right now, singing. It's like her body's here but her mind has scattered out over the prairie."

Liddy hated to ask, but did. "Grace, have you heard from Mitch? The last letter I got was dated April 17th. I wrote him about the tornado, but I haven't heard back."

Grace blushed. "I got a letter a week ago, but he didn't mention the storm."

"Did he say whether they're still in North Africa, or anything about what they're doing? His letters never tell much, but I know he's not supposed to say anything."

"No, no details. But he talked about freezing at night in his tent, then being able to fry eggs on the tarmac during the day."

"If you hear any more, will you let me know?"

"I'm not staying. Hal and I are…getting a divorce." She turned away. "I'm going to try to sell the ranch."

Liddy pulled her purse to her chest. "Where are you going to live?"

"In Tulsa, where my mother is. I've rented an apartment." Grace turned back and put out her hand out. "Mrs. Field, I'm so sorry your family's had to endure so much; Marvin hurt, and your store and house—*and Lola.*"

She didn't mention the baby. Had she heard? Liddy pushed a strand of hair out of her eyes.

"Lola's death is terrible for everyone. Cassie's *real* broken up. But the baby is fine. You know about the baby?"

"I heard she was saved, and Lola wasn't."

"Grace, the baby is Dan's. Evidently they fell in love without anybody knowing. And Cassie took care of her...not far from here." She gazed off in the direction of the Farrow farm. "What our family's lost isn't much, compared with some people."

They walked together to Grace's car. "Liddy..." This was the first time she'd ever called her "Liddy"—probably an acknowledgment of the closeness of their ages. What was Grace now— thirty-eight, thirty-nine? "I know I'm too old for Mitch. I love him, but when he comes back I'll make myself scarce."

It took all the forgiveness Liddy had, but she said, "Grace, your life is yours to live, and Mitch is a grown man." She moved a step closer and took Grace's hand in hers, then released it. "I'd better go in and do what I came out here for. But to tell the truth, I'd just as soon be hung!"

She walked to the entry, and the last she saw of Grace she was at the wheel of her convertible, driving past all the collapsed outbuildings and blown-down barbed-wire fence.

○

It was the middle of the night, three weeks after the tornado, when Dan came into Cato on the train from Oklahoma City, having managed to hitch a ride on a transport plane to Tinker Air Force Base. The train from O.C. was jammed with servicemen heading toward the Pacific coast.

Homer stepped out of the depot in the dark. "Glad we finally got aholt of you, Dan. It's been pretty bad around here, you'll find out goin' home. Wish I could drive you, but I gotta stay here." Homer's voice broke. "I lost Connie, and I know you—"

Dan felt Homer's knobby hand on his. "I was gone from March Field when the tornado came, Mr. Botsin. I guess that's why they couldn't find me." He didn't tell Homer he was with a group of pilots being briefed at an airplane plant in Los Angeles on a new bomber's maneuverability and speed.

Since there wasn't much moonlight and only half the town had electricity back, Homer lent Dan a flashlight. He walked along, occasionally stumbling on a tree limb or a splintered board. It was dangerous going, but finally he found his old neighborhood. Could that splintered building be *their* house? He located the back door and went into the house. He flashed the light around the room, then tiptoed over, knelt, and gently shook Liddy's shoulder.

She sat up. "Dan!" She threw her arms around him. Cassie woke up, too, and Dan gave her a fierce embrace, his beard scratching her cheek. Marvin limped out of the spare room, and hugged his son.

"I forgot how tall you are!" exclaimed Liddy. Dan's uniform was rumpled, but his pilot's wings, bars, and visored cap were impressive. Cassie thought he looked like soldiers she'd seen in movies.

Liddy seemed unable to move. She stayed spread out on the couch, looking limp from shock. Cassie lit a candle, and Dan took off his cap and stood over the laundry basket. They watched as he picked up Dulcie. He held her away from him, looking at her a long time, and kissed her cheek. This was a scene Cassie had played over and over in her mind's eye: Dan holding Dulcie. *Dan holding Lola's and his baby.*

"Gonna fix hot chocolate." Cassie brushed at the tears in her eyes. Why wasn't Lola here?

Dan sat down on a kitchen chair holding his child, who was still asleep. One foot had loosened from her blanket, and a fat leg hung out. In her sleep, Dulcie gave a little kick.

"It's so hard to believe she's mine. Even harder to realize..." He handed the baby to Liddy, took out a handkerchief, and blew his nose. "Sorry, everybody, wakin' you up like this."

"We're just glad you could get here! Isn't she a lovely baby?" asked Liddy.

"I think so. Kinda hard to tell, in the dark."

"She's six weeks old now," said Cassie from the kitchen.

Marvin, too, seemed overwhelmed by Dan's homecoming. He sat down next to him, trembling, and lit a cigarette. "Everybody's real sorry about Lola."

His words met silence. Evidently Dan didn't want to talk about her now.

"How you feeling, Dad? I'm sorry you got the worst of it. You okay?"

"Better."

"If you don't mind, I'd like to get to sleep now. We'll talk about everything tomorrow."

They tried to give him blankets from their own bedding, but he refused, saying it seemed warm here, and that he was used to the cold night air of the California desert. Liddy insisted on giving him her pillow, however. Dulcie hadn't awakened, and Dan curled up on the floor near her.

Next morning, Dulcie's crying woke Dan. He gave her her bottle, and Marvin came in. Now they talked about Lola, and Dan allowed himself to weep. "I can't imagine her drowning like that in Wolf Creek—it's usually low as bedrock! Maybe I didn't take care of her enough." His words came rushing out. "Maybe I was an idiot, but it didn't seem like there was any *wrong* to it!"

Marvin looked down, studying his bedroom slippers. He didn't comment.

"How long can you stay, son?"

"They gave me four days."

"Why didn't you come sooner?" asked Cassie.

"My commanding officer broke all of this…bad news…to me when I was doing something in…another place. It was heavy training, that's all I can say about it. He told me the training was important, and I had to finish. But it was hard not to be able to come home!" Dan dropped his head into his hands. "I talked to the chaplain, and to a friend in my squadron. If I hadn't been able to finally come, I woulda gone nuts!"

Liddy went into the kitchen to fry eggs and make toast, and soon the smell of coffee filled the room. While they ate, they told Dan every story there was to tell about the twister; the effects on the town and countryside, the funerals (they didn't dwell on the funerals). They told him how Sally and Charlene had made Veterans Hall into a hospital, and how everyone had pitched in. They told about Stuffy being blasted out the back of the drugstore, and how Walt Zimmer's wife had come to town, *alive*. And about Charlie and Louise Detwiler being carried over a grove of trees and living to see another day.

"I can't believe *that* one! I'll have to go see 'em. And ol' Walt Zimmer, dead."

Dan suddenly remembered going out to Walt's to get the well water.

He was getting more comfortable with Dulcie; now she nestled against his chest, sleeping. She woke up and fussed a little, so he gave her part of another bottle. After Liddy showed him how to burp her, she fell asleep, and he put her back in the basket.

"Is she always this good?"

"*No!*" said Liddy and Cassie together.

Liddy was pleased when Dan admired the new bathroom. She said, out of Marvin's hearing, "I paid for it, and new paint on the house, out of my needlework commissions!"

He looked up through the roof at patches of sky, and at the gaping front wall of the house.

"Mom, you don't deserve this. Maybe I can help pay for some of the repairs."

"No, you just worry about flying airplanes," she said. "That's plenty for you to think about. We'll take care of Dulcie and rebuilding, and you fight the war."

Dan read all of Mitch's most recent letters. Liddy had stored all his letters in an old leather train case, had found it safe in the backyard, the day after the storm. He told her, "Don't worry, Mom, Mitch isn't anywhere near the fighting. Besides, he's too tough—they'll never lay a glove on him."

Later he confided to Cassie, "Looks like Mitch is right in the middle of it."

"But you said…"

"I know, but she worries so much."

He wanted to know more about Lola, and walking around outside, they talked for long stretches of time. She told him everything: how Lola had made a home in the cabin, weaving baskets every spare moment while she waited for Dulcie, never complaining of hardship or cold.

She told him about Lola's moods as she went through the months of pregnancy, her delight in the letters he'd written, and her great joy when she at last delivered the baby.

He wanted to know how Cassie had delivered food, and she told how they were constantly afraid of being discovered. She didn't mention Duke Farrow.

They talked about the catastrophe. Why, she asked Dan, would God punish the town like this? She plopped down on a section of surprisingly green grass, and Dan sat down too, long legs bent, hands hanging between his knees.

"Cassie, there's no rhyme or reason to things that happen, like this twister. Do you think some Great One ruling the universe was trying to punish Cato? *No!* It just *was!* Tornados and floods and earthquakes and hurricanes, they're all just...just fate—and nature! You're not important enough to be the cause of Lola's living or dying. She stayed out there of her own free will."

That night, before she went to sleep, Cassie remembered Dan as a boy, putting a curse on Mitch's friends. And now Mike and Dooky were dead. But that was all kid stuff—she was sure he would be the first to say so. Some people believed in astrology, but her mother said you couldn't be a true Christian and plan your life around the stars, that it was all hocus-pocus.

But her dad thought religion was hocus-pocus! So what *could* you believe in?

O

Dan walked around town looking at the wreckage. He couldn't believe his eyes. Trees uprooted—some of them so big and old they should have withstood any amount of wind! Goosebumps stood up on his arms as he gazed at familiar buildings, now shattered, pieces of them strewn about the landscape. Main Street looked as if it had been bombed out, and he wondered if the town would ever recover. He noticed the old flagpole was gone.

At the drugstore, things were a mess. While Marvin watched, Dan spent part of one day rebuilding the prescription counter, but Marvin said a new piece of marble might have to be ordered. He didn't want

Dan to spend any more time that way. "Stop workin'," he said. "Your furlough's too precious to waste it doin' carpenter work."

"Dad, how about insurance? You better call your company, or write 'em pronto."

Marvin mumbled something and limped away.

O

Cassie's parents had never questioned her as much as she'd expected they would about the doctor Lola went to, how they got there—any of it! Could it be they didn't *want* to know everything? She'd never volunteered any information, so they knew nothing of Floyd Weston's involvement.

But now she told Dan the whole story.

"You mean you got him to do all that for Lola, just because you saw him and Eula screwing in the car when you were a little kid?"

She nodded.

"Well, I'll be a son of a gun," he said, laughing out loud.

She knew that eventually he would comment on her hair. When she told him she'd cut it off and worn his and Mitch's old clothes to fool Mrs. Weston, he said, "You've seen too many movies, Castor Oil! You better grow your hair long again; you look way too much like a boy."

"I might and I might not," she said, and for once he didn't reply.

She knew Dan was grateful for what she'd done, but she could tell he was uncomfortable about it. He covered his discomfiture with a gruff manner that was all too familiar. The third morning he was home, when she was changing Dulcie, he stepped in and started telling her how to fold the diaper a different way, and he wasn't very gracious doing it.

Her dad overheard, and later he said, "Dan just has 'lieutenant-itis'."

One afternoon Dan asked, "Wanta drive with me out to the Weston farm? I need to square things with Floyd, but I'm dreadin' it. That man must think I'm a prize number one jackass, getting Lola into this— then staying away while he took care of her, him and you!"

"I don't want to see them!" said Cassie, with feeling. "And remember, Mrs. Weston doesn't know!"

"You don't have to go in. I want to talk to him alone, anyway."

"I'm pretty sure that's the way he'd like it too."

They left the baby with Liddy and drove north in a car Dan borrowed from Stuffy Byers. He couldn't fit into the bashed-in Plymouth. Dan wore civvies, and Cassie wore slacks and her old yellow sweater. On the way, Dan took a flask out of his back pocket and took a long swig. When she stared at him, he held up the flask and said, "Picked up some courage from Stuffy."

They got to the bridge and started across. Cassie looked down for one second; that was all she could manage. The water was low and moving slow, not like that day, but it looked deep and menacing to her. Her body stiffened, and from then on she kept her eyes straight ahead.

Dan took her hand and held it.

"You're gonna have to face it, Cassie. It's like getting back on a horse after you've been thrown. You'll prob'ly have to cross this bridge a lot more times in your life."

What did *he* know about it? And how many times had he been on a horse? But he seemed truly sorry for her. They were over the bridge now, and they didn't speak for another mile or so, passing destroyed sheds, bloated cows, fields covered in debris.

Suddenly he said, "I really appreciate everything you did for Lola and the baby."

"That's okay." The silence lasted for awhile; then she said, "I loved Lola too, and I feel like I'm to blame for her death. Nobody else thinks so, but I can't help it, I just do!"

Now she had to cry, so Dan handed her his handkerchief. "I know you loved her, Castor Oil. If I remember right, you said the doctor wanted her to go up to Wichita to that home."

"I talked her out of it, but she'd be alive if I hadn't!"

"She might be alive, but if she'd decided to give up the baby, like she might have if she'd gone up there, she would've been unhappy forever about that!"

"Maybe I shouldn't have been such a know-it-all!"

"Did you know it was me all along?"

"No. She told me the father was Bobby someone, from another town. She didn't tell me about you because she didn't want our folks to find out. But I wouldn't have told!"

She asked if he wanted to drive farther and see the cabin, but he said, "I can't. I want to remember it the way I imagined it all those months with her there, happy and alive."

He brought out the flask again and took a long pull.

They turned into the Westons' farm and parked, and when Dan went to the house and knocked, Cassie slid all the way down in the seat. Mrs. Weston looked at Dan suspiciously, but she took him around back where Floyd was working near the barn, then went inside the house.

Floyd Weston was bent over a sawhorse, cutting a two-by-four. He straightened up abruptly at the sight of Dan.

"Mr. Weston, I'm Dan Field." Dan stuck out his hand and waited. Floyd seemed to know who he was, and gave him a lukewarm handshake. They stood in silence for a few seconds until Dan realized the man was not going to make things easy for him.

"That tornado was awful, huh!" Dan ventured.

"It was awful for ever'one—folks in town, too," agreed Floyd.

"My folks' house doesn't look too good, but it sure looks better'n a lot of others." He braced himself. "Mr. Weston, uh, I know you took care of Lola—takin' her to the doctor and the hospital and all, many times. I just—I c-can't thank you enough."

He stood on one foot and the other, while Floyd stood wiping his sweaty face with a rag. He walked farther into the dark barn, and Dan followed, holding out a wad of bills. "So...here, this... I hope this'll partially repay you for all you d-did."

Floyd hesitated, then took the money and thrust it into his overalls. Standing next to a tractor, hands deep in his overall pockets, he said, "Hope you didn't mention to my wife what you're doin' out here. It's kind of a tetchy subject."

"No. I just wanted to say thank you, and try to pay you back. I hope that covers it."

Floyd took the bills out and counted them. "Oh, yeah, 'at's plenty. The hospital and doctor bills came to 'bout fifty, is all."

"The extra's for the gas, not to mention all your trouble." Gazing at the split barn door, Dan said, "I wish I could stay here and help you as kind of a repayment, but I have to fly back to the base tomorrow."

"Oh, 'at's okay," said Floyd. "I'm goin' to hire me some help. That there Swede in town said he'd send me somebody."

"Okay. And thanks again. I owe you a lot more."

Floyd walked over close to Dan, and in a low voice asked, "How's the baby?"

"Fine, just great. Her name's Dulcie."

Floyd's face broke into a broad grin.

Dan started to walk back to the car, and it wasn't until he'd rounded the corner of the barn that he noticed Mrs. Weston hovering nearby. She'd evidently been trying to eavesdrop, and from the expression on her face, she must have succeeded.

As they left the Westons and turned back toward town, Cassie glanced up the road in the direction of Lola's cabin. Beyond it was the Sandy Flats ranch, and Duke Farrow.

Should she mention her suspicions about him to Dan? She opened her mouth to speak, then closed it. She had no proof. It would worry Dan unnecessarily, get him all heated up when he was just beginning to adjust to Lola's death. And what could he do about it, anyway?

Crossing Wolf Creek was just as hard this time.

They picked up Dulcie and stopped in for a hamburger at the Mistletoe Café. It was operating with a hot plate, boarded-up windows, and with borrowed tables and chairs. Ben looked just the same, except that he had new thick glasses with horn rims. His dad Reuben wouldn't let Dan pay. "You're out there fightin' for our country," he said. "Wish I could give you more'n a hamburger!"

As they were leaving Dan said, "Ben, I been thinking about it. I'd like to give you my arrowhead collection. I don't have any use for it anymore."

Ben looked stunned, and with eyes as big as an owl's, he nodded his thanks.

"Great. Cassie'll bring it over to you, won't you, Castor Oil?"

Liddy finally told Dan that Mike and Dooky had died in action in the South Pacific, and Cassie wondered if Dan's giving his precious arrowheads to Ben had anything to do with that.

Dan left on the train the next day. He would catch a transport plane at Tinker Field to fly back to California. They all went to the station see him off, Dan holding Dulcie until the last second.

The last glimpse they had of him, he was hanging out the window, waving his pilot's cap in the air. But though all three of them were smiling and waving, and Liddy was waggling Dulcie's tiny hand up and down, Dan didn't smile. He looked somber and serious, the way he used to look when he was a young boy and always in trouble.

O

Cassie remembered Lola's baskets one day when she heard Liddy describing for the hundredth time how her bowl of fruit had sat undisturbed while the front of the house blew off. A vision of Lola's scratched hands pointing to the willow cradle appeared before Cassie, and it suddenly occurred to her to wonder if any of the baskets were out there. Lola had the baby in the cradle when they'd been blown off the bridge, so that was lost, but what about all the others?

She had no bicycle to ride out on. She'd thrown it into the bushes near the Weston's, and probably it had flown to Kingdom Come. She went to Fiona's and asked if she could borrow her bike, and she said sure. When she got to the bridge, she tried closing her eyes at the place where the Chrysler had been blown off, but she kept bumping into the railing. She tried to prepare herself for the cabin's wrecked appearance, but was still shocked by the devastation. Trees were down, and bushes uprooted, and it was hard to look at the collapsed cabin; parts of it were tossed about the yard. Walking around to the kitchen side, she stepped over a pile of boards and went in. What could be left? A few pans, some old furniture, the mismatched teacups? She decided not to try to retrieve the rag rug; Liddy hadn't missed it yet anyway. Making her way around loose boards, she stepped onto the porch where Lola had done her basket weaving. The table was gone, and long strands of willow were tossed about, but the baskets were nowhere to be seen.

She stepped off and paced about the yard, looking up into the trees, as if the baskets might be perched there like birds' nests. Yards from the cabin, she found the remains of the table, now missing two legs. She continued to search a wide area, in back and in front. Something caught her eye. It was the big market basket, caught in some fallen limbs, and looking remarkably undamaged! She didn't find any others near the house, so she wriggled under the barbed-wire fence into an adjoining field, tearing a trouser leg as she did so. Miraculously, she found four more baskets snagged in catclaw and mesquite.

She was overjoyed! There had to be a few more, but she was lucky to find these. All were a bit warped from the wind and rain, but only one was beyond redemption.

There was one basket that looked different from the others. This must be the honeysuckle- vine basket Lola said she was going to make for Aunt Flo! Her aunt wouldn't have Lola again, but she would have this.

Another was the two-colored basket she had picked when Lola said she should choose one.

"That one's mine," she said aloud.

She nested the baskets together, then took her shoelaces off, tied them together, and attached the baskets to Fiona's handlebars.

The tornado had turned over a tractor at the Sampson ranch, it had left her mother's bowl of fruit untouched, and now, remarkably, she had found Lola's baskets. Pedaling energetically toward home, she tried to riddle out the strangeness of it all.

25

Sweet is revenge—especially to women...
     —Lord Byron
     Don Juan

In the wake of the killer storm, several businesses had to temporarily relocate. Herb Richards ran the post office in the front part of the bakery, where Davy had sold his baked goods. The *Cato Enquirer's* press was moved to the back of the bakery, where Davy had his ovens, and Billy Saltman managed to print a couple of pages a week.

Violet and Reuben, taking only Ben along, had gone off to the Justice of the Peace in Red Arrow and gotten married. Violet, one of the Hall's hardest-working volunteers, told Liddy and Rowena that one day when she was emptying trash out back, she got an idea about where to put the new Mistletoe Café and Grocery. Looking across the alley, she noticed the abandoned laundry building, with its two hawthorn bushes loaded with pink blossoms and framing the big double doors. She was overcome, she said, seeing all that unexpected beauty only a few yards from the devastation that was Main Street.

Reuben had received his insurance check in the mail the day before, and that morning he had sat up in bed and waved it around like a little boy with a new toy airplane. The thought occurred to Violet, whose grocery had been hit also, that *her* insurance check would be coming any day now. She said she got so excited she could hardly breathe.

"Why can't you and me put our checks together and fix up that big old place?" she said. "Make it a combination grocery and diner!"

That afternoon she got the key from Harold Cutter, and she and Reuben looked around. The laundry was immense and open, with a high ceiling. Violet envisioned another level above the main floor, with wide stairs, and shops on the top floor going all around. With a few skylights in the roof—she'd seen some in a magazine—ample light would flood in. She told Liddy that when she started describing these grandiose plans to Reuben, he yelled, "Slow down, woman, *whoa!* It's just two insurance checks—we didn't win the Kentucky Derby!"

The next day Liddy, Rowena, and Flo were invited to the laundry to hear Violet's plan. They wandered through the dust while Violet described her ideas for remodeling the place.

"You know, Violet?" said Liddy, "I could open a shop here! People all over are getting interested in my ladies' needlework. I could have a shop to show things!"

"And I don't have near enough to do," Rowena said. "Livin' with Herb is like livin' with a big tongue-tied rabbit. Could I help run it, Liddy?"

"Sure. I'll be busy a lot of the time, out collectin' stuff." Slyly she said, "And I'm sure Violet won't charge much rent."

"Let me get the place built first; then I'll tell you what your rent's gonna be," said Violet.

○

Marvin was able to work a few hours a day now, still limping, but on the mend. Liddy was beginning to fret about rebuilding the store. She had been quizzing Marvin repeatedly about their reimbursement from the insurance company, the same company that had already paid off Violet and Reuben.

The day Marvin told her the awful news, it was five o'clock, and they were both at the store. Peggy had left, and Liddy and Marvin were tallying figures, adding up everything they had lost. It was a big job, because they'd lost a lot. Marvin was trying to estimate the loss on furnishings —shelves, counters, tables and chairs, and Liddy sat next to him, working on the totals for medicines and all other merchandise. They were grateful that the soda fountain, except for the stools, was unscratched.

Once, when Marvin cleared his throat, Liddy looked up, but he dropped his head back to his numbers. They continued to work. then he cleared his throat again. This time when she looked at him, he put down his pencil and folded his shaking hands on the table.

"Honey, I'm afraid I didn't quite...keep up the, uh, the policy... on the drugstore. I kinda reduced the amount of insurance, back in...I think it was 1939. Since then I been sending most of the amount of the premium..." His voice dwindled away.

"You *what*!" Liddy's expression of horror scared him even more than he had imagined it would. "You haven't been paying for the *insurance*?"

"...payments to Joe Kelly—to invest in an oil drilling company. The... uh...the investment didn't do quite as good as Joe and I expected."

"I do not believe what I'm hearing." Liddy's voice was flat, and her eyes were hard and unblinking.

"It—it didn't do anything. All the holes were dusters. I'm afraid we lost all our money." Marvin rubbed one eye over and over.

Liddy jumped up, overturning her chair. "What do you mean, *we* lost all our money? *I* didn't lose it, and I'll bet Joe Kelly didn't lose *his*! I bet he found a way of getting *his* money back! How much insurance have we got left? And did you use the house insurance, too? Please tell me we're going to be able to rebuild our house!"

"There's two hundred left on the store, but I didn't touch the house insurance," Marvin said miserably.

"Of fourteen hundred dollars' worth of insurance we had on this store, we only have two hundred left?" Her lips tightened in a hard line. "I guess we'll lose the store, then." She wrenched the chair to one side, sat down again, and began to write figures on a piece of paper. She did some adding, then some subtracting. Then she stood up and walked to the cash register. She stood there for a long minute and finally rang it open. While Marvin watched openmouthed, she scooped up every cent of change and flung it all over. There was a long clatter as the coins rained down and rolled everywhere— under chairs and tables. and under the one sales counter they had left. Then she pulled out all the bills and walked over to Marvin. "If that's what you think of all the money we've worked so hard for, then here's what *I* think of it!" She tore up a twenty and threw the pieces and the rest of the bills in the air like confetti. Without waiting for the paper to settle, she stormed out.

When she got home, she was angrier than when she'd started. She strode purposefully through the backyard to the dog pens.

"Here, you sons o' bitches! Come here!" She threw open the gates and watched as the bird dogs ran out. Yelping madly, they scampered crazily through the yard and out into the street. She didn't know where they were going, and she didn't care. She would have been happy if a whole fleet of trucks had rumbled through and run them down.

She went inside and cried for the rest of the day. Marvin, wisely perhaps, didn't come home at all, but slept in back of the store. Cassie heard her carrying on, but Liddy didn't care.

What would they do? They wouldn't be able to rebuild the store, not the way it should be! He said he hadn't touched the house insurance. But where would they get the money to send Cassie to college, and how would they have anything to live on in retirement, if they used their meager savings to pay for the store's rebuilding and refurbishing?

She would have to be strong again.

Liddy sat on the side of the bed and began to do the only thing she could think of to save her sanity. She began to count her blessings.

No one in her family had been horribly injured, and their precious grandchild had survived. They could rebuild the house. But the list of blessing quickly ran out, and she was left with Marvin again. He was a no-good, swindling double-dealer, and a flimflamming bunco artist. *He was a humbug, a black-hearted rascal, a thieving rogue.*

No, all of that wouldn't stick. Marvin was a weak person, carried away by misplaced trust in a friendship, with a childish desire to get rich quick. He had blundered into a costly mistake with complete disregard for his family's well-being. He wasn't a no-good, swindling double-dealer or a flimflam man. He wasn't even a humbug, rascal, or rogue.

He was a man.

○

Floyd Weston was busy with repairs to the hay barn, the cowshed, and all the other damaged buildings on his property. The biggest event to interrupt the Westons' peace and quiet had not been the terrible twister, but Dan Field's visit.

What a revelation! After tiptoeing over and standing near, Winifred couldn't help overhearing the conversation in the barn. Floyd had helped the Mallory girl when she was in trouble, had even taken her to Antelope to have the baby! And of course the Field girl had been involved, right up to her elbows! Floyd hadn't asked Winifred's permission for any of it, but at least he wasn't the father.

So why did he help the girl?

Every day Winifred walked out to the road to pick up the mail, and one warm day in June she reached into the mailbox and pulled out an envelope addressed to her. It had no stamp, and the note was unsigned. It read, "You think you're so high an mity, but gess what—yore husban is didlin Eula Tully."

She read it over twice, trying to figure out the handwriting. The script was more feminine than masculine, as if made by little birds' claws. Could this be from Smiley? It sounded just like him. But Smiley was dead! Looking around and seeing no one, she brought the paper up and sniffed it. It smelled like permanent wave solution, and there was a smear of orange on one corner of the envelope.

Winifred stumbled inside, sank down on the settee in the hall, and tried to catch her breath. She believed every word: Smiley's hints, Alvin's veiled slanders, and all the years of his leaving the farm for flimsy reasons.

That evening Floyd came into the kitchen and plopped onto a chair without removing his cap, wanting only a long drink of iced tea and some supper. He had spent the day reroofing the hay barn. Winifred stood by the big chopping block, cutting a beef roast into chunks. She turned to face him, knife in hand. "So it wasn't that Mallory girl you were carrying on with—it's someone else!"

"What? What in the world are you *talkin'* about!"

"I thought it was her making you hurry out of here all hours of the day and night. I even thought it was your baby Alvin and I saw at the Farrow place—but then I heard it was Dan Field's! But now I know you've been carrying on with…with…" Winifred stabbed the knife, tip down, pinning the slab of beef to the butcher block.

Floyd sat very still. So far, she had used no real information. "With *who?*"

"With *Eula Tully!*"

The kitchen was quiet for too long. "Where in blazes are you comin' up with stuff like that!" he asked, in a tone of deep indignation.

"Never mind where I heard it! What do you have to say for yourself? And why, *why*, Floyd, would you disgrace me in front of the whole town with someone so…so slovenly and *low!*"

Floyd took off his hat and wiped the sweat pouring off his face. Slowly it dawned: it would have been a whole lot better if he'd been fucking someone higher up on the social ladder.

Realizing he'd better say something, he temporized: "Winnie, I don't know what yer talkin' about. Somebody's jes' tryin' to make trouble. Now I gotta git me a bath."

○

Marvin was silly with love for Dulcie by now and would barely let her out of his sight. He even changed her diapers on occasion—something he had never done for his own children.

Liddy was glad of his attentions to their grandchild, but she would never forgive him for his treachery and stupidity with the insurance money. He would have to redeem himself, or she would leave. The only person she really trusted was Harold Cutter (Rowena or Violet might tell one other person) so she went to his small office next to Veterans Hall—like the Hall itself, miraculously untouched—and bared her soul. When she'd finished complaining about all Marvin's shortcomings, which stretched over many years, she asked him if he knew any good lawyers in Red Arrow.

"Yes, I do, Liddy, but think it over. Think it over a long time."

○

The Methodist hierarchy was corresponding with the insurance carrier, and while construction bids were coming in for replacing the steeple and the stained-glass windows, local church members vowed to do something about the mess. Harold Cutter and Liddy put out calls for a cleanup committee, and half the church members signed up.

Eula Tully wasn't regular in attendance, but she had been on the rolls for years, and Liddy, who felt a certain protectiveness toward Eula since bandaging her head, felt she should be given the opportunity to help out. When Cassie learned that Eula was coming to the church cleanup, she asked, "Is Mrs. Weston gonna be there, too?"

"I guess so. Why?"

Cassie couldn't think of a good answer. Evidently it hadn't gotten around town about Eula and Mr. Weston, because her mother would know about it if it had.

On the day of the cleanup, Cassie donned the most outlandish-looking outfit she could find: overalls and a ragged-looking shirt, and she put on the boy's cap she'd worn the night Lola had Dulcie. Would Mrs. Weston *get* it—would she remember? She wondered if she might be doomed to Hell for being so dangerously provocative.

"I don't know why you want to look like that," Liddy said. "Seems like you're determined to look like a scaggly ragamuffin." But she didn't tell her to change; since Lola's death, her mother had seemed to soften toward her.

Everyone arrived at the church carrying buckets and rags and wearing old clothes. The women and girls started cleaning the inside, and the men went outdoors with pushbrooms, rakes and shovels. Sure enough, when Mrs. Weston saw Cassie, her mouth set in a thin line, but she ignored her for most of the day. Cassie was relieved that Mrs. Weston and Eula weren't working close together. She noticed that Mrs. Weston, instead of giving out orders as usual, seemed a bit subdued.

The clean-up committee worked all day. They had brought food and coffee so they could keep going until dusk, and old Mrs. Dickens went to the parsonage and brought back a big devil's food sheet cake.

It was while they were all standing around enjoying the cake that Mrs. Weston reverted to her old ways. She said to Eula, "I thought you were cleaning that part over there. It looks a mess!" and pointed to a corner near the choir loft. Obediently, Eula went there and started sweeping.

At the end of the day, everyone stood around admiring what they had accomplished. Their clothes were filthy and their shoulders ached, and even though the church was still missing a chunk of its roof, and they hadn't been able to raise the steeple, the church was tidy now.

It was when they were all leaving that things got out of hand.

Liddy and Cassie had just climbed into the Plymouth when Liddy exclaimed, "Oh, shoot! I forgot my bucket! Cassie, go back and get it."

Cassie went back into the church, then stopped, caught by what she saw. Eula and Mrs. Weston were alone in the dark sanctuary, and Eula was trapped between Winifred and a pew. Mrs. Weston was wagging a finger in Eula's face and saying in a shrill voice, "...thought you could get away with it! You young girls, all of you doing immoral things—debauched, perverted things—you're a *canker* on the face of this town!"

Eula's hand was covering her mouth, and her eyes were round and frightened. She caught sight of Cassie, and for the very first time, Cassie felt sorry for her. This was a melodrama she had long hoped to see played out, but now that it was here before her eyes, it seemed vulgar and coarse. Their roles in the scene were well defined: Eula was the slow-witted slattern, Mrs. Weston the shrieking harpy. But why couldn't Eula figure out how to escape? Cassie riveted her eyes on Eula, willing her to fight back. But she only gaped, her head swiveling from Winifred Weston to Cassie and back again.

Mrs. Weston turned to see where the girl was looking. "And *you*, Miss High-and-Mighty Field, you're just as bad! Helping that immoral Lola Mallory, who should have left town when she knew she was pregnant! You girls are a scourge on society—thumbing your noses at all upright, self-respecting people!"

The desecration of Lola's memory was too much. Cassie felt her face get hot, and suddenly her fury at all the years of Winifred Weston's nastiness boiled over. "Don't you *ever* talk like that about Lola, you old witch!" she yelled. "Why don't you just mind your own business and stop tellin' everybody in God's creation how to act!" Looking down, she saw a mop bucket at Eula's feet. Without another word, she picked it up and flung the bucketful of brown, murky water all over Mrs. Weston. As the woman sank to the floor, Cassie took Liddy's empty bucket and walked out the door.

○

The news spread like wildfire: the Westons were getting a divorce. Hetty Saltman had got it from the switchboard and told it at Tootie's Beauty Nook; Charlene Byers heard it there and told Rowena Richards, and that was all it took. Another divorce besides the Sampsons', and this one between such paragons of the church!

Winifred Weston had evidently gone bonkers. She had marched out to the barn at night and sliced open all the feed sacks; then she'd taken a sledgehammer and hammered the doors, hood, and roof of Floyd's pickup. After that, she'd driven the pickup into the side of the barn—the barn Floyd had been repairing for two solid months.

○

Liddy continued to think about leaving Marvin, this time for good. No more running away, then coming back full of forgiveness and hope; this time it would be for keeps!

What she would really like was to get *him* to leave. But where would he go? He'd have to live in a shack somewhere. But she *deserved* the house. She had worked for years to preserve what they had, while he had frittered everything away! *She* paid for the new paint, the shutters, and the new bathroom. The house at least was insured, and that would pay for the repairs. Sure, he had traded a bird dog to get her some furniture— now it was all blasted to the four winds. But when it came to making any sacrifices, she had always been the one. But did she want to be put in a category with Winifred Weston and Grace Sampson, or Marvin's sister Hannah— disgraced divorcées?

Yet she couldn't hang on like an old dishrag; she had to show some spunk.

They had so many expenses. She didn't feel right, leaving Marvin to rebuild the drugstore on his own. If she stayed, she could scrimp more, and try to make more money with her business, and put it back into the drugstore. She'd always helped him, and it looked as though she would have to keep on helping him…forever.

It was during these uncertain days that the unthinkable happened. She was washing diapers when Marvin called out. He sounded as though he was choking. Cassie was gone. She found him in the breakfast room on the sofa, his legs sprawled at an unnatural angle, head thrown forward, both hands pressed against his chest.

"Call Doc—I'm havin' pains!" he croaked. "But first…get those pills in my room!"

She knew he'd been doctoring himself with nitroglycerin pills. She got the pills and put one on his tongue, then called Doc Ledbetter. The next twenty minutes felt like a day. Finally the old doctor came, checked Marvin's pulse and color, looked at the bottle of pills he'd been taking, and ushered Liddy into the next room. "He's fine. Just keep him calmed down, and he'll be all right."

"Was this a heart attack? I didn't know he was this sick!"

"He's takin' the right dosage of nitro, but you're goin' to have to keep him quiet. Marvin's the kind of man gets worked up about things, you've got to keep him from gettin' agitated."

Doc Ledbetter went to the door, then turned. "Oh, and try and get him to quit smokin'."

Several days passed, and Liddy made up her mind. She would forget about divorce. Besides their financial situation and Marvin's health problems, the children wouldn't like it. Or at least Cassie wouldn't. What did she mean, *the children?* The boys were gone, and would probably never come back to live with them; Cassie was the only one it would affect. And Cassie loved her father—didn't know him, really, didn't see his faults. Probably that was how it should be. Probably that was how all children loved their parents: with blinders on.

And there was Dulcie. She didn't have it in her to take the baby away from Marvin. Was it called love when you couldn't bear to hurt someone, when it felt like shredding your own heart to cast him or her out?

Stop kidding yourself, Liddy thought. Of course you love him. Not because you don't want to hurt him, or you're afraid of hurting Cassie, or because he's sick, or you don't want to send him away from Dulcie.

You love him.

She would stay.

26

Since slavery-time, long gone,
You been calling me
All kinds of names,
Pushing me down.
I been swimming with my
Head deep under water—
And you wished I would
Stay under till I drowned.
    —Langston Hughes,
     "Jesse B. Semple"

When Uncle Fred and Carlton parked in front of the drugstore in mid-July, it was three months since the tornado, but the town was still torn up.

Cassie was glad to see both of them. Uncle Fred gripped her by her arms, then took her chin in his hand and said, "I hear you're still tryin' to take the blame for that girl dyin'—now, you quit it! Wasn't *none* o' your fault!"

Uncle Fred was on his way to Kansas to look into buying another small newspaper, and he said he brought Carlton along because he needed help toting his suitcase. Since he had only one small bag with him, that didn't seem like much of a reason. He told Liddy and Marvin the real reason later on, when Carlton and Cassie weren't around. Carlton's father Jesse had been shot in a race riot in Beaumont. Uncle Fred said, "He's hurt real bad; the bullet pierced his kidney. You think Feemy isn't in a state? He's bein' tended by our doctor, and Feemy's nursin' him in their apartment. Carlton's been awful upset, and he was kinda underfoot, so I thought maybe seein' how bad your town got wrecked would take his mind off his dad."

He told Liddy and Marvin about the riot. A colored man had been arrested for the rape of a white woman, then lynched by a white mob. When rumors of a second rape went through the town a few days later, violence broke out, then escalated. Several hundred white men marched from the Beaumont shipyards to the jail, where they discovered that no Negro was in custody, so they then marched out to a colored neighborhood. Businesses were torched, and a barber was badly burned in his shop. The next day martial law was instituted, and two thousand Texas National Guardsmen, Texas Rangers, and police tried to keep order. Fred said whites roamed the streets and coloreds barricaded themselves at home, armed and ready to defend themselves. In the end, a white man and a colored man were dead.

"I talked to Henry Bier, the owner of the newspaper in Beaumont, and he said the trouble started because whites workin' in the shipyards couldn't abide coloreds like Jesse makin' good money, fillin' jobs that coulda been filled by all the white crackers from the East Texas hills."

"It's just like that riot up in Detroit last month, where Roosevelt had to send in the troops," said Marvin, shaking his head. "That's what they get, bringin' all those colored folks up there to work in the war factories. There were nine white people killed up there."

"But weren't some Negras killed up there, too?" asked Liddy.

"Twenty-five," said Fred. "I don't think anybody brought 'em up; it's just that the war wages are so good; that's why Jesse went to Beaumont. Plenty whites from the south went up north, too."

"But I bet the whites didn't cause the riots," said Marvin, having the last word.

○

They all rode home in Uncle Fred's Cadillac to have sandwiches and iced tea, while Marvin stayed at the store. The house insurance had a clause for household furnishings, and Liddy was glad the new roof was on, and that her new furniture from Montgomery Ward had arrived. Cassie made the sandwiches while Liddy fed Dulcie, and Liddy talked with Fred while Cassie and Carlton were in the backyard. She had written, him telling him and Bertha everything. Not just about the twister, but about Dan, Lola, the baby, and what she knew of Cassie's role in it all.

"How come Dan didn't know better'n to get that girl knocked up?" asked Fred.

"Lola didn't exactly use good judgment, either, did she?" retorted Liddy. "But look what we have here!" She kissed the top of Dulcie's head.

"She's a doozy, all right. Looks like you're getting the house put back together! What about the store?" Liddy hadn't meant to tell Fred about Marvin letting the insurance lapse, but somehow it came out. Fred was furious. He said he would talk to Marvin and see if he would accept some financial help.

"No. I—I think he'd resent it, Fred. He was hurt pretty bad in the storm, and Doc Ledbetter doesn't think he's snapping back as fast as he should. It's his heart—he's dosing himself with nitroglycerin pills. Don't talk to him about it, please, and whatever you do, don't offer him money!"

"Liddy, Marvin shoulda been lookin' out for you and Cassie. I knew those dogs would get him in trouble someday!"

"This time it wasn't the dogs—it was dreamin' about oil!" Liddy put Dulcie in her borrowed crib. "And we all have our faults."

She came back and sat down, looking out the window as Fred lit up a cigar. They could see Cassie and Carlton walking around on the grass.

"Poor little Carlton," Liddy said, "his daddy getting hurt so bad!"

Carlton wasn't little now; he was almost six feet. She wondered if she should reproach Fred for bringing the colored boy up here again. Marvin was furious about it, and, truth be told, she didn't like it, either. People would see Cassie with him, and after what she'd done with Lola, they'd think she and Marvin had completely lost control! No doubt they already thought it. But she did feel sorry for the boy.

She turned back to Fred. "You still gamblin' on horses?"

Fred sipped his iced tea, the big diamond in his Masonic ring flashing in the sun. "Uh-huh. But I can afford it."

"Marvin and I will figure it out, Fred. I've learned something about myself after all these years. I've learned hope makes you happy. We'll come out of this somehow."

○

Cassie and Carlton spent the afternoon in the backyard. Cassie wore shorts and a red bandanna halter; Carlton was in what looked like a new green and yellow plaid shirt. He wasn't talking, like usual. It seemed like every time she saw him he got quieter. They ambled around on the dried-up grass, carrying glasses of ice water, crunching the ice between their teeth.

Cassie said, "I'm sorry 'bout your dad."

"Uh-huh." Carlton turned his head and looked around, his liquid eyes finally settling on the dogs in the pen. After Liddy's mad act, people all over town had returned them.

"Yo' daddy's dogs didn't get hurt none in the to'nado?"

"Nuh-uh. Mama said it was a downright dirty shame."

Carlton never laughed. A sense of humor didn't seem to be part of his makeup, although Feemy had a high-pitched, girlish laugh, and Cassie remembered Jesse chortling at something Uncle Fred had said years ago at the barbecue. Of course he had been drinking whiskey.

The sounds of summer flowed about them, cicadas droning, and bees humming around the sunflowers, a few crows squawking. Carlton dropped to the ground. They were both silent for a long time; then he said, "My daddy say a white man try to git him to dance fo' pennies."

"*What?*" Cassie sat down, too, mindless of the possibility of chiggers.

"My daddy say one night a bunch o' white men down theah try to get him to dance fo' pennies."

"Down there in Beaumont?"

"Yeah."

"That's awful! Your daddy isn't young, and he works hard! It's *disgusting!*"

"When he wouldn', they beat up on him."

Cassie couldn't think of anything to say.

"Did you hear 'bout that cullud doctah in Dallas went to be on a jury, and some white men kicked him all the way down the co'thouse steps?"

"No. In *Dallas?*"

"Yeah. Couple yeahs ago. My daddy say Mr. Thu'good Marshall, he come down theah an' took care of it."

"Mr. Marshall who?"

"He a big Washin'ton lawya. Thu'good Marshall. He come down, an' he got the gov'nah to call out the Texas Rangahs!" Carlton stood up and walked around, casting a tall shadow in the late afternoon sun.

Cassie lay back stretched out, her arms behind her head.

"Bet you didn' know, Cassie, ah'm gonna be a baseball player."

This was the first time Cassie had ever heard Carlton issue a statement with such flat certainty. In fact, the amount of conversation coming from him in the past few minutes was downright shocking. "D'ya think you can? Be one?"

"I sure am *hopin'*." A wide grin spread across Carlton's face, and his hands reached up together and swung an imaginary bat in the air. "Coach at my school, he think so. He gittin' me a spot on the Kansas City Monarchs, to be a batboy. They got all these colored baseball teams playin' 'gainst each other all over the United States. Tha's *this* year. Then *nex'* summer, I gonna play down in Houston with a young colored team. All the players little bit older'n me, but Coach say I kin do it. Coach say I the best hitter he ever had."

"Hey, Carlton, that's terrific! I didn't know 'bout any o' this! How come you never tol' me!"

"Dunno."

"Let's celebrate. Let's go to the drugstore and get us a malt. The soda fountain's workin'."

While they walked downtown, and while everyone who passed them on the road stared as if they'd seen the reincarnation of the Holy Ghost, she told him all about Lola and the baby. She told every bit of her role in it, even the part where she pretended to be a boy.

Carlton stopped on the road, laughing with his head thrown back. "I sho' would like to seen that! You dressed up like a boy! You crazy, Cassie!"

She'd finally done it—she had made Carlton laugh.

When they got to the store, Cassie scooped up three dips of vanilla ice cream each, plus chocolate syrup, milk, and malt powder, into two metal mixers. After running the mixers, she poured the malts into tall chilled glasses, and led Carlton to the front table. Marvin limped out from the back of the store, looking as though he was going to deliver some pronouncement or other, but at the sight of the two kids happily spooning up their malts, he closed his mouth, turned, and walked to the back again.

Liddy and Fred came downtown with Dulcie that afternoon to see more of the storm damage. Fred walked up and down Main, kidding in his jovial way with shopkeepers, repairmen, and carpenters, charming everyone in sight. He also tended to some business. Obeying Liddy's request, he said nothing to Marvin about the insurance. But he visited the Cato Mortgage and Loan and put a thousand dollars in Liddy's account, swearing Henry McCallum to secrecy. Back at the drugstore, Fred announced that he and Carlton were going to spend the night.

"Oh, no!" said Marvin. "I don't think that's wise."

Fred ignored him, lit up another cigar, and turned to impress Peggy and Cassie by recounting a number of Texas tornadoes, all bigger and more terrible than this one. "Back in 1927 there was the one down in Rock Springs, 'tween San Antone and San Angelo. That was *really* somethin'! Killed 'bout fifty people and caused more'n a million dollars' damage!"

Marvin took Liddy by the arm and walked her back to the prescriptions desk. "I don't want Fred and the boy here overnight. And there's sure no extra beds at our house. I don't want that boy with us at the café, even if Reuben *would* let him in! You tell Fred to get on out of here. Bringin' that boy up here when he knows better! *Tell* him!"

Liddy shook his hand off her arm and said, "I don't think so, Marvin. Why don't *you* tell him?"

"Because he's *your* brother!" They went back up front, but Liddy didn't say a word.

The supper problem was solved when Marvin said the adults would eat at the Mistletoe, and Cassie and Carlton would eat their hamburgers in the drugstore. While the three of them were eating at the café, Fred said he was going to spend the night at the hotel. Marvin's voice rose. "You mean you're goin' to try to put that boy in a *room?*"

Fred waved his cigar in the air. "'Course not. He'll sleep in the Cadillac, in the parking lot out back."

Back at the drugstore, Uncle Fred told Carlton, "Let's drive over to the hotel now, son—I got some paperwork to do. You're gonna sleep in the car." Carlton's expression didn't change, and he didn't say anything in protest, just got up and followed Uncle Fred out. Cassie wondered if he always slept in the car on these trips. But she was delighted that Uncle Fred was pushing things this far. *Carlton was going to spend the night in town.* It occurred to her that Uncle Fred must like upsetting her dad.

They found out from Stuffy Byers what happened later.

Fred couldn't sleep, so at midnight he went down to the lobby and asked Clyde Spokes how he could get some liquor. Clyde said Stuffy

Byers lived nearby and would probably sell him a bottle. Fred woke up Carlton, gave him a five-dollar bill, and told him to go pick it up. Clyde pointed Carlton to Stuffy's place half a block away. It was visible from the hotel, the only house on the block with the lights still burning.

O

On hot summer nights, the Cato Shores stayed open until eleven. It was the only swimming hole for miles, and young people from all over the county came to swim or lie by the side of the big pond with their blankets and radios, and make out. Tonight a group of boys and a couple of girls from Red Arrow had been swimming until late; then they'd piled into a pickup, four in the cab and six in the back. For more than an hour they'd been carousing around the countryside, throwing beer cans in all directions. When they drove through Cato, they spied Carlton on his way across the street and skidded to a stop.

"Hey, there, jigaboo! What you doin' 'roun' *here?*" yelled the driver.

"Walkin'."

"Where you walkin' *to*, coon?" another boy yelled.

"Ah'm jes' goin' on a errand fo' Mistah McIvor."

But nobody knew who Mr. McIvor was, as they would have in Waxahachie. He hurried along, the pickup following him slowly, blinking its headlights on and off. One boy leaned his head out and yelled, "Wanna go for a ride, nappy-head? Come 'long with us! We got *us* a errand, too!"

Carlton ran. He made it to Stuffy's, where he pounded on the door until Stuffy opened it and found him, shaking and terrified.

Stuffy had met Fred at the races years ago and again earlier that day. He put Carlton and the whiskey in his car and delivered both to the hotel room. When Fred answered his loud knock, Stuffy said, "You got two choices, Mr. McIvor. You can let this boy sleep in your room, or you can take him right now and leave town."

Clyde Spokes stood in the hall, peering around Stuffy's bulky shoulder at Fred, looking worried. "I don't want no trouble," he said.

Fred took the whiskey and packed his bag, and he and Carlton drove away in the dark.

O

Cassie walked along the road, the eagle bone whistle stuck in her jeans pocket. She had assumed that it blew away along with so many other things, but she'd found it just now in a closet downstairs, nestled inside a box of other treasures.

The thing that had happened to Carlton yesterday upset her terribly. She had been in a pensive mood all day, distressed that she hadn't gotten to say good-bye to Carlton and Uncle Fred. Mr. Byers had told them what had happened, and it made her so angry! She was going to write Carlton a letter and apologize, tell him those boys were from Red Arrow, not Cato. But she doubted if it would make much difference to Carlton where they were from.

She needed to get out into the air, needed to walk and walk. Maybe she would take a hike down Wolf Creek—not anywhere near the bridge, though. She could try to find Dan's Indian grave, though she'd never gone there alone.

Cassie had to admit it—she missed her brothers. Yesterday they received Dan's new APO number; her dad said that meant "Army Post Office." Dan had shipped out of the States, and her mother had gone into one of her tailspins.

After all Cassie had been through, her parents wouldn't have the nerve anymore to declare Wolf Creek off limits to her, but they didn't have to know where she'd gone, either. Reaching the bridge at the end of Main, she kept walking east and soon was on the path Dan had shown her so long ago. After a five-minute walk, she came to the creek crossing and began to pick her way over the flat rocks. It didn't seem as tricky this time to hop from one stone to another.

The only good thing that had happened lately was a letter and fifty dollars from Mitch. That had cheered her up a lot. She was going to use the money to buy clothes—she'd have to look good as a sophomore. And he'd written her some news he hadn't told the folks yet, about his promotion to staff sergeant. He sounded proud and, at the same time, as though trying not to sound proud. She let Liddy read the letter, and you would have thought Mitch had been promoted to general. Daddy was pleased, too. He said that sounded like his son, all right, a leader of men. Yup, her dad was getting soft in his old age.

Cassie was walking across the same territory she and Dan had hiked, but after several minutes she realized she was lost. She retraced her steps and, with a lot of wasted time searching for some scenery she remembered, at last found the trail.

Walking for another half hour, she came to the low sandstone hill and started to climb. These tennis shoes didn't slip and slide quite as much as the old, worn-smooth hand-me-downs she had on when she was with Dan, and after a bit of a struggle, she reached the top. She walked across the flat tableland until she found the boulders marking the grave. She was breathing hard, and her cotton shirt was soaked through, but she felt invigorated and alive for the first time that day.

She stood near the rocks and thought about how everything had changed.

If only Fiona hadn't left! Fiona's dad had opened a dry-cleaning shop far away in Boulder, Colorado. Since both their house and business had been hit hard in the twister, Mr. Bannister had cashed in on his insurance and moved. Cassie and Fiona had already exchanged six letters apiece. Fiona wrote that she liked Boulder. There were college boys there, but her folks wouldn't let her go out with any of them, so she was biding her time until she turned fifteen. She said Aura Lee was still a giant pain in the butt.

Cassie wondered why the Bannisters wouldn't let Fiona date college boys when they had let her go out with Seth Scruggs. Did they think Seth was harmless? Boy, were *they* wrong! Fiona had confided to her that Seth liked to put his tongue in her mouth. *Ugh!* No way would Cassie let some boy put his disgusting tongue in *her* mouth! Maybe she would put off growing up after all—that was what Daddy wanted anyway.

For weeks her mother had been hinting that her dad wasn't well, but she wouldn't say what was wrong—just something with his heart. He didn't seem very energetic anymore, which seemed odd because her mother was downright zippy. Talking to Sven Sundersson about the remodeling had gotten her all revved up again.

Cassie wasn't sure—did her mother have the approved and acceptable kind of female strength? When she was *too* strong—hardheaded, Daddy called it—he didn't like it, but when she was vulnerable, when she worried too much about Mitch and Dan, he didn't like that, either. She thought about all the powerful women she had known besides Liddy. Mabel for sure, and Lola, too. She had to wipe her eyes, thinking of

Lola. Winifred Weston was strong, too, but in a nasty kind of way, and all those movie heroines—Bette Davis in *Jezebel*, Dorothy in *The Wizard of Oz*, Scarlett O'Hara—*they* were spirited and strong-willed. The best was when you could be strong and soft at the same time. But Cassie was pretty sure men just wanted the soft part.

It was getting dark—she hadn't realized it was so late. Stars were beginning to appear. She sat down cross-legged on the warm, dry earth, remembering Dan's solemn air when he'd shown her the grave. She took out the eagle bone whistle and ran her fingers up and down it. The beaded pendant and the feather were exotic and intriguing—from another time. The whistle had belonged to the Indian warrior buried here. Was he a Kiowa, as Dan thought? Or was he Pawnee, like the Pawnee warrior chief her class studied in Oklahoma History class last spring?

The chief would always be the first of all the warriors to take up the medicine bundle around the ceremonial fire. He would tie it around his waist, shake his head and shoulders, and dance. While he was dancing he would recite:

I have killed an eagle and consecrated it to my enemy, and I have taken the enemy's scalp and consecrated it to the gods in the heavens. And the gods received my smoke.

Cassie tried to imagine the warriors dancing near the flames, their bodies painted with bold designs, feathered headdresses shivering and shaking in the firelight. Maybe Mitch and Dan were like those mighty Indian warriors. But what if they ended up buried, too? It was hard to imagine Dan as a pilot, and it was almost impossible to imagine him as a hero, but she had to admit it, he was one.

She picked up the whistle and blew it, making a few tentative warbles, and tapped her finger against the little holes to make quick, staccato chirps; then she held one long, high note that sounded so sorrowful it made her start to cry again. She blew on the whistle for a long time, pretending she was an Indian girl trying to give herself courage.

The round, white moon was coming up, and a few bright stars glimmered low in the charcoal sky.

Epilogue

Dulcie had her first birthday on March 9th, 1944.

By that March, Anzio beach was taken, and tanks were on their way to Rome. The invasion of Normandy by Allied Forces was only a few months away. Dan was flying bombers in the Pacific, and Mitch had been dead for eight months, killed in an accident at his airfield when a shot-up P-38 had tried to land with only one engine. It had skidded, smashing directly into the hangar where he was working.

Harold Cutter walked over to the drugstore and found Marvin sitting at one of the new ice cream tables. He was holding Dulcie on his lap, while directing Peggy's reorganization of his prescription counter. Almost a year after the tornado, the marble top had finally been replaced.

"Marvin, I want you to be quiet and let me talk," Harold said. "I don't want any arguments. Tonight I'm going to repay you for that slug of whiskey I had here the day of the tornado, when you were laid out on the floor lookin' like you'd been kicked by a horse. You and me are going to have us a snort over at my office, and the ladies aren't invited. After that, I'm taking everybody to the café to celebrate your grandchild's birthday."

That evening the Fields and Harold ate at the new Mistletoe Café, which was now located in the old laundry. The new booths weren't installed yet, so they ate at a card table. Stacks of boards were piled against both walls, and the smell of wet plaster and wood chips lent the chili a unique flavor.

Ben ran into the kitchen and out again with a highchair for Dulcie, then stood by grinning while Cassie put her in it. For most of the evening, Dulcie made her presence known by banging on the metal tray with a tablespoon, with Liddy repeatedly trying to shush her. Liddy had turned completely grey in the last year, and Violet and Rowena thought she was way too thin.

Across a wide hallway was Violet's new grocery store, which had begun business a month ago, and upstairs, Liddy's new shop A STITCH IN TIME was almost ready to open. Women from all over the county had delivered a deluge of needlework, quilts and crochet work for Liddy and Rowena to sell.

Some of Reuben's old signs had made it through the tornado, but Violet told Reuben the state wouldn't renew his license if the food inspector ever laid eyes on them. So Reuben ordered new ones. Three of these were prominently displayed near their table:

IT'S NO USE CRYING OVER SPILT MILK; IT ONLY MAKES IT SALTY FOR THE CAT

WHAT IS THE DIFFERENCE BETWEEN A WOMAN AND AN UMBRELLA? YOU CAN SHUT AN UMBRELLA UP

YOU CAN'T GET THERE FROM HERE, AND BESIDES, THERE'S NO PLACE ELSE TO GO

With their chili they had hamburgers, and for dessert they had Reuben's bread pudding.

Liddy thought the best part of the evening was that Marvin didn't have to pay for a thing.

About the Author

Marianne Gage was born in Oklahoma. She was educated at Oklahoma State University, Stillwater, and later moved to California, where she continued her studies at California College of The Arts, San Francisco State, and Cal State Hayward. She taught for several years in the Oakland schools, and has for many years been a portrait artist and printmaker in the San Francisco Bay Area. She is married to illustrator Ed Diffenderfer, and has two grown children.

Photo by Paul Fillinger

Breinigsville, PA USA
27 July 2010
242543BV00002B/2/P

9 781935 514466